A Bride Worth Taking

Also by
Rebecca Connolly

An Arrangement of Sorts
Married to the Marquess
Secrets of a Spinster
The Dangers of Doing Good
The Burdens of a Bachelor

Coming Soon
A Wager Worth Making

More romance from
Phase Publishing

by
Emily Daniels
Devlin's Daughter
Lucia's Lament

by
Grace Donovan
Saint's Ride

A Bride Worth Taking

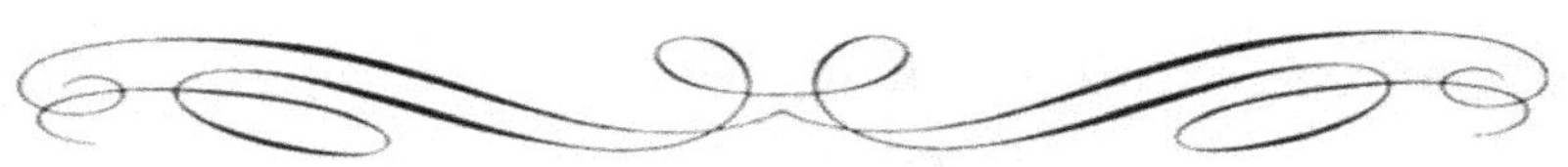

Rebecca Connolly

Phase Publishing, LLC
Seattle

Phase Publishing, LLC first paperback edition
July 2017

ISBN 978-1-943048-30-4
Library of Congress Control Number 2017945407
Cataloging-in-Publication Data on file.

Acknowledgements

For my grandma Velma, who did not live to see me do so many things, let alone publish a novel, but whose generosity, love, and inspiration has been felt by her children and grandchildren every single day. I love you, and I know you would love this one in particular.

And to Five Guys, which I happen to be eating now, much to my very great delight. You never fail me or let me down. Also, you were the working title for this series. Here's to you.

Shout out, gratitude, and love to the regulars: the epic Phase Publishing team, the incomparable Deborah Bradseth of Tugboat Design, and the gracious Whitney Hinckley. All-stars all around.

And thanks to my Musketeers for keeping me sane on this one. Well, sane enough, anyway. Chocolate helps, and you know that. Thanks, guys.

Chapter One
Yorkshire, 1822

$\mathcal{A}$nthony Marksby was not at all husband material.

A paltry statement to make at this point, given all that had passed.

Of course, if she had considered that detail properly two days ago, it would have saved her a good deal of trouble.

But Marianne Bray had never been a particularly intelligent creature, not even when she was a little girl. Oh, she was clever enough for the ballrooms and parties of London society, and no one would ever accuse her of being *un*intelligent, should they have been bold enough to attempt it, but neither would anyone invite her to an evening of puzzles and riddles. Nor would she wish to go to such an event. She had no patience for such things.

Nevertheless, at this moment, she rather wished she had put more effort towards improving her wits and cleverness. Her situation at present was entirely of her own making because she had not been intelligent or clever enough to see the truth of the matter.

But what girl of considerable looks and more considerable means is sensible when a handsome and dashing suitor pays her a marked degree of attention, even if it does lead to her ruin?

Sitting confined in this poorly furnished, cheap room at the coaching inn near Leeds, she felt quite the fool, actually. What had started off as a rather grand and impulsive adventure had just as quickly turned into a waking nightmare.

Marianne had not wanted for admirers in six years, not since her very first Season, and had a great deal too many, as a point of fact. It was something she rather prided herself on. But after spending a Season practicing a more reserved nature two years ago, which had only been natural considering the horrific events surrounding her sister-in-law and friend Annalise, she had found that she had lost a good many of her favorites to other girls with less charming natures.

As such, she had redoubled her efforts last year to regain some of the footing she had lost. Oh, she had still been popular, immensely so, but it did not have the same gripping excitement as it had in former years. Nor was her coterie so entertaining.

Then Anthony Marksby had come across her path. His arrival in London had caused quite a stir, particularly with him arriving so late in the Season that some of the more eager families had departed for their country homes. It had proven quite a delight to her, and to her best friend Fanny Hayes. They had grown weary of the endless strings of peacocks vying for their attention, and Mr. Marksby was fresh and exciting, and added a bit of mystery to the thing.

Fanny was not as pretty or as popular as Marianne, and she never would be, and her fortune was really quite a pittance by comparison, but she was so skilled in the navigation of a crowded room that she drew men to her with barely a half look. Her family was set up well enough, with a fair reputation, so she could make quite an eligible match if she ever settled upon one. This past Season alone, she turned down three proposals because they did not suit her.

Marianne herself had turned down five, but she did not generally make that public.

The rumors took care of that for her.

Fanny had tried for Mr. Marksby first, with her usual voluptuous and brazen ways, forgoing the subtle cuts that typically accompanied her tricks. Marianne had chosen a more coy and unaffected approach, using secret glances and hints of a smile, lying in wait for his actions to prove his intentions. She could hardly have called her behavior reserved, as she had not shown one moment of modesty in her attempts, but she had long ago learned that there was some benefit in being careful and cunning in the matter of attracting men.

It had been a very skillful game they had all played. Fanny and Marianne had vied for the same men before, and considering they had such different ways of going about it, they never felt they were in particular competition. On the contrary, it became a sort of game to them. May the best player win, in cards and in life.

Marianne had won Mr. Marksby, though long after the excitement and fever of the Season had worn out. He had been one of her most challenging captures yet, and would have put quite a feather in her cap.

Then winter had come, and boredom had set in. Duncan and Annalise had gone off to Scotland to visit her cousins, taking her adorable little niece Tillie with them. Her aunt, Lady Raeburn, had taken up her past habits of travelling every three or four months, and was at present in Italy, no doubt looking for her fourth… or was it fifth?… husband. It was hard to keep track with Tibby.

With no family and very few friends to entertain her, Marianne had been left to her own devices, which had not proven to be sufficient. One could only go to the theater and to small house parties and card parties and pay calls so much before tedium struck and there was nothing left to do.

Mr. Marksby had come in handy there, and after Christmas he had taken up a charge to entertain Marianne in whatever ways he could come up with, some of which were very creative indeed. She found herself growing very fond of him, and not just amused by him, as she usually was.

Oh, she was not foolish enough to have thought herself in love with the man, not in the least bit. His habit of smoking was perfectly disgraceful to her, and she had told him so on several occasions, and he raced about in his phaeton much too wildly. Those traits, combined with his sadly-tailored clothing and his scar under his left ear, solidified the impossibility of her ever falling in love with him.

She was not entirely sure she could love, not romantically, at least. She loved her family, and her brother's friends had become sort of half-brothers to her, and she found herself more devoted to those people than any other creatures on earth. She would be fiercely loyal to all of them until the day she died.

But as far as the rest of the world was concerned, she could not have cared about love at all.

She rather found more satisfaction in being loved than in giving love herself.

Perhaps that made her heartless, but there it was.

She had not left Mr. Marksby under any illusion of her feelings, and Mr. Marksby made no secret of his feelings for her, which were a mad passion, fervent and burning desire, and hoping to make her the toast of London for decades to come. He was of such an attractive and charming nature that on his arm, she would have soared into an entirely unmatched level of status and reputation.

No love, never anything so sentimental, but the base and honest confessions of his daring heart had woken something exciting and bold within her, and she had jumped at his suggestion that they run away together and marry, starting a scandalous life together that would only increase their popularity.

It was a delicate balance, keeping one's reputation and becoming a household name. There would have to be a period of pretended shame, but it wouldn't last long, particularly with their elopement being declared a brilliant love match and her extensive fortune securing them entrance into any and all events. She was too desirable by half to be ignored and shamed.

So, two days ago, they had ventured off, sneaking out right under the nose of her current companion, Mrs. Gordon, who was rather old, slow, and dim, and laughed their way out of London, their impetuous future awaiting them.

At least, those were the ideals she had set stock by in this whole scheme.

She'd allowed some passion, and had rather enjoyed the moments of it, but her wildness only extended so far. She might have been bold, daring, and heartless, but she would keep her virtue until they were man and wife, and hadn't allowed him any sort of liberties that could truly compromise her.

Tony, as she'd taken to calling him, had not liked that at all.

And that was when things had turned.

He'd never forced himself on her, thank heavens, but he'd lost the pretense of caring about her. He would kiss her any chance he got, sometimes quite violently, and what had once stirred something in her now only made her ill.

He was cruel, crass, and had no aversion to hitting her, if she bothered him too much.

She had annoyed him to such a degree hours ago that he had struck her across the face and left the room, locking her in without food or water. The first night had been spent in the coach, and the second she had been forced to share a bed with him, but he had become so drunk that he'd been unconscious the entire night and never touched her. She hardly hoped for such luck this evening.

A knock on the door startled her and she jumped, skittering back on the bed and slamming her head into the headboard.

"Are you decent, my love?" slurred the all-too familiar voice of her intended as he entered.

However attractive he may have been in her eyes before, he was now disintegrated into a monster. He was unshaven and unkempt, and his eyes raked over her with indecent light and thoroughness. It didn't matter that she had on her thickest day dress, she felt entirely and shamefully naked under his gaze. He staggered into the room and leaned against the wall, cigar in his mouth, collar of his shirt so wide open the hair on his chest might have been his weskit. And he grinned wolfishly at her from his position.

"The company wants me to present my intended to them," he said, winking a bloodshot eye at her. "Surely you won't deny the gentlemen downstairs such a treat."

"No, thank you," Marianne said, trying to keep her tone as stiff and haughty as she ever would. She had to make a show of a spine, no matter how imagined it was.

He laughed wildly. "You stupid chit, I was not asking. We've taken a break from our games. I've told them some of the stories of our adventures in London, and they don't believe I've actually secured you. So you will come on down, give them a bit of a show, and then, if you do it well, I shall give you dinner. And then bed. For both of us." The glint in his eyes left no doubt as to what would follow.

Marianne swallowed down the sudden wash of bile and tried to tuck herself into the headboard more tightly. "Did you lose at the tables?" she asked, unable to keep the bite out of her tone.

"'Course I did," he snorted as he sauntered over. "That's why I have no money, and why I'll need all of yours, darling. My wild, passionate, cold-hearted heiress, that is why you will do for me quite well."

He seized her wrist and yanked her towards him, her loose hair falling over her eyes like a thick, black veil. She resisted, twisted and thrashed, but he was stronger. He tossed her hair behind her, pulled her up to him and kissed her deeply, the taste of his sour, ale-strewn breath seeping into her.

Disgust and rage rose within her and she bit down hard on his lip. He yowled in protest and shoved her against the wall, her head cracking back on the corner of the aged bureau. She crumpled into a heap on the floor, and he kicked her repeatedly, spewing forth streams of curses as his boot repeatedly met her ribs and her face, which she shielded as best as she could.

"You'll pay for that, my minx," he rasped, staggering away. "Put on your best frock and be downstairs in ten minutes, or you'll get the worst of me, dearie."

The door slammed behind him, and for only the second time this whole trip, Marianne gave herself up to desperate tears as she cradled her own head as best as she could. She made her way back up to the bed and curled up into a ball, willing the world to shut itself out. How had she been such a blind fool?

She could not escape, not from this inn and not from him. The windows did not open, and she could not break them, she'd already tried. The door to her room opened up into a landing just above the common room, perfectly within the view of everyone. She'd never make it out while he was down there, and she was not a girl with endurance for physical activity. Why had she never become a great walker?

She was trapped here, trapped with him, and he would ruin her, then marry her. Not that the order of events would make any difference once her brother found out.

She groaned and covered her face with her hands. *Oh, Duncan…*

Her brother had always been kind and generous with her, if a bit heavy handed and overbearing, but he had given her freedom, despite his concerns for her behavior. He did not deserve the hell that would come crashing down about him.

And Annalise! She had only just gotten into the good graces of Society, which Marianne had long given up arguing and resisting, and now it would all be wrong again.

Even Tibby would be ashamed, and might actually cut her off this time. She was always threatening to, and had been for years, but it was entirely possible that she would at last follow through with it.

Overcome with shame, regret, pain, and fear, Marianne clutched at her suddenly quaking abdomen and sobbed, burying her face into the counterpane.

The door to her room suddenly burst open and she jumped back again with a surprised scream, crossing her arms over her chest, trembling and eyes wide.

The sight that met her eyes was at once dearer than anything she had ever seen and infinitely the worst.

Colin and Kit Gerrard stood there, expressions thunderous, both in an eerily matching state of disarray, chests heaving with exertion. Colin still wore a hat on his head, but Kit's was long gone and his hair was disheveled.

The Gerrard twins were not identical, but in this moment, they might as well have been.

Her brother's best friend, who had always been a favorite of hers, and his brother, a man doomed to ever torment her, stared at her for the space of several heartbeats, and she stared back at them. They showed no pleasure at seeing her, which meant they knew exactly what she had been about. Yet they were here, which meant they cared enough to come for her.

Marianne slowly and awkwardly slid from the bed, wincing and gasping at the sudden searing pain in her ribs, the wince drawing forth further pain in her jaw and cheek. She bit her lip and straightened, sniffing back the last of her tears, and turned to face them. She trembled like a dried leaf in the wind and her fingers toyed anxiously with each other.

A muscle in Kit's jaw ticked ominously. Colin removed his hat and tossed it into the corner, and started stripping off his gloves, still looking at her steadily.

Was she supposed to run to them as she wanted to? Or was she to stand judgment first as she deserved to?

A stray tear rolled down her throbbing cheek, but she made no move to brush it away.

She couldn't move at all under the combined force of their storming expressions.

"Are you well?" Colin asked in a surprisingly calm tone.

Marianne swallowed and bit her lip. She sensed he was not asking after her health. "I am w-whole," she answered carefully.

The immediate release of tension in Colin showed her she was right.

"And are you hurt?" he asked, seeming slightly more concerned than he had been previously.

Her eyes flashed to Kit briefly, who had not relaxed in the slightest, then returned to Colin. They had seen her get off of the bed; she could not hide her pain, nor the bruises on her face, nor the tattered, tangled mess of her hair. She could not lie, but neither could she tell them all.

Colin, she knew, could raise a temper when he was of a mind to, and whatever she said would be reported back to her brother, who *did* have a temper, and took very little provocation to rise to violence.

"Only a little," she whispered, the words hitching on her breath.

Colin looked to Kit, who nodded once and left the room. Then Colin turned back at her, and said with a severe look, "I left my very tired and expectant wife to find you. If she has suffered any upset because of this, it will be your head she wants, not mine."

Knowing what she did of Susannah Gerrard, that was undoubtedly true. Marianne nodded and looked down, tears burning at her eyes.

Colin sighed and opened his arms. With a soft cry, she ran to him, burying her face against his shoulder.

"There, there," he soothed, holding her in a surprisingly tight grip and running a hand over her hair. "It's all right, minnow, I'll take you home."

A soft kiss on top of her head brought a small smile to her face. Colin had always been the most demonstrative of her brother's friends, and the only one she would ever let call her by Duncan's pet name, though he had not done so in years.

"How did you find me?" she hiccupped.

"Oh, we rallied forces and raced off in various directions," Colin said dismissively, rubbing soothing circles on her back. "Half of the men are headed towards France, the rest towards Scotland. Kit and I followed a lead we had that said you might take the more direct path through Leeds, and here we are. Your Mrs. Gordon is not as dumb as you think, despite evidence to the contrary."

Marianne sagged against him. "I've never been so glad to be wrong," she murmured.

"Nor I, minnow."

After waiting a few long moments for her tremors to settle, she sniffed again and pulled back, rubbing at her eyes. "Where did Kit go?"

Colin's face wrinkled a little and he wrapped an arm around her shoulder. "He is taking care of something… unpleasant." He patted her shoulder once and gave her a small smile. "Come on, let's get you out of here. Duncan is heading down from Scotland, he should cross paths with us in the morning if not sooner."

Colin picked up her bag with his free hand and nudged his head for her to start out of the door.

"How much trouble am I in, Colin?" she asked in a very small voice, reaching for her shawl and wrapping it tightly around her.

He gave her a very shrewd look that held no encouragement. "Not sure, pet. Quite a lot, I would think."

Marianne nodded once with a hard swallow, a small shiver running down her spine.

Two agonizing days after they had discovered Marianne and dealt with Mr. Marksby… well, when *he* had dealt with the blackguard… the men gathered at Lord Loughton's rarely used Yorkshire estate, and Christopher Gerrard was not any less furious than he had been before.

He'd given Marksby the best thrashing he had ever given another living soul, and ironically, his first outside of a boxing ring, and still he burned with the desire to hit something.

The moment Colin had called upon him at his house in St. James and told him of the situation, Kit had been wild and disorganized and utterly unhinged. All within the confines of his mind, of course. He would never have been so far gone as to publicly display anything so uncontrolled, not even to his twin. He'd known full well that Colin was to be Marianne's warden if things got out of hand while Duncan was away, but he'd made it a point to stay as far out of the way of Marianne Bray's destructive path as he could. It did not work all of the time, as he was still inexplicably drawn to her, no matter how disgusted it made him.

He was only grateful he had never as yet been physically drawn to her side. His connection to her was entirely internal, and thus remained his secret, as it should be.

But hearing that she had run off with Marksby had released something within him that had long been dammed up. He had been as driven and relentless as any of the men who had rallied to the rescue, though how most of them had managed to be in or around London at such an unpopular time was miraculous.

The exception had been the Earl of Beverton and his family, but their estate in Hampshire was not too far off for him to be called upon.

Duncan and his wife had been with relations in Scotland, and so he had played no part at all in the hunt for his sister, for which he was furious and deeply embarrassed, despite the assurances from the rest of them, and any consolation they attempted was waved off. Kit could understand that. If one of his sisters had fallen into such a way, he would have felt guilt beyond anything else.

He had no idea what sort of conversation had occurred between Marianne and her brother, and he did not care to. He had his own opinions on how Marianne had been raised, which would be of no use to anyone at this point. All that mattered was that she should understand what the consequences of her actions would be.

And as they all sat together in the study, the situation unfolded as being very bleak.

Kit knew it would be. He knew something of being a topic of rumor and having a standard reputation among Society's circles, however unfounded his was. Marianne had gleefully earned her place, and everything she did, from a new gown to a harsh word, was instantly known and flittered about London as if on a breeze. She was quite proud of it.

Her reputation would likely never recover from this idiocy.

He clenched his hand into a fist for the thousandth time this morning as his mind flashed back to seeing her in that inn. He'd feared the worst when he'd seen the state of the place, and not knowing if she had been willful or ignorant had eaten away at him. The information they had received about Marksby had terrified him, and he knew Marianne could not have been aware of the whole truth.

But would she have cared?

Her state and distress had haunted him for days, and her soft admission that she was whole had gone a long way to smooth things over. But just because she was whole did not mean she was well, and he might never know the entire story of what she had been subjected to.

Therein lay his horrors.

The woman he loved, no matter how he hated himself for it, had been grossly abused, and he could do nothing about it. He certainly had taken care of the man at whose hand she had suffered, but as far as soothing her, nursing her back to herself, ensuring she need never feel so victimized again… None of those things were in his power.

Granted, he did not think he could have held her or soothed her if he had the power to do so. Perhaps he could have at first, when she was so distressed, but he could not do so for long. He rather was more inclined to give her a few solid swats on the backside for her stupidity, but he would never raise a hand to a woman, not ever, not even if it was deserved. She had behaved foolishly, recklessly, like a rebellious child, and her punishment should be treated as such.

But as he listened to what the room as a whole was thinking, there would be nothing of the sort. She would be protected as she always was, and she would never know just how bad things were.

She never had.

"So I think," Geoffrey Harris was saying now as he sat back in a chair and rubbed at his eyes, "that really, the only solution to her problem is to get her a husband. Quickly."

The entire room seemed to groan and Kit looked around with a bit of interest at the sound.

"Why does it always involve finding someone a husband?" Derek, the Marquess of Whitlock, grumbled as leaned forward and put his head into his hands.

"It does not," Nathan, the Earl of Beverton, scoffed with a crossing of his ankles.

Derek gave him a rather direct look. "Doesn't it? We needed Susannah to marry Colin. We needed Annalise to marry someone, preferably Duncan. We needed Mary to get married and save Geoff the trouble of murdering someone. You took Moira to Preston so she could get married."

"And what about Kate?" Colin asked, folding his arms and looking intrigued.

Derek grinned unabashedly. "Well, we needed to find her a husband worth having, didn't we?"

That earned a round of good-natured chuckling.

Kit had heard some of the stories these men had with finding, or keeping, their wives, but he'd not been close enough to hear them directly. Oh, he'd been friendly enough with them over the years, and he certainly had the highest respect and opinions of them, and of their wives. But they had been Colin's friends, not his. He had grown closer to them in the last year and a half, with Colin's marriage and the sudden appearance of their three half-sisters, but there was still distance between them.

"Do you really think we need to proceed with marriage?" Nathan asked with a look at Geoff. "It seems a bit drastic."

The fair-colored man raised a brow and snorted softly. "Do you really think she would ever be admitted into Society again when word gets out that she ran off on an elopement that was foiled? And I do mean when, for it will come out."

Derek made a face. "It will be brutal. They aren't kind about her anyway, behind her back. Now it will confront her head on, and we haven't exactly let her in on that secret."

Kit grunted softly, but only Colin marked him, and gave him a warning look.

She ought to have been told ages ago that she wasn't popular for the admirable reasons she thought. If she knew the stories that swirled about her… If she had any idea what they actually thought…

He'd never taken any pains to inform her of them. It was not his place to do so, and he didn't care.

Unless there was a direct attack. Then he cared quite a lot.

Secretly, of course.

"Do we *really* have to find her a husband?" Derek asked, whining a bit, which made the others smile. "They don't exactly line up for this sort of thing."

"Marriage is the only option," Geoff answered back, shaking his head.

Kit stole a glance at Duncan, who looked impossibly larger than he was as he sat in his chair. His eyes were unfocused and he seemed miles away. The worries and stress on his mind at this time had to be extensive and consuming. Whatever Kit believed about how Marianne had been brought up, there was absolutely no denying that Duncan Bray was a caring brother who loved his sister very much, despite her obvious faults and failings, and had only wanted to do right by her.

There was nothing to find fault with in that.

"You say that as if it were like buying a pony, Geoff," Colin said with a snort of derision. Then he perked up suddenly, "Oh, could we do that instead? Nathan, can we buy a pony from your stables?"

Someone threw a pillow at Colin, which he caught easily with a smile.

"Duncan, what do you think?" Nathan asked quietly, watching his friend with concern. "You have been very quiet."

Duncan sighed, and the house nearly shook with the weight of it. "I don't know what to do. She has ruined herself, there is no doubt about that, but she is also a victim. Of her own making, it is true, but had she known what sort of man she had trusted…" He shook his head and pinched the bridge of his nose. "No one will be as forgiving or understanding as the people in this room."

That was a sobering thought for Kit. As much as he felt, as angry as he was, it was true. He wanted what the rest of them wanted: what was best for Marianne.

"What is her fortune these days?" Geoff asked Duncan, suddenly all business.

"Somewhere around forty thousand," Duncan replied modestly,

looking a bit sheepish when someone whistled, "and that doesn't consider what Tibby might give her. If she forgives her this."

"That should help matters," Derek muttered as he sat back. "Fortune hunters are everywhere."

A severe light entered Duncan's eyes and he raised a finger. "I won't sell her off like cattle just because we are desperate," he told the group firmly. "He must be a good and decent man, a gentleman of quality. I do want her to have a husband she can tolerate, maybe even come to love, if she ever grows up. She should be happy, eventually."

That earned a round of understanding nods, and Kit suddenly felt the slightest bit uncomfortable.

Colin sighed and rubbed at his forehead. "And how do you propose we do that, Duncan? We have not the time nor the resources to give her a real courting Season."

"And who is desperate enough to take her as she is, even with her fortune?" Geoff murmured.

"Well, whom do we know that might be persuaded?" someone else said.

"Are we really going to make a list of eligible men?"

"I feel like my mother."

"Don't say that, I feel bad enough as it is."

The voices faded into a buzzing as Kit sat there, outside of the group, yet suddenly inside of it. Was he really supposed to help them come up with a man who could marry the woman who haunted his thoughts whether waking or sleeping? He could not do it, not even pretend at it.

There was no solution here. There was no man in England that could marry Marianne Bray, as she was, as she had been, extensive fortune notwithstanding, and honestly have a chance at making her happy, let alone having her fall in love with the poor soul. Marianne was a prideful creature; she would never go quietly, not even with her reputation in tatters. She would never obey a husband, she would hardly even care for one. He would be used by her, for status or grandeur, as if it made her somehow more respectable.

No one should be subjected that fate. No one knew her well enough to be able to properly manage such a future.

The only thing to do was…

Was to…

"I have an idea," he heard himself say.

The room was suddenly deathly still, all eyes on him, curious, as if they had forgotten he was there.

He was an idiot for what he was about to do.

There would be no going back.

"Well, go on, Kit," Geoff said, looking interested, but encouraging. "Speak up."

Kit barely spared a glance for his twin, who suddenly looked terrified, before leaning forward and meeting Duncan's eyes calmly. "I will marry Marianne."

Chapter Two

"WHAT?" three voices cried out, with varying volumes.

"Are you mad?" asked Nathan from his left.

Duncan was gaping at him openly. "Kit, are you sure?" he managed, his voice noticeably lower than normal.

"Of course he's not sure," Geoff said with a hard laugh. "He couldn't possibly…"

He trailed off when he saw Kit's expression, which had stayed perfectly composed and calm, and now he only raised a brow at him.

Geoff gave a weak cough. "You are sure?"

Kit nodded once.

"We were not asking for volunteers," Nathan said faintly.

"Kit…" Duncan tried again, still appearing to not understand.

Their reactions to such a statement ought to have given them a great deal of insight into the severity of the situation at hand. If he, who knew and understood both the circumstances and the woman they were attempting to marry off, had earned this much concern and protest, how could they expect any other man to take it on? They would have no idea what they would be agreeing to.

"I will marry her," Kit said again, still calm and controlled, though something inside was beginning to burn.

Derek was shaking his head desperately. "Your reputation…"

"…is already unclear," Kit finished firmly, looking around at them all. "All that is known for certain is my association with you lot, which, granted, has declined in recent years, but it is still there." He turned back to face Duncan directly. "Your sister knows me well. We were friends in her younger years, there is no reason either of us should be unhappy. And I have needed a wife for some time now. Marianne would suit my purposes well enough. No doubt better than I had expected from marriage at all. And I will treat her well and keep her protection my prime objective. So, yes, I am sure. I will marry her, if she will have me."

"Oh, she'll have you," Duncan said without hesitation. He sat back in the large wingback chair he occupied, a smile touching the corner of his mouth. "I may not have expected you to volunteer yourself for the job, Kit, but now I consider it, I am not sure there is a better man suited for this."

That was not exactly what Kit needed to hear at this moment. He hoped that Duncan did not have any notions of love or felicity in this union of theirs, for he could hardly promise that.

"This might be the best idea any of us have ever had," Nathan laughed, clapping Kit on the back.

"Or the worst," Geoff murmured, seeing Colin's face.

Colin suddenly stood, his hands almost visibly shaking. "Kit, a word, if you please." Without waiting for a response, he exited the drawing room and turned down the hall towards the study.

The room quieted, all of them watching Kit now.

Kit twisted his lips a little. "I suppose I should have spoken with Colin first," he said slowly, rising to his feet, "though there was hardly opportunity."

"Does he have the ability to change your mind?" Duncan asked him, not looking concerned or upset, merely interested.

Kit shook his head, exhaling softly. "No, and that might drive him mad." He gave Duncan a wan smile. "We will be back momentarily, and then perhaps we can see to details."

He followed Colin out of the room, determined to settle himself before he had to explain his actions to his brother. To be perfectly honest, he was not entirely sure he could explain it to himself. It was the right course, he had no doubt of that, but what had possessed him to do it?

All he had known was that no one else could have Marianne. He might not want her, not particularly, but he would not... indeed, he *could* not... let someone else have her.

On what level of insanity did that place him?

He entered the study to find Colin already pacing. That was a sign of Colin's turmoil if there ever was one. If he ever became perfectly still, that was dangerous. This was panic.

Kit took a seat in one of the open chairs. "Need a drink, Colin?"

Colin glared at him, eyes wide, and shook his head. "I don't see how you can find amusement in any of this."

Kit scoffed softly. "What else am I supposed to do? Will you not congratulate me, Colin? I am about to become engaged!"

"Don't say that!"

Kit sighed and decided to take pity on his brother, just for the time being. Colin really was very distressed, and Colin was rarely distressed. "You are upset," he said, propping his ankle on his knee.

Colin shoved his hands into his hair. "Of course I am upset! I don't like this one bit!" he cried, suddenly whirling to face him. "You have just volunteered to marry Marianne Bray! Are you completely outside of your mind?"

It was a valid point, he could grant him that. He probably was mad for doing this, but that did not mean he would change it. "What don't you like about this?" he asked with the same controlled tone. "My becoming a husband or Marianne becoming your sister?"

Colin put his hands on his hips, staring at him in confusion. "Honestly? Both."

Kit snorted. "Stop."

His brother sank into the opposite chair, shaking his head. "You haven't been thinking of getting a wife. You've never even attempted to court anyone before. And now you decide it is time? Like this?"

Kit shrugged one shoulder. "Why wait? The opportunity presented itself."

"The opportunity presented itself?" Colin repeated in disbelief. "This is your idea of a marriage of convenience? Kit, if you want an easy time of it, we can take you back to London and let it be known that you are in need of a wife, and proper candidates will appear."

Kit shook his head, smiling at his poor, confused brother. "No, Colin, this will do. Why shouldn't I marry Marianne?"

His brother gave him so sardonic a look it was comical. "Would you like me to list reasons by date or by category?"

Kit rolled his eyes. "Marianne is not as bad as all that."

Both of Colin's brows rose a little. "And this coming from you?"

"Have a care," Kit warned, his tone going a bit darker than he would have liked.

Colin snorted softly and rubbed his temples a little. "Of all the women in the world, Kit, really?"

"I say again, why not?" He shrugged his shoulders. "You care about her, don't you? You rode like mad to find her, rallied the forces to chase after her, and you yourself comforted her when we found her," he pointed out.

"Yes, and never once during all of that did I think 'I would really love to have this girl as my sister.' On the contrary, I think I thanked God she was not my sister."

Kit smiled drily. "God has a sense of humor, Colin."

"Apparently. He gave me you for a brother."

That drew a smile from them both.

Colin sighed and leaned forward, hands pressed together. "Why are you doing this, Kit? I mean, really."

He felt the real concern in his brother's words, and knew he could not play this off a moment longer. His twin needed truth from him, something to settle his newly rattled sensibilities. Well, he supposed it was long past time to admit something that Colin might have suspected, but had never actually put into words. And he would find absolutely no comfort in what he was about to reveal.

"I love her," Kit said blandly, a bitter smile on his face. He nodded once in confirmation when his brother's mouth dropped open at the seriousness of his tone. "I always have."

Slowly, Colin's features contorted into a mixture of surprise and disapproval. "You are... not supposed to say those words looking like that," he told him unsteadily, pointing a finger at him.

Kit exhaled without mirth. "Believe me, if I derived any pleasure from that statement, I would show it openly."

"But you don't?"

He shook his head. "I do not. More than that, I cannot. Because I feel no joy, no thrill of excitement, no visions of hope from it. It is more a curse than anything else."

"Love is not supposed to do that," Colin murmured as he rubbed his temples.

"And yet..." He shrugged helplessly.

Still Colin looked concerned. "How did I never know that you were in love with her?"

Kit turned his head towards his brother so fast Colin jumped. "Not *in* love, Colin. I love her, I am not in love with her."

Colin's brow furrowed. "I do not understand the difference. We are talking about romantic love, correct?"

Kit heaved a pained sigh. "Yes, unfortunately. I have not been *in* love with her for years, but I cannot stop loving her. As complicated as that sounds, it is even worse to feel. You knew something had gone on between us, and you knew that I was still drawn to her."

Colin only nodded, obviously still confused.

"I could not bear to admit aloud what my feelings for her were. You accused me once of being obsessed with her."

"You asked me never to speak of it again, and I never have," Colin interjected with a defensive gesture.

"I know, and I appreciate that," Kit told him with a nod, "but it does not change the fact that you were right, though you may not have understood. I might have denied it, but truth is truth. My ears strain for news of her, my eyes search for her, my heart skips three beats when I see her, and my stomach clenches like a nervous, lovesick puppy when she speaks to me. And I hate every single moment of it. I have loved her for years. Hated her, been bitter about my traitorous heart, wished that I could root it out of me, but there it is." He smirked bitterly at his brother. "Shouldn't this be the happiest moment of my life? I am to marry the woman I love. Is that not the height of all glorious things?"

Colin slowly shook his head, his face contorted with concern. "Not like this, Kit. Not like this."

Kit's smirk faded into a tight smile. "Well, it's too late for that now."

"No, it is not," Colin insisted, canting forward even more. "We can find another solution."

That drew a snort from him as he looked away. "Right. Because there is another man out there who would take Marianne as she is and give her the chance at happiness we all want for her."

"Do you want it?"

Something in his brother's soft query brought Kit's head slowly around, the hair on the back of his neck standing on end. "What is that supposed to mean?" he asked, defenses suddenly raised and at the ready.

Colin gave him a knowing look. "Why are you doing this?" he asked again.

Kit returned his look with a rather mocking face. "Because it is my chance at being heroic."

Colin frowned and his brows snapped together. "Heroic," he repeated slowly. "I am afraid I am going to need more than some chance at glory for you. You won't become a martyr, will you?"

"I guess I could be a bit of a sacrificial lamb," he considered thoughtfully. "I will certainly have the sympathy of all Society, perhaps even England as a whole…"

"No, don't you start that," Colin snapped, pointing a warning finger at him. "If you do this, *if* you do this… you do not get to wave your so called martyrdom like a badge of honor or feathered plume. You do not get to do this so you have an excuse to be miserable for the rest of your life."

"Shouldn't I be the one to decide if I will be miserable forever or not?" Kit asked, leaning on his hand a little and watching his brother with interest.

"You already have."

Kit straightened up and frowned at Colin. "I have not."

The return look of disbelief and blatant understanding made him shift in his seat.

"Yes," Colin said firmly, "you have. I do not care what your real reasons are for this marriage, but you will not make this a hellish existence for Marianne just to make yourself feel better."

"I thought you did not want her as your sister," Kit sneered, folding his arms.

"I don't," Colin said bluntly, "but that does not mean that I don't care about her. There is a reason why we are not selling her off to the first man we can find."

Kit started to raise his hand to indicate he was that man, that that was exactly what they had agreed to, when Colin gave him a look, and he lowered it once more.

"Marianne is not wife material," Colin continued, folding his arms as well. "You know this, or you would have married her already, as you want her so badly. Debatable at times, yes," he said loudly, as Kit began to protest, "but even you wouldn't be doing this if you did not want to, somewhere. I am telling you right now, Kit, that you cannot marry her if all you intend is to make her life hell because that is what she did to yours."

Kit sat in silence, staring at his brother for a long while. Somehow, in some impossible way, Colin had become the sensible, responsible brother, and Kit the reckless bachelor. Not that his rashness would ever match what Colin had accomplished, but it did not change the fact that he had never in his life expected Colin to be the one talking sense into him.

"You owe it to yourself to try for more," Colin said softly. "And even Marianne, as impossible and maddening and spoiled as she is, deserves a chance for more. Even if she does not take it."

"I have no intention of making her life hell," Kit answered, his voice sounding hollow even to his own ears. "I hope to teach her a lesson or two, see if I can't bring some sense into her head, but I know full well she will never change unless she wishes it. I will not intentionally make her unhappy, but I cannot promise that she will be particularly happy either."

"I doubt anyone knows that," Colin muttered, shaking his head again. "Not in this situation."

Kit nodded soberly, then gave his brother an open, honest look. "I can't explain why I am doing this, Colin, not even to myself. I suppose I hope that somewhere inside is the girl we once knew, the one that I *did* fall in love with, before she became strangled by the dragon that currently exists in her form."

"Marianne is not a dragon," Colin protested with a brief flare of temper.

Kit scowled and leaned forward, bracing his elbows on his knees. "Do you have a better word to describe her?"

Colin's mouth worked, but no sound came out.

Kit nodded firmly. "Exactly."

"You can't speak of her that way once you are married to her."

"I know. And I will not." He sighed and put his face into his hands for a moment, then brought his fingertips to his lips. "I am resigning myself to the fact that I will have a wife that might not care for me at all. But then I remember who she was… and I find I still have hope, somehow. I cannot give that up. I cannot give *her* up." He peered at Colin, who looked thunderstruck. "Does that make me a fool?"

"Probably," Colin managed, tempering it with a smile. Then he cocked his head. "Do you even know how to be a husband?"

Kit laughed a little. "No, not at all, but neither does Marianne know how to be a wife." He smiled at his brother, then groaned. "This is going to set London aflame with talk."

"Yes, it will. So you had better prepare yourself, Kit. I will stand up with you and support you, if it is what you want. If you are determined to marry her, in spite of everything, with a full understanding of what you are undertaking, then I will defend you both as valiantly as I have ever done." Colin looked appropriately determined, and almost seemed to be glowing with his sudden valor.

This would take some getting used to.

"I am doing this, Colin," he said firmly, keeping his eyes steady on his twin.

Colin smiled thinly. "I know. I knew that the moment you said it."

Kit raised a brow. "How did you know that?"

Colin shrugged, his smile growing. "You are a man of your word, Kit. Honorable to the core. You would never have suggested it to Duncan if you were not going to follow through."

Kit found himself smiling in earnest at his brother. "I'm getting married," he said on a laugh.

Colin made a face. "We need to secure the lady's acceptance first."

Kit scoffed and waved a hand. "You heard Duncan. She'll have me."

A slow, mischievous, very Colin-esque grin spread across Colin's face, and Kit was suddenly very wary. "What is that for?" he asked.

"This is going to be a very interesting marriage," Colin said, settling into his chair as if to watch it unfold before his very eyes.

"Of course it is," Kit replied, confused, "but why should you say it like that?"

Still Colin's smile remained. "You say that you know Marianne. Better than most of us, I should assume. Do you really think she will be as easy to persuade as Duncan seems to think? And that she is going to quietly and meekly enter into this union as appropriately compliant as she ought to be?"

Kit's jaw suddenly ached and it took a great deal of effort to keep his mouth from dropping open.

Of course, he'd known it would be difficult, but he hadn't thought it through in great detail. Marianne was emotional and headstrong and naturally rebellious, and he had very little comfort to offer her in that regard, should she have sought comfort from him at all. She might have wanted his head on a platter instead.

It could be a very ugly beginning to this marriage.

And he had not exactly envisioned it starting off well.

"She will come around to the idea," he said roughly, rubbing at the back of his head.

Colin's smile grew a little. "Not before a rather loud, drawn out, and vicious fit ensues."

Kit swallowed and tried for a smile. "Perhaps I have not thought this through as thoroughly as I should have."

"Oh, I know you have not," Colin laughed, getting to his feet, "but I can promise you that I will very much enjoy watching."

Kit looked up at him with a frown. "That is all you have to say?"

Colin mirrored Kit's typical sardonic brow raise. "You said the same thing to me not too long ago."

"Yes, and we see what sort of trouble that led to," Kit remarked dryly as he pushed himself to his feet as well.

Colin grinned at him. "But you are always saying how you are so much wiser and more responsible than I am. Surely you would never make such disastrous mistakes as your younger brother."

"Why do I confide in you?" Kit muttered as he started out of the door, glancing behind him with a glower.

"Because your only other option is Rosie, and that would not go well at all," Colin said with a faint skip as he caught up to Kit.

"It's going to be hard enough to explain this marriage to her," Kit muttered.

Colin clapped a hand on his shoulder. "Don't worry. I will be right there with you when you tell her."

Kit shrugged his hand off. "That does not give me any comfort." He shook his head and the pair of them returned to the room with the others.

They all looked to them as the brothers entered the room.

"All settled?" Duncan asked with a searching look between the pair of them.

"Quite," Kit clipped, settling back into his chair.

Colin only nodded as he did the same.

"Do you want to inform her of the news?" Kit asked Duncan. "Or shall I?"

The entire room seemed to shudder. "I will," Duncan groaned. "She is my sister, it is my responsibility."

Colin looked somber and solemn as he gazed at his large friend. "You should eat something before you go, Duncan. A last meal, if you will."

Kit glanced at his brother, wondering if he was supposed to start scolding him about speaking of Marianne that way.

The others in the room laughed in agreement, and Kit opted to sit back and let them.

He would have to do enough defending for a lifetime very soon.

"Duncan, I have another question, and I have wondered it for several months now. What in the world possessed you to name your daughter after Tibby?" Derek asked with a shudder.

"Absolutely," Nathan chimed in. "One was quite enough."

Duncan smiled and shrugged. "Annalise wanted it. And we will never call her Tibby. Just Tillie."

Colin snorted and flagged down a servant to request a tray. "Right, until she gets old enough to know Tibby well, and then you'll be in quite the mess, my friend."

Kit resisted the urge to rub at his forehead again. They were unknowingly bringing up another thing he was worried about.

Tibby.

Marianne agreeing to the marriage would be a trial enough.

Tibby could be a nightmare.

Chapter Three

"Married? I thought we just prevented my getting married, now you've changed your mind?"

"*We* did nothing," Duncan pointed out sternly, sitting as he was in the chair beside her in the sitting room adjacent to the bedchamber she had been using. "And you do not get to claim that your illicit attempt at elopement compares with this plan."

Marianne stared at her brother in abject horror, slowly shaking her head. "I apologized to you for my blindness and my rash behavior, Duncan, and you said…"

"I said I would find a solution," her brother overrode, his expression not at all comforting. "And I have."

She did not appreciate the finality in his tone. She folded her arms and glared back. "And your brilliant solution is to marry me off?"

The storm brewing in her brother's face should have warned her, but she had never been particularly adept at obeying unspoken warnings.

"What a novel concept!" she said, mocking amazement. "A girl causes trouble, and the only plausible solution a group of men can come up with is to get her married."

"That's enough."

"This is a punishment, isn't it?" Marianne cried, getting to her feet. "You've been warning me again and again that I was going too far, that my actions would someday prove to be my downfall, and you did not know how to save me. Is this your idea of saving me, Duncan? Selling me off like a common animal?"

Her voice broke on the last word and her emotions got the better of her, which was almost unheard of for her. She was a consummate actress by now, and never showed emotion at all, except, it seemed, for her brother.

"Marianne," Duncan said softly, surprising her with a gentle tone and more gentle expression.

She had expected thunderbolts and roaring and the power of Zeus to rain down upon her head. She had provoked him, goaded him intentionally because a fight was far more comfortable for her than this. And Duncan never backed down from a fight, particularly not with her. They'd had some perfect rows in their past, and the apologies came after, as did the solutions.

She was not sure how to do this without a fight.

She met her brother's eyes and the fight went out of her, the dam in her chest bursting into tears that she could not contain. She sank to the floor beneath her, and put her face into her hands, crying rather pitifully.

Duncan was soon sitting on the floor next to her, pulling her tightly against his side. "Oh, minnow," he sighed, handing her a handkerchief, "I wish I could have spared you this."

"Then don't make me do it!" she begged, leaning her head on his shoulder and wiping at her eyes.

She felt him shake his head. "There is no choice, Marianne. You have run away from London without the knowledge or consent of your family, and even Mrs. Gordon, try as she might, cannot keep that from getting out. Your own popularity will be the rope they hang you by, I am afraid."

She pushed at his chest a little, not quite willing to remove his comforting arm, but disturbed by the picture he had painted. "That was unnecessary," she protested stubbornly.

He looked down at her with a quizzical brow. "Was it? You know Society, Marianne. You have seen what they do to others in your situation, and you know how bad it can get."

That was secretly what terrified Marianne. She did know. She had been part of the throng that had called for the metaphorical blood of those who had behaved as she had, without any sort of sympathy or pity. She had furthered rumors of such things, had possibly been one of the chief causes for some rather painful falls from Society's good graces, all without batting an eyelash.

But surely, with the influence of others in the rooms downstairs, there could be something better than marrying her off…

"If you were anyone else," Duncan said, reading her thoughts with perfect clarity, "then there might have been something we could do that was less drastic. Between Colin and Derek alone, they have enough influence to change someone's fate. But you, my dear sister, are the height of Society, and everyone cares about where you go and what you do."

Her heart sunk deep into the pit of her stomach as the reality of her situation set in.

"You don't have a choice, Marianne," Duncan continued softly. "Not even I can save you from this."

And as wrong as it felt, she knew he was right. Her own willful nature had been her undoing, and there was no alternative but for her to marry, if she had any hope of retaining a shred of respectability. Or living in seclusion at Brockleton House or, more likely, some cottage on its expansive lands. Shropshire was full of expansive lands, and nobody asked questions there.

But she would be miserable in seclusion.

"What if I went to stay with Graeme?" she suggested in a small voice.

Duncan gave her a look. "You want to go to MacLaine Keep and stay with our cousins for the rest of your life?"

Marianne winced, her nose wrinkling up. As much as she loved her cousins, and she did love them, they had a rather harsh life, and they thrived in it. They would never be properly behaved for the London Society, but they could be passable. They were generous and kind, loyal to anyone with family ties, and would protect her from everyone and everything that could potentially harm her. They would not even judge her for her actions. Others might, but never her cousins. Of course, they lived in an old castle that was practically medieval in its design and construction, which was all well and good for visiting. But to live with them…

"And you would still have to marry someday," Duncan added with a soft nudge. "Even Graeme wouldn't be able to sustain you forever."

Marianne groaned and rubbed at her head. "I'm sorry," she murmured for what felt like the thousandth time.

"I know."

She glanced up at her brother's face, and saw that, to her astonishment, he did seem to know. He accepted her apology. Not many would have.

Her brother knew her better than anyone in the world, which she could not always have said. Someone else once held that position of prestige.

No more.

Not for years.

But her brother knew her, good and bad, and loved her in spite of it all.

She leaned against him more fully, sagging a little, forgoing her usually perfect posture. "Then I will do it. I mean, I have to do it, obviously, but I agree to it."

He patted her back softly. "Thank you, minnow." He pressed a soft kiss to her hair and got to his feet. "I will see to the arrangements."

She frowned, confused. "Arrangements?" she asked, looking over her shoulder at him as he headed for the door. "What do you mean?"

He raised a brow. "For your wedding, of course."

Marianne turned herself on the floor to face him completely and gave him an exasperated look. "My wedding? What wedding?" Her eyes went wide and her heart stopped. "You don't mean you've found a husband for me already?"

Duncan tilted his head as if he were concerned for her welfare. "Yes," he said slowly, "which is why I came up here to tell you about it."

Marianne's mouth was suddenly dry and it was several seconds before she could speak. "Who?" she eventually managed.

Duncan seemed to take a breath, held it, then said, "Kit Gerrard."

Her entire world stopped spinning on those words and she was completely frozen, immoveable, unable to breathe or think or blink.

From bad to worse, the absolute and very worst.

This was a nightmare.

This was *her* nightmare.

"No," she squeaked, her voice sounding as if it came from a great distance. She cleared her throat, though the powerful pulsing in her ears would not clear. "No," she said again, more firmly. "No, no, absolutely not."

Duncan frowned and his brow furrowed. "I don't understand. No?"

Marianne wanted to laugh, but there was absolutely nothing in this to laugh about, not even in mockery. "No," she said again, her voice and her panic rising. She scrambled to her feet. "Not Kit, no. No, Duncan, please. Anyone else, quite literally, anyone. But not Kit."

Her brother's frown grew and he folded his arms across his broad chest, looking rather disgruntled. "What is wrong with Kit Gerrard?"

She opened her mouth to reply, but what could she say? *Nothing* was wrong with Kit. Anyone else in England, or the entire world, could marry Kit Gerrard, and they were welcome to him. He was a fine gentleman, with a vast fortune, a good family, and well respected by those who were not idiots. There was absolutely nothing wrong with him.

Except he hated her.

No, he himself was not the problem. They would be. Together.

He would make her miserable, and love every minute of it. And she would no doubt make him miserable, just by being his wife. They had once been friends, and back then, they might have suited, but that was ages ago. After what had passed between them, what they had once been, and what fracture had come to that… and after experiencing his bitterness firsthand when he'd finally returned to England, when she had not expected it, she knew they could never be friends again.

But how could she possibly have known that he would have taken a refused proposal so personally?

And how could she ever explain *that* to her brother?

"Marianne?" Duncan prodded without patience.

"I don't love him!" she thought up quickly. And it was true, she didn't. She could not stand the man any more than he could stand her.

Their reasons were different, but the facts were the same. There was no love between them.

Duncan gave an odd sort of snort. "You were expecting to find love in the short time we have? You didn't even love the man you ran away with, Marianne. Love was never going to come into this arrangement, and you know that. But love can grow."

Love could grow? With Kit? The idea was laughable. Some people might be that fortunate in their marriage of convenience, but it was certainly rare, and would not happen here. The best she could hope for was a silent marriage of avoidance.

"Surely you don't wish me to be unhappy in my marriage," she protested, folding her arms to match him.

He had no doubt been spending too much time with Derek, for one brow slowly rose rather imperiously. "Why should a marriage to Kit make you unhappy?"

Why, indeed.

Marianne whirled away, covering her face and groaning. "I can't marry him, Duncan. I can't."

"Why?"

She could never tell him how or why or what reasons there were for this, not if she wanted him to love and trust her. This was one detail of her life she had never shared with him, and never would. After what had passed between them, she knew that six years was not long enough to deaden the sting of her behavior, not for Kit, and not for her. Rumors had swirled about them from that day on, but she had never said anything.

And Kit… He would…

"Why?" Duncan asked again. "Is there something about Kit Gerrard that makes him unfit to be a husband?"

She swallowed hard. "No," she whispered honestly.

"Does he squander money or mistreat people?"

Her aside? She shook her head. "No."

Duncan pushed off of the door and came to stand just a few feet behind her. "Is he an honorable man?"

He knew the answer to all of these questions, and she could not answer any differently. "Yes, of course, he is," she said impatiently. "In fact, I doubt a man has ever been more so, unless he was Geoffrey Harris."

Duncan put a hand on her shoulder and gently turned her back to face him. "Then why should you, in your situation, not marry a man like that?"

A man like that was not the problem.

It was that particular man that was the problem.

She looked into her brother's eyes and saw that he was waiting for an answer. One she could not give. "It is personal," she murmured, averting her eyes.

Duncan made a small noise of disapproval. He waited for her to look at him once more. "And does Kit know these personal matters?"

She looked down at the buttons on his weskit, and nodded once. "Then it is settled."

Her head shot up and she looked at him in horror as he stepped away, again heading for the door. "What?" she cried.

He glanced at her without concern. "Kit is willing to marry you, knowing the reasons why you should not. If he suggested it, despite those matters, then I have no concerns about it."

Suggested? Surely he was not saying that...

There was no possible way that Christopher Gerrard would suggest himself as a candidate for marriage to her. Not after what she had just done, and not after what had happened before.

"What?" she said again. "Kit suggested it?"

"It was his idea," Duncan said with a nod. "I wouldn't have thought of it, and it really is much simpler this way. You marry Kit here, and we all go to London without a fuss, rumors are at a minimum, and you are taken care of. I asked Kit if he was sure, it seemed so illogical, but he was determined." Duncan shrugged, still watching her carefully, despite his apparent nonchalance. "He will marry you."

Marianne had to reach out and grip the chair next to her for balance. Kit Gerrard had volunteered to marry her. He had not been forced, he certainly had not felt duty-bound, and there was no hint of sentimentality in it. Before the scandal had ever really touched any of them, he had put himself on the chopping block for her.

Her mind whirled in confusion. She could still hear his chilling voice from that day at Tibby's musicale, could feel the icy glare of his blue eyes disapproving of everything about her, as he said the words she would never forget: *"I do not tolerate heartless creatures who care only for themselves. Go back to your menagerie and leave me in peace."*

They had not spoken since.

She had taken great pains to avoid him, and he had done the same, it seemed.

Now he would marry her?

An apprehensive shiver raced across her skin and she resisted the urge to rub her arms against the chill.

Her future was bleak indeed. His sentiments could not have changed so, not when he continually looked at her with the same expression of disgust and superiority. She would be in a shell of a marriage to protect her from scandal, when the partner in her marriage had the power to give her more misery than the scandal itself.

They thought this would stem the rumors? It would enflame them.

And Kit had to know that.

Still he said he would marry her?

Very well, she would accept. And she would give London something to talk about.

And perhaps then her would-be husband would think twice about his superiority.

"All right," Marianne said stiffly, folding her arms yet again. "If he has no objections, then so be it. I will marry him. But I shall not like it."

Duncan gave her an incredulous look. "Did you expect to like it? You would not like marrying anybody."

She sniffed, no longer feeling emotional or distressed. Merely enraged. "And I like nothing less than the idea of Kit Gerrard as my husband."

Duncan rolled his eyes and wrenched open the door. "Your opinion on the subject is noted."

"And ignored," she pointed out.

He turned and she saw his jaw tightening. "You have lost the right to choose here."

Slight tremors of fury started in her fingers and toes and made their way through her limbs. "I don't love him."

"Well, you had better get over that, or start trying to, Marianne," Duncan barked, "because no one else will have you. Do you even know what he is sacrificing by marrying you?"

"No more than I sacrifice by marrying him. Believe me, Duncan, if anything works out in this sham marriage, it will be in spite of Kit Gerrard, not because of him."

The door slammed behind her brother and Marianne whirled to the toilette, picking up various objects and throwing them against her bed, grinding her teeth together to keep from screaming.

Marriage to Kit Gerrard? She was sick at the very thought of it.

Why must a woman be so helpless and voiceless? Why could she not return to London as herself, wiser and only slightly soiled, and continue on without ramifications?

Why had she been stupid enough to think that a salacious elopement with a scoundrel would be a brilliant addition to her reputation?

She grabbed a pillow and screeched into it until her frame shook with exhaustion. She flung it, and herself, on the bed and seethed until she fell into a fitful sleep.

Chapter Four

The wedding day dawned bright and beautiful, as if to mock everything Kit had ever wanted out of life. He had avoided thinking too deeply on what it was he was about to do, and it seemed to calm his anxieties. He had not seen Marianne since becoming engaged to her, and he was not certain if his bride was going to claw his eyes out, ignore him completely, or dissolve into a mass of tears that would now be his duty to see to.

All he knew was that she had agreed to the match.

No one would tell him more than that.

Duncan was much easier now his wife and daughter were back with him, though he was surprisingly reserved on the subject of Marianne. Even Annalise, who had always been very kind and open with him, would not discuss her.

He supposed that was a sign in and of itself.

Marianne was not pleased.

Well, neither was he.

It was truly a grand day for this wedding.

He sat in the finest clothes that could be acquired on this short notice in a vestibule off of the chapel, waiting for his bride to arrive at the church. Colin's friends were the only guests in attendance, and Marianne's only female companion would be her sister-in-law. Colin had agreed to stand up with him, but Kit rather wished everybody would stop pretending this wedding was actually something to celebrate or deserving of the usual niceties.

Even Derek had gone to the exorbitant length of riding hell-bent for London and back to procure the special license from the

Archduke of Canterbury for them, as he held more influence than all the rest of them put together; he had arrived only this morning. Kit could have done without the extremes.

Why could the minister not just pronounce them man and wife and send them on their way?

That, he supposed, was reserved for Gretna Green, and only those simplified circumstances could have it with ease.

Pity.

He sat forward and rubbed at his brow with a heavy sigh. They were leaving directly after the service and all heading back to London. It had been highly debated, but Kit was adamant that he would ride his horse and Marianne would have the carriage to herself. They would travel separately from the rest of the company, which the others were quite relieved about, including Duncan, but it did not mean they would do so sharing the same space.

Enclosed spaces with Marianne would make him nervous for quite some time, until she accustomed herself to being married to him.

So perhaps in ten years they would share a carriage.

Ten years with Marianne as his wife…

Would he live that long?

"Not even married yet, and already you look ill."

He almost groaned aloud. She was here.

He slowly sat back and gave her a bland look, pretending his heart didn't lurch at the sight of her in a pale muslin, her hair curled and pinned and strewn with small flowers, and a simplified veil draped down the back of her bonnet.

She was a beautiful bride.

His stomach clenched in distress.

She folded her arms and raised a brow at him. "What?"

He shrugged one shoulder. "I am simply looking at my bride, is that so wrong?"

She snorted and moved further into the vestibule, leaning against the wall, looking stubborn and irritated. "Don't say that as if it means something."

Ah, so this would be how it was going to go. Excellent. He could fight just as well.

"Aren't you concerned about bad luck?" he asked in a completely unconcerned voice. "You know, the bridegroom seeing the bride before they are at the altar?"

Her expression nearly made him grin. It was perfectly emotionless and left no doubt in his mind how she felt about this situation. "Things couldn't possibly get any worse than they are now."

The clipped bite in her tone strummed an intriguing chord within him, and he felt a little unsettled by it. "I beg to differ."

She pursed her lips. "Pray, do tell," she drawled, as if she truly wished he wouldn't.

"Marksby."

She hissed and a slight wince twisted her features, but then she was back to her usual haughty, beautiful self, her rich blue eyes steady on him. "Yes, about that. I wanted to discuss some things with you before I am bound to you."

He slowly rose and clasped his hands behind his back. "Naturally."

She took in a small breath and released it quickly. "First and foremost, we will never discuss that man again. I was an idiot, he was a villain, and the matter is finished."

Kit smirked. "Is it? I rather thought it was just beginning."

Marianne glowered. "I mean the man himself, you troll. The situation in which I find myself, as well as the scandal from it, cannot be helped, but Marksby will never be brought up again."

If she was willing to admit that she was an idiot, he could agree to that concession. "Very well, as you wish. Next?"

Marianne nodded, but did not look pleased. "I shall retain my independence."

Kit frowned. "I have not the pleasure of understanding you."

"You'll get used to that," she bit out sharply.

He gave her a look and waited for her to explain herself.

She did in short order, her brow furrowing. "What I mean is I shall not be biddable. I am the same creature I was before, and I shall keep my societal interests and entertainments with or without you. I am not going to be only your wife and nothing more."

Kit felt a cool smile cross his lips. "No, indeed, continue to be who you were before, as that worked out so well for you."

Her upper lip curled in a hint of a snarl. "Toad…"

He shrugged as if it did not matter. "I will not restrict you unless you get out of hand. I mean to let you have your way in many things, mostly because I do not care. But if you bring shame or dishonor to me or to my family name, I shall have a great many things to say about that."

She gave him a mulish sort of look.

He returned it with one of significant warning. "I mean it, Marianne. I will have your word. It is not only me that you must think about now. I have three sisters who depend on me for their futures. You will not ruin their chances simply to spite me."

Her expression cleared and she seemed to think on that. "I can live with that," she finally said with a nod. "You have my word. I only ask that I receive fair warning before you do something drastic."

"What, or you might change to prevent the punishment?" he asked mockingly.

"I might," she snapped. "Depending upon what it is I have done or you expect."

"Just don't make me regret this, Marianne," he growled, raising a warning finger and stepping closer.

She smirked up at him. "I cannot promise you that. You shall regret this in about fifteen minutes, I should think."

He returned her smirk with one of his own, which made her rock back. "Surely you don't think me such a weakling as that."

"No," she said in a low voice that set his hair on edge, "I simply know your opinion of me, sir, and the affliction my presence must be for you. And while your tolerance of heartless people who think only of themselves might be low, you cannot completely avoid me unless you escape this marriage."

She remembered those words? That was uncomfortable. He'd been harsh, but the first time seeing her after two years away had unnerved him and he'd lashed out. He had never taken it back, and he would not now. Still, it was not a particularly pleasant memory.

"Are you trying to dissuade me from our marriage?" he asked softly, keeping his voice controlled.

Her eyes suddenly became wide and pleading, her expression soft. "Can I?"

Her eagerness steeled him. He raised his chin a touch. "No."

As he thought, her wide-eyed softening vanished in a moment and her arrogance was replaced. "It was worth a try." She glanced back out into the chapel, then back at him. "Do you have anything to say or shall we proceed with this comedy?"

He exhaled slowly, willing his anger back firmly. "As I said, so long as you do nothing to shame me or my family, you may do as you wish. I will not be overbearing, and I shall leave you to your own devices. Except for one thing."

"I knew it," she muttered, tossing her head a little. "What is it?"

He leveled her his most serious glare, and she stiffened under it. "No lovers, Marianne."

Her brows shot up. "What?"

He shook his head with determination. "No lovers. Not one. I will not be mocked in that way. Do you understand me?"

Something in his tone or his expression seemed to startle her. She swallowed hard and nodded. "I do. And I shall not squander your fortune away, either."

Kit scoffed and started past her. "Good. Though you could not manage to, no matter now hard you tried."

Marianne made a soft sound of amusement. "You underestimate me."

He stopped and glanced behind him. "I tried to have them remove love and obey from the vows, but the minister refused adamantly. Pretend for his sake that you actually will."

Now she barked a hard laugh. "Simple recitation of empty words means nothing to me. I rather think I shall hold to our conversation just now as the best sort of vow we shall attain. We will not kill each other and we will not ruin each other. Simple enough."

Kit exhaled roughly in irritation. That was no way to begin a marriage, but it was the best he could do. "I did, however," he continued as he started walking again, "manage to convince him that a special license trumped his psalms, so we will be spared the sermon."

"Well, well, you may prove useful after all."

He whirled to glare at her, but she had already gone down the hall to the front of the church so she could proceed in properly with her brother.

He squeezed his hands into fists at his sides, and turned on his heel to assume his position at the front of the church. Colin was instantly at his side, and the man at the organ struck up pompously.

"You look as though you might punch the minister," Colin muttered out of the corner of his mouth.

"If this is not the fastest wedding service in the history of the Church of England, I might," he replied in like manner. "And if you do not shut up, you might get some too."

"What has you so agitated?" Colin hissed.

Kit grunted in response.

Not three seconds later, Colin sighed. "Ah, yes, I see… A very beautiful dragon, your bride."

Kit closed his eyes and exhaled slowly, fighting for control. He did not need to be reminded of that. He knew full well how hauntingly beautiful she was, particularly today. There was no equal, and he did not have to turn and look in order to know how she entered the church and walked towards him.

She would have all of the grace and poise of royalty, a perfect bride despite the special license and rushed arrangements. No one ignorant of her situation would have suspected anything amiss. She would triumph here just as she had done in every ballroom and sitting room in London.

She was Marianne Bray.

She never did anything less.

"Don't," he growled when his brother opened his mouth once more.

Colin gave him a look that was a mixture of amusement and concern, then he glanced down at Kit's folded hands, which were clenching once more. Then Colin nodded once, his expression cleared, and he obediently faced the minister.

Marianne reached Kit's side and he turned to shake Duncan's hand, and glanced at his bride.

She was staring straight ahead, and he saw the firm set of her perfect jaw.

And the upturn of her pert nose, raised higher than normal.

"This is your last chance," she murmured for his ears alone.

"No, my dear," he replied, facing the minister himself. "I am yours."

He would swear later that he heard her screech, but no one else seemed aware of it. Still, it made him smirk as the service began, and it only faded when the vows commenced.

Well, it was all done and over now, and she was officially and forevermore Marianne Gerrard.

She wrinkled her nose up at how that sounded in her head.

She'd never really imagined any particular surname as becoming hers, but she had certainly never considered that one.

The service had been fairly straightforward, exactly as it had been for every wedding she had ever attended. The exact words and vows, the same boring intonation of the minster ringing in ears, and even the exchange of a ring, just as every wedding did. She had no idea she would be getting an actual ring from Kit, given the hastiness of the marriage, but the simple gold band with sapphire and diamonds was surprisingly elegant.

And quite perfectly suited to her tastes, actually.

And more than she thought Kit would ever give her.

If it hadn't been shoved onto her finger with such haste and efficiency, she might have taken a moment to properly appreciate it. As it was, she could only gasp softly and look up at Kit in surprise, but he had already turned back to the minister, face impassive as ever.

Even during the vows, they had only made a show of looking at each other. Kit's eyes had been somewhere on Marianne's bonnet, her eyes on his cravat. It was by unspoken agreement that they did not meet eyes. That would make these vows more real, when they were anything but.

Oh, she would be a fine wife, as far as it went. She had no intention of throwing the Gerrard name to the wind, despite the temptation to do so. She had too much respect for Colin to do that, and Kit's mention of his sisters had struck something in her. She could not ruin those girls. She might not know them, and certainly had no particular love for children in general, but it was not their fault that their older brother was so insufferable.

She would run his house with the same efficiency and finesse by which she had managed her family home before Annalise had come, and she could make the servants love her quite easily. Despite her manners towards those of her own station, she had a firm rule to never berate or injure those in her service, and in fact, preferred a gentle touch with them. And several conversations with her personal maid and her brother's housekeeper had reassured her that it was much appreciated.

It would no doubt come as a great surprise to her husband that she had quite a bit of skill with the running of a house. And when he discovered that she had swayed the entire staff of their house to her side, he would be quite put out indeed.

And that thought cheered her immensely.

Of course, they would have to find a staff for their house first. She might not have known much about the arrangements, as they had all happened so quickly, but she knew full well that Kit Gerrard had no residence in London. Not one she could remain in, at any rate, which meant even if he did have a house, it was a bachelor's residence, and thus fairly sparsely staffed.

All told, things were lining up fairly well for her as a wife, despite the unfortunate husband selection.

Kit's assurances that he would let her have her way had comforted her somewhat, but she had long ago learned never to trust the word of a man without the proof to reinforce it.

Oddly enough, that bit of wisdom had come from Kit himself.

She sighed and leaned her head back against the carriage as it barreled its way towards London. Kit, as he had been in those days, had been a godsend to her. Gentle, kind, considerate, encouraging, and even charming, which seemed impossible to contemplate now. He'd always made time for her and she had never felt rushed by him or that he ever wished to be elsewhere.

Colin and Duncan had become friends when they were thirteen and fourteen respectively, and Kit usually followed where Colin went, mostly to keep him out of trouble. Many of their adventures took place in London, but occasionally, the boys were invited to Shropshire, when their aunt Agatha allowed it.

She'd never met Aunt Agatha, but Kit and Colin's stories about her were horrifying enough.

Marianne had been a fairly timid child, but pretended at bravery for her brother's sake, and even so young, she had been an accomplished enough actress that he had never suspected how insecure she truly was. But being eight years younger than her rambunctious brother had often had her feeling left out, and only one person noticed.

It was only after a gentle, teasing prod from Colin's quiet twin that she opened up at all. They started a sort of secret friendship, the two of them, and while their loud siblings carried on, Kit worked tirelessly to see that Marianne had a companion, encouraging her voice and her opinions.

He'd been so much older than her that it should have been the height of inconvenience for him to entertain the imaginative child she had been, but he had never given her the slightest indication of any such thing. Once she opened up to him, she'd never quite shut up.

They'd never been particularly regular visitors, but their pattern became routine. Marianne would find some corner of the house or grounds away from where Colin and Duncan would go, and Kit would find her and stay with her until the visit was completed, or they would join in with the others. He always seemed to know where to find her. There was never anything romantic in their visits together, for she was a child and he only ever treated her with politeness and light teasing. No, he had simply become her closest confidante and the brother she had always wished for, despite her love for Duncan.

He had not laughed when she'd told him of her plans to be a grand lady, as Duncan and Colin, soon joined by Derek and Geoffrey, all had. Kit had seen to it that she felt encouraged when she learned a new skill, brought her the gossip from London, though she knew nothing about it, and had even been her first dance partner, when Tibby had seen fit that she should learn.

Kit hated dancing, but for Marianne, he had done so.

They'd laughed far too much to ever actually learn anything.

But she was twelve, and dancing at all was such fun.

The visits became less and less frequent as they both grew older, as was proper and as the business of their lives required. But he had always called when he could, and listened to her tireless complaints about her aunt and her governesses, her stories of Duncan's time in the army, and had comforted her when she confided her fears that she would lose her brother to the French, despite his being stationed far from them.

Kit had always known what Marianne was thinking, and could usually warn her off of a course before she ever opened her mouth about it. It had infuriated her, but only so far as that he always knew, not that he kept her from it.

Where Colin had teased her, Kit had nurtured her.

She had loved them both as brothers.

But Kit... He had been something special to her.

At her first ball, her brother being away with his regiment, Kit had been the one to claim the first dance. She had been terrified, but his calm and steady voice, and the certainty in his eyes, had set her to rights. Hardly anyone else had asked her to dance, but Kit had made sure she never wanted for entertainment. He teased her endlessly about several gentlemen in attendance, and any nerves or tension had eased from Marianne's shoulders, and she had very much enjoyed the entire evening.

The Season as a whole, however, had been a disaster. Not a single man showed interest in her. Her callers had been older women and other girls in their first Season. No hints of courtship or romance, or even friendship.

Kit had not been able to stay the full Season, his duties to his estates requiring his attention, but Colin, as usual, had remained for all of it, and had taken up the charge to be Marianne's protector, chaperone, and court jester. Not that he was needed, of course, as Marianne had rarely been invited anywhere.

Her next Season, she determined, would be much different. She would pretend at confidence, even if she did not have it, and she would stop waiting to be noticed, but command attention.

And when Kit came in the midst of her second Season, he had found an entirely different Marianne from the year before.

She was at the height of fashion, was noticed, invited, and

praised. This Marianne had no flaws or faults, no insecurities, and three offers of marriage, six of courtship, and a steady stream of male callers weekly, none of whom would have done for any creature of sense.

And that had become Kit's favorite topic. He teased her endlessly about the men swarming her, his dry sense of humor studiously analyzing each one as if for serious consideration. It had provided her with hours of amusement, and she found herself collecting men just to see what Kit would say about them.

Then that horrible, hot summer day…

The carriage jerked to a halt and Marianne jolted awake, having been entirely unaware of ever falling asleep. She sat upright and rubbed at her eyes, glancing out of the window to find it was nearly dark.

The door was opened and Kit appeared, looking rather too perfectly put together for riding his horse all day.

"Would you like to stop for the night?" he asked stiffly, his eyes meeting hers, but not seeing her. "Or drive on through?"

Still sore about the memories that had plagued her, and rather wishing he would go away, she scowled. "I do not care."

A muscle twitched in Kit's forehead, but nothing else in his expression altered. He nodded once. "Very well. We will stop." He held out a hand to help her out.

Marianne sniffed and took it with the bare tips of her fingers just for the sake of steadying herself, and snatched her hand away the moment her feet hit the ground. "Trying to be considerate?" she sneered.

"Yes," he said simply.

She looked up at him in disbelief.

He did not look at her as he straightened his gloves and brushed at his coat. "My horse is exhausted after riding so hard all day. He deserves a good night of rest before doing it again."

He strode towards the inn, leaving her gaping in indignation behind him.

If she had the power to burn with her eyes, she would have been a widow already.

She huffed, lifted the hem of her skirts, and followed him,

wondering what sort of scandal a secret marriage of less than eighteen hours that ended in murder would cause.

It might have been worth it.

Chapter Five

*L*ondon had never been a more welcome sight for Kit, and he was ready for the seclusion it could provide him. Hiding from his wife would be so much easier when she was distracted and when he had the freedom to move and go where he wished. Travelling with only her for company had tested his will and patience, and their life together would only make things worse.

But it was London. All of the best hiding places were there.

Thankfully, he and Marianne had been able to avoid having much conversation with her being in the coach and he on his horse, and each inn that they had visited had blessedly had separate rooms privately situated from the rest of the patrons. They had seen very little of each other over the course of the trip, for which he was grateful. Most of their communication had been through glares and brief head movements, and it had worked well enough.

All in all, it was better than he had expected it to be.

But still, riding alongside or near a carriage containing a woman he unnaturally pined for, who was now his wife, of all things, was a torment he had not been prepared for.

He breathed a sigh of relief as they entered Berkeley Square and pulled to a halt before their new home. He'd sent word on ahead to his staff of the change, and things ought to have been at least partially ready for them.

He hoped, at least.

He dismounted and went to the carriage to help his wife down, only to find her already down on her own.

His fingers slid against each other awkwardly at his side.

Marianne brushed at her skirts absently, then looked up at Kit with a scowl. She opened her mouth to say something, but caught sight of where they were and her eyes widened. She looked around, turned to glance about them, and then took in the house before her.

"Are we… in Berkeley Square?" she asked in a squeaky, breathy voice.

Kit forced back the urge to smile and opted for a nod instead. "Very good. We are."

She whirled to face him, her eyes still round as saucers. "You got us a house in Berkeley Square?"

He tilted his head a little. "No, I simply thought you'd want to walk the rest of the way now that we are in London."

A tiny furrow appeared between her perfect brows. "Kit Gerrard, so help me, if this is a cruel joke…"

"Yes," he overrode with a roll of his eyes, "this is our house, and it is in Berkeley Square."

Marianne clamped her lips together on a tiny squeal. "And how did you manage that?" she asked in a would-be composed voice.

He offered her his arm, which she took lightly, and escorted her towards the house. "Very easily. The Duchess of Falmouth had no more use for it now her lover has died, and she is retiring permanently to Surrey."

"Of all the luck!" Marianne said with a skip in her step as the ascended the stairs to the house. "She always was a bit strange."

"Your aunt likes her well enough."

"That should tell you a good deal right there."

That, at least, was true.

"Imagine retiring to Surrey," Marianne mused with obvious disdain. "It is so close to London, you might as well remain here. I have never once thought of Surrey as anything of great value."

"Surrey is quite lovely," Kit informed her as he rang the bell, "and I have a house there."

She sniffed and adjusted her lace gloves. "Well, we are never going there."

"You do not have to, if you wish it," he informed her, the place her hand touched him starting to itch and burn. "I, however, have duties to attend to there on occasion, and quite like it."

She shrugged. "As you wish. It probably smells of pig anyway."

Kit closed his eyes in exasperation, then turned his head to nod at the coachmen to take the carriage and his horse to the mews, which they did at once.

The door to the house was opened and his trusted butler Caldwell answered, looking well and whole, and a bit too delighted to be answering the door of this house.

Caldwell's furry black brows rose as one when he saw them. "Mr. Gerrard! What a pleasant surprise! We were expecting you this afternoon." He stepped back and bowed.

"Yes, well, we pushed on," Kit muttered as Marianne brushed past him anxiously. "Caldwell, may I present my wife, Mrs. Gerrard?"

Marianne had been too busy gazing around the grand entrance to pay the butler any attention at all, and did not turn. Less than that, she did not mark either of them as her eyes and expression seemed to glow with a sort of malevolent satisfaction.

Kit cleared his throat. "Mrs. Gerrard?"

Still she did not turn, her eyes running over various aspects of the hallway and taking in the house as a whole.

Caldwell turned to look at Kit with wide eyes.

Kit tried not to grind his teeth as he removed his hat and tossed it onto the table nearby as the butler closed the door. "Marianne," he barked.

Marianne whirled in surprise as she untied the ribbons of her bonnet. "What?"

Kit indicated the butler with a nudge of his head. "Caldwell would like to meet the lady of the house."

Marianne looked over at him, as if she had no idea he had been there, and her perfect smile appeared, brightening her entire countenance. "Of course! I do apologize, Caldwell, I am never so rude or thoughtless." She handed her coat and bonnet to a maid who had appeared from the hall.

Kit barely avoided snorting and removed his riding coat, handing it off to the same maid.

"I am afraid I have not adjusted to my new surname as yet," Marianne continued, blatantly ignoring Kit and walking over to the butler, who now seemed at least a foot taller and had more perfect posture. "It will undoubtedly take some getting used to."

"Yes, madam," Caldwell intoned with a small smile.

Marianne dimpled and held out her hand. "It is a pleasure to meet you, Caldwell. I trust the new arrangements have not caused too much difficulty for you?"

Caldwell took her hand in surprise and bowed over it. "Not at all, madam. The former staff have been adjusting well with the rest of us, and you shall find the entire house in perfect order, I think."

Marianne frowned a little. "Former staff?" She turned to look at Kit. "The former staff stayed on?"

Kit nodded at Caldwell to explain.

"Yes, madam," Caldwell said, gesturing for them to come with him. "The duchess had no use for them in her country residence."

Kit heard Marianne snort under her breath and mutter, "Country residence, indeed."

Caldwell, however, did not hear. "Had I known you would arrive this early, I would have had them all available to be presented to you for your inspection." He looked over his shoulder rather apologetically at them both.

"It is not necessary," Marianne said with a wave, her voice surprisingly natural. "If you do not have concerns about them, neither shall I. The house appears to be in rather perfect order, and you seem to have things quite in hand. No need for my interference."

Kit looked down at her in surprise, but she paid him no heed.

"I will, however," Caldwell continued on, "be sure to present Mrs. Wilton to you. She is the housekeeper, and worked for Her Grace for many years. I have found her to be quite capable and firm of hand."

"Excellent, Caldwell," Marianne praised, still looking around at the house with a smile.

Kit was bewildered. What was she doing? She was warm and friendly with the butler, pretending as though these changes had been perfectly natural and she had been expecting them. She was being… matronly.

And doing it well.

They met the housekeeper in short order, and she, too, was upset that the staff had not been prepared for them, but assured them that all of the rooms were ready, and their luggage, such as it was, would be taken to their rooms and unloaded without delay.

A light meal was also quickly produced for them, and they were shown into the dining room to enjoy it.

A strapping footman helped Marianne with her chair and she gave him a dazzling smile of gratitude that the poor lad could only blink at.

Kit snorted softly and tucked his serviette into his collar. "Don't do that," he scolded.

Marianne actually looked surprised. "Do what?"

He gave her a look. "That. Flirt with the servants. Smooth Caldwell's feathers. Don't do that."

Marianne huffed a little in her seat. "Well, pardon me for being polite and kind to the servants, Mr. Gerrard. Did you expect me to huff and puff and order people about the first three minutes in my new home?"

"Yes, actually," he said simply, as he began eating. "Or demand to be shown to your rooms so you could cry some more."

Marianne shook her head with a roll of her eyes and laid her own serviette in her lap. "I have not cried in ages, Kit. I have quite got over the whole thing, as, I think, should you."

He raised a brow and opened his mouth to retort that her behavior was something one did not simply just get over when she raised her hands for him to stop.

"The point is," she said with a steady look at him, "that I am trying to get acquainted here. So put aside your pitchfork for a moment."

He replied by taking another bite of food.

"Did you intentionally retain the duchess' staff?" Marianne asked him with interest. "Or did that happen by chance?"

"Intention," he said with a nod. "I brought over my own limited staff, put Caldwell in charge, and let him make the decisions about who stayed and who went. I did not want to be troubled with it, and I hardly thought you would either."

"I might have," she muttered, pouting childishly over her plate.

"You wouldn't before," Kit assured her with a bit of a sneer. "You were so busy fighting with your brother and resisting this marriage that you had no energy for house details."

Marianne's fork came down with a clatter and he received a bold glare. "I could have been consulted!" she argued indignantly. "Or were you just so occupied with taking care of everything without reference to me, the marriage, the house, the journey back, that you just could not be bothered?"

He shrugged a shoulder and took another bite. "A simple thank you will suffice."

She screeched between clenched teeth, flopping her hands into her lap.

"You will also find," Kit said simply, as if his wife's behavior was normal, "that the duchess left all of her furniture. Do with that what you will. Some of the rooms will probably be overdone, but if your tastes run in that course, feel free to keep them as such."

"Oh, thank you for giving me an occupation," Marianne replied with dripping sarcasm.

Kit smirked at her. "Incidentally, the house is fully staffed, but if something displeases you, I am sure Mrs. Wilton would be happy to secure whatever you need."

"I will need my things from home," she sniffed, beginning to eat once more.

He nodded once. "It is already being brought over. Your lady's maid will also come."

She looked surprised. "Anna? You are letting me keep her?"

Kit scoffed. "Did you think I would have a jail keeper for you instead?"

"I did, actually."

He shook his head, and sighed. "No, as charming an idea as that is, we could not have the rumors. Your lady's maid seems to like you, which might be hard to find elsewhere, so Duncan released her to us."

Marianne made a face that must have matched the thoughts in her head, but not his words. "Well," she finally said, "at least someone here will like me."

That seemed rather petulant, but he let it pass.

It might have been true.

"I think it will be a most fortunate staff for us," Kit mentioned absently as he ate. "After all, the duchess lived here quite comfortably without anyone hearing the faintest whiff of detail or scandal."

Marianne looked up at him with a stubborn expression, the effort to remain controlled causing a visible tension in her forehead. "How fortunate for us. No one will know how vilely we suit."

"That is the idea, yes."

She pursed her lips for a moment, and her face cleared as she thought. "The duchess seemed to leave in quite a hurry," she said carefully, returning to her meal.

Kit nodded slowly, dabbing the corner of his mouth with his serviette. "She did indeed. Most distressed, I think, about losing Lord Rodale so suddenly."

Marianne frowned. "Lord Rodale did not die in this house, did he?"

Again, Kit nodded, though it wasn't true. "Tragic, isn't it?"

Marianne's eyes widened. "He died here?"

"Not in this dining room, no," Kit said with a light laugh, rising from the table. "Upstairs in the bedchambers, of course."

He saw Marianne's delicate throat work in horror. "Is that where I am sleeping?" she asked with a half-panicked, half-mocking look.

He thought about lying and telling her yes, thought about playing up the story to make it more horrifying, and even thought about stroking her cheek, oddly enough.

He forced a placid smile instead. "Of course not, my dear. You are quite safe. He died in one of the guest rooms, though I cannot remember exactly which…"

He left before giving her another chance to ask him anything or argue another point, but he heard her sputtering madly, and a proud smirk found its way to his face.

The next morning, Marianne was forced awake far too early, still absolutely exhausted. She'd spent the entire day yesterday organizing her things, getting to know her new home, and consulting with Mrs.

Wilton on various changes that ought to be made.

Mrs. Wilton knew absolutely everything about the house, and she was more than pleased to discuss it with Marianne as they went from room to room. She had been very reserved in her own opinions at the beginning, letting Marianne ask the questions rather than offering up information or suggestions, but once Marianne had invited her to be as forthright as she wished, she had done so. She had strong opinions on certain pieces of furniture, mostly begging for replacement of them, particular layouts of rooms, and even some color choices.

"The duchess did not use you to your full potential, it seems," Marianne had suggested as the two women had shared a tea tray in her receiving room.

Mrs. Wilton had shrugged her slender shoulders, and her warm brown eyes held a smile her lips did not. "She had her own opinions on things, the duchess. She was an excellent mistress, and we shall miss her."

Marianne had smiled. "But…" she prodded.

A ghost of a smile formed on the housekeeper's face. "But it will be wonderful to have a young couple with active lives here. And to update this old place. It has long needed a change, and Her Grace was not inclined to alter anything. I understand Mr. Gerrard has young sisters that may be joining us as well?"

Marianne had been somewhat flummoxed about how to answer that, having never discussed that, or much of anything, with Kit, but she pandered a bit about how the guardianship between the brothers was still new and a long-standing arrangement had yet to be settled on, but the girls would undoubtedly be staying at the house on occasion.

She had changed the subject before further details about those particular rooms could be inquired about. She had no idea what sort of nursery or rooms the girls kept to at Colin's house, and they may want the same thing here. Or perhaps something different. It was difficult to say with girls, and Marianne had never had sisters, so knew nothing of what to expect.

She had always had her own rooms, and knew very well that her life had been far different from the young Gerrard sisters.

Dinner between her and Kit last night had been a fairly silent affair, but the food was excellent, and she had made a mental note to ask about the chef and the kitchens, if not see to them herself.

To make the evening even more pleasant, she had not seen Kit the rest of the night. She'd been concerned that once they'd come to London, he would wish to exert some husbandly rights. She was rather pleased when that did not seem to be the case.

She was, however, not pleased to now have her sleep disturbed at this ghastly early hour by Anna, who had pulled back the thick curtains of her room and was now shaking out a dress for her.

"What are you doing?" Marianne asked her groggily, her mouth and throat dry and rough.

Anna, who had not quite forgiven her for her illicit elopement and thereby abandoning her, gave her a look. "Getting you ready for the day, miss. I mean, madam."

Marianne frowned and sat up against her pillows. "But it's early."

Anna made an impatient noise. "Yes, madam, but your husband insisted you not sleep all day and that I was to wake you."

She put her hands to her head and blinked blearily. "When my husband decides to keep to his word about not being overbearing, I shall consider listening to whatever else he says. Until then, I am resisting his orders."

That cracked a smile on Anna's face and the girl folded a dress over her arm, her fair hair catching a bit of sunlight through the windows. "He also said it was time for breakfast, madam."

Marianne made a face and twirled a lock of her hair around her finger. "Breakfast at strict times, waking at specific hours… It all seems rather structured to me. What is the point of being the mistress of a house if I have no flexibility or authority, hmm?"

"Surely a bit of food would not do you harm, madam," Anna said with a tilt of her head, her tone noticeably warmer than her first words, though still not quite friendly.

That was a thought for consideration. If she was to be up this early anyway, for there would be no returning to sleep after this, she might as well eat something.

"Perhaps you are right," she mused. "Yes, I will take a tray up here, if you would be so kind."

Now Anna smirked a little, which caused some uneasiness somewhere in Marianne's stomach. Her maid rarely smirked unless mischief was happening.

"What?" she asked slowly.

"Mr. Gerrard has forbidden trays, madam," Anna said as she came closer to the bed, smoothing the dress on her arm more.

Marianne's brows snapped down. "He what?"

Anna's eyes widened. "He expressly said there will be no trays in rooms for breakfast unless you are ill."

"Then tell him I am ill," she ordered coolly. Her husband, with all of his claims of not ordering her about, was doing a great deal of ordering about. He was not going to control her life, not like this.

Now Anna's mouth drew into a tight line. "I would, madam, but he said you would claim to be ill, and he knows you are well, so you must come to the breakfast room and eat."

Marianne groaned and leaned her head back, then reached for another pillow and covered her face with it, screaming into its downy depths.

She could try to refuse him, but knowing Kit, he would come up to her rooms and carry her over his shoulder down to the breakfast room, or force-feed her.

She tossed the pillow aside and yawned. "Why does he want to see me at all?" she grumbled, eyes still closed. "Why does he even care?"

"He said proper couples take meals together."

Marianne raised her head and gave Anna a doubtful look. "Show me one couple in London that was not married for love that breakfasts together."

Anna bit back a laugh, then frowned. "You were not married for love? I thought you eloped."

Marianne snorted and flung aside her bedcovers. "I meant to elope, but not with him. The whole elopement was a plot by Mr. Marksby to get my fortune and make me a sort of mistress bound to him legally."

Anna looked horrified by the thought. "Oh, madam…"

Marianne waved off her concern as she rose from the bed and stretched. "It is enough, I was spared that, and had to marry Kit instead."

"Mr. Gerrard married you to protect your reputation?"

The warmth in Anna's voice made Marianne stop, and she narrowed her eyes at the maid. "Do not paint him as a hero, Anna. He is intolerable, insufferable, and quite possibly the worst man in the world with whom I could be joined, excluding Mr. Marksby."

"He *is* a dreadfully handsome man…" Anna prodded, a hint of a sigh in her voice.

Marianne grunted and moved past her maid to fetch her yellow wrap instead. "Tolerably attractive at best. You need to see more men, Anna. Your opinions will drastically change on Kit's features."

Anna seemed to realize her impertinence and held out the gown on her arm. "Will you not change, madam?"

Marianne looked at the dress, a pale pink that was her favorite, then smiled up at Anna. "No, Anna, I will not. My husband asked for my presence at breakfast, and interrupted my sleep to get it. He never said anything about being dressed for the occasion."

Anna gaped, but Marianne grinned. She tied her wrap about her waist, tousled her hair a bit more, and left the room, barefoot and yawning as she was.

Her husband was already at the table in the breakfast room, properly dressed for the day, and enjoying the plate before him.

Marianne sleepily made her way to the seat prepared for her at the opposite end, and heard her husband's reaction before she saw it. His fork scraped against the plate just loudly enough for it to be unnatural, and she made a face at the noise. She adjusted her wrap a little as she sat in the chair and began to eat her own food.

Kit cleared his throat quickly. "Good morning," he said, his voice apparently unaffected.

"Early morning, more like," she grumbled as she cut herself a piece of ham.

"I thought you might like to enjoy as many hours in the day as you can," Kit replied calmly. "Productivity is a noble quality."

Marianne snorted at his pompous platitude as she chewed. "Leave the lectures for the preachers, Kit. I would much rather sleep than be productive this early."

"Yes, so I see from your choice of wardrobe."

Ah, there it was.

Marianne finally looked up at him, and while someone who did not know him might have thought him composed, she noted the tightness in his jaw and the hardness in his features, the coldness in his eyes.

He was livid.

She hid her thrill of pride and offered him the best stubborn glower she could. "You had me practically dragged out of bed to eat with you, knowing that I tend to sleep late. It was either come down as this or not at all."

"In the future, you will be properly dressed," he ordered, his nostrils flaring slightly as his fork twisted absently in his hand.

"For all other meals, yes. For early breakfasts like this, if you insist upon them, no. I shall come just as I am."

"Marianne…"

She shook her head slowly, then went back to eating. "Choose your battles, Kit. I come as I am or not at all."

He was silent for a long time, but she could feel his glare.

"Don't glower so darkly when we are eating," she told him, as if he were a moody child. "You will turn something rotten and I have no desire to be ill."

Kit suddenly shoved off from the table and stormed from the room, and Marianne fought the urge to smile.

She sat back in her chair and saw one of the footmen struggling against a smile as well. He looked at her, and she winked conspiratorially, which made his struggle worse and he fixed his gaze straight ahead once more.

She finished her breakfast, then sighed in thought. For all her distress the night before, she really had slept quite well. Her bed was comfortable, her room spacious, and her fatigue had been so complete she had hardly dreamed at all.

She frowned a little as she considered that Kit was going out, no doubt to see his brother. Colin had many sources for gossip, and would know what to expect when Marianne went out in public once more. She winced as she realized that she'd goaded Kit, making him less likely to be accommodating for a favor, but she had to try.

She rushed from the breakfast room, and asked a maid where

Mr. Gerrard had gone, and was directed to the front of the house, as he was leaving.

She caught him just as he was taking his hat and gloves from his valet.

"Where are you going?" she asked, slightly breathless from her running.

He barely glanced at her. "To see my brother and my sisters. You object?"

"No, of course not," she replied, folding her arms.

"You wanted me to stay here and entertain you?" he asked pointedly as he pulled on his gloves.

She snorted, bringing a surprised quirk of brows from the valet. "Hardly."

Kit turned and sighed impatiently. "Then what is it, Marianne? You wanted your independence, I am letting you have it."

She gave him a skeptical look.

"Breakfast and servant selection aside," he allowed with a roll of his eyes.

"I had a question I wanted to ask," she said simply.

He gestured irritably. "So ask."

"I was wondering if you might speak to Colin about… rumors."

Kit sighed impatiently. "What?"

"About us." She rolled her eyes at his look. "Me, then. I… I don't know what people are saying about me, and I find that I am worried about going out in public without knowing."

Kit eyed her carefully, and Marianne bit her lip before she could stop herself. It was a childish habit, but she felt very young all of a sudden.

Kit exhaled again. "Very well. I shall inquire, but I make no promises." He inclined his head and spun on his heel and was out the door before she had blinked once.

"Thank you," she muttered to the closed door. "So considerate. Very husbandly." She pushed a loose tendril of hair behind her ear, tucked her wrap around her, and returned to the breakfast room, worry suddenly gnawing at her stomach.

Chapter Six

"*So* how was your trip?"

Kit gave Colin a baleful look, and turned back to hear the rest of Bitty's story of what happened to one of the maids when Freddie and Rosie had a footrace in the hallway. He wasn't actually listening, and she knew it, but she appreciated the show of it.

Rosie was refusing to speak to him at the moment, as punishment for his getting married without her presence or permission, and was reading in the corner instead.

Bitty had no such bitterness and thought the present her brothers had brought for her an appropriate apology. Ginny couldn't have cared less either way, but she was torn between the attitudes of her sisters and settled upon wandering aimlessly about the room, jabbering to herself.

He made some noncommittal reaction to Bitty's story and Mrs. Creighton summoned the children for their lessons, leaving Colin and Kit alone in the room.

"So it was bad?" Colin asked as he pushed to his feet and gestured for Kit to follow.

"Did you not understand my look just then?" Kit asked him in return. "I clearly don't want to talk about it."

"And I am clearly ignoring that and asking anyway," Colin replied with no small amount of cheek, leading him into their newly refurbished drawing room.

"It was tolerable," Kit allowed with a sigh, taking a chair.

Colin raised a brow. "Well, that tells me a lot."

Kit snorted. "I'm not discussing my marriage with you, Colin."

"Will you discuss it with me?" asked a feminine voice from the door.

He turned and saw Susannah entering the room, looking more pregnant than she had last he'd seen her, but with a healthy glow that was quite becoming on her.

He smiled fondly and rose to kiss her cheek. "Perhaps, depending on what it is you want to know."

Colin barked a laugh and sat down, pulling Susannah into his lap as he did so. "So? How is it?" Susannah asked.

He sighed and made a face. "It's only been a few days."

"Bad already?" Colin asked.

Kit wavered between vagueness and honesty. "She is… complicated."

"We knew that beforehand," Colin pointed out.

"Difficult."

"Knew that."

"Contentious."

"And that."

"Driving me insane."

"And that as well."

Kit gave his brother an exasperated look, and Colin only grinned in response.

"I don't know how to be a husband," Kit admitted.

"Neither does Colin," Susannah assured him.

"What?" her husband cried.

Susannah winked and struggled up from his lap. "I am going to leave you two to a discussion that I probably should not hear." She turned to Kit with a smile. "Lovely to see you. Staying a while?"

He nodded and returned her smile. "For dinner, I think. I owe the girls."

She suddenly had a knowing look in her eyes that he wasn't sure he liked.

"What?" he asked defensively.

She shrugged and rubbed at her belly absently. "Most men having been married four days would rather spend their time with their wife."

His expression soured. "I am not most men."

"True." But her voice still rang with disapproval, and she gave him a look as she left the room.

Colin sighed and set both feet flat on the floor. "All right, Kit. What is the trouble?"

Kit rubbed at his eyes, suddenly feeling a weariness seep into him. "I married Marianne."

"Did you forget that?" Colin quipped with a laugh. "I can remind you whenever you like. I was there, I saw the whole thing. It was rather like a funeral. Only less crying."

Kit glared at him and leaned back against the chair. "I knew it would be difficult, but I suppose I did not fully comprehend how it would affect me."

Colin raised a brow slowly. "What is affecting you?"

Kit debated telling him what had him so irritated this morning. After all, the private matters of his marriage were not his brother's concern, unless they related to the family as a whole. Still, Colin had some insight into loving and hating the same woman, and perhaps this madness might actually make sense to him.

He could still see the glorious vision in his head. Marianne coming into the breakfast room, rumpled and sleep-tousled, in naught but her nightgown. The cream gown seemed to fit her perfectly, and yet not fit at all, and the gold details on the bodice had echoed the gold embroidery in her wrap. He could still see her padding barefoot and sleepily into the room, apparently unaware of the tempting picture she presented, and sitting down at breakfast as if it were a perfectly normal thing to come down to meals so dressed.

Somehow he had been composed outwardly, but if this was what he was to expect from his marriage…

Choose your battles, she had said.

But which side was he on?

Carefully, he wetted his lips. "This morning was… interesting," he said slowly.

Colin seemed to sense this was important, for he remained silent and nodded in encouragement.

A faint exhale escaped him, and Kit winced. "I forced her to rise early to eat breakfast with me."

"Good heavens," Colin exclaimed softly, eyes wide.

Kit looked at him in surprise. "What?"

Colin laughed in a bit of disbelief. "It's a wonder you are still alive. Why did you do that?"

Kit shrugged and rubbed his hands together. "I wanted to have some sense of order. And I wanted to provoke her a little."

Colin's laugh faded softly and he waved for him to continue.

"She fought back, but not in the way I expected." Kit held his breath, wondering how to politely say what had happened. "She came… but…"

At his fumbling, Colin sat up straighter, his expression expectant, and a touch intrigued.

Kit sighed heavily. "She was… *sans* proper attire."

Colin's face was entirely blank and devoid of emotion. "Meaning…?"

"She was in a nightgown and wrap," Kit grumbled, wishing the recollection would not cause such warmth in his chest.

"Oh!" Colin cried softly. "Oh… well…" He trailed off, eyes suddenly full of laughter.

Kit looked at him again, gesturing for him to elaborate. "What? Well, what? It is shocking, isn't it?"

Colin shrugged a little, a pert smile forming on his lips. "You're married to Marianne. I expect nothing and I am surprised by nothing."

He glowered at his brother, his teeth grinding softly. He needed no reminder of the woman he married, or the insanity of his choice. He needed advice, he needed space, and he needed to find ways to cope with her maddening ability to drive him to distraction.

He needed his brother to be on his side.

Colin's smile grew to nearly a grin. "And just for the sake of argument, I actually enjoy it when my wife comes to breakfast like that."

Kit muttered incoherently and shoved up out of his chair, going to the fireplace. "Changing the subject," he said firmly.

"If you must," Colin said, still laughing.

"Marianne wants to know… and I confess, I do as well, what is being said about her."

Colin sobered at once, which made Kit look back at him.

His brother appeared hesitant, which was more of a warning than Kit was expecting. "Well?"

"If you want to know the whole of it, Kit," Colin said in a low voice, "I am not the person to ask. But you know who is." He widened his eyes meaningfully, and Kit knew his intent.

The Gent would know.

That was certainly no help at all, but it did give him some scope. He shook his head slowly. "That bad?"

Colin nodded once. "More than likely. What whispers I have heard have been what we expected to hear, and it is not good."

Kit bit back a curse and ground his teeth. This was not what he wanted. Marianne had a cold exterior, but he strongly suspected she was far more sensitive than she would ever let on. This could destroy her.

"I cannot add to it," Kit muttered, moving back to his chair. "This will be hard enough for her, I cannot be so unfeeling as to make home a burden as well." Feeling suddenly drained of everything, Kit leaned forward, putting his face into his hands. "What did I do?" he moaned.

"I don't know," Colin said simply. "I tried to warn you."

Kit glared at him, which Colin only smiled at. Kit sighed and rubbed his hands together. "I know I need to be better. I may have underestimated what it would be like to be married to her."

"The situation is hardly typical," Colin told him, looking far too understanding. "I do not think expectations come into play here."

Kit nodded soberly. "If I want something to be different, I cannot blame or control her. I can only control myself. So, I must be controlled."

"That would follow, yes."

Kit ignored his impertinent twin. "I think… I need to stop resenting her so much. Not *everything* she does is an evil."

"Don't go soft, now," Colin protested, grinning as he relaxed in his chair.

Kit snorted and shook his head. "I will do no such thing. I don't have to be nice to her, I simply need to stop being malicious. Does that make sense?"

"Oddly enough, given your situation, yes it does." Colin sat up just a little bit. "In fact, Derek says…"

Kit held up a hand, silencing him. "I am not interested in what Derek has to say on the topic of my marriage," he warned.

"The more you cast blame on others, the less you can see it in yourself," Colin said quietly, staring at Kit with sober eyes.

He sniffed, shaking his head again. "I don't need lectures, Colin."

"Then what do you need?"

Kit exhaled heavily, rubbing his hands together again. "I have no idea."

"Right," Colin drawled slowly. He waited for a long moment, watching Kit with an inscrutable expression. Then he sighed heavily. "So we're going to have a baby…"

Kit laughed suddenly at the thought, and, grateful for the change in topic, he started to let his brother know just what he thought of that.

It was full dark when Kit ventured back into the Berkeley Square house, having made very little progress with Rosie at all, but at least she had hugged him farewell.

It was not much, but he had to start somewhere.

Rosie, it seemed, did not forgive easily, not even for her brothers, and it would take some time to set her to rights once more.

Perhaps she was more like him than they had previously thought.

His conversation with Colin had replayed over and over in his mind, and he knew what he needed to do. He had to know what people were saying, not for Marianne's precious curiosity, but for his own means. If there was anything he could do to salvage her reputation for the rest of the world, he would have to know just what they thought.

He jotted down a quick note and handed it off to Pearce, who had long been used to running these sorts of errands for him, and then they both left the house, going in opposite directions.

The London streets were dark and cold, and yet he could not feel it. While he had fully expected others to have jaded opinions of

Marianne, he had not realized just how shaped by them his own had been. But he, at least, could change himself. After all, there had to be something in Marianne that was still worth loving if he could not let her go.

Or was there?

It did not matter, he supposed. He was married to her, and that was something he could not change. Whatever his feelings, he would most certainly have to desist with the childish behavior himself and start acting like a married man.

He reached the designated place, long ago established for him, and did not have to wait long for his companion to show.

"My congratulations," the man said in a Cockney accent, strolling into the opening of the trees, "though I am surprised."

Kit looked at his oldest friend, no longer shocked by the cheap clothing or disguises, or speaking in accents in all ranges and tones. He had seen and heard the most extraordinary things with this particular friend over the years.

"Gent," he greeted simply.

His friend removed the cap from his head, shoving it into the back of his trousers. "What can I do for you?" he asked at once, his voice returned to his usual tone and accent.

Softly, Kit told him the basics, knowing that he would know the details of everything else soon, if he did not already, and he knew he'd been right to fear when there was no shock, awe, or dismay.

"I think you will find worse tales than the truth out there," his friend said, nodding slowly.

Kit winced and pinched at his nose. "I need to know for certain."

The Gent pressed his tongue against his lip and raised a brow. "Are you sure?"

Kit nodded rapidly. "All of it."

"You've never wanted to know all of it before."

"She was never my wife before. That changes things." He looked down at his boots for a moment. "Who else should know but her husband? If I cannot bear it, who can?"

"I am not your personal gossiping harpy, you know," his friend said lightly, trying for teasing. "I actually have duties to see to. Important ones on very high levels."

"Rafe…" Kit murmured, raising his eyes to plead, knowing using his real name was not supposed to occur under these circumstances. "Please."

Rafe exhaled slowly, then gave him a tight smile. "Of course, Kit. You should hear from me in a day or two." He waited a beat, then said, "The Gardiner's party should be small enough for you to take her out. See what the tone is in her presence."

Kit nodded obediently, a small portion of the weight being lifted from his shoulders.

"You have time before the Season," Rafe reminded him. "We can clear up a good deal before then."

"But I should be concerned," Kit said. There was no question of that, and he was not asking.

Rafe pulled his cap back out and tugged it back into place, becoming the Gent once more. "You would not have married her if you did not know she would need protection."

Kit nodded again. "Thank you, Gent."

He touched the brim of his hat. "You know where to find me."

Kit watched his friend disappear into the night, and then, breathing a little easier, started the walk for home once more.

There was work to be done.

Chapter Seven

$\mathcal{J}$t was even worse than she had imagined it to be.

Oh, Mr. and Mrs. Gardiner had been welcoming and warm, but even they had exchanged a surprised look at seeing her arrive with her brother and his wife. A warm press of hands, a fumbling of her name, and before any faux pas could be committed, Annalise had linked arms with her and begged them to excuse them to the other rooms, where she had seen a friend.

She had seen no one, but had been observant enough to know that things were only going to get worse, and her kind heart had wished to spare the Gardiners any discomfort and Marianne any distress.

That had been the easiest maneuvering of the night.

The Gardiner's small ballroom had been opened up into a very comfortable space for any who wished to sit and socialize or for those who felt more inclined to dance, and some of the younger guests had proceeded to dance a great deal, accompanied by Lord Viskin, of all horrid things.

But even Lord Viskin would not be tempted by Marianne.

Indeed, the entire room had been whispering about her as she entered, and it had not stopped.

She had no idea what to expect from her first venture into society. She had always known there were people who would say horrid things about her, or anyone, and she had never paid them any mind. She did not have the time, energy, or desire to think on them. But she did very much care about the general opinion of Society as a whole, and the select few whose opinions had come to matter very much.

She could hardly leave after being here for only an hour, but how long could she sit and be so mortified?

What had possessed the Gardiners to invite Lady Cavendish? While not as vile as Lady Gerversham, she was a notorious gossip, who had no notion of what whispering was or what ought to be discussed in situations such as these. And though she had not Tibby's range or influence, a great many people listened to her. And they tittered and whispered, and none of it was kept from Lady Cavendish.

Marianne was now, it seemed, rather notorious.

No one seemed particularly offended by her presence, but neither was she being approached. The only person who had spoken to her since she arrived was Annalise, and she had just been called away by Duncan about some matter. People were looking and whispering, even those that were dancing, and they spoke of her elopement, her now infamous marriage to a man she did not elope with, and various details about said elopement, some of which were true.

"The window, I heard tell. She made a rope of bedsheets."

"For pity's sake, Frank, she is not your brother."

"Marianne Bray would *never* use the window. She has a terrible fear of heights."

"Broad daylight. Mrs. Gordon was asleep when they left."

"They had to marry her off at once. Marksby fled the country before her brother's wrath."

"Did you know she got married in the same bedsheets from the inn?"

"Oh, now you are being ridiculous."

"I thought she had more sense than that."

"No sense."

"Marksby?"

"Desperately in love."

"She was ruined. Entirely ruined."

"Ignore them," hissed a voice near her.

Marianne turned her head slowly to see Mary Harris taking the vacant seat next to her, and she blinked uneasily. "What?"

Mary took her hand and glared around the room fiercely. "Ignore them. All of them."

"I can't," Marianne whispered, feeling a faint tremor coursing through her arms and legs. "How can I? It's true."

Mary gave her a very severe look, and Marianne saw the delicate jaw of her friend work for a moment. "A young woman I like very much once told me to never let them see your distress," Mary reminded her firmly, her clear blue eyes steady and even.

"That girl ran away with a man who would have ruined her," Marianne whispered, the fabric of her gloves suddenly feeling like shackles on her skin.

"You are more than that," came another voice from the other side.

She turned to see Susannah Gerrard, her new sister-in-law, taking up position on the other side. She had apparently foregone convention by going out so near her confinement, which had probably driven Colin mad.

"What are you doing here?" Marianne managed to squeak. "Your baby…"

"Would want me to support his aunt," Susannah finished with a kind smile. She leaned back a little with a wince, then made a stubborn face across the room, no doubt at her husband. "I may be uncomfortable, but I believe the entire room is at the moment."

"I should go," Marianne murmured, adjusting her skirt. "I am ruining everything."

Both women held her in place. "No," Mary ordered. "That was not what Susannah meant."

"Marianne Bray? I happen to know she tried to run off with George Oliver only last month. It's habit for her now."

Marianne closed her eyes slowly, surprised to find moisture beneath her lids.

"Idiot," Susannah hissed under her breath. "As if anyone ever listened to Lord Darlington's opinion on anything."

"And George Oliver?" Mary added with a snort. "Please. The man isn't even in England right now, he's on the continent with his sister."

"But it's being said," Marianne whispered, feeling ill.

"You knew people were going to talk," Mary murmured, rubbing her hand softly. "You know better than anyone how hard this would be."

"But now it's me as the target," she told her, opening her eyes again and gasping softly when a tear fell.

Mary wiped it away immediately and shook her head slightly. "Smile. Or pretend one."

With great effort, she curved the corners of her lips a little.

"There," Mary praised with a smile. "Now you merely look tired."

"Where is Duncan?" she asked, looking around.

"All of the men are somewhere," Susannah said with a slight wave. "Even Derek and Nathan came."

"Not Lady Whitlock or Lady Beverton?"

Susannah shook her head. "Their babies are so young still, they most likely will not do much until the Season starts. But Kate says David is easy enough that she could leave him with Alice and be comfortable."

Mary laughed, but Marianne was completely lost. "Who?"

Susannah gave her a look. "I was under the impression that you knew everything."

Marianne opened her mouth, her mind whirling with connections she would have known only days ago.

"David is the new baby," Susannah told her before she could even exhale. "He is almost four months now. And Alice is…"

"A Wittinham," Marianne recollected suddenly, nodding to herself. "She is Lady Whitlock's niece, and the only tolerable member of that family."

"There she is," Mary said proudly, squeezing her hand tightly.

Marianne nodded again, exhaling slowly. If her mind could return to its old self, perhaps one day the rest of her would as well. And perhaps Society would let her.

"And Moira's little Charlotte is but two months old," Susannah continued conversationally, her voice rising to cover the voices behind them. "But she is good natured and quiet, so I anticipate us seeing Moira before long."

"Polite society won't accept her now. Not after this."

"And poor Mr. Gerrard will have to suffer for it."

"I think we need to move," Mary murmured to Susannah, taking Marianne by the arm, and Susannah did the same on the other side.

"No," Marianne said firmly, trying to shake loose from their hold. "Leave me, both of you."

The women looked at each other, no doubt feeling helpless.

Marianne couldn't blame them. For all their kindness, it was not worth it. They could not keep the people from talking, nor could they change the opinions and feelings of the rest of Society. She knew only too well how damaging mere speculation could be, and the rumors would only get worse until someone else sinned worse than she had.

Her head suddenly felt too heavy for her neck and she was tempted to sag, but years and years of training prevented her from sacrificing that bit of pride. Her feet were chilled, her fingers numb, and her cheeks burned with a heat that did not seem to reach any other part of her.

She did not know if Susannah and Mary left or not, and it did not matter.

Not really.

The whispers and titters suddenly increased in volume, and her eyes fluttered shut as if to brace her for a wave of more slander.

Then, just as suddenly, it stopped.

She opened her eyes to see her husband standing before her, hands behind his back.

He looked as pristine as he ever had, every aspect perfect and untouchable. His strong jaw was taut, his chestnut hair perfectly placed, and his clothing immaculate and tailored with precision. His stirring eyes were fixed on hers and she saw in them a surprising amount of gentleness.

"I cannot believe my wife has not yet danced this evening," he murmured quietly, but others could hear him with ease, "and that I cannot allow." He extended his hand and bowed. "Will you dance the next with me, Mrs. Gerrard?"

There were a few hisses of surprise from around her, but Marianne could only stare at him with wide eyes. She had danced with Kit years ago, but never again since. And as far as she could tell, Kit had danced less than a dozen times since then.

She let her composure slip a little, unable to completely conceal the hurt that she felt deep within her, the bleakness of their situation, and regret she was starting to feel creeping into her soul for this marriage, not only because of what it did to her, but because of what it would do to him.

"I know it is not seemly for a husband to dance with his wife," he said, his voice carefully warm, "but perhaps you might make an exception?"

He dipped his head just enough that the message was clear. He knew what she could not say. And then he smiled.

And it felt as if the entire room gasped.

Marianne felt a bare smile cross her lips and she set her gloved hand in his. "If you insist, Mr. Gerrard."

Again came the brief dip of his chin. "I do."

He led her out to the dance floor where five other couples waited, wide eyed and staring.

The music started up and Marianne stared at Kit in surprise. "This is a waltz," she whispered.

"So it is," came his reply, entirely unconcerned.

She frowned in confusion. "You don't waltz."

If they had not been in public, he would have shrugged. "Tonight, I do."

And waltz they did.

The room buzzed around them, but Marianne was too focused on this turn of events to listen. Kit was waltzing. With her. And he was actually quite talented and graceful, which she would not have suspected. They had never waltzed when they had danced together before, and certainly never when she had learned. She did not even know he knew how to waltz, or that he was inclined to. Some still held the belief that a waltz was scandalous, despite it being so popular recently.

She had always assumed that Kit would be among them.

They did not speak during their waltz, and for that she was grateful. What sort of small talk would they make at an event like this? They were a spectacle apart, together they were shocking, and for them to be willing to stand up together, knowing that, showed a complete disregard for everyone and everything else.

In short, this could have been the miracle she needed.

This could set her feet back on the ground.

And if that was the case, she could most certainly be Mrs. Gerrard.

A spattering of applause rang out when the waltz was completed, and Kit returned her to her chair, bowing deeply over her hand once more.

"Thank you," she murmured for him alone.

He looked surprised, then his lips quirked a little and he nodded. He hesitated a moment, as if he would say something, but then he left, disappearing into the people lining up for the next dance.

"Did you see that? Gerrard danced with her!"

"I thought it was a marriage of convenience."

"Kit Gerrard danced with her!"

Marianne felt the smallest bit of smiles start and it only grew when Colin started towards her, smiling as fondly as if she were really his sister.

"Well, Mrs. Gerrard," he said with a noted emphasis on her new surname, "would you like to dance with the graceful Gerrard twin next?"

"With pleasure," she told him, and she meant every word.

Kit heaved a sigh of relief when the party started to disperse, and went over to collect Marianne. He would make another statement, and one that had better be remembered. She may have come with her brother, but she would leave with him.

Let the gossips and rumors feed on that for a while.

Oh, he had no expectation that they would ever think much of it, and certainly it would never be called love, but it would settle their presumptions concerning his feelings about this marriage.

No matter how it had begun, Marianne was his wife, and that was enough.

She had not danced much, but he hoped the few times she had would make it a point with those that witnessed it. He could do without her being a sensation, but he did not want her to be a pariah, either.

The men had settled it this evening that the rumors, which Gent had confirmed to him in the promised letter, needed to be dealt with if they were going to remain in London, or ever return. So Kit asked Colin and Derek, the most influential men in the group, to spread a different sort of rumor. Marianne had not, in fact, eloped, contrary to popular opinion. She had been abducted by Marksby, who had intended to marry her solely to gain her fortune, and sought to ruin her along the way.

It was not a lie. They simply would leave out the part Marianne had played.

After all, she had been tricked, and she had a woman's heart, no matter how she might have locked it away.

Sympathy would be far better than slander.

Marianne said very little as they left and loaded into the carriage, but he could already see some color back in her face, and it encouraged him.

"Was it as bad as you expected?" he asked in as gentle a tone as he could manage.

She nodded, shrugging. "I've seen others with damaged reputations return to Society, felt the embarrassment at their appearance, and snubbed them myself, but I never knew it would feel like this. I never knew just how it would sting."

He stared at her for a long moment, wondering that she was not tearful about it. "I am sorry you had to endure that."

She looked at him in surprise. "Why are you sorry? You had nothing to do with it, and you solved quite a bit of the problem yourself."

And at great cost to his control, but he would not tell her so. "I am sorry that I cannot stop them from saying such things."

Marianne smiled a little. "Well, I can easily forgive you for that, as it is an impossible task."

He shook his head. "Impossible or not, I should be able to do something. You've been a reigning member of Society for so long, I cannot believe they are so quick to slander you like that. And to be unable to change it? For heaven's sake, I beat a man to a bloody pulp for insinuating less with you."

"You did what?" she cried, bracing one hand on the side of the slightly swaying carriage.

He clamped his mouth shut and silently cursed himself for letting that detail escape.

She gaped for a moment. "You don't mean…"

He cleared his throat and looked away.

"You beat Marksby?" she asked in a small voice.

"Only a little," he murmured.

He heard the sharp inhalation, and imagined that she heard the echo of her own voice saying those same words that night at the inn, as he did now.

She hesitated, still looking confused. When he did not say more, she offered him a nod, which he took to be an acceptance, and he found himself breathing easier.

Then she surprised him further with a very small smile. "I should thank you again for the dance this evening. I fear your reputation might suffer."

He snorted softly. "For dancing with my wife? Hardly."

She shook her head, her dark ringlets bouncing. "No, for dancing with *me*. You had to know what people were saying."

"I think we have already learned that people know nothing and what they say is worth just as much," he said with finality, bitterly recalling their behavior this evening. He could still see how drawn and miserable Marianne had looked, which was more haunting than it should have been in a ballroom. And he dreaded how long the Season would be for them both if nothing changed.

"But where Marianne Bray is concerned, they are not entirely wrong," she pointed out, her voice going a little raw.

He gave her a hard look. "Where Marianne *Gerrard* is concerned, they know absolutely nothing, and they had best remember that."

Her mouth worked for a moment, and then another tremulous smile formed. "Thank you."

Reminders of the girl she had once been flickered into his mind at her expression, at her soft words, and he looked away. That girl was gone, but his wife remained, and he had a duty to her.

"Everybody deserves a second chance," he murmured, almost to himself, knowing that she would hear it.

And he could not have said if he were speaking to himself or to his wife.

Chapter Eight

$\mathcal{I}$t soon became evident that the tactic the men had employed of posturing Marianne as a victim rather than an accomplice had worked. The idea had taken hold and whatever the opinions people held of Marianne, their curiosity would not be slaked. Within a week, all had changed.

Invitations had come in steadily after the Gardiner's party, and Kit had nothing to do with any of them. Marianne was discerning enough to know which of the invitations ought to be accepted and which would not matter. She was encouraged by them and was quickly back to her old liveliness, which had its benefits as well as its drawbacks.

He did not have to worry over her or ask Mrs. Wilton to be mindful of her, which was a welcome change. Marianne had returned to her preening, carefully cultivated persona, and he was back to glowering about it.

He was continually reminding himself that if she were strong and bold once more, it would mean less intervention would be needed by him.

And that he could be satisfied with.

Oh, if the rumors or Society got out of hand again, he would step in, he meant what he had said to her. The usual gossip surrounding his wife could remain, but anything surrounding their marriage or her elopement would be quashed at once.

When he had seen Marianne come down to breakfast in her nightgown and wrap the second day in a row after Gardiner's, he knew she would be quite well. And when she had barked at him about the earliness of the hour, he'd hid a secret smile of satisfaction.

His wife was back.

But when she'd started fussing about the sheer volume of people she would have to call on now that she had returned, and who would have to come to her, and which apologies and sympathy she would accept, Kit was done.

He'd started to escape to his study daily, which he had finally situated exactly as he liked it. It had become his ritual ever since and usually kept himself occupied for several hours therein, or seeing to business about London. The house became more ordered and Marianne directed more and more of the room arrangements, starting with their receiving rooms, and working her way to the back of the house. She had not ventured to appraise the upstairs rooms as yet, but he'd heard her ask Mrs. Wilton to examine each and let her know of their states.

She was a remarkably efficient taskmaster for claiming to hate productivity.

Workers were constantly in and out of the house, hanging wallpapers and painting, moving furniture out and in, altering draperies, and he would have sworn he saw a man replacing panes of glass the other day. Kit never asked what was going on, nor was he approached for his opinions or for funds. From what he could see, Marianne had surprisingly elegant and uncomplicated tastes with the rooms, and he had nothing to object to. He'd always known she was fashionable, but he would never have thought sensible. No doubt the cost would reflect her true tastes.

They'd had little to do with each other of late, but still met regularly for meals, though their conversation was stilted and strictly light and business-related. On occasion, she would tell him details about the refurbishing of the rooms, and what she'd heard of other people doing. His lack of enthusiasm did not impress her. She was usually sharp with him in the mornings and more inclined to ignore him at dinner, but he could manage either extreme quite well.

Marianne meeting his sisters hadn't gone particularly well for them, but he wasn't sure what he had expected.

Rosie had been livid the entire time. She sat in the furthest corner of the room from Marianne, reading to herself, and never smiled once. Bitty wasted no time in getting to know Marianne, asking her questions about dresses and fashions, what was polite and what was not, and if she truly did need to wear a bonnet. Ginny had surprised them all by measuring Marianne quietly with her sober eyes, and then climbing onto her lap and chattering in her mix of words and nonsense about the doll she held in her hand.

Marianne hadn't known what to do, but somehow she'd managed to come through unscathed.

Kit had tried to coerce Rosie into getting to know Marianne, but she'd adamantly refused.

"If you really wanted me to know her," she'd insisted, "you would have waited to marry her until after I'd met her."

There was no polite way to explain that, so he'd given up trying.

Eventually, Rosie had walked over to where her sisters and Marianne were, choosing to sit on the smallest portion of the settee, staying as far away from Marianne as possible.

Marianne had seen Rosie, but seemed to understand that she would be harder to win over than her sisters, and kept the conversations between them minimal, though she did try.

Rosie participated just enough to avoid getting in trouble, but not enough to be praised.

According to Colin, that was better than he could have expected. Apparently Rosie had been raging about the house before they had arrived, and he'd expected no less during their visit.

Either way, the duty was done, and if Bitty's attentions were anything to go by, he would have to restrict their visits, or Bitty would become too fascinated with her new sister-in-law. Nothing could make Kit shudder more than the idea of Bitty becoming apprentice to his wife.

"Sir?"

Kit looked up to see Caldwell in the doorway to his study, looking somewhat apprehensive. "Caldwell?"

"A visitor, sir," Caldwell said, clearing his throat.

Kit gestured for the card, but Caldwell didn't move. Kit raised a brow. "No card?"

The butler shook his head. "No, sir. She… said she didn't need one here."

"Who said?" Kit pressed, wondering who in the world would call on them without the politeness of a card.

Caldwell cleared his throat once more. "Lady Raeburn, sir."

Kit stared at him for a long moment, then cursed under his breath and moved quickly out of the room.

"Your aunt is here."

Marianne jerked up from her writing desk to look at Kit in horror, as he stood in the doorway of her sitting room. "What?"

Kit swallowed hastily, his eyes belying the fear that his outward appearance hid so well. "She is in the west drawing room."

Her pen clattered out of her hand and Marianne sat back hard, staring at the new wallpaper as if the vine-like details had suddenly come to life. "She was supposed to be in Italy."

"She was."

"There is no way to return from Italy that quickly." She did the math again, and shook her head. It had been two weeks since her wedding, just over that since her elopement. It was an impossible feat. "She had to have been elsewhere."

"Wherever she was, I can tell you where she is now."

Marianne looked at him again, feeling color draining from her face. "What do we do?"

"I think we had better go down and see her," he said simply, which made her frown up at him. Of course, they would go down, she would hardly think of ignoring Tibby altogether. That would ruin them faster than anything.

"Or else she will come up here, and who knows what chaos would ensue," he finished, not watching her at all, but staring unfocused into the room.

Ah, so he was not intentionally being difficult. He was truly unsettled by Tibby's sudden appearance. Marianne could understand that.

She looked at the pile of invitations before her wistfully. She would much rather sort through them and start planning for events. It would take some strategy to do so, as these invitations would lead to more once the Season started. Why, most of the higher Society had not even returned to London yet! And they would not wish to be overrun by invitations or activity. Selection of the most important events and connections was critical.

But all of that must wait, for Tibby would not.

"I suppose we must," she sighed, pushing aside the stack and rising. She brushed at her gown nervously, wishing she had time to change or fix her hair or something, but it would have to do.

Kit waited for her to pass and then followed just to her left. They were silent as they proceeded out the hall and down the stars, and Marianne could feel her nerves beginning to shred already.

Tibby was the closest thing to a mother she had anymore, and she had twice the emotions of one. This could ruin her more than any scandal.

Kit seemed to sense her nerves and offered her his arm without a word, his eyes firm with a hint of encouragement, though he had to be as uneasy as she was. And they were not exactly pleased with each other at the moment.

Still, there was strength in numbers, she supposed, and Tibby was a terrifying force they had to face together. She took his arm with a short nod.

Once they reached the drawing room, however, and she caught sight of Tibby's back as she examined their fireplace, the nerves soared once more. Tibby was wreathed in bronze fabric today, shimmering boldly even in the evening light, and her hair seemed more vibrantly red than normal. She had forgone the turban she was so fond of, and instead wore a bonnet of a rich orchid color adorned with bronze ribbons and feathers.

She looked just as imposing and impressive as Tibby had ever looked.

Kit lowered their arms, and their bare fingers brushed as they did so. The grazing of skin seemed to jolt something in them both, and anxiously Marianne's hand seized his, forging the connection between them once more as she squeezed tightly.

She heard Kit draw in a surprised breath, felt him stiffen, and just as quickly she released his hand, her face flaming.

What had prompted her to do such a silly, girlish thing? She was strong enough to face her aunt. Tibby loved her, and it could not possibly be as bad as she currently feared.

Tibby suddenly whirled about, her skirts dancing with the motion, and the cold, thunderous expression on her face caused them both to fall back a step.

Perhaps it could, Marianne faintly considered.

Tibby set her hands on her hips and looked between them both with her pale eyes.

"I will not speak to you in this room," Tibby sniffed suddenly. "The color clashes dreadfully with me. You must refinish the room; Sophronia had no idea of interior décor. I trust you will do better than she."

She started passed them, marching towards a different room, when Marianne suddenly blurted, "How did you get back so soon?"

Tibby leveled her with a cool glare. "I have ways," she informed her as she continued on.

Marianne opened her mouth, then turned to Kit and hissed, "How do you think she…?"

"I wouldn't question it," he muttered out of the corner of his mouth as they followed Tibby to the nearest sitting room. "It's Tibby."

"I know," she sighed grumpily. "She is my aunt, after all."

"It is a miracle you survived adolescence."

Marianne smiled without mirth, and then prepared for the wrath of the most terrifying woman on the planet.

It took Tibby a full minute of looking at the two of them, in a room much better situated for her wardrobe, before she spoke again.

"The pair of you," she said in a stiff voice, "are the biggest idiots I have ever known personally, and possibly even professionally. I can hardly think of a worse situation than we are in now."

"Tibby," Marianne started in a placating voice, ignoring her husband's warning shake of his head.

"You!" Tibby barked, bringing an accusing finger to within centimeters of Marianne's face. "You do not get to speak. Are you entirely without wits, girl? Running off like a common strumpet with that man… entirely improper match there… and then! To be married in Yorkshire? No one is married in Yorkshire!"

"Tibby," Kit tried in a rather worthy soothing tone.

"And you!" Tibby cried, twisting to bring her finger into his face. "You know better!" She suddenly slapped him hard, drawing a gasp from Marianne and a wince from Kit.

Tibby started rubbing at her delicate lace gloves, no doubt feeling the sting against her skin more than she'd anticipated. "Really, Christopher, you know better! Marianne is not the sort of girl you should have married! You know how she is, what she is like, and for her to be so willful, and you marry her anyway? That blasted honor, Christopher, is going to kill you! She did not deserve your saving!"

"I am right here," Marianne muttered.

"Don't think I have forgotten that!" Tibby shrieked as she turned back to her. "Marianne, what were you thinking?" She seized Marianne's upper arms and shook her with a surprising amount of force, given her slight frame, nearly slamming Marianne's teeth together. "I could wring your neck, you stupid girl!" She shook her hard again, then suddenly pulled her to her for a tight hug. "You stupid girl," she whispered again, her voice choked.

Marianne had barely time to get over her astonishment and return Tibby's hug before her aunt pulled back, serious once more.

"Well," she sighed, looking disapproving at them both, "I am most seriously disgusted with you both, but out of the goodness of my heart, I shall make the best of it. Marianne shall *not* be cut off, despite my vowing the entire trek back to do so this time."

Marianne breathed a very small sigh of relief, but Tibby's expression quelled any further good feelings.

"If anyone can make a positive out of this dismal thing, it is I," Tibby continued, one hand still on Marianne's arm, squeezing too tightly. "The idea of Marianne being abducted and not an accomplice is good, I applaud whoever thought up that one."

Marianne reared back a little in shock. She hadn't heard that, but she would most certainly let it continue on without issue.

"All we have left to do is to show the world we are not ashamed of this union," Tibby was saying, looking at Kit with a knowing expression. "The murky details shall be bandied about for a while, and we will never discuss it, but so long as you idiots keep your chin up, and save your spite for the privacy of home alone, things shall quiet down soon." She shook her head, as if she could not believe she was going along with this. "I have only just arrived and am really quite fatigued, but thanks to you two, I now have a party to plan. We must keep to expectation, and had my niece married under *normal* circumstances," here she paused to glare at Marianne, "I would certainly have thrown an elaborate celebration."

"There is no need…" Kit tried, but Tibby silenced him again with another slap, nearly as fierce as the first.

"There most certainly is," she barked, scolding him with another finger in his face. "Therefore, Friday you will come and we will celebrate this ridiculous scheme." She looked at them both disapprovingly. "You dear children, I adore you, but do not test me. I may still cast you off. And for pity's sake, Marianne, wear something elegant. Not that lawn ornamentation you currently have on." She shook her head once more and swept past them both, calling for Mrs. Wilton loudly.

They stood there for a moment, staring where Tibby had been, and tried to catch their breath.

Tibby had slapped Kit. Twice! Marianne felt as though she should apologize for her aunt, if she could only manage to turn and face him.

Kit suddenly exhaled heavily. "That was actually not as bad I expected it would be," he said, rubbing at his jaw.

Marianne couldn't help it; she burst out laughing, wrapping an arm around her midsection and another at her mouth as she did so.

Kit smiled at her briefly, then craned his neck. "Well, I had better go and save Mrs. Wilton. Lord knows what your aunt is raving about now."

"Block your face next time," Marianne gasped, still laughing breathlessly. "She would never forgive you if you went to her party with bruises on your face."

Kit shuddered a little, and disappeared.

Marianne fell into a chair near her and sighed. Her aunt was a wild woman of high status, and a party for them with her as hostess would go a long way.

But more than that, she had faced the dragon and come out relatively unharmed.

Perhaps things would be well after all.

"Madam, you have additional visitors," Caldwell intoned from behind her.

Marianne frowned a little, turning to him. "Who is it?"

He handed her a tray with cards on it, and she took them, her fingers trembling slightly. After Tibby, she wasn't entirely certain anyone else could be endured without disaster.

Marianne swallowed as she read the cards. It was unfathomable, these two women had never spoken more than five words to her at most, and yet they had come together to call upon her. There was no reason for them to do any such thing, particularly when she had only avoided being cast out of London for scandal by clever thinking and stratagem.

She would never have refused them, but neither would she have necessarily sought them out.

And yet…

"Miss Gemma Templeton and Miss Lily Arden," Marianne read faintly, looking down at the cards with wide eyes. "I barely know them."

"Would you like me to send them away, madam?" Caldwell asked, eager to please.

Marianne shook her head before she could dwell on it too much. "No, Caldwell. I will see them. Thank you."

Caldwell nodded and led her to receiving room, where the two girls waited, looking pretty and innocent, and very young. She knew they were not too far off of her own age, but at this moment, she felt positively ancient by comparison.

"Miss Templeton, Miss Arden," she said with a broad smile as she entered.

The two turned and gave her respectful curtseys. "Mrs. Gerrard," they murmured in unison.

Marianne gestured for them to sit, and they did so. "I was surprised to get your cards," she told them without any sort of preface.

Miss Templeton grinned, while Miss Arden merely curved the

corners of her mouth. "We thought you might be," Miss Templeton said, untying her bonnet ribbons. "We hardly know each other, and have never done anything like this before, have we?"

"No, we haven't," Marianne replied, still smiling, but now curious.

"Gemma and I do not know each other all that well either," Miss Arden spoke up in her soft, demure voice, "but we have become more acquainted this winter, and are now friends. And we thought, after what happened… well…" She trailed off and looked embarrassedly at Miss Templeton.

She smiled at her friend and took her hand, then looked directly at Marianne. "We thought you could use some friends, Mrs. Gerrard, and we wanted to be them. So, here we are."

Chapter Nine

$\mathcal{A}$s the entire world would have expected, Tibby's party was the height of spectacle, in the most elegant, fashionable, and envious of ways.

Kit had tried to prepare himself for what this event would be like, knowing Tibby's tastes were far more extravagant than his, but also knowing there was no stopping her.

After her visit the other day, he had not been sure what sort of reception he would receive on subsequent visits from Tibby, but the moment she had seen him this evening, she had clasped his hand, touched his face, and given him the most pitying of looks.

"My poor boy," she'd whimpered a little, patting his cheek. Then she'd snapped back into her tart character and ordered him to stand in this exact spot until she advised him otherwise. She'd positioned a rather flustered Marianne next to him and then began ordering the rest of their friends about.

Marianne was positively radiant, and it irritated him. She had chosen the palest possible shade of pink muslin adorned with delicate rosettes along the comparatively modest neckline, with more rosettes in her nearly ebony hair. With Tibby wearing a brilliant burgundy, Marianne looked like a fairer, nymph-like echo of her aunt, and her complexion glowed with it. Her dress was a little too close cut to her figure, but it only heightened her innate loveliness, and her eyes sparkled in the splendor of the candles abundantly scattered throughout the room. She was far simpler adorned than usual, which somehow made her more beautiful than ever.

She looked far too much like the girl he had proposed to six years ago, down to the shade of her dress and the curl of her hair, and the echo of the laughter of that day, mocking and hysterical, resounded in his ears when he looked at her now.

Well, her idea of a joke was now the reality for them both. What a lark.

He could not keep from scowling, and no doubt those who greeted them wondered at his displeasure. But as most of them wished to speak with his wife instead, he could not bring himself to care enough to adjust it.

Some of their friends required introduction to one or the other, though the names of each were familiar, and Marianne had far more than he did.

All told, he only had to officially introduce the Viscount Blackmoor, who had silently communicated to Kit that they would speak later, and Lord Marlowe, whose presence was causing a bit of a stir, but he would soon be forgotten, as he always was.

"Lord Blackmoor didn't really kill his wife, did he?" Marianne whispered through a false smile as more people approached.

Kit stiffened. "We are not discussing it," he hissed back. Really, were people still under that impression? Blackmoor had suffered enough in the last few years because of that woman, he hardly needed that accusation to still be hanging over his head as well.

"He certainly is mysterious enough to have done it," Marianne continued, "and he is always so cross."

"He is not cross," Kit insisted with little patience. "He is reserved and reticent. As am I."

"Case in point." She sniffed and flipped open her fan. "Who was the other man you know?"

"Lord Marlowe," he reminded her for at least the third time. Poor Rafe, to be always so easily forgotten. It suited his purposes, though, so it might have been his greatest asset.

"He is shockingly handsome," she said as she looked at him from across the room again. "Yet no one speaks with him, and I cannot recall ever seeing him at anything. Is he foreign?"

"No."

"Odd…"

Kit looked over at Tibby with the sort of longsuffering look that begs saving, and she ignored him for the moment.

The room began to fill with more and more people, some of whom swirled about them, and seemed to forget they were standing there.

"Gerrard finally got what he wanted," someone said with a hint of surprise. "Looks like the second time was the charm."

Kit's spine stiffened of its own accord as one of his hands formed a fist by his side. He forced his face to remain composed, eyes scanning the room as if looking for a familiar face.

A lady nearby tsked. "I thought she had better taste."

"He has a fortune," some man pointed out.

"And the looks," a female sighed.

Marianne shifted slightly beside him, and he slid his eyes to her, finding her perfectly poised, smile fixed, but obviously attentive to them.

"He's wanted her for years."

All seemed to still behind them, and Marianne with them. Kit nearly groaned. *Not here, not now…*

"You're lying," someone laughed.

"No, really, he proposed six years ago and was refused."

Kit saw Marianne's mouth tighten into a thin line, and his jaw echoed that same tightness.

"Can't say that I blame her," another said with a snort.

"Well, he's managed it now. He is the luckiest man in England."

"Or the most foolish."

"Either way, he has what he wanted."

"The Gerrards always get what they want."

Just as Kit had been about to snap, the group began to disperse, now speaking of some other idle reports, and he fought to find rational thought again.

How could they have been so unlucky to stand by the one group of people who still talked of that rumor?

He'd heard bits and pieces like that before, but never all put together, and never with Marianne near him. Not when he'd been married to her.

He exhaled slowly, his breath halting with every pounding beat of his infuriated heart.

"What were they talking about, Kit?" Marianne whispered sharply, her fan flicking in agitation.

"Nothing," he said in a firm tone. "Gossip."

"Gossip has its roots in truth," she pointed out, smiling with a delicate flutter of her lashes and resting a gloved hand on his arm, putting on a show for public eyes.

He wrenched away as discreetly as he could. "Leave it, Marianne," he snapped, giving her a small nod, his eyes pointedly averted, and then marched away. Tibby looked at him at last, her expression fraught with unspoken tension, and he raised a taunting brow at her, daring her to command him to remain.

She did not.

He walked passed his brother and his friends, who all looked the tiniest bit unsettled by his expression, and only Colin followed him.

"Aren't you going to dance with her?" Colin asked quietly, seeming surprised.

"No."

"She is your wife."

"And I don't dance. There will be a line soon enough, and you are more than welcome to stand in it, if you think it so important."

Colin stopped tailing him, and Kit was grateful for that. He needed space from everyone who connected him with her, for at the present his mind swirled with memories, and he could not bear it.

He found an empty hallway just off of the ballroom that was partially obscured from view and leaned against the wall, filling his lungs with the cooler air and closing his eyes.

He would never know how word had gotten out about that day. He did not think Marianne had told anyone, and he had certainly never let anyone know his feelings about her. Yet the truth was out there, swirling amidst rumors and lies and speculation, and seemed so far-fetched to everyone that it was ruled as the same. It had risen up once more when he had returned to England three years ago, and followed him everywhere he went.

If Marianne attended the same events as he, the stories resurfaced.

She had to have heard something about them before. Yet she seemed completely uninformed. Either she was ignorant or she simply sought the confirmation of whatever truth existed.

He could not give it.

He would not.

Did she remember that day? Did she have any idea what she had set in motion?

It had been a miserable day, long before he'd spoken a word to her. Hot and damp with no breeze to lighten it, and Marianne had been trapped in Tibby's poorly ventilated drawing room, receiving caller after caller. Kit had been growing more and more agitated as the days had gone on that summer, his feelings growing wild and straining against his control.

He could not go away that Season, could not bear to be parted from her. Day after day, week after week, he would play his same part of being her friend and confidante, able to stay close to her, closer than any other soul, for their past relationship. He could make her laugh with a single look, could read her as easily as she might a novel, and could make her see what a frivolous thing the parade of preening fools was. He knew she had begun encouraging men simply to see what he would say about them, and he ever delivered, knowing she would never seriously consider anyone that did not perfectly suit.

That day, just another in the endless streams of blissfully tormented days, he had broken form.

"Marry me," he'd said without any elegance or ceremony, bearing his heart without any preparation.

Looking back on it now, he could see the insolence of such a presentation.

But it was no excuse for the response.

"What?" Marianne had cried with a hint of a smile, her color still rosy from the last embarrassment of a suitor, about whom they had laughed heartily.

He had stepped forward, closer to her than he'd dared go in weeks, and simply said again, "Marry *me*, Marianne."

"That is it?" she'd said, laughter flittering through the simple words. "Nothing else? Oh, Kit, now you are being dreadful! No one would ever say it like that and be accepted!"

And then she had dissolved into laughter, peals and peals of it, falling against the sofa in her mirth.

He ought to have stayed, to profess it more and assure her of his affections, but her laughter at his expense had been too much for his fragile pride. He'd stormed from the room, hearing her call after him laughingly, still thinking it all a joke.

He had left London that night without even a feasible excuse for his twin. Shortly after that, he had left England altogether, and did not return for two full years, when he knew he was immune to her.

Mere weeks after his return, he'd been faced with seeing her once more, and the same adoration, love, and passion had burned within him just as fiercely as it had before he'd left.

More for the long absence.

And he had hated himself, and her, just as much. He'd been able to maintain his cool demeanor, cut her with biting words, and she'd not approached him since.

And he had married that woman? Oh, he was a fool, and worse than that, a glutton for punishment. Would he always wait for a look or a smile or a kind word, despite his desire to offend and insult?

Would he always want and hate his bride as he did now?

And what of their children? Their children. It drew a chilling shudder of apprehension from him. He'd always thought of fatherhood as a prime objective in his life, but now a life of celibacy was far more appealing to him.

Perhaps not appealing, but certainly the safest, most reasonable alternative.

"Gerrard," a low, familiar voice rumbled nearby.

He opened his eyes and saw Lord Blackmoor coming towards him, and he straightened.

"Blackmoor."

Blackmoor raised a dark brow and waved him back. "Please, you were comfortable, and this is no ceremony."

Kit did as he was bid and leaned back once more.

"Under the circumstances, I think I had better ask you if you need a drink," Blackmoor said with a marked casual air.

Kit exhaled a soft laugh. "If I started, I might never finish."

"I know how that is," his friend sighed, matching Kit's pose against the opposite wall, then drawing one leg up against it for support.

Kit watched his friend for a moment, having not seen him so relaxed in years, and certainly never since his marriage. Or what had transpired after. "Were you sent to fetch me?" Kit asked after a pause.

Blackmoor curved his bare smile, pale eyes unreadable. "No, not even Lady Raeburn dares to order me about, and your brother knows me only well enough to acknowledge me. Beverton I know a little, our country estates are neighboring, but he was dancing with his wife at the moment."

"So why seek me out?"

There was a faint look of surprise. "You seemed distressed, which is not like you. I thought it my duty to see to your aid."

"Most men would rather see to my wife," Kit muttered, glancing back out at the ballroom.

"If I cared for your wife, no doubt I would," Blackmoor replied without concern.

Kit turned his head to look back at him. "Why should you dislike her so? What harm as she done you?"

Blackmoor shrugged one broad shoulder, nonchalance not entirely suiting his athletic frame. "Nothing at all. I do not like her, I do not dislike her. Despite her popularity, I have never seen any reason to think well of her. Now that we have been introduced, I shall acknowledge her as I would any acquaintance of value. More than that is unnecessary at this point."

Kit measured that for what it was worth, and compared it to Marianne's gossiping inquiry about Blackmoor. "She is my wife," Kit murmured.

His friend gave him a quizzical smirk. "Indeed, she is. I wondered about that, but I assumed you had your reasons."

"I did," Kit said with a nod, then offered a slight smile himself, "though I may forget them from time to time."

Blackmoor nodded with a surprising degree of understanding in his eyes.

"If you could remind me that I had reasons on those occasions," Kit sighed, giving a sardonic look to his friend, "I would be most grateful."

Looking amused, Blackmoor nodded once more. "I shall." He glanced towards the ballroom, then back at Kit. "Did I see Marlowe here tonight?"

Kit nodded. "You did."

"So I take it he is…"

"Yes."

"Still?"

"Yes."

"And he's never…?"

"Not as far as I know."

"Amazing," Blackmoor murmured with a shake of his head. "I had better speak with him before he vanishes for four months again." He looked at Kit once more. "Are you yourself once more?"

Kit nodded, smiling with a newfound degree of warmth for his somber friend. "As much as I ever was."

Blackmoor smiled back, which would have shocked the rest of the world. "Well, that is all that we can hope for these days." He bowed slightly, and returned to the ballroom.

Kit waited a few moments more, exhaled slowly, and did the same, his carefully composed self once again.

Marianne was irritated, and no amount of amusement from her peers could help that.

Oh, she had been swarmed by people ever since Kit had left, all begging her for the story of her horrific abduction, wanting the details as to how they all could have been so deceived by Mr. Marksby, and even the faint scattering of felicitations on her marriage. She had all the attention she could want, and from some people who had never bothered to speak to her before. She was under no illusions about those gossipmongers, and she was not about to give them the merest sniff.

She had managed to play the entire group off with coyness and false modesty, claiming it was too distressful to recall, and she was only grateful to have been saved from it. Which had sparked another series of questions about *that* particular venture.

Who had saved her? How did they find her? Was it terribly heroic?

Was it gratitude that had sent her flying into her husband's arms?

She'd tried to be as delicate as possible, vague and off-putting, and it worked, for the most part. She could see the disappointed and sometimes exasperated expressions of those who had hoped for grand tales, but she'd kept them all entertained with tales of their new home. Particularly when she reminded them that the last occupant had been the Duchess of Falmouth.

They had seized upon that subject gratefully, no doubt hoping she would let something slip about her marriage, but also keen to hear about the scandalous death of Lord Rodale.

She had danced several times, and was pleased that most of her old favorites still hung about. Even Fanny had come to this event, though she looked a trifle distracted and a little pale. Poor thing, she'd never quite recovered from hearing the truth about Marksby. She alone knew what had really happened between him and Marianne, and she had vowed to keep it a secret.

Fanny might be a bit of a simpleton, but she never broke a confidence.

And then there had been that vile Lord Darlington. He'd thought this particular evening an appropriate time to attack Kit, much to the delight of others, and though she had been furious with Kit, though there wasn't a single reason for her to do so, Marianne had flown at him in a rage, and were it not for Annalise's calm intervention and quick thinking, a true scene might have broken out.

Clearly there was more to be done in repairing Marianne's reputation than she thought.

She'd made Annalise promise not to tell Kit anything about that, which her sister-in-law had agreed to, though her disapproval was clear. The gossip of the incident might reach Kit anyway, but Marianne couldn't do anything about that. She just couldn't bear to have Kit think that anything was changed between them.

Not when there was more about their past to discover. With all of that going on, she'd not managed to get another hint of what the people had been saying about her and Kit before.

He had got what he wanted? How was that even possible?

Kit despised her! Well, perhaps that was too strong a word, but he certainly barely tolerated her. Yes, they had been close once, but he had become stiff and disapproving the more popular and sought after she became. He did not like the way she behaved in public, and she did not care.

How anyone had managed to hear about his proposal was a mystery, and the fact that anyone had taken it seriously was even more mysterious. It was an embarrassing time to remember, for her and for him, and only one person had ever been so crass as to confront her about it. Thankfully, Mr. Townsend had not been to London in ages, and he'd never spoken a word about it again.

She regretted every moment of that day, and though she had no idea at the time, it had been the end of her treasured friendship between her and Kit.

But they thought he had actually meant to marry her? As if he had truly sought her hand?

It truly was laughable. Surely someone like Kit would have done a proper job of romance.

She scanned the guests in the room, searching for the men whom she had heard speaking before. If Kit would not tell her what they meant, or what he knew, then she would go to the source of the gossip. She highly doubted these men in question were the instigators of the rumors, they merely spread the stuff.

She felt a rush of satisfaction when she caught sight of them and started in that direction.

Before they saw her, however, her arm was forcefully seized and she was steered away. She gasped and looked up to find her husband hauling her off, his expression bordering on the murderous.

"What are you doing?" she hissed, looking around to see if anyone was aware of his manhandling.

"Taking my inquisitive wife home," he replied in harsh, clipped tones.

She glowered up at him as they exited the ballroom and headed for the entrance. "Afraid that I will discover something?"

His icy glare stole her breath for half a moment. "Afraid you will cause more trouble, Mrs. Gerrard, and you really must behave yourself."

"I am not a child," she reminded him pointedly as she took her cloak from the servant.

Kit nodded as he took his hat and set it on his head. "I am well aware of that. A child is far more obedient."

She screeched between clenched teeth and marched out to the carriage ahead of him, climbed in without help, and settled herself, wishing, for once, that she could walk home.

"Kit, tell me what they were talking about," she demanded once he entered the carriage.

"No."

"Yes! Or I will continue to seek for answers on my own at every event and outing I attend!"

He snorted and rapped on the ceiling for the coachman to depart. "You know the gossip."

She frowned, starting to seethe a little. "Of course, I know the gossip," she snapped. "I've been fighting the torrent about you and me for years, and I've never heard that little detail."

He gave her a very serious look. "Do you believe every detail about every life you hear?"

That was a fair point, but she would not be swayed. "No, of course not…"

"Then do not believe that."

His avoidance only made her more determined. "You are hiding something from me, Kit," she said in a low, hopefully dangerous tone, and folding her arms, "and you cannot stop me from finding out. You cannot corral me forever, not from every event and every circle. We have danced around this subject long enough, and now that we are married, it will only get worse."

He stared at her without expression, though his jaw worked and his grip on his walking stick tightened. She could see how the words had affected him. Things *would* get worse, whether she had anything to do with it or not. So long as they were married and together, it would always come up.

He knew that, however reluctant he was to admit it.

Which meant this could be her only chance.

"Why would anyone ever assume that you wanted me?" she asked him without hesitation.

"Because I did."

Her eyes widened at his low response, simply stated with marked coldness.

"What?" she cried in a breathless, weak exclamation.

A sneer curled on his features. "Surprised, are you? All of London seems to know that I was in love with you, but not you. And you are thought to be so intuitive."

"You loved me?" she managed to stammer, suddenly going cold.

He scoffed and shook his head. "The idea that you were ignorant about that then and still are now is the most preposterous thing in the world."

"I didn't know that, Kit," she insisted, wringing her hands a little. "How was I supposed to know that?"

"You have eyes," he suggested bitterly.

"What?" she cried, her hand going to her throat. "You never said anything!"

"If I remember correctly," he drawled with false casualness, "I did propose to you."

"Hardly!" She shook her head in astonishment. "You *never* said you loved me."

His lip curled, making her feel ill. "And you never thought of me. You laughed at me."

"You had been teasing me about proposals and suitors!" she protested with a wild gesture of her hands. "I thought you were mocking them!"

He sat back and surveyed her without pleasure. "Well, I wasn't."

Her whole world had been turned upside down. He had actually proposed to her? In all sincerity?

Suddenly the words he had spoken to her upon his return three years ago echoed once more in her mind.

I have a very low tolerance for unfeeling creatures who care only for themselves.

Oh, Lord, she had been exactly that. Unknowingly, it was true, but… "I never meant to hurt you," she said softly, feeling an ache well up within her.

"I know that," he bit out, his composure cracking for the first time. "Don't you think I know that? But that was worse. You didn't take me seriously. You never even thought of me. I burned for you with such love, such passion." He shook his head, seeming to laugh at himself. "And you didn't even think of me."

Good lord, what had she done?

"Kit…" she breathed, suddenly and inexplicably wanting to reach out and touch him. To mend something. To feel something.

He seemed to know her intentions and scoffed, surveying her with cold eyes. "It makes no difference now. They can say whatever they want about us. We know the truth."

Her brief turn towards tenderness vanished and the desire surged to wound him as he had wounded her. "That I was a fool and you saved me from ruin by marrying me," she recited in mocking tones. "A convenient marriage, aren't I lucky?"

He raised his chin in indignation as they arrived home. "If you want out, be my guest. Lord knows, I suffer enough for it." Without another word, he exited the coach, yet he still waited to help her down.

Still a gentleman. He ought to have left her here and gone on ahead, storming away in his fury. She would have preferred that.

But no, Kit Gerrard was a gentleman, even when he was cruel.

Reluctantly, and with a look of hatred, Marianne took his outstretched hand, then released it the moment she could. They silently walked into the house, said nothing to the servants, and separated for the night without a word.

There was absolutely nothing more to be said.

They'd said quite enough.

Chapter Ten

"Kit! Did you see? We have received invitations to a masquerade at the Rivertons!"

Kit looked up from his solicitor's letter in irritation, not at all amused by the way his wife was fairly bounding on the balls of her feet, her pale pink dress swishing with her motions.

"Pardon?" he inquired with a would-be patient sigh.

She waved the pair of invitations in the air, looking eager. "Invitations, Kit! To the Rivertons! On Saturday!" She looked at them again, her features alight. "I've never been invited to an exclusive event of theirs, only their open soirée every other year. This is something entirely different, and after all the commotion being made about us, I cannot imagine how we have each garnered an invitation."

He frowned and set down his pen. "Each?"

Why in the world would they garner separate invitations? Was that what they had come to now? Everyone thinking they could spend so little time together, they would invite them as individuals and not as a couple… and perhaps sometimes invite just one. Not that he was pining for invitations to anything, as Marianne was, but to be separated by the public in such a way…

"It's an anonymous masquerade," Marianne explained lightly, handing him the invitation with his name on it. "All attendees must present their specific invitations before being admitted."

"How anonymous can it be with our names on them?" he mused, grudgingly looking it over.

Marianne huffed and rolled her eyes. "The invitations are within, Kit. The names are not on the invitation themselves."

"Wasteful extravagance," Kit muttered, shaking his head. "They ought to have sent one letter, with a request for attendance in the body of the letter, rather than include an additional card within, and certainly should only have sent one per household."

"Kit," Marianne scolded as if he were a simpleton, "it's the Rivertons. They are all extravagance." She hummed a little and looked away in thought. "I wonder what I should wear... I should not like anyone to know me."

Kit sighed and set the ridiculous invitation on the desk. "Wear whatever you like. I shall not be attending."

Marianne's head snapped back to face him, her eyes wide. "You cannot be serious."

He shrugged a shoulder. "I cannot abide masquerades. I never attend them."

"But..." she sputtered, looking bewildered. "But it's the Rivertons."

"Yes, so you have said."

She took a step forward and put a fluttery hand on the desk nervously. "No one refuses the Rivertons. How can you?"

"Like this," he said simply, taking his invitation and tearing it in half, then again, tossing the pieces into the air.

He thought Marianne might swoon, she was suddenly so pale. She gasped almost silently as the pieces fluttered to the floor, then seemed to shake with rage or distress or both.

She screeched between clenched teeth. "You are going to ruin my life!"

He sniffed a mirthless laugh. "I am not. An anonymous event with no announcement of arrivals? I won't be missed. No one will know you are there, and no one will know I wasn't."

Marianne screeched again, stomped her foot, and whirled from the room, drawing a small smile from him.

Goading his wife was really too simple.

But at least they were speaking to each other again. That was progress, was it not?

Part of that seemed to be Marianne's newfound friendship with Miss Gemma Templeton and Miss Lily Arden, two young ladies of whom Kit thought very highly, and hoped they might persuade

Marianne's behavior down to a more respectable level. He was already accustomed to seeing them about, or hearing of ventures with them, but only time would tell how it affected her.

He shook his head and returned to his letter. There were some issues with the estate in Somerset, nothing too disastrous or challenging, but he would need to pay a visit soon. There was only so much he could accomplish through a letter, though his estate manager and solicitor were both highly capable men. He would need to discuss things with Colin first, however. Though Somerset was one of Kit's estates, when it came to matters such as these, the brothers shared details and counseled with each other.

Loughton did not care for anyone or anything, by his own admission, and had given up all properties and duties to Kit by law, and Kit had arranged matters several years ago so that the management of the estates was equally divided. He was the elder brother and heir, it was true, but he had no desire to rule and reign. Both Kit and Colin, though gentlemen by heritage, fortune, and nature, were deeply invested in their estates and the management of them, taking a far more active role than anybody would have expected of them.

Nobody knew that about the Gerrard brothers, and they liked it that way. No one remembered who their father was, except those of the oldest set. They'd been a reclusive family before their mother's death, and after… Well, things had only gotten worse after that.

But so long as there were more pressing scandals and people like Marianne running about London, Lord Loughton and his reprehensible history were quite forgotten.

If the life he currently lived was any indication, Kit would greatly enjoy being equally forgotten.

Given the identity of his wife, however, he doubted he would be so fortunate.

Wherever she went, people would speak of him, and when they spoke of him, they would revisit the past, both his and hers, and they would wonder what had possessed him to marry her, and what had become of him.

He couldn't be entirely reclusive until his sisters were married off. Despite Colin's unfathomable popularity, it was Kit that was the eldest, and the responsibility of his sisters' future, however small a portion it was in reality, lay with him. He would have to venture out into Society more and more as the years passed, and he had accepted that fate.

But a masquerade he utterly refused. He wore enough of a mask in his everyday life, as did the rest of the world, and hardly needed an excuse to wear more of them. Nor would he ever wish for the freedom that such a disguise afforded those in attendance. Inhibitions and respectability were too easily stripped away by the simple adornment of a mask and a costume.

It unnerved him.

The Rivertons were entirely respectable, and he admired their sons, Lord Sheffield and Captain Riverton, as well, but he did not see the need to hold them to the impossibly high standard as the rest of the world. They were only people, the same as everyone else, and their home was no more elaborate than the Whitlocks, so there was no need for such a fuss.

And so, on Saturday evening, his wife would go, and he would stay, enjoying the solitude with a good book by a warm fire.

He had no doubt he would hear all sorts of details from his gossip-addicted wife upon her return.

Marianne could barely contain her excitement as she ascended the majestic stairs of the Riverton estate. Though Kit had adamantly refused to accompany her again, she was beyond caring at this point. She had settled on the perfect ensemble, one that would allow her to be perfectly disguised from anyone expecting her usual brazen costumes and enable her to hear the gossip and rumors people were actually saying about her behind her back.

Ever since that fateful carriage ride, she had been more curious about perceptions of her and Kit. His revelation of the feelings of his past had unnerved her, particularly when others had been the first to reveal it to her. If Society as a whole could find such truth in their whisperings, what else lay therein?

And what would people say if they did not know her identity?

She was very plainly dressed, and entirely modest in all things. Her hair was pulled back and only barely curled, without any finery or elaborate adornments, only black ribbons. Her dress was one she had made over from Tibby's old things, and still held that old style of dress long out of fashion, and required Marianne to fasten her corset more tightly so as to make it fit.

It was a deep midnight blue, with black lace trimmings that was actually quite flattering on her, which made her consider more of the same style of dresses for the future. She had chosen black elbow gloves and a simple black domino that covered most of her face, her lips and chin being the only visible features.

She could have been a nun or a mournful widow for all her blandness.

And it was exactly how she wished it.

Imagine the shock when people discovered her!

She fought to keep from biting her lip as she handed the requisite invitation to the servant at the door, who then stepped back with a bow to let her pass. The house and the ballroom were just as exquisite as she remembered, even more so, perhaps, for the brilliance of the candlelight, the mystery of the masks, and the feeling of freedom cascading through her frame.

She had never thought she would be admitted here again.

The room was already filled with people, and she slowly, shyly, ambled her way around, waiting for the moment when someone knew her gait or her figure. Then they would call out to her or approach her, as had inevitably happened before.

The moment never came.

A satisfied smirk spread across her face. Her disguise was even better than she had predicted. She had perfect anonymity tonight.

She could say anything, be anything, and no one would ever know.

She searched the room for anyone that she might know, and was a bit discouraged that everyone else seemed to be just as well disguised. Not that she had expected to immediately know anyone, but she wished Gemma and Lily had received invitations as well. The three of them were becoming better friends than she would have thought, given their vast differences in personality and experience. But Gemma was so overtly friendly and cheerful, and Lily gentle yet witty, that it was impossible to be anything but warm with them. They had even been so bold yesterday as to take her down a few notches when she had said something too haughty, and she had not even minded it.

She had not minded at the time that they had not been invited, and promised to share details with them. She doubted she would have spent much time with them anyway, considering how she would be flocked.

Now, however, she was rather desperate for their company.

A scant few moments into the event, and she was already feeling eerily similar to the shy, retreating girl in her first Season who had attracted the attention of nobody at all. Despite her perfect figure and posture, her effortless gliding, all of which had taken her years to perfect, not a single head turned in her direction.

No one looked for her. No one marked her.

No one missed her.

She frowned and was tempted to fling off her mask, but she could not risk endangering future invitations from the Rivertons. If they wanted an anonymous masquerade, then she would comply with those wishes.

Eventually, someone would know her. She was one of Society's brightest gems, as she had been told repeatedly, and her popularity was unmatched. This idea of complete anonymity was not as entertaining as it had once been. Surely she could not be this invisible.

She floated amongst the groups, ears straining for anything of value, but people only spoke of costumes, of the heat of the room, and of recent decisions of Parliament, of all things. Who spoke of the government at an event such as this? Whoever that was, she made a note to avoid them in the future.

"No, I heard it from Colin Gerrard's own mouth. Miss Bray had been carried off by Marksby against her will, and her brother rallied his friends to save her from certain ruination."

Marianne's ears perked up and she moved closer to the masked group of people nearby, a small, secret smile forming. Now, at last, she might hear something worthwhile.

A derisive snort escaped from someone in the group. "If she was unwilling, I will eat my hat. That girl has been an impudent hoyden for years. Takes after her mother, you know. She was a harlot as well."

"Surely you are not suggesting that Miss Bray is a fallen woman."

"All I am saying is Mr. Marksby would not have been inclined to pay any interest in her without the proper inducements. And given her family history, it is little wonder that she is so without morals."

Marianne was too stunned to even gasp and hid herself behind a pillar, allowing her to listen without being seen, despite her costume.

"She *is* rather cold and cruel," a man said in a tone of reluctant consideration.

"Her talents for polite society are minimal at best. All the accomplishments she can boast are for things about which we refined persons do not speak. I have no doubt her mother taught her well. Perhaps even her mother's lovers."

"Lovers? I thought there was just the one."

"Yes, the one the late Mr. Bray killed before her eyes, and then dispensed with his wife afterwards."

"Idiot. Do you think Eleanor Bray only had one lover? Scores, gentlemen. Scores of men seduced by her wiles and then tossed aside, entirely ruined. And the daughter is on the same path, mark my words."

"But her brother is so fine a gentleman."

"Duncan Bray is a wild man dressed in a gentleman's clothing," retorted the same, sharp voice. "Do you know how many men he has thrashed to keep his sister's supposed honor intact? Townsend, for example…"

"If she has had so many lovers, why do we not know of them?"

"Are you disappointed to not have been one of them?"

The group chuckled darkly, and Marianne felt her face burn with shame and embarrassment. She raised a gloved hand to her cheek and found no relief from the cool fabric covering her numb fingers.

"Not at all, I have no desire to be among the unfortunate souls taken in by such a woman. I tried to court her, you know, before her true nature was known. Even then, she was a heartless wretch."

"She always has been. Not a single friend, and I doubt anyone would miss her if she were gone."

"I rather think London would be more polite for it."

"Why is she so popular then?"

"Oh, because she says what nobody else dares to, and one never knows what she will do next. She is more of a spectacle than anything else."

"Her aunt is quite eccentric…"

"Yes, but Lady Raeburn also has grace, class, and encourages accomplishment. She fosters goodwill and brings a spark of life to dull events such as these. Her niece lacks all that is good and polished for a well-bred lady."

"She is not well-bred. Her father was a tradesman!"

"He was the son of a very respectable family."

"Yes, and was cut off! Nobody knows why, but that should tell you how serious it is."

"To think, Marianne Bray parades herself around as a fine lady. She has no accomplishments, you know. Nothing to recommend her but a fortune."

"A man would have to be truly desperate to want such a creature, no matter how vast her fortune."

"How do you explain Kit Gerrard, then?"

"Simple. He could get her for an easy time of it. She was quite ruined, you know, whatever the circumstances of her departure from London. Gerrard fancied the girl, and her brother knew no one else would have her. One should know by now that not even a respectable marriage could save such a woman. She will never be truly admitted by polite society, not even her husband can stand her."

"She will have to bear him children…"

"It will be impossible. He will never know which children she bears are legitimate."

"From bad blood comes bad blood. The whole family will be ruined because of her. Shame it's the Gerrards who will suffer."

Marianne could hear no more. Her ears rang with the mocking laughter, the flagrant lies that this particular group was so lightly tossing about. She could not feel her extremities, all of her sensation focused on the erratic and painful beating of her heart.

She wandered to another portion of the room, and found others discussing her marriage, and not politely. Still others were delighted that she had not attended, feeling they might actually enjoy the evening. And still another, with people she recognized as being among her circle of regular friends and admirers, criticizing everything about her, from her laugh to her nose to her accomplishments, or lack thereof. She had known she was a household name, but she had never expected this.

What would be the point in remaining now?

She moved back towards the entrance as if in a daze, occasionally being jostled or bumped by people who did not see her, or had imbibed too much. She managed a glance at a large clock in the entryway, and found she had not even been at the party for two hours. But it was enough.

Her carriage was summoned, her dark cloak fetched, and wordlessly she loaded herself in, ignoring the questioning looks from her footman and driver.

She felt nothing as she rode back, her eyes seeing nothing though she stared out the carriage window. There was nothing around her, nothing touching her, nothing in her head…

Nothing.

It was as if no time at all had passed before she was back at the house, wondering faintly if this place might become a refuge for her. This home that was not yet a home, but could it become a source of comfort and hope? Or would it become a prison for her?

The footman, sensing she was not quite right, escorted her inside and wordlessly took her cloak and mask, and asked her something, probably feeling the need to see her safely to her rooms, but she waved him off, and he disappeared.

She started towards the stairs, but found her step faltering. She teetered on her slightly heeled shoes, feeling as if she had not eaten in days. Her chest ached and her dress felt too tight, her legs too weak, her arms too heavy. She managed to reach the stairs and the railing, and hand over trembling hand, she pulled herself up the stairs, tripping over her long and heavy skirts at scattered intervals. Her lungs started to work in a frantic, heaving pattern, and dry sobs soon found their way out.

Everything burned and ached, and her eyes flooded with hot

tears of shame, embarrassment, guilt, agony… She could not bear the load suddenly thrust upon her, the weight pressing against her back and her chest and her shoulders. How could she not have known? How could people say and think such horrible things about her?

Was it the truth?

Had she really given such impressions?

No wonder Kit hated her.

That, it seemed, was the final blow, and at last, safely in her bedchamber, she crumpled to the floor awkwardly, her feet tangling in her skirts, sending her crashing down hard. She did not care, though her shoulder ached from the impact. She wrapped her arms around herself, curling into a ball, her frame wracked with sob after sob.

It could not have been long after her fall that her husband appeared, though time had ceased to hold any meaning or significance to her.

"What was that noise?" he asked, not seeing her in the dark of the room. "It sounded as though…" His feet shuffled a little. "Good Lord… Marianne?"

She could only answer with more sobs. Embarrassed at being discovered so, she flung an arm over her face and mouth, desperate to stifle the pitiful sounds emanating from her and hide her face from him.

"Did they not light your room before you returned?" Kit asked, sounding irritated. "Idiot staff, they will wind up killing one of us. To be fair, you are back earlier than expected, but that's no excuse. We can train them better. I will speak with Caldwell and Mrs. Wilton about it. At least your fire is still going, but what did you trip over? Are you hurt?"

He entered the room more fully, shutting the door behind him softly, then seemed to notice her state. He stopped, and then she felt a surprisingly gentle hand on her shoulder. "Marianne?"

The soft surprise, even kindness in his voice undid her, and the painful sobs returned with a vengeance. She twisted away from him, burying her face into the hard floor beneath her.

Kit muttered to himself softly, and tried to get her to look at him. "Marianne, look at me. What is it? Are you injured?"

She shook her head frantically, wishing he would just go and leave her in peace. She could not face anyone now, perhaps ever again.

She heard him shift, and then suddenly she was lifted from the ground and into his arms. A bleating cry of protest was wrenched from her and she struggled in his hold, her hands now fists.

"No, no," he scolded, though his tone sounded odd. "Easy. It's all right."

She needed him to be hard, to be unfeeling, to kick her while she was down, to join the others in their condemnation of her. Not this…

He carried her across the room, his hold on her sure. "Relax, Marianne," he ordered softly, still not sounding himself.

Something about his steadiness shook her and the stubborn resistance evaporated. She found herself curling against him, turning her face into his coat and sobbing even harder, her lungs gasping for air that she could not find.

His hold shifted and tightened briefly, then she was set on the divan near the fire. Kit ran his hands along her shoulders and back. "Are you hurt?" he asked again. "Did the fall injure you?"

She shook her head, now swimming in faintness, and covered her face with her hands.

His hands slid down her arms and her hands were suddenly pulled from her face and held in his, his grip nearly clenching. "What happened, Marianne? What is wrong?"

Eyes still closed, she shook her head again, unable to bear his inquisition. She was broken and still breaking, and he could not see it.

She heard Kit swear softly, which was impossible, for Kit never did any such thing, and her forearms were suddenly seized, and she felt him on the floor in front of her.

"Marianne, what is it?" he asked again, sounding almost panicked now. "For heaven's sake, tell me!"

She hiccupped on a few more sobs, unable to draw in a full breath and swaying a little from the effort. Even with her eyes closed, she could almost see dots before her eyes and her blood pounded in her ears.

Kit made a noise of irritation and went around the divan, his fingers suddenly at her back and unhooking her dress, then loosening her corset laces. She inhaled sharply, the acute relief washing over her. She heard him give a satisfied grunt, then felt a shawl being draped around her, which he proceeded to pull tightly around her when he faced her again.

Back on his haunches before her, he took her hands. "Breathe, Marianne," he murmured, rubbing her hands a little. "That should help you now."

She obeyed his calm directions, and found herself settling a little.

"That's it," he praised softly. "Can you look at me?"

She slowly shook her head, her frame still shaking with unreleased sobs.

He sighed, then got to his feet. "I will call a servant to light the room and help you change."

"No!" she cried, her hand shooting out to seize his arm. She could not bear to be seen in this state of disarray and distress by one in her employ. It was bad enough to be seen by her husband this way, but that she could get over.

And for some inexplicable reason, she wanted him to stay.

She forced her eyes open and looked up at Kit through her tear dampened lashes, more tears falling from her eyes down her cheeks. "Please stay."

Kit stared at her for a long moment, then he slowly nodded once. "All right. Let me light the room while you settle yourself."

She dropped her arm with a nod, closing her eyes against the urge to cry again. She heard Kit moving about the room, lighting several candles and stoking the fire. It must have been a sight, the proud gentleman and master of so many now acting a servant. What had gotten into him? She ought to have laughed at the sight, but she could not even bear to see him brought so low for her.

She ought to be alone in the darkness, laying where she fell.

"There, you already seem more yourself," Kit said at last.

Marianne looked over at him, standing with his hands on his hips by the fireplace, watching her intently.

She swallowed as she realized there were no more hysterics, no more frantic pounding of her heart and lungs. Tears were still there, but they now fell slowly down their path across her cheeks.

Kit came to her again, slowly going down before her, and taking her hands in a comforting hold. "Tell me what happened," he said gently.

Marianne looked into his blue eyes for a long moment, then nodded. Haltingly, she confessed to everything she had heard this evening, recalling every blistering second with perfect clarity. Kit remained silent through the entire telling, though his hold and his features tightened occasionally. She told him how she had felt in the room before she'd heard anything, the strange sort of loneliness that she had long forgotten and had no wish to feel again. She told him how betrayed she had felt by people whom she had known for years, and had thought well of, and the shocking discovery about what people truly thought of her. She had wanted to be popular in society, but hardly notorious.

When she had finished, she sagged against the side of the divan, Kit's hold on her hands the only thing keeping her upright.

"You didn't know?" Kit finally asked in a quiet tone, his head tilted, looking curious.

She frowned and tried to glare at him. "How would I know that?" she demanded.

He looked a little lost for words and shrugged. "I thought…"

His uncertainty gave her pause and she stared at him wordlessly. "You thought I wanted to be that?" she finally whispered.

He met her eyes steadily. "No, but I thought you would have heard," he admitted softly.

She groaned and shook her head, looking away. "I have been so blind. I'm such a fool."

He squeezed her hands tightly. "No, you are not a fool. We have all taken such care to protect you that we have left you ignorant." She looked back at him with a doubtful look, but he nodded earnestly. "You should not have had to discover it this way, we should have warned you."

"I wish I'd known," she murmured, shaking her head again, her hands finally warming in their gloves beneath his touch. "I don't want them to think those things. But it is too late." She sighed and let her shoulders slump a little.

"Why does it matter what they think?" he demanded, his eyes

flashing. "What do they know? You know what they say about me, I presume."

She snorted. "Yes, and it is absolutely ridiculous. As if you would ever resort to piracy."

He reared back, then a slight smile appeared on his face. "Oh, that's a new one. I had not heard that."

How could it be so comfortable for him? It had to bother him, at least a little, to know he was so maligned. "Doesn't it vex you? That they don't know you?"

His half smile remained as he shrugged one shoulder. "Well, I am not particularly inclined to let them." He gave her a serious look, his smile fading a touch. "I know myself well enough, and I know you well enough. That suffices."

Marianne stared at her husband as if she were truly seeing him for the first time. She was tempted to reach out and touch his strong, angular jaw, where not a hint of stubble marred his smooth skin. She saw a warmth in his blue eyes that had been vacant for years. She noticed how the years had aged him, how he was more handsome now than he had been in her youth, and would grow handsomer still as the years passed.

"You have always known me, haven't you?" she murmured, feeling an odd surge of tenderness welling up inside.

He seemed to soften further still. "I thought so once. Haven't been so sure in recent years."

She felt more tears welling up in her eyes, and her heart seemed to burn beneath her ribs. "I am so sorry," she whispered, her voice choked with emotion.

Kit shook his head and rose to give her a hug, which she returned tightly. "Never mind me," he murmured, his voice low in her ear. "I can take it. But be yourself."

Marianne sniffed and buried her face against his shoulder. "Why are you still nice to me?" she muttered against him.

He laughed once and rubbed her back. "I haven't been nice to you. I've been ignoring you."

She hesitated a moment, then pushed back from him. "I know."

He sat back on his heels, one brow raise in query. "You do?"

She nodded, rubbing at her eyes. "I deserved the worst from

you," she confessed, her voice and her throat suddenly raw. She swallowed hastily, needing to get this out before they were back to their old selves. "Had I known what… what you meant, what you intended, I would never have said or done what I did. You had every right to destroy me. But you chose silence. Avoidance."

Kit snorted in derision, shaking his head slowly. "It was stupid."

She reached out a hand and put it on his shoulder. "It was noble," she assured him, wanting him to know what it meant to her now that she knew what it must have cost him. She offered as much of a smile as she could manage. "I know it was probably self-preservation, and rightfully so, but it saved me. And I know you did not mean to…"

"Yes, I did," he overrode at once.

"You did?" she asked, eyes going wide.

He took her hand from his shoulder and gave a light kiss to her glove, then rubbed it softly. "How could I destroy you, do anything to harm you, simply because you did not want me? That wouldn't…" He trailed off, shaking his head again. "I couldn't do that. I could never hurt you or see you hurt. Because I really did love you." His voice caught, and he cleared his throat, his brow furrowing slightly. "And that means something."

Marianne's fingers fluttered slightly in his hold, her heart mimicking the action. "Thank you," she murmured, hoping her eyes could convey just how much gratitude she felt.

He nodded once. "I cannot promise that you will never feel pain from my hand, so to speak. But I can promise that I will never intend to cause you any. Can you live with that?"

She smiled a little. "Yes, Kit. That will be enough."

He swallowed quickly, then gave her a brief smile of fondness. "You barely ate a thing at dinner, I presume you were too excited?"

She flushed, which drew a chuckle from him.

"I will have Anna bring you something and help you change. What in the world possessed you to wear that thing? I am surprised you could breathe at all."

She drew herself up taller. "I will have you know that it was a far cry better than what most of the other women were wearing. You would have been scandalized beyond repair, had you seen them."

His mouth curved in a crooked smile. "Yes, I suppose I would. Though I should have been there for you, I cannot regret my ignorance of such matters."

"I can manage things myself, Kit," Marianne told him with a sardonic smirk. "There is no need for you to suffer through an event you abhor for my sake."

He returned her look with a very serious one of his own. "If Society thinks they can say such things about my wife and I will stand idly by, then they, and you, are sadly mistaken."

Marianne stared at him, a surge of gratitude and confusion, bordering on tenderness, rising within her, and if she was not careful, it could turn her head.

Kit suddenly cleared his throat, and did so a bit awkwardly. "Now, you have yet to tell me…" he trailed off, watching her.

Her body stiffened, and her eyes grew wary.

He tilted his head just a little. "How was the Rivertons?"

She grinned and without any further encouragement, she prattled on and on about the house, the décor, the guests, the costumes, every single detail until Kit no doubt wished he'd never asked.

Kit would have to be more careful with encouraging his wife in matters such as this.

She really did not need it.

Chapter Eleven

*K*it walked briskly down the Mayfair streets the next morning, before many were up and about, which was just how he liked it. He'd slept fitfully at best last night, his mind whirling with questions and possible solutions for Marianne's situation, unable to forget the sounds of her distress or the sight of her crumpled on the floor.

It had been far more unsettling than he had let on, seeing her that way.

Marianne was a woman of strength and determination, prone to emotion, it was true, but never like that. She was high-spirited, but she was not particularly inclined towards dramatics. That was a trick for her aunt. He had been helpless in the face of such distress and grief, and he had to help her.

He could not regret caring for her as he had done, nor sharing so much with her. And during the night, he had wondered if he ought to have done more. He could not change Society, and he would have been afraid of the attempt, knowing he would not come out unscathed. But he felt sick when he recalled what Marianne had heard when she had only meant to enjoy an evening out before the Season began. How she had managed to get home before letting her emotions free was beyond him.

He had to do something. So, he had made the decision sometime in the night to go to the person who knew Marianne as well or perhaps better than he did, and had a significant interest in her well-being.

Her brother.

He had not spoken with Duncan much since their return, and he was glad for it. As much as he liked the man, it was a relief to not have an overprotective brother watching the marriage over his shoulder.

He would not have liked what he had seen.

He reached the Bray family home and rang, having only to wait moments before being shown in. "Good morning," he said to the smiling butler as he gave him his hat and gloves. "Is your master available?"

"Here, Kit," came a soft call from the stairs.

Kit looked up to see Duncan descending the stairs, casually dressed in breeches and an open-collared linen shirt, no weskit or cravat in sight. Against his shoulder was his small daughter, her fair hair almost hidden by a blanket.

Duncan smiled at Kit's perusal of him. "Tillie had a rough night," he explained as he reached him. "Annalise is still sleeping, so I've got the little one."

Kit had to smile at the soft gurgling sounds from the child in question. "Is she well?" he asked politely, indicating the baby.

Duncan grinned swiftly. "Well enough. Just teething. Annalise insists on getting up with her in the night, so this is the least I can do." He patted her back a little when she fussed again. "What can I do for you?"

Kit sighed reluctantly. "Do you have a moment? There is something I need to discuss with you."

Duncan's eyes flashed briefly and his jaw tightened, but he nodded. "Of course. If you don't mind Tillie joining us."

"Not at all," he said with a hint of a smile.

"Good. I promise she will keep your confidence."

"That is a relief. Takes after her mother, then."

Duncan grinned swiftly. "Blessedly so, in all things. Come with me, the study is down here." He turned and started down the hall. His daughter looked over his shoulder and her green eyes met Kit's and he smiled a little, which earned him one in return.

A gentle tugging started somewhere in the middle of his chest, but he shook it free as they entered the study. Duncan situated himself near the fire, speaking softly to his daughter.

Kit remained standing for a moment, staring at his brother-in-law and wondering how to approach the subject.

"I'm sorry that I have not come by," Duncan said suddenly, his mouth curving up in a smile. "Annalise advised me several times to go, but I always found a reason not to. I wasn't entirely sure how Marianne would react, and I was hesitant to interfere."

Kit nodded in understanding. "There is nothing to be sorry for. It has been a tumultuous time, and I think we may be settling into a semblance of normalcy now. Or at least, we were."

That perked Duncan up and his smile faded. "Were?" he asked cautiously.

Kit nodded firmly once. "Marianne knows," he told him.

"Knows… what?" Duncan inquired, though his eyes and expression showed a tension that spoke volumes.

"Everything."

Duncan looked as though he would swear, but looked at the baby and bit it back. He closed his eyes and the tension in him increased momentarily, then seemed willed away. "How?" he asked in a barely controlled hiss.

Kit gave him the brief version of what had transpired at the masquerade without revealing any of the particulars. Knowing Duncan's temper and defensiveness over his sister, it would not be wise to give him further excuse.

"How did she take it?" Duncan asked him in a hollow voice, his eyes still looking a bit murderous.

"Well…" Kit started to say slowly, which made Duncan get to his feet and start walking, then look down at his daughter in consternation.

Duncan looked absolutely miserable, and Kit could understand. If it were his sister in this situation, he would not want to sit still when hearing this. Against his inclination, he stepped forward and held out his hands for the baby.

Duncan gave him an odd look.

"You want to pace and rage and probably hit something," Kit explained, gesturing in invitation. "Give her to me, and I'll tell you the rest. I've come to terms with it, I can be calm."

"She doesn't really like strangers," Duncan warned as he handed the infant over.

"I'm no stranger," Kit informed him, and her. "I'm her uncle."

Duncan watched for a moment as Tillie situated herself against Kit, then shook his head with a smile as Tillie yawned and began gnawing on Kit's jacket buttons without a peep of distress.

Kit smiled and looked back at Duncan with a satisfied smirk. "You were saying?"

Duncan grunted and began to pace the room. "How did Marianne take the surprise?" he asked in a low growl, his thick brow furrowing.

Kit watched him pace, somehow seeming larger without the typical gentleman's clothing. "Not well, as you can probably imagine. To her credit, she made it home before showing anything outwardly. It took quite some time to set her to rights."

Duncan winced and rubbed at his forehead. "Tell me you were gentle with her," he begged, his voice suddenly raw.

"I was," Kit assured him, meeting his eyes calmly when Duncan looked over. "I might not be the husband Marianne wanted, or worth any sort of salt as a husband at all, but seeing her like that…" He trailed off, shaking his head as a surprising amount of emotion rose within him. "I was gentle," he managed.

Duncan nodded his thanks.

Kit cleared his throat, patting the baby softly. "Once she was calm, we discussed it, and she seemed to handle it fairly well once the shock wore off. I think she will be all right."

"Think?" Duncan asked sharply, folding his arms in his agitation.

Kit shrugged one shoulder. "Well, it was just last night, and I have not seen her this morning yet. I have no way of knowing how she truly is until I see her. Assuming she wishes to discuss it at all."

Duncan rocked back on his heels for a moment, considering that. Then he released a slow breath. "So what do we do?" he asked, starting to pace once more. "I haven't thrashed anyone lately, I may be out of practice."

Kit shook his head and looked down at his niece. "I worry for you, my dear. When you want to start courting someone, come see your aunt and me."

Duncan glowered at him. "That was a very Colin thing to say."

"I am a Gerrard," Kit said simply. "It is a non-exclusive trait."

That earned him a brief flash of a grin. Then Duncan sobered. "What do we do, Kit?"

"Nothing, I think." Kit sighed and tried to look encouraging. "If we pretend that they are only whispering about a poor choice in fashion or a social faux pas, then all of the fervor dies down at once. If we give them nothing to feed the fires with, why should they keep talking on the subject? You of all people know that the reason Marianne is such a subject for discussion is…"

"…is because she always gave them something to discuss," Duncan finished, looking uneasy, but calmer. He rubbed his hands over his face and groaned a little. "These were supposed to be her friends."

"Friends and foes are all mixed together in London," Kit sighed, patting Tillie gently for good measure. "It is a treacherous place."

"I hate it."

Kit shared his brother-in-law's vehemence. "Trust me," he said with a bland smile, "I know the feeling. Better than anyone." He hesitated, then hesitantly asked, "Do you think Marianne would take to removing to the country?"

That shook Duncan out of his gloom and he barked a loud laugh that made his daughter jump. "Marianne in the country during the Season? Good lord, Kit, I hope it doesn't come to that. You'd be dead or mad in a week."

Kit failed to see the humor in that.

Mostly because he knew it was likely the truth.

He opened his mouth to say something about that when a soft throat clearing came from the door. They both turned to see Annalise standing there, looking as soft and welcoming as she always did, and she smiled curiously.

"Good morning, Kit," she offered, taking in the sight of him holding her daughter with interest.

"Annalise," he greeted with a nod.

Tillie stirred restlessly and her mother grinned and stepped forward to retrieve her. Then she gave Kit a rare teasing look. "Are you trying to be her favorite uncle? You're far and away better with her than the rest."

Kit grunted softly. "That's because I *am* her uncle, unlike the rest."

Duncan scoffed a light laugh and came to press a kiss to his wife's brow, then wrapped an arm around her waist.

"Staying for breakfast, Kit?" Annalise asked as Duncan started to steer her out of the room.

To his surprise, Kit found himself shaking his head. "No, thank you. I think I had better go home and see to my wife."

"Well," Annalise said with a curious smile, "I think I need to tell you something before you do. About an incident that happened at Tibby's party, if you don't already know."

Marianne was waiting for Kit at breakfast when he returned, properly dressed, and not altogether unwell. She could not smile when he came in, but neither was she particularly downcast.

She was just... there.

"I apologize," he said rather stiffly as he took his seat. "I thought you would be sleeping later."

She shrugged a little, her eyes almost meeting his, but not quite. "I did not sleep well. I mean to busy myself today and not dwell on it."

He nodded soberly and tucked his serviette in. "If you think that is best, by all means do so."

"I do," she replied. "I can hardly wallow around forever."

"No," he allowed, as he started on his breakfast, "not forever. But you could certainly take a day or two, if you wanted. Though I hardly think you would wallow."

She snorted and sipped her tea. "Have you met me, Kit? I would most certainly wallow, if I wished it."

"Perhaps you're right."

Her head shot up, indignation rising, only to find him giving her a bit of a crooked smile.

She opened her mouth in a retort, then sighed and her lips

curved into a smile. "You're teasing me."

He scoffed and shook his head. "Over breakfast? I would never. It's far too early." He shook his head again and made a show of focusing on his meal at hand.

"Of course. My mistake."

Marianne smiled to herself as she returned to her meal as well. Her husband was teasing her. Well, well, that was a pleasant surprise.

"What is on your agenda for today?" he asked politely. "Wallowing aside."

She pursed her lips as she thought on it. "I hope to finish all of the drawing and receiving rooms, if I can. There is really not much else left on them. Then I really must take stock of the bedchambers, Mrs. Wilton has said some are in a sad state." She paused for a bite of ham, then made a face. "And then I must decide what to do about Lady Cavendish's card party tomorrow."

Kit raised a surprised brow. "You still intend to go? You could easily cry off, feign an illness or some such. After last night, you need a respite."

Marianne threw him a stubborn look. "I cannot cry off, and I am never ill," she informed him with all of the haughtiness her aunt carried so well. "Lady Cavendish is one of the biggest busybodies in London." She settled a little, her towering indignation exhausting her strength. "But I really don't know that I can endure it. Particularly not after..." Her cheeks flushed and she focused on her food intently.

"You don't have to," Kit murmured softly.

Marianne's cheeks burned at his gentleness, and she couldn't find a response.

"I was wondering, Marianne..."

At his hesitation, Marianne chanced a glance up at him to find that he was watching her curiously. "Did you really scream at Lord Darlington at Tibby's party and call him a duck?"

She gasped. "How did you hear about that?"

He grinned without reserve. "Your sister-in-law has a remarkable memory for gossip, it seems."

Marianne blushed furiously and muttered, "I might have known. Traitor. You were never supposed to know."

"But a duck?" he asked, grinning still.

She shrugged a shoulder. "He is rather duck-like. It was more a confirmation than an insult."

Kit suddenly barked a laugh and sat back, covering his eyes as more laughter emerged. Surprised as she was, Marianne joined in with him, and they laughed until tears began to form in both of their eyes and rolled down their cheeks.

"Why would you do that?" Kit asked as his laughter began to fade, wiping at his eyes.

She shrugged, still grinning madly. "He was being repulsive and ridiculous and someone had to stop him. He just continued to carry on and on."

Kit smiled and shook his head. "What about?"

She sobered and looked away quickly. "It doesn't matter. Nothing of great importance."

"I doubt that," Kit murmured, still sounding amused and curious. "Tell me."

Marianne stared at her husband for a moment, wondering if she dared. She'd been so careful to ensure he never heard of it, and now... What would he think?

For the first time in a very great while, she felt unaccountably shy.

"Marianne..."

The surprisingly gentle timbre of his voice struck her and she exhaled slowly, all resistance suddenly fading.

Quietly, she began to tell him, and she could not help but become more and more animated as she described Lord Darlington's rudeness and hateful words, his coldness and his ridiculous assertions, the memory raising her temper with surprising swiftness.

Kit stared at her steadily throughout, his smile gone, his eyes intense, everything about him still and unmoving.

When finally she was finished, and she still huffed with the remains of her rage, she looked up at him, wondering why he hadn't responded.

Slowly, almost hesitantly, Kit rose from his seat and came over to her. He took Marianne's free hand and held it for a moment, his thumbs absently stroking her knuckles. Then he brought it to his lips and brushed a feather light kiss to the back of it once, then again.

"Thank you," he murmured, his lips brushing the skin in a way that sent tingles all the way to Marianne's toes.

"For what?" she half gasped, staring at his lowered head and finding herself somehow without the necessary air for thought.

Still he looked down at her hand and stood in silence for a long moment. "For thinking enough of me to defend me."

She could not mistake the earnest nature of his words, nor the slight hollowness to them. As if he would never have expected her to do so. And that was something she absolutely could not bear.

"I have always thought very highly of you, Kit," she told him quietly, "and I will always defend you. To anyone and everyone."

That, at least, was something she had never told a single living soul.

Kit seemed a bit taken aback by her words and stared in disbelief. Then he carefully turned her palm over and gently kissed it, warming her entire body in an instant.

Before she could do more than exhale her surprise, he pulled a chair next to her, sat, and laced his fingers with hers. "What a mess," he chuckled softly.

Marianne giggled and found herself settling rather comfortably against her chair, her fingers twining with his. She could not pretend this solved all of their problems, for she was still willful and he was too proud, but in this moment, they were friends again.

She sighed and looked at her hands, her nails still perfectly formed and pristine, despite her recent adventures. "I don't think I was ready for London."

"No?"

She shook her head. "No. It's quite different being at the center of the gossip, and not in a good way, and knowing what is truly being said… I don't think I fully understood what it would be like."

He exhaled and rubbed her arm a little. "I'm sorry."

She nodded, and bit her lip, wondering if she dared to voice what she had been thinking all morning. "In fact…"

He stiffened at her hesitation. "Yes?"

She met his gaze steadily. "Can we go somewhere, Kit? I don't want to be in London, and no one will miss me. Take me someplace that I can breathe."

He pulled back, staring at her in shock, his eyebrows raised and his mouth open. Then his eyes narrowed and gave her a searching look. "What if I told you the only house open would be in Surrey?"

She resisted making a face and exhaled noisily. "At this point, I would even take Surrey over London…" She waited for a moment, then wrinkled her nose. "Do we *have* to go to Surrey?"

He chuckled and toyed with her fingers. "No, we don't."

She sighed heavily with her relief, for truly, Surrey might have been the worst.

Kit leaned back against the seat and pursed his lips a little, watching her. "How would you feel about Somerset?"

She looked up at him with a half smile. "You have a house in Somerset?"

"*We* have a house in Somerset," he corrected with a nod, a hint of warmth flashing in his eyes. "Glendare Court. It's a relic, though we've refinished it comfortably. No doubt you will enjoy getting your hands on it."

Marianne grinned fully and gave him a speculative look. "You'd let me change things?"

His face was carefully composed, as ever, and he shrugged one shoulder as if he were carefree. "You've done a fine job with the house here, so I don't see why I should fear for any of the other estates. Don't prove me wrong, though."

The offhand compliment warmed her and she grinned once more. "Tell me about Glendare. I've never been to Somerset, and I want to picture everything."

"I am hardly the person to tell you," he sighed a little sadly. "I've not been there often, just enough to keep it up. The only reason I've suggested it is because I have business with the estate manager there that needs my attention."

"Ah, so we shall both find ourselves suitably occupied, is that it?" she asked with a bit of a laugh.

"Something like that," he answered, his fingers gripping hers more securely. "But let me see if I can give you an idea of the place anyway. What I remember is the gardens seem to stretch from the back of the house to the front, as if the house were merely a fixture in the garden itself."

Marianne found herself enraptured by him at the moment, as he used his hands to gesture, emphasizing the descriptions, and his voice was warm with fondness. Despite what he said about not knowing the estate well, his voice betrayed him. He was attached to this place, no matter how he tried to play otherwise. And she suddenly wanted to know everything about it.

"The gardener there is probably seventy if he's a day and all he's ever wanted is to take care of Glendare, and he does a masterful job of it. We'll never get him to retire. Nor will we be rid of the cook. The kitchens are the most elaborate I've ever seen, including the brief glimpses I've had at Tibby's kitchens, and those belonging to the Duke of Ashcombe."

"When have you seen the kitchens of the Duke of Ashcombe?" Marianne asked on a laugh.

Kit sniffed dismissively. "I wasn't always a stodgy, reserved man. And Derek had some very fine ideas for amusement when Colin and I were young."

Marianne could well imagine that, but the idea of Kit participating was preposterous. Intriguing, curious, yes, but hardly realistic. Hardly Kit.

And yet...

"The grand hall is very grand," Kit continued with resignation. "Marble everywhere and statues that I am desperate to be rid of, if you don't mind..."

Marianne snickered. "I shall reserve judgment until I see them, but your opinion is noted."

He sighed as if she had already forbidden their removal. "There is also a very fine staircase in the family wing that many a young lad would be tempted to slide on."

She jerked her head up to look at him. "Did you?"

"Did I what?" he asked, mildly surprised.

She rolled her eyes. "Slide the banister."

"Never," he said very succinctly. His mouth quirked and a brow lifted. "Colin did, and almost broke an arm. After that, I saw no need to do so."

Marianne laughed and fell back a little against her chair, her fingers sliding from his. "It sounds lovely."

"It is," he said on a swift exhale. "The grounds are vast, and partially border the seaside, so it is really quite picturesque in places."

"And the nearest village?"

"Rifton. A few miles away. Two, perhaps three. You can partially see the main thoroughfare from the terrace sometimes in the evenings, all lit up and sometimes quite festive. It is small, but the people seem warm enough."

Marianne nodded again, warming to the idea already. She bit her lip, hesitating. "I may not behave well, Kit. I've never done well in the country."

He laughed softly. "Yes, Duncan warned me."

"He was right to do so." Really, they both ought to be nervous about it. Could she endure rustication and only Kit for company? Or would this be the proof they needed that this marriage was a foolish idea?

"I'm not sure I'll behave either," Kit finally said, "but we won't know until we try."

That, in the least, was very true.

Chapter Twelve

The manner in which Marianne left London was far different from how she had arrived. Oh, the carriage was similar, though this one was far and away more comfortable than that beastly rented hack. And she was dressed rather similarly to that day, though her grey travelling gown was really much better suited to her figure than the horrid, dark wool creation she'd worn then. She'd been tempted to burn that one after the inns along the way and those awful days in Leeds and Yorkshire, and she still might.

The distance they travelled was less, but so was the pace of the horses. Her heart was racing, but this time it drew a smile from her rather than a grimace. Also, this time she was not riding alone.

Nothing had shocked her more than when Kit had followed her into the carriage. He'd caught her shocked expression and merely smirked at it. "Don't think anything of it," he'd said rather gruffly as he adjusted himself against the seat. "Last time it hurt to walk for a week, I am not about to do that again."

Her surprise had been all the more compounded by the fact that they'd hardly spoken since their decision to leave had been made. He'd gone about his usual manners and activities, reserved aloofness and all, practically ignoring her and letting her do as she pleased. It hadn't been unpleasant, but she had wondered why he should be so warm… kissing her bare hand and palm, after all!… and then to go back as if it had never happened. But Kit had always been a mystery, and his resistance to emotions of any kind was typical, and strangely comforting.

But riding in a carriage with her? That was progress, despite his return to normalcy, whatever he might say.

They had been travelling for three days now, and conversation had been limited, but pleasant enough. He asked after her comfort at fairly regular intervals, ensured they had food and rest aplenty, did not plague her with inane conversation, and gave her the best of the rooms at the inns, which were a wonderful change from before. This, she had thought several times, was how a married couple should travel. Whatever had occurred before had been... unfortunate.

They'd seen a great number of people before they had left, each of their family calling to consult and wish them well, no doubt wondering as to what would send them off so suddenly. But by unspoken agreement, they kept their reasons quiet, and only said some time away would be good for them.

Bitty had been quite upset about their going, though Rosie could not have cared less, and Ginny did not understand any of it and was not perturbed in the least. Annalise advised Marianne to enjoy herself, and to try and find peace between herself and Kit. Marianne didn't know if peace would ever be in her future, but she had nodded and promised to try anyway. Duncan had hugged her tightly and told her not to kill Kit, which she felt quite safe to promise. Tibby... well, Tibby thought they were mad to go anywhere together, and vowed she did not know how she would explain their absence.

Marianne had no doubt she would come up with something.

Armed with several pieces of music from Lily, who secretly swore that some might be scandalous, and some entertaining suggestions of ways to pass the time from Gemma, she thought she could actually quite enjoy the country. It was an astonishing notion, as she had always found herself quite bored when they'd been forced to Duncan's country house.

She'd always preferred the excitement and pull of London and stayed there whenever she could, no matter the season or popularity. Considering what she knew of London and Society now, however, the country had a great deal more charm for her than it ever had.

After three days of being in this lovely and spacious carriage, however, she was desperate to be rid of it, and longed to stretch her legs. But dozing as she was... as well as any woman in a corset and a bonnet can ever doze in a moving carriage cramped by a long-legged husband… was almost comfortable. Kit had somehow managed to make himself fit into the smallest place possible considering his size and that of the carriage, so she had far more space than she would have otherwise. It was really rather sweet of him, all things considered, though it could hardly have been comfortable for him. If this was his way of trying to make up for being a lackluster husband and not giving her the wedding she liked, then he was sadly…

"Marianne."

She stirred and squinted over at Kit, suddenly realizing his hand was on her arm. Had she really fallen so completely asleep under these conditions?

He smiled at her, which was impossible under these conditions, and he indicated the window with his head. "We are approaching Glendare Court." He sat back and raised a brow at her, as if her reluctance to excitement amused him. "I thought you might like to see the place straightaway. And right yourself before meeting the staff."

Marianne sat up and rubbed at her cheeks, feeling very sluggish all of a sudden. But as she processed the words he'd said, she nodded in agreement. She absolutely wanted to take stock of her house while she could, and not have several servants watch her gape at it. Heavens, she must look a fright. She smoothed her hair under her bonnet, adjusted her bodice and cloak, then patted the skin beneath her eyes so it might not seem so puffy from sleep.

She nodded again, ignoring Kit's look, and sat forward to catch a glimpse, grateful that the day was clear and bright. Surely the house would prove at its greatest advantage under these circumstances.

The sight before her caught her breath in her throat. Never had she seen a place look so magnificent as this. Kit's description, though quite accurate, had fallen far short of the glory and splendor of its reality. The sun seemed to glint off of the majestic arches and peaks, sparkling off of the windows like on water, and even the faded stone façade seemed brightened by the light. It was an older house, as she had anticipated, but with none of the cold formality she had come to expect from such a place. Even her brother's house was more marble than anything, and though she loved it, and always would, it had never quite felt like home.

This sprawling estate, expanding before her eyes as they approached, was all warmth and welcome, with just enough grandeur for her more worldly tastes. Hardly the ruin she had expected, from Kit's assertions, and it seemed to come alive before her very eyes. It was as much a part of the glories of the countryside as the rich treasures Somerset afforded, and seemed just as natural. As Kit had told her, it was as if the garden had created the house for its own use. But instead of seeming overgrown and wild, it was as if someone had taken a charming country cottage and made it grow into this fine testament of architecture, taste, and refinement. She had seen grander homes, more majestic homes, and some homes that would be better served to be called castles, and she had envied each and every one of them, thinking she could make such a place a very fine mistress, and make it her own.

But this… This bit of magic before her was something else. Something entirely different.

"You're quiet," Kit murmured as they reached the circle drive and the servants filed from the house. "Well?"

Marianne sniffed back the barest hint of tears that had begun to form, and the sudden congestion in her throat. "Well," she said simply, trying for her usual tone. "It is better than Surrey, at any rate." She waited a moment for his steely irritation to rise, then gave him a soft look. "It's wonderful."

She did not expect the rush of relief that escaped him and he tried to hide a smile as he exited the carriage, then held a hand out for her.

She took it and forced a fine smile on her face, and allowed herself to be presented to the very long line of ordinary looking servants. But they all seemed very capable and pleasant, and their uniforms were quite smart. Not one sour face amongst the whole of them, and the housekeeper, Mrs. Dinstable, was the most matronly sort of woman she had ever laid eyes on. Though she could not have yet been fifty, and her hair still held all the richness of its amber color, the faint lines on her face and warmth in her eyes spoke of a life well lived, and Marianne suddenly wanted to get to know the woman over a pot of tea.

The butler, Reynolds, was a tall and stately man with almost no hair, save for his eyebrows and the back of his head, and his voice was rather like the growl of a rather large dog, but his smile was sure, despite the almost drooping sag of his skin the smile produced. He seemed very pleased and proud to receive them, and made all of the proper introductions. And it was evident he was well respected by the other servants, and took great pride in Glendare, which was all they could want.

As they entered the house, Kit let her hand fall from his hold. He stepped back and bowed to her, expression implacable. "I'll let you get settled, then." He turned and started away almost stiffly.

"What, you're leaving already?" she called.

He turned back to face her, his expression giving no sign of his emotions. "I told you before, I know little of this place, and I'm not in any sort of favor to give a tour at the moment. There is work to be done, and I am keen to get started on it."

Marianne frowned and moved closer, wanting to keep her voice down so as not to alert the servants to their issues already. "We have only just arrived, Kit. We should both get settled in, take a meal, perhaps, and then let things progress as they will. Such a distinct separation so quickly will be cause for comment. They will think you cannot stand me."

He slowly raised a brow at her. "Are you really that concerned about what the servants think?"

"Yes," she said simply. "Particularly when I don't know them, nor they me."

He exhaled a quick breath. "So get to know them."

"Kit…"

"They will talk no matter what we do, because servants talk," he overrode as if she had said nothing. "We will meet for meals, as we always have, and I will converse as I see fit, or not. I have spent three days in a carriage, my head is splitting, and yet I still have work to do. I mean to start on it now."

Marianne ground her teeth together and lifted her chin just enough to make a point. "Forgive me. I thought we were past our differences in this marriage." She gave a hard laugh. "I shall stay out of your way to avoid making your head worse than it already is, since that is apparently all that I do."

She gave him a mocking attempt at a curtsey and swept away, towards the great marble stairs that made up a fair portion of the great hall. Her boots echoed ominously on the floors, and gave a great distinction to her steps, much to her satisfaction. But after this, she would most certainly see the room redone. So much marble was quite intimidating.

"That is not what I meant, Marianne," Kit hissed, his voice echoing about the hall.

She tossed a glare at him over her shoulder. "Go do your work, Kit. As you said, you have much to do." Her voice sounded sad and fatigued, even to her ears, and she hated herself for sounding so pitiful. But she had no fight left in her.

Not anymore.

A small, bitter smile played at her lips, and she fought down the twisting sensation in her stomach. They were just out of sorts from travelling, she considered. After a day or two here, once they had recovered and settled, a normal routine would commence, just as it had in London, and they would not be quite so at odds.

Surely that would be so. They could not possibly manage any length of time anywhere if they always behaved like this, let alone expect a marriage that would be worth anything.

But how many marriages did she know of that barely existed in name only? Countless members of society lived apart from their spouses, and quite willingly. Would that be her fate?

It could be quite a good thing, if their behavior was any sort of indication.

So why should the idea make her a little sad?

He should have sent Marianne away by herself. This was by far and away a worse torture than London had ever been. Oh, she was vastly better protected here, and no one would injure her, which meant his more gentlemanly impulses would grow dormant, and he was contented that they should do so. But he would have absolutely no sense left when they left here, if his wife continued on like this.

Two days at Glendare and he was already finding ways to leave the house. Meals were completely silent, Marianne still insisting on being indecent at breakfast, and he had stopped attending luncheon, as he had been seeing to business with the tenants or his manager or taking stock of the repairs needed to the estate. Dinners were perhaps the worst, as neither of them were sleepy and had passed a full day, but with no desire to share anything. He'd noticed the beginning of some changes to the interior, but hardly anything worth commenting on. The statues in the great hall were still present, much to his disgust, and he would swear he saw a footman dusting one of them.

If Marianne meant to keep them, he may just have to cause an accident involving all twelve.

How had they fallen back here so fast? They had been doing fairly well in London, not altogether easy, but the fighting had lessened. Not that they were fighting now, they were not speaking at all, but this tension between them was maddening. His pride would not let him speak first, and nor would hers, and so they were locked in this stalemate that only disaster would break.

He was fully aware that he could not blame Marianne for their situation. Why was it that he could not settle on his behavior around her? Why did she bring out the absolute worst in him? He had spent two years away to find his control, and had only improved it in the years since, and yet she found ways to break through and set him at odds. He was driven to rage so quickly by her hand that he would seem a man with a temper, when in reality, he was quite calm and unruffled by nature.

The only other person in the world who could provoke him with such skill was Colin, and even he did not press Kit to these extremes.

"Begging your pardon, sir," intoned Reynolds from the door.

Kit looked up from his desk in surprise, wondering how he had not heard the door knock, nor open. He set down the papers he had obviously not been reading and raised a brow. "Yes, Reynolds?"

The older man frowned, his sagging skin moving with the fluidity of honey. "It is Mrs. Gerrard, sir."

Kit sighed and pinched the bridge of his nose. "What has she done now?"

"Well, she's gone for a walk, sir, and I am growing concerned."

Kit looked up again and his brow furrowed in confusion. "Why should that make you concerned? I should think it a good thing that she's got out of the house."

Reynolds nodded, the sheen of his head nearly glowing from the light through the window. "Indeed, sir. Only she has been gone several hours now, sir, and I do not believe she knows her way around the grounds."

"Perhaps she has gone to the village or to call on our neighbors."

"No, sir, she said very clearly that she wanted to see the grounds. And she would not take anyone with her."

Kit sat back in his chair heavily and chewed his lip a little. "How many hours?"

"Nearly three, sir."

He swore under his breath. Marianne wouldn't know her way around the estate, and she was no walker. He'd taken care to be so busy that he would not be available should she have sought him out for any sort of tour. He'd always presumed that if she had really wanted to know, she could have asked one of the servants. But he'd neglected to take into consideration Marianne's pride and independence. She would have gone out on her own to explore without consideration to anyone, and his estimation of the estate's grounds had not been entirely accurate.

Truth be told, it was one of the largest estates in Somerset, and involved quite a bit of foliage, rises, and moors, not to mention a precarious stretch of shoreline if one was unfamiliar with it.

If she had stuck to the gardens by the house, it would not have been an issue. But Reynolds would not have brought this to his attention had Marianne been so wise as to remain in the gardens. And three hours was worrisome.

"Have some of the stable hands ride out," Kit said after a moment of consideration. "It's likely she has become turned around and…"

"But sir…"

A low rumble of thunder stopped them both and Kit rose slowly, his gaze fixed on the window. He walked towards it, a feeling of dread rapidly unfurling in his stomach. Rain pattered against the glass, and larger streams fell from the roof above, large and impressive puddles catching it beneath.

"How long has it been raining?" Kit murmured, his breathing the slightest bit unhinged.

"Almost two hours, sir."

A violent burst of cursing flew from his lips as he nearly flew from the room. "My horse, Reynolds! And get those damn stable hands out!"

Marianne's teeth began to chatter more viciously and her head throbbed, to say nothing for her feet and legs. She ought to have been in Devonshire by now with how far she'd gone. She had long accepted that she had been a fool to wander so far from the house for her own curiosity and without someone to accompany her. She'd never been to Somerset herself, but she knew from others that the terrain could not be trusted and could, in fact, prove quite treacherous. But she'd never considered that their property would be so, nor that it would have been so vast.

And when it had occurred to her, she'd turned back to return the way she had come, only to have no idea how she had gotten to this point.

All she had wanted was to see the coastline, and she had done so, miraculously not breaking any bones or even turning an ankle, though it was not for want of trying. She had forged on through the rain, and when the first ten minutes of rain had soaked every article of clothing and inch of skin, she'd decided that was not a wise course and tried to find her way back.

She did not know how long ago that had been, but she knew that the moment she stopped, she would give up and dissolve into tears. Not that she hadn't cried a little already, for there was no stopping the helplessness and embarrassment that transcended whatever mistaken independence she'd come out with. But to give in to the fatigue in her legs and the aching in her chest would rob her of any strength left, and she could not afford that.

Would anyone know to come for her? She'd told Reynolds where she was going, but she hardly knew him well enough to know what his memory was like, or if he would act in her interest. And Kit… Oh, Kit would be furious when he found out.

She hiccupped a small sob and swiped at the tears in her eyes, though it made no difference, as the tears and the rain all mixed on her chilled skin. Kit might not even know she was gone. He was avoiding her at all costs, saving meals, and she could hardly blame him.

Yet another crash of thunder erupted, seemingly from all around her, and she whimpered, clutching her sodden cloak more tightly around her. It did nothing for the wind nor the chill, but wrapping it around her made her feel smaller, and that was a comfort.

The rain poured down more steadily upon her, falling from her bonnet like waterfalls over rocks and stones, and that tattered thing provided no shelter anymore. Nothing did. She was wet, cold, filthy, and had no way of getting home. She did not know which direction she had come from, nor in which direction she was headed, and her boots were growing so caked with mud that soon she would not be able to do more than slide through the inches of thick muck on the ground.

Another, much louder, roll of thunder caused her to jerk and she lost her footing, tumbling to the grass and barely catching herself before her face hit a standing puddle. She bit back a cry and pushed up on her trembling limbs, tenderly setting herself back on her feet.

That was enough, she finally admitted, clutching her bonnet with both hands. She could not do more. She would have to find a place and wait for the weather to pass. Her lungs heaved with panicked breaths as she stumbled towards a large tree nearby, its thick trunk a welcome support for her. She tried to ignore her tears as she scraped what she could from her boots against the rough bark of the roots, and when they were as clean as she could manage, she leaned back against the tree, looking out at the vast expanse before her.

The clouds were so low they mingled with the mist of the ground, and the whole panorama looked like something from a fairytale. The rain's melodic pounding against leaves and grass and rocks would have soothed her had she not grown weary of the noise. A pair of large raindrops fell from the branches overhead and landed heavily on her shoulders, and she felt the weight of them sink against her.

What a dismal prospect she was and had.

Impossibly, over the noise of the storm, she heard a different thundering. Something more like hoof beats. With a wild gasp of hope she did not know she still possessed, she stepped away from the tree and looked behind her.

A great black horse approached, and its rider was at once the most wonderful and most horrid sight of all. Kit rode recklessly, his greatcoat billowing behind him, his head looking all around. Then he caught sight of her and turned the horse in her direction. When he was close enough, he reined the animal in, and stared at her for a long moment, his expression maddeningly impossible to read.

Then, to her utter relief, she saw his chest move with a massive exhale and his shoulders slumped just a little.

Her tears would not be restrained and she covered her mouth to keep from embarrassing herself with hiccups and gasps, though her body shook with the sudden force of her emotions.

Kit swung down off of his horse and came over to her, and only when he was near her could she see the concern and relief in his face.

"I'm so sorry," she gasped, her voice breaking and clogged.

Kit only shook his head, his throat working on several swallows. "Are you all right?" he asked quietly, reaching out to take her arm.

She swiped a filthy hand across her cheeks and then nodded. "A little wet, a little cold, and very lost, but yes."

He nodded, squeezing her arm gently. "I should have shown you the estate before letting you go out, my apologies."

"I wouldn't have listened," she admitted with an attempt at a smile.

He tilted his head, sending a torrent of water falling to one side. "And you are more apt to listen now?" he asked, reaching up to wipe mud off of her cheek.

Her face crumpled as she nodded, and she gasped on unrestrained sobs, her cleaner hand finding its way to encircle his wrist, as if he could anchor her, steady her, as if to remind herself that he was really here.

He was still for a long moment, his fingers curling against her cheek, then scooped her up into his arms easily. "I can walk, Kit," she managed, shaking her head at him.

"Don't rob me of my opportunity to be husbandly," he scolded at once as his arms hefted her into a more comfortable position. "This seems the least I can do."

Marianne swallowed back more tears and tucked her chin in embarrassment. "I've not been a wife that deserves such a husband," she whispered.

They reached his horse, and Kit set her down on the ground, removed his greatcoat, and wrapped it around her tightly. She stared at him as he adjusted it, his eyes avoiding hers, but taking in everything else about her state, muddy mess and clinging clothes and all. He sighed and nodded reluctantly, as if it was the best he could do. He turned and mounted the horse, then reached down for her and pulled her up to join him, settling her in his lap.

He picked up the reins and hesitated, meeting her eyes for a long moment, as if the rain weren't pounding all around them.

"What?" she asked him, her cheeks heating under the intensity of his gaze.

He exhaled briefly. "I am doing something I should have done a long time ago," he told her, his voice low and a bit rough.

She gave a soft snort despite her tears. "What, going to punish me for being a spoiled child and say 'I told you so'?"

He shook his head slowly. "No. Forgiving you."

The severity in his tone left no doubt as to what he was referring, and it had nothing to do with today's excursion. She gasped a little and swayed, forcing him to hold her more securely. "You cannot possibly…"

His hold tightened, silencing her at once. "I told you before we left London that everybody deserves a second chance. It's time I gave you one." He cleared his throat and turned the horse. "Now, hold tight," he murmured. "We will be home soon."

Fighting more tears, Marianne looped her arms around his waist and clung to him, wondering if it were possible that her husband was a far better man than she had ever believed or imagined. Gratitude unlike anything she'd ever known rose within her, and she buried her face against him. Impossibly, his arms tightened further, and he quickly and capably carried them home, the rain no longer seeming to bother either of them.

Chapter Thirteen

$\mathcal{G}$lendare Court was all a bustle with their arrival, and Kit insisted on carrying Marianne up to her rooms even as he gave orders. Mrs. Dinstable was hot on his heels, echoing his wishes on a bark of sorts to the servants, and gave a few additional commands of her own. Marianne still shook in his arms, and Kit rubbed where he held her as best as he could.

Once they were in her rooms, he set her down, stripped his damp jacket off, and immediately went to work on her clothing. He untied her bonnet ribbons and flung that across the room, then did the same with her cloak. He bent to the ground and said, "Put your hands on my shoulders."

Marianne did so, shaking all over and fighting to keep her teeth from chattering audibly. "I c-can do it," she managed to stammer out as he worked at the laces of her boots.

He paused to look up at her with one incredulous brow raised. "You are barely able to stand." He went back to her boots and lifted her feet one at a time to take the filthy footwear off, setting them aside and wiping his hands on his trousers.

He rose and turned her around, his fingers suddenly flying along the buttons at her back. She made a weak sound of surprise, but he did not pause now. "I'm not being forward," he murmured. "I am just trying to get you warm and dry. It will be much faster if I do it than to have you try."

She nodded jerkily and forced herself to keep still. Her head was throbbing and her body ached, and her fingers burned with the pain of cold. "You c-could have a servant do it," she reminded him, biting back a small gasp when his fingers brushed the thin material of her chemise as he divested her of her corset.

"I could," he said in a very off-hand way as he moved to the hem of her chemise and started to draw it upwards. "Arms up. However, doing so would draw attention to certain ideas about our relationship, and I know how you feel about servants gossiping."

Marianne bit out a short, shaky bark of laughter as he tugged on the wet garment that clung to her, finally getting it over her head. She clamped down on her lips as she covered herself, ignoring another accidental brush of his fingers against her back, and glanced down at the sodden chemise, now crumpled on the floor. An instant later, the warm fabric of her velvet-lined dressing gown was draped over her back and shoulders and she shivered in appreciation, pulling it around her and sliding her arms into the sleeves.

"And turn to face me," Kit said with politeness.

Marianne obeyed, her cheeks feeling oddly warm despite freezing everywhere else. If there was any situation more mortifying than this, she didn't know it. But he was right, she could not have managed by herself, and calling for a servant would have been a cause for comment, considering how Kit had brought her in.

Still, she could honestly say she had never expected this.

Kit crouched and quickly unlaced the ties of her drawers at her waist, then immediately crouched further to finish his task with her garters and stockings, sliding them down her legs with more efficiency than any maid in the world. One light tug on the material of her drawers, and she was entirely naked beneath her robe, which she clutched to herself as tightly as possible.

An embarrassed blush rose on her skin, every conceivable inch of her, but Kit had already turned away from her, gathering all the scattered articles of clothing and forming them into a pile near the door. He grabbed a blanket set down by one of the servants, opened it fully, and turned back to her.

"Come here," he said firmly, his eyes running over her in assessment.

Marianne obeyed, the blanket as welcome a sight as Kit himself had been earlier.

He wrapped it tightly around her, then moved her over by the fire. With speed and remarkable ease, he removed every one of her pins and had her hair hanging to its full length in moments, then wrung the whole length out onto the rug beneath them. To her surprise, he moved her over to a nearby chair, sat down himself, then pulled her onto his lap and wrapped his arms around her once more, rubbing her arms rapidly.

"You're freezing," he muttered, shaking his head. "I may turn to ice just holding you."

He, on the other hand, was wonderfully warm. Marianne moved some of the blanket to cover his shoulder so she could lay her head against him without further drenching his clothing. "I'm not being affectionate," she murmured as she found herself nuzzling closer, "but I'm very cold, and you are very warm." She couldn't resist a helpless giggle as her words mirrored his earlier ones.

Kit did not miss it either and he smiled. "I know. That's why I'm allowing it."

She raised her head to look at his clothing, and frowned. "You're all wet."

He exhaled in amusement. "I wonder why."

She winced and covered her face with part of the blanket. "I'm sorry."

"Stop that," he said gruffly, his hands stilling momentarily. "No more apologizing. It was not your fault."

She nodded and gasped a little as another strong tremor passed through her.

"How long until that bath is ready?" Kit barked as he resumed rubbing her arms.

"Don't do that," she murmured, nudging at him. "They're doing the best they can."

"You'll catch your death if it's not soon," he grumbled, turning them so she was closer to the fire.

She pulled the blanket more tightly around her. "I will not." She shivered hard against him. "How long did it take you to find me?"

"A little less than an hour."

Marianne suddenly turned her head. "Agnes!" she bellowed, making Kit jump beneath her.

"Madam?" Agnes replied quickly with a bob as she reappeared.

"Do we have two baths?" Marianne asked in a much more polite tone.

"Yes, madam."

"What are you doing?" Kit asked with a smile.

She ignored him. "Have the other set up in Mr. Gerrard's room straight away, if you please."

"Yes, madam." Agnes bobbed again and left them as more maids filled the bath.

Marianne turned to look up at Kit. "You're not catching your death either. You gave me your coat on the ride back in, and now you are sitting here in sodden clothing. The moment you see fit to release me to the care of the maids, you are to see to your own bath and health." She smiled at his surprised expression. "You see? I can toss around orders as well as you."

He smiled and shook his head, and rubbed her arms gently. "Yes, you can."

Agnes reappeared, rubbing her hands together for warmth and smiling. "We are ready for you, madam."

Kit rose with his arms still around her and did not release her until he was assured of her steadiness on her own feet. Agnes took Marianne's arm and helped her over to the bath.

"I will see you at supper, Marianne," Kit said with a nod.

Marianne winced and gave him an apologetic look. "I'm not sure I am up for fine dining this evening, Kit. I'd rather have a tray in here, if you don't mind."

His eyes were surprisingly warm and Marianne bit her lip in hesitation. He'd told her before they would take meals together, and there were no excuses save for illness. But surely, just this once…

He nodded once more, a slight hint of a smile on his lips. "If you wish it." He looked at Agnes with mock sternness. "You stop her shivering, Agnes. I want her pink and warm and no hint of chattering teeth."

Agnes grinned openly. "Yes, sir. I'll not leave her until she steams herself."

He nodded politely, gave Marianne one last look, his expression rife with something she could not identify, and then he left the room, shutting the door behind him.

"You poor thing," Agnes half whimpered as she drew the robe from Marianne's shoulders and helped her into the tub. "I'll set you to rights, see if I won't. Me and my girls will have you back to yourself in no time."

"You are the senior upstairs maid, then?" Marianne asked with a hiss as she sank down into the tub's hot water, her skin tingling in its numb appreciation of the heat.

Agnes nodded once and rolled her sleeves. "Aye, I am. And don't you feel that you need to talk to me, madam, unless talking eases you. You just relax yourself and let me see to you."

Marianne nodded and leaned back against the edge of the tub, and did her best to relax as Agnes and the other maids helped her to bathe. They scrubbed every inch of her skin until she felt as though she was new all over, and her hair had been washed and rinsed and wrung until she could feel every strand. Then she was ordered to remain in the tub afterwards and let the heat seep into her aching limbs, and bonelessly she obeyed, rather feeling that any movement at all would be impossible.

True to her word, Agnes did not leave her side the entire time, her warmth and kindness as soothing as the bath itself. She offered Marianne her choice of any of the girls she'd met to act as her lady's maid, as she'd left hers in London, and Marianne smiled at that prospect.

Mrs. Dinstable appeared and asked after her, then helped Agnes towel Marianne off and remove her from the tub. The two older women helped Marianne into a new chemise and nightgown, followed by a fresh robe that she didn't recognize.

"This isn't mine," she protested, rolling back the thick sleeves that extended beyond her hands.

"It is your husband's, madam," Mrs. Dinstable said as she ushered Marianne to sit so Agnes could rub the towel through her hair.

"My husband's?" Marianne repeated, looking down at the fine garment, so thick and warm. "But what will he wear?"

"I understand that he is dressing as per usual, madam, and has no need of it," the woman replied, handing over a comb to Agnes.

Marianne pursed her lips in thought as they worked on her hair.

She didn't dare think Kit was being preferable, but he was being inordinately kind towards her, and she so little deserved it. But he had forbidden any further apologizing, so she supposed she would have to do so by her actions instead. And she would not refuse any goodness that he gave.

If he could try, so could she.

Then again, he had completely undressed her only an hour ago. Surely *that* was not insignificant.

Mrs. Dinstable came around to the front and smiled at Marianne. "There, madam. You look much more to rights."

Marianne smiled up at her in return. "Thanks to your good care, and Agnes's ministrations, I feel more to rights."

"Your husband was vastly concerned," Mrs. Dinstable said with a sad shake of her head. "You should have seen him tearing out of the house as wild as anything. I told Agnes he would be the one to find you, what with determination like that, and find you he did."

"I'm right glad he did, too," Agnes echoed emotionally.

Marianne smiled fondly at the two women who had cared so well for her. "So am I," she murmured softly.

They collected the toweling up and a few maids entered to take the tub away. Mrs. Dinstable smiled from the door. "I will see to your supper tray, madam."

Marianne sat for several minutes staring into the fire, letting the warmth of it continue to heat her, no longer feeling the chill from outside or the aches in her limbs. She was fatigued into an unknown state of weariness, but her pain and her distress were all melted away. She drew her legs up beneath her and folded herself more deeply into Kit's robe, sighing softly as she felt herself relax even more still.

The tide between her and her husband had to turn now. After what he'd said today, about forgiving her and a second chance, and holding her so close, helping her with her clothing, and being so genuinely concerned about her... Everything about his behavior indicated that he was certainly not indifferent to her, and far from it. Was it possible that he had decided to change at last?

Given his behavior today, she rather expected he would be the one to bring up her tray and see after her. If he did that, she would be more than capable of convincing him to stay and partake with her.

Perhaps they could even talk and she could test the waters a little, so to speak. It was high time she knew her place in her husband's opinion and estimation.

The good opinion of one's husband was surely not such a shocking thing to wish for, was it?

A light knocking at the door brought her head around with a smile.

"Come," she called softly.

Mrs. Dinstable entered with a warm smile and a heavily laden tray, and Marianne was surprised at the crush of disappointment she felt.

Where was Kit?

She forced herself to smile and spoke lightly with the housekeeper as she bustled about getting things situated for her, and only when she prepared to leave the room did she bring herself to ask about her husband.

"Oh, he had himself a hot bath, and a fresh set of clothes, and he is taking his supper in the dining room," Mrs. Dinstable said with a smile. "He asked if I might check in on you and let him know if you would be needing a physician. Shall I tell him you wish to see him?"

At this moment? No, she did not wish to see him. She would probably throttle him. Eating in the dining room without her? After what she had been through today, he was giving up her care to the housekeeper?

After he had very swiftly stripped her clean and made it his own personal duty to keep her warm? Good gracious, had he even *looked* during that time? He must have. But as she thought back, he had treated her as he would have a child, perhaps one of his sisters. Firm but gentle orders, swift and methodical changes, and no apology or real concern for mortification or embarrassment because he would not think it was called for under the circumstances.

And yet she was a full woman and no child at all.

Either his control was truly one of the great wonders of the earth or he was as cold blooded as a fish.

She barely managed to hide a scowl. "No, thank you, Mrs. Dinstable. You are too kind. Truly, I think I am well. I expect we shall know more in the morning."

Mrs. Dinstable smiled again and bobbed a little. "Indeed, madam. You get your rest now and I'll send Sophie up to collect your tray and help you prepare for bed,"

Marianne returned her smile, nodded, and when the door was closed once more, she let the smiled fade and glowered into the fire.

She rather hoped she would take ill. It would give her an excuse to avoid her husband and perhaps let guilt start to grow within him.

Assuming he was at all familiar with the emotion.

Kit knew he was in trouble the next morning when Marianne came down to breakfast fully dressed, hair pulled back a bit severely for her, and her eyes already full of indignation. She glared at him as if he had somehow greatly offended her, though he had no idea what he was supposed to have done between yesterday and today.

After all, he *did* save her, and he *did* go to a lot of trouble to get her back safely and took great consideration for her health.

And he did sacrifice almost an entire night of sleep on account of his mutinous memory replaying a certain part of the day repeatedly and in great detail, at much slower speeds.

His inability to catch his breath after leaving her room, even in his own hot bath, was the chief reason why he did not go back to check on her. He was feeling things again, and he could not feel things for her.

Oh, he meant what he said to her. He did need to forgive her, and he was working on it. Her humiliation and sorry state yesterday had shaken him and he would never forget the look on her face. He really should talk to her about it, find out how bad it was, but he couldn't bring himself to do that. He might find himself going to his knees before her and saying all sorts of things that he would never be able to take back.

She did deserve a second chance, and he would give her one.

Just not until he could get control of himself.

After all, she hadn't changed all that much. The way she looked at him at this moment proved that. He'd been damn heroic yesterday and she was mad at him. No doubt he'd forgotten to bring her flowers or warm her bed or walk her down the stairs so she would not injure herself.

How dare he.

"Good morning, Marianne," he said pleasantly, rising from his chair and giving her a bow. "How did you sleep?"

"Like hell," she snapped, sitting in her chair with a thud.

He blinked in surprise. Marianne did not swear, as far as he knew, and yet… "I am sorry about that," he replied sympathetically as he retook his seat. "Are you taken ill? The physician is not far, I can send for him if you wish."

"I am fine," she replied, waving a footman over to scoot her chair in for her. "And if I wasn't, I would tell Mrs. Dinstable so she could give you a report of it."

He tried not to smile as he took a bite of his eggs. "You sound as if you might be getting a cold."

She gripped her fork so tightly he thought it might bend. "My nose is a little stuffed up," she said slowly, forcing a smile that was more of a grimace, "but it is nothing I cannot bear. A token of my little adventure yesterday."

"That is a pity."

"Isn't it?" She resumed eating and then made a face. "I forgot to thank you last night for… you know."

"For what?" he asked, feeling rather impertinent.

"You know very well what," she ground out.

He pursed his lips in confusion, and shook his head. "Sorry, I don't."

The glare he received was worth every bit of impertinence. "For riding out into the rain, at the risk of your own health and safety, to come and find your poor, lost, soaking wet wife who had been wandering for hours because she had no idea that her estate contained the entire county of Somerset in its grounds." She gave him a simpering smile even as her eyes skewered him with daggers. "It was really quite dashing of you."

He fought a smile and inclined his head. "You are quite welcome. I don't recommend you do it again, but at least you saw some of the estate. What was your favorite?"

Her eyes narrowed and she carefully sipped some water. "The shoreline was quite lovely."

He jerked and looked at her in shock. "You went all the way to the shoreline?"

She nodded, her eyes widening as if it should have been obvious.

Now he was the one fighting to control his emotions. The shoreline of their estate was full of rocks and crags, and the ground was not entirely stable. She could have injured herself in so many ways, and he would never have known. He adored the shoreline, it was a breathtaking view, but he knew it well enough to know where to go and where to mind his footing. Marianne would know nothing of that.

"I am glad you enjoyed it," he managed, pleased by his calm tone. "I would advise you not to return there, however, until you know more of it. You could find yourself in danger."

"Oh, what, more than yesterday?" she asked sarcastically. "Nobody cared about it then, not until I was gone so long it drew comment."

He stiffened and set his fork down carefully. "And did you ask anyone to show you around?"

She made a face. "No," she admitted reluctantly.

He didn't smile, which was miraculous. "Any of the stable hands could have ridden out with you. The estate manager was even available."

"Surely the lord of the house could show the lady of the house the grounds of the house in which they reside…" Marianne suggested with so much derision that the room felt several degrees cooler.

"And yet you did not ask me," he said, magnanimously deciding not to comment on her blatant declaration of his apparent transgression.

She tilted her head sharply. "And if I had, you would have shown me?"

She had a point there. "I would have considered it," he muttered, wrenching his gaze away as his neck began to heat a little.

"I see." There was a pause and he heard her fork scrape against her plate. "It is a wonder why you came riding after me at all. I am

such a trial for you. To *consider* showing me the estate *if* I asked...
How you managed to bring yourself to marry me at all is quite the
mystery of our time."

Kit rolled his eyes and sat back in his chair hard. "Come off it,
Marianne. Don't do this now."

She looked back at him with fire in her eyes. "And when should
I do it, Kit? When would be convenient for you? Shall we work it into
your schedule? I cannot keep track of which days you like me and
which you don't."

"And I am not entirely certain to whom I am married," he shot
back. "Which version of you comes down to breakfast or comes
home from a ball, it is all a surprise."

"You knew what you were getting into when you married me."
She shook her head and sniffed. "I am quite sure my brother, and
your brother, had several things to say on the subject."

"They did, as did everyone else."

She sneered a little. "And do they know what horrible things I
have done to you, Kit? Did you share all your secrets with them just
to prove to them that you are the strongest person on earth and the
only one who could possibly withstand being married to a creature as
horrifying as me?"

Something rather cold and desperately uncomfortable settled
upon him and he stiffened. Carefully, he pressed his tongue to his
teeth and watched his wife for a long moment, keeping his eyes
steady, trained on her face. He noticed every blink, every twitch of an
eyelash, every breath that passed her lips. He noticed the small lock
of stray hairs that had escaped her tight chignon, curling against her
will. Independent and willful, just as she was.

She slowly raised a brow at him, daring him to answer her.

He let himself exhale entirely, still fixed on her. When she shifted
in her seat, uncomfortable with his silence and his gaze, he replied,
"No."

Her brow furrowed slightly. "No?"

"No," he said again, measuring his breath again. "I did not tell
anyone. I have never told anyone. That is a part of my past that I do
not treat lightly, or use it as a reason to sway me from a course I have
determined to be correct." He cleared his throat and lowered his chin

a little to stare more directly. "I have never called you any names. Nor have I permitted others in my presence to do so. Can you say the same?"

Her eyes widened and her lips parted further.

Now it was his turn to raise the questioning brow.

"No," she said faintly. "No, I have never spoken of it. And I did everything in my power to avoid any conversation concerning you at all. I will admit to not stopping the gossip, but anything truly vile I would not allow. No one could injure you in my presence. I believe I said as much in London."

That should have appeased him. It did, a little. He remembered her rage in his defense and that had touched him far more profoundly than anything had in years, but it did not change what lay between them.

"So the only people who know the extent of our animosity is ourselves," he said simply, ignoring the sudden warmth in the pit of his stomach. It would vanish soon enough. It always did.

Marianne swallowed hastily. "So it would seem." She closed her eyes for a moment, swallowing again, then she looked back at him. "You said you were forgiving me. That I deserved a second chance."

He tried not to be moved by the hoarseness of her voice. After all, this was Marianne. She was a consummate actress. Still, something stirred.

He nodded slowly. "So I did, and so you do. But in doing so, it does not mean that I am going to revert back into the man I was before. It certainly does not mean that I am going to love you again."

She flinched as if he had struck her, and his stomach seemed to drop. It was harsh, but he could see that was what she had been expecting. And it was better that she know now than to continue anticipating that he would dote on her like one of her former lapdogs. He would never mistreat her, but it hardly meant he would go out of his way to treat her especially well. She would always be well cared for and respected under his care. If she deserved the respect.

"I thought we could at least be friends again," Marianne said carefully, averting her eyes.

He could see the stubborn set of her jaw and felt himself wishing for the same.

If only they could.

"But apparently," she continued in a much softer tone, "that is too much to ask of your pride."

That nettled him quite neatly, and his sympathy evaporated. "You don't want friendship," he said with a fairly icy smile.

She looked up at him with a mixture of surprise and fury.

His smile grew just a little, taunting her. "You want an admirer. A little pet to follow you around and make you feel better about yourself. Someone who falls at your feet and thinks you walk on gold dust and the clouds of heaven. That is not me, and it will never be me."

Her mouth dropped open in outrage, but no sound came out.

No longer hungry, Kit rose and untucked his serviette, tossing it onto the table. "When you find a way to understand the proper definition, perhaps we will have a chance at friendship, but not before."

With the most perfect and polite bow he had ever given anyone in his life, he strode from the dining room, head held high, studiously avoiding looking at the frozen and slightly quaking form of his wife as she sat so rigidly proper in her chair.

He needed to go for a hard ride, something to work off this rage that seemed to surround him, something that would drive his inexplicable pain at her distress out of him, something that would at the very least keep him from thinking about how soft her skin had been yesterday and what heaven it had been to touch it. And if there were any mercy at all in the world, something that would keep him from dreaming of her again.

His obsession was going to kill him.

Colin was right.

And that was the most infuriating part of all.

Chapter Fourteen

The days following their breakfast spat were not comfortable ones, and Kit was fairly chafing with the desire to be away from the place. Marianne was everywhere and looked at him with coldness, if she looked at him at all. They spoke very little to each other, but when they did it was with forced politeness and with the same unaffected air he'd heard dozens of couples in London use with each other. Why that should perturb him, he could not have said, but so long as he and Marianne were not arguing, he supposed that was an improvement.

She seemed to be taking up her responsibilities in the house with much more enthusiasm and energy, and Mrs. Dinstable was very keen on every project. Kit hadn't thought it, but the house seemed to be in need of some change and repairs, though the exterior and the grounds, which were his responsibility, were well enough off. His tenants, on the other hand, had needed quite a bit of help, as he had expected from his solicitor. Much of the troubles had already been addressed, but there were still many to see to, and a firm relationship of trust to establish and maintain.

For the moment, he could only pore over the accounts again, though his estate manager had not found anything out of the ordinary, and pray something would come to him. Mr. Jennings was very capable and highly thought of, but as he was not the landowner, very little power rested with him. He was gathering reports that would help them prepare for the harvest, and Kit was strangely glad to be alone today. There was far less pressure to be decisive and maintain authority when one was unobserved.

He shook his head as he set aside the accounts and rubbed his hands over his face. There was nothing here, which meant there would be no quick and simple solution. He would have to do some unconventional thinking and planning with Jennings when next they met, or else they would struggle to have any sort of profit from the estate at all this year.

And what would that say about the master of the estate?

There was a firm rap against the door of his study and it opened before he could respond. Marianne entered, looking every bit the lady of the house in her pale blue day dress, and the dark pinstripes along the fabric made her seem taller and thinner than she was. Her hair was back to her usual elegance, which was strangely comforting to him, and he smiled as she absently fidgeted with the lace fichu at her modest neckline.

"The post," she said without preamble, looking at the letters in her hand and not at him. She shook her head and a ringlet near her ear hooked itself on the delicate lobe. "I cannot make out much on this one, so I must presume it is from Colin."

She came forward and handed it to him, still not meeting his eyes.

What was this, he wondered. She'd been defiant and willful at every turn since they quarreled, and yet here she was being almost demure. Almost, because he could still see the muscles in her throat and neck tightening, so there was some spirit and resentment in her. That, too, was comforting, in a way.

He took the letter, and could not help but to laugh a little. "Yes, this is Colin's hand. He never did have patience for legible writing."

"I know," she replied, setting another letter on his desk. "I remember trying to discern his attempts to write Duncan when you all were away with Aunt Agatha. I always just assumed he was drunk."

Kit looked up at her and raised a brow. "At thirteen?"

Finally, her rich blue eyes met his and her full lips spread into a small smile. "Why not?" she said with a light shrug. "It's Colin."

Somehow, he forgot to breathe, and when had he taken notice of the fullness of her lips or the richness of her eyes or how her figure looked in certain gowns? He must be more fatigued than he thought. Still, he had to smile back. "You have a point there." He saw she held a letter herself and indicated it. "One for you as well?"

She nodded and looked down at it. "I cannot think who it is from. I've already had letters from Lily and Gemma, and this is not in either of their hands." She returned her gaze to his, tilting her head slightly. "Does Colin share London reports with you?"

He broke the seal of his letter and opened it. "Sometimes. But in this case, he would have very little to say. They are in Hampshire at the moment, staying at Amberley House."

"They removed to Hampshire?" she asked in surprise, still standing before his desk.

He nodded as he scanned the lines before him. "Susannah decided the remainder of her confinement would be better spent in the country. I understand several of the ladies have sworn to attend her at a moment's notice, so they would not let her venture too far from London."

Marianne was quiet for a moment, though he could see her fingers toying with various items on his desk. How elegant her hands were, how long and fine her fingers. Her nails were always so perfectly manicured, and she never wore rings, which allowed anyone with an appreciation of hands to savor any glance they could of such a sight free from the concealment of gloves.

"I would have thought she would go long before this," Marianne was saying, drawing his thoughts away from her hands. What in heaven's name was coming over him? He moved his gaze to her face, which surely would be safer territory. "She certainly ought to have, in her condition."

Kit frowned and readied a response, but as he looked into her face, he could see no malice in her words. Just an honest, forthright admission of her opinion.

Well... in that case...

"Susannah is not one to be persuaded one way or the other," he heard himself reply in resignation. "I know Colin suggested it some time ago, but she was not of a mind to. Now that we are gone, and her time is closer, she found herself wanting to be away."

Marianne nodded, a bit of a furrow between her brows. "Did they take the children?"

"Yes."

Her eyes widened. "All of them?"

Kit offered her a curious hint of a smile. "You think they should have left some in London? With your aunt, perhaps?"

She shuddered delicately. "Heaven forbid. No, I am only surprised. I cannot see how her confinement, or her recuperation, will be very restful with the house filled with children. Between Rosie and Freddie alone there will be chaos, and Bitty would want to know everything about the baby and will drive Colin mad with questions, and Ginny…" She frowned a little. "Ginny, I think, they could manage. She's quiet enough."

Kit hid a smile at the mention of his youngest, and most mysterious, sister. "For you, perhaps." He took in the sight of his wife with a new sort of appreciation. Her predictions were fairly aligned with his, and that she should be so intuitive about them, having never before taken an interest, was deeply surprising. Not troubling, just surprising.

"They do have Mrs. Creighton," he reminded her as he folded the letter back. "She is more than capable of handling them."

Marianne nodded again, seeming lost in thought. "Quite right. I'd forgotten about her." She shook herself and looked back at him, her cheeks looking pale against the sable darkness of her hair. "Will you go to them when her time comes?"

Kit sighed and nodded, rubbing his head. "Yes, it seems. Despite having four friends ready to ride at a moment's notice, Colin has requested that I be there." He shrugged a little, helplessly smiling. "And I must admit, I have a certain degree of interest in seeing how he handles the whole thing."

That drew a smile from Marianne, a true smile that brightened her countenance so it fairly took his breath away. "Now that is a sight I would pay a great deal to see." She shook her head and tapped his desk once. "You shall have to tell me all about it," she said a bit airily as she turned and exited the room, her attention now fixed on her own letter.

For the briefest of moments, Kit considered asking her to stay. Why, he did not know. What he would have done if she had, he hadn't even thought about. But seeing her, speaking with her, without the strain and tension of resentment between them, had been a breath of fresh air.

And he hadn't breathed that in such a long time.

Marianne suddenly made an odd moaning sound of distress, keening as if in pain, and she gripped the wall.

He was on his feet in a moment. "Marianne?"

She held out a shaky hand to stop him and he heeded it, waiting on the balls of his feet in his study, watching her back carefully.

Her head was bowed over the letter, but he could see a flush of distress rising on her neck and her shoulders were suddenly tense. He heard the letter crinkling in her hold.

"What is it?" he asked in a low voice.

She drew in a slow breath and half turned towards him. The color in her face was gone, but the pink flush continued to rise upwards. "It is a letter from Edward Hayes. Fanny's brother." She swallowed with great difficulty, wet her lips, and straightened a little. "Fanny has run away from home. With Mr. Marksby."

It was as if the floor had vanished beneath him. His breath suddenly felt hot, and burned his lungs and chest with every exhalation, and his pulse began to pound in his head.

"He asks me to prevail upon you," Marianne half whispered, still reading, "to aid him and his brother in finding her and stopping him. They are for Gretna, as is expected, and given my… history with the man, they assume they will take a less direct route. If you agree, they request that you meet them at the family home in North Oxford as soon as possible."

The letter, and the hand that held it, fell to her side. She leaned her head back against the wall and closed her eyes. "Damn you, Marksby," she rasped.

"My sentiments precisely," Kit muttered in clipped tones, running a hand through his hair. He exhaled a short breath and shook his head. "The Hayes family will never recover from this."

Marianne looked at him, her eyes dull and flat. "Will you go?"

He hid a shudder and shook his head again. "No."

The letter in her hand suddenly crumpled as she balled her hand into a fist. "Kit, they have asked for your help."

He shook his head more firmly, leaving no doubt. "No, Marianne. I am not going to go chasing after him again. I have no desire to reacquaint myself with him or his damages."

Marianne pushed off of the wall and turned fully towards him, folding her arms over her chest. "Kit…"

He took her arm and led her back into the study, shutting the door behind her.

"You have to go, Kit." She stepped towards him, her hands shaking as she brushed back a stray tendril on either side of her face. "Are you really going to let another woman be subject to him?"

"Why am I to be the deliverer of justice for all things Marksby?" he asked, desperately trying to ignore the part of him that was enraged by her distress. "She has brothers, and they have friends, all of whom are more than capable of mounting a rescue."

"They asked for you!"

"Why?" he demanded, as if she would know. "Why me? Why not Colin or Duncan or literally anyone else?" He shook his head again, whirling away from her. "I *cannot* see that man again, I swore that the last time I put my fist in his face."

"I have not told you all that I suffered at his hand!" Marianne suddenly cried, her voice cracking.

The utter silence was deafening and he was suffocated by it. Slowly, and with more fear than he'd ever felt in his entire life, he turned back to face her.

She was pale as death, still as the marble in the great hall, and her hands were clenched tightly before her. The only thing that moved was her chin as it quivered with unshed tears.

"What?" he managed in a broken, hoarse voice.

She closed her eyes and a tick of a wince flickered across her face. "There was so much more to it, Kit, than anything you saw. What I endured, what he… promised in my future, the violence, the threats, all that he anticipated from me…" She shuddered and put a fist to her mouth, fighting for control.

He ought to take her into his arms. He ought to sweep her up and promise that she was eternally safe and nothing would ever harm her.

"Marianne…" he managed roughly, willing his feet to her side, though they ignored him.

How could he bear hearing more?

"How I managed to escape without actually being ruined is a

miracle," she managed, sounding stronger, if only just. She met his eyes at last, and the fire in them seared his soul. "Fanny is not me, Kit, and I am afraid for her. There may not be anything left to save, and I know that, but please try. For her sake, for her family's sake… For me, please try."

A lesser man would have fallen to his knees at such a request. Anyone else would have immediately taken up the charge.

But Kit could only stare at his wife, heart pounding furiously in his chest.

She had no air of superiority or expectation of reward. She was a tower of strength and yet exuded humility. This was not the woman he married. This was the girl he fell in love with.

And he could never refuse her anything.

He exhaled heavily and a great weight came off his shoulders and settled in his chest. He came forward and gestured for the letter, which she gave him, eyes wide.

He scanned the pages for pertinent details, then nodded. He handed it back to her, unable to speak. Equally unable to leave her without anything, he took her hand in his, squeezed it in what he hoped was a gesture of comfort, and then brushed his lips over her brow quickly.

The faint whisper of a gasp that escaped her would have unmanned him had he not already released her hand and started away. As it was, his lips tingled with the feeling of her skin, and his thoughts were awhirl as the subtle fragrance of her flooded his senses. He was utterly mad to be going after the foolish chit, especially considering Marksby. He wasn't sure he had the strength to face the villain again, but for his wife, he would try.

He called for his horse to be readied, and he was gone within a quarter of an hour. He did not see Marianne again, for which he was grateful. He would rather remember her as he left her than see her change into the wife he had known.

But all that rested on his mind was the picture she had presented when he'd ridden to the inn at Leeds, when Marksby had done with her.

And a cold fear began to grow within him.

It was a strange thing to be at Glendare without Kit, but Marianne managed well enough. She continued with the refurbishing of a few rooms, but pointedly left the horrid marble statues where they had been in the great hall. Despite her adding the carpets and softening the great marble overload of the room with tapestries and some plants, the room was still oppressive, and until the statues were removed, it would be so. But Kit hated them, and she was not ready to give in yet.

She wandered the house and the grounds at length, within reason, and found herself feeling rather at home here, despite being in solitude. There were no neighbors in residence, and she was not yet brave enough to go into the village on errands. But she did let the estate manager introduce her to some of the families under their care, and she had never been more grateful for her ability to read people and sway them into liking her. She had never been a lady with real responsibility, let alone responsibilities involving other people, but she found a sort of affinity for it. There was something to be said about people being in need and being the one to whom they could turn for solutions and relief.

According to Mr. Jennings, she had quite a knack for this, despite her initial doubts, and he thought her husband would be quite pleased with the progress she had made. It seemed that some of the families she had visited had been some of the more troublesome ones, and she may have gone a long way to smoothing over some rather ruffled feathers.

Well, if she could do something to be of use to Kit when he was doing so much for her at the moment, she would be quite content.

She could not have said what had persuaded him to go, but she was so grateful for it. She hardly slept while he was gone, worrying over Fanny and her fate. And if she were being entirely truthful, she was worried about him as well. He had never told her all that he had done to Marksby, but considering what depth of feeling he once had for her, and the responsibility he had felt to her, it was no wonder he had taken it upon himself to thrash the man. Seeing him again, knowing that she had not told him all…

She would be surprised indeed if Marksby lived much longer.

But she could not tell him all of the horrible whisperings that Marksby had laid upon her, the vulgar and base illustrations he had created with his words, the physical beatings, chokings, indecent touches… He had been determined to ruin her entirely before he ruined her in truth. He had been so very persuasive, and she had been tempted more than once to give in, but pride and a firm resolve had preserved her.

If Kit knew all that she had suffered, in detail, he would always feel guilt and pain. He would always see her with pity. He would never be the same sort of man again. She could not bear that.

There was no word from him, or either of the Hayes brothers, but she hardly expected any. There would not be time, and they certainly should not have made communication with her any sort of priority. Not when Fanny's fate was hanging in the balance.

Still, wandering the house and playing the pianoforte and examining the gallery could only be done so many times before she was like to go mad with wondering. She was never very good at being helpless.

But the time in the house alone with the servants had given her opportunity to get a better feeling for the flow of the house and the sort of energy that resided here, and she quite liked it. She spent a good deal of time with Mrs. Dinstable and the cook, Mrs. Paul, and they regaled her with all sorts of stories, some of which gave her a very interesting insight into the man she married. She thought she knew him very well, but the man they knew was kind and considerate, remembered details with exactness, and cared about the welfare of his estates and tenants with a veracity that endeared him to everyone.

This was the man who treated her with coldness and disdain?

That was the Kit she had known in her youth, not the one she was married to.

Not the one she had wounded.

Marianne had gone to bed troubled, suddenly desperate to find something she could do to attempt to mend this mess of a marriage they had created. Their odd moments of harmony and companionship had been flanked rather soundly on either side with some rather vehement spats, which did not reflect well on either of them.

But she knew one thing: her husband was a good man, despite his complicated and confusing feelings towards her. And despite her attempts to prove to the world the contrary, she had a heart, however infrequently she had used it.

Perhaps if they stopped hiding so much, they might actually get somewhere.

Sometime in the night, she found herself coming awake, which was highly unusual for her. She usually slept like the very dead without any interruption. But tonight, something had roused her. She turned over and gave a little start as she made out a shape by her bedroom door. Blinking quickly, she peered more closely, and was further shocked to see her husband there, leaning against the wall, his eyes on her.

"Kit?" she murmured softly, sitting up against the headboard and rubbing at her eyes.

He did not respond, but continued to stare at her, his expression almost fearful.

She took in the state of him, faintly illuminated from the dying light of the fire in the hearth and the candle in his hand. His cravat was gone, his jacket and waistcoat were open, his linen shirt wrinkled and crumpled, his hair was windswept and disorderly, which left him looking very young, despite the growth of whiskers on his face. His corded throat worked in a swallow, and he looked utterly exhausted.

If he had just arrived, surely he needed to rest and could see her in the morning.

Unless...

She swallowed and considered him with newfound concern. "What's wrong?" she asked softly.

His head jerked in an uneven shake of his head. "I didn't mean to disturb you," he replied, his voice hoarse and unsteady. "It can wait."

Yet he did not move, and he barely breathed. He watched her still, steadily, as if he were afraid she would disappear. Obviously, whatever it was could not wait. Not for him.

A surge of tenderness enfolded her, and she held out a hand to him. "Come here, Kit."

He moved so quickly it almost startled her, and he seized her hand at once. The contact seemed to shake him and he sank onto the edge of her bed, his grip tightening.

"What's wrong?" she asked again, squeezing his hand as she took the candle from him and set it on the nightstand beside her.

He stared at her face for an uncomfortably long moment, his eyes tracing her features. Then he looked away, his hold on her clenched, and started speaking. In quiet, controlled tones, he spoke of meeting with the Hayes brothers in Oxford and making plans for the direction they would head. They had been hopelessly lost as to how to proceed and where to go, and he'd been able to advise them as to a proper plan. They'd used several resources, both monetary and informational, to finally track the elopers down in Carlisle, just before the border. It was unfathomable that they had stopped so close to Scotland, but once they had found them, they understood why.

Kit inhaled slowly and closed his eyes, swallowing again.

Marianne sat up a bit more and rested her other hand on his arm, giving him a gentle squeeze.

"She was worse off than you had been," he said flatly. "Far more bruised and battered, particularly in her face, but she clung to Marksby as if he were the one who should protect her. She loves him, despite everything. Even with the evidence of his brutality upon her, she turned to him like a dog to his master, with adoration and eagerness. They had already been to Gretna and back, man and wife, for better or worse. And she is… She is carrying his child. Already confirmed by physician. I believe that is what convinced Marksby to settle for her fortune, which her brothers have no choice but to confer upon him. They plan to live at his house in Staffordshire until the child comes, and then…" He shrugged and shook his head. "Who knows what will happen after that."

They sat together in silence for several long moments, as Marianne tried to digest the information. She should have seen it, how devoted Fanny had always been to Marksby, and how little she wished to believe her when she told her the truth. She ought to have been more emotional about it, and she felt the odd burning of tears in her eyes, but most of what she felt was a hollow sort of emptiness, and a great deal of pity.

"Poor Fanny," she sighed, absently stroking Kit's hand and forearm. "She has no idea what she has gotten herself into."

"I'm sorry we couldn't save her," Kit murmured bleakly, his free hand rubbing at his head.

Surprised, Marianne tugged his hand, forcing him to look at her. "Save her? Kit, I told her what happened to me. Everything. She knew exactly what she was doing, so there was nothing to save. And if my calculations are correct, she was already carrying his child when he carted me off. And she knows that."

Kit swallowed and shook his head. "It could have been you," he rasped. "That was the thought that tortured me the whole ride. It could have been you and I couldn't save you."

Realization now dawned on her and she clung to his hand tightly, holding it against her. "It reminded you of looking for me."

He shuddered a little. "Every blistering second of it. I'll never be able to forget it. From the moment I had heard you were gone, I was beside myself. I could barely rein in my emotions. Could you see that?"

Had she seen that? Had she seen any of it? Reluctantly, wishing she could answer any other way, she shook her head slowly. "All I remember from that moment was my shock at seeing you there at the inn. That you had come for me. I've never known shame like that before, wondering what you thought of me." Her voice broke a little, but she swallowed it back.

Kit stared at her with such intensity that she could barely draw breath. "I was tormented the entire time we searched for you, furious that you'd run away, terrified you were in trouble, desperate to throttle you…" He shook his head, his eyes still fixed on her but somehow distant. "Then I saw you, the state you were in and the terror in your face… and all I could think of was killing him, and holding you." He blinked hard, his face tensing at the memory. "My mind was filled with images of hauling you into my arms, carrying you out of that place, looking over every inch of you just to assure myself that you were well and whole… My hands literally itched to touch you. But I couldn't. So I did the only thing I could do." A dark, satisfied sneer broke across his face. "I thrashed Marksby until my hands bled, and then I threatened him with worse if he ever came near you again. And as much as I hated to admit it, I knew you were mine from that moment on. More than that, I knew that I belonged to you." He suddenly focused on her again, pinning her in place. "I'll never regret coming after you, Marianne. Seeing Fanny Hayes, and learning that I don't know everything you endured... It makes me ache in places I didn't know I could."

His tortured whisper ripped at her heart and she found herself suddenly choked up, her eyes swimming with the tears that would not fall for Fanny. She pulled him closer, and to her surprise, he came. She tucked his head under her chin, wrapping her arms around his neck and broad shoulders, and he curled against her like a child.

"I am right here," she whispered, softly stroking his thick hair. "I am safe and here with you. I'm sorry to have given you cause for such worry."

His arms suddenly latched around her waist tightly. "I am so sorry I couldn't get to you sooner. I'm sorry you had to marry me, I'm sorry we have had such trouble together..."

"Shhh," she scolded, shaking her head and holding him tight. "I'm far happier than I would be otherwise. Now be quiet and hold me."

He stilled at her command, but did not lift his head. "What?"

She sighed, wishing she had a better talent with words where her husband was concerned. She ran her fingers through his hair, and felt some of the tension leave him. "We have had a rough start, Kit," she murmured, "but we were friends long before any of that. We can be friends again."

He settled against her for a long moment, sighing heavily, wearily. Then he pulled back a little, his eyes wary, but in all other respects looking utterly exhausted. "Do you... want me to leave?" he asked carefully, his voice a mere echo of his usual tones. "I can, if you wish."

Marianne shook her head, smiling softly. Even now, with all he was suffering, he was controlled and polite. A gentleman to his very core. The hint of hesitation in his voice told her all she needed to know. "Did you hear me?" she asked with a mock exasperated sigh.

She leaned forward and took his face between her hands, meeting his gaze firmly. "You are distressed. You need to be held, and you can only reassure yourself if you hold me. So stop being so polite, Kit Gerrard, take your boots off, and come hold your wife for as long as you like."

His eyes suddenly glinted and he laughed briefly, nodding. He stepped away from the bed and stripped his boots, coat, and waistcoat, and then he hesitated, looking back at her.

There were a hundred emotions she could have read in his eyes and expression, but she chose not to. Tonight, she was in charge, and pride had nothing to do with any of it. She gave him what she hoped was a stern look, then smiled and held out her hand. "Come here, Kit," she said as gently as she could.

He came to her at once, put out the candle, and slid into bed beside her. Immediately, Marianne moved into his hold, and he gripped her tightly against him. "Don't ever leave me," he whispered harshly, his hands stroking her back and hair.

She peered up at his darkened face in surprise. "Why would I?"

He shook his head and pressed his mouth into her hair. "It's not a love match, everybody knows that, but…"

His frantic breathing and more frantic words concerned her. She rested a hand over his erratic heart and rubbed soothing circles against his chest. "Kit, I'm not going anywhere. I am yours now."

Again came the quick shake of his head. "I don't want you to think you are a possession."

She smiled at his words. "I don't," she said softly, "but you need to stop worrying that I will run, or that I resent this marriage. I'm not that girl anymore. I am your wife, and I will stay your wife forever."

She hadn't meant for it to come out so earnestly, such a heartfelt vow at such a moment. But neither could she regret having said them, nor would she take them back. She felt him swallow, press a kiss to her hair, and heard a relieved sigh that made her throat tighten again.

"I'm sorry you doubt me, though I know I deserve it," she whispered, tucking her face into his chest.

"Shhh," he soothed, finally sounding more like himself, even with the evident drowsiness. "That's enough. Just let me hold you now. We'll be all right."

Whether those last words were meant for her or not, they brought her a measure of comfort. Something had changed between them, something rather significant. The next few days would tell all, but she would not worry about that now. She could not. Wrapped in the protective embrace of her husband, and protecting him herself, she felt nothing but satisfaction and a little flame of hope that had sprung to life once more.

Relaxing completely against him, she sighed, closed her eyes, and drifted off to sleep once more.

Chapter Fifteen

The next few days were quite different at Glendare Court. Kit felt no different than he had any other day of his marriage, except now he did not find Marianne quite so vexing. It could have been that she actually had not been quite so vexing, but he was more inclined to look at her with concern than with criticism. She conversed politely, smiled more, and seemed to lose that part of her that was so inclined to airs and superiority. Oh, she had not lost her nature, by any stretch, but she was warmer somehow. Softer.

She still refused to dress for breakfast, but that did not seem to bother him as much. It was becoming amusing, actually. Aside from how distracted he grew by the all-too appealing picture she presented.

They continued their separate duties, for the most part, though he did not take any pains to avoid her. He could see the progress she made in the few rooms she had decided to redo, and her comfort with the servants and the housekeeper made him smile. She certainly had a way with people, no matter what she might have tried to portray. She was no more heartless than he was unfeeling. How that would surprise people if they knew.

He made it a point to seek her out at some point during the day now, and she never once seemed to mind. Once he had been certain she truly was not going to fall ill, he'd taken her out for that tour of the estate he'd sworn off before, both of them on horseback, and despite what he'd thought about her taste for the outdoors, she had been observant and fascinated, taking in every aspect with a sense of appreciation. She'd asked thoughtful questions about the estate and the tenants, and ridden with a surprising amount of grace, if not skill.

The marble statues still remained in the great hall, much to his disgruntlement, and he made a mental note to bring that up at a convenient time.

He smiled as he shook his head, wondering what she planned to do with them. He looked down at the book in his lap, forgetting that it was there, not quite sure what he'd been reading. The library at Glendare was fairly respectable, and he had decided to take advantage of his unoccupied hours there, but it seemed his thoughts were going to take him elsewhere.

The door to the library opened and he looked up, not surprised at all to see Marianne enter the room. She saw him at once and smiled a little, sending stray sparks and jolts in various directions throughout his body.

"Mind if I join you?" she asked, waiting in the doorway.

He smiled and shook his head. "Not at all. Please."

Her smile grew and she came to sit on the sofa opposite from the chair in which he sat. He thought she would have sat as prim and properly as every English miss, and the way he'd seen her do time after time. But to his surprise, she drew her legs up under her and lounged comfortably, laying her book in her lap. She propped herself up on the edge of the sofa with her elbow and laid her head on her hand, completely oblivious to his observations of her.

The country had done wonderful things for her appearance. While she had never been anything less than beautiful, she had begun to look almost forced and unnatural amidst London's fashion-addled society and the demand for thinner, more made-up females. She'd not looked any different from any other girl with her same nature and situation, painting her eyes and rouging her cheeks, even powdering her complexion to seem paler. He'd never liked that sort of look, no matter how popular it was.

Now, however, she was completely devoid of such things, her complexion healthy and rosy of its own accord. Her figure, which he'd never fully appreciated until certain events, was too perfect and needed no corset or accessory. Her eyes seemed to carry all the richness of every shade of blue within them, and dazzled more brilliantly for the lack of paint.

His wife was a stunning woman just as she was.

He had always known that, but now that the resentment surrounding her had faded, now that he was seeing her clearly, he felt the unmistakable draw that she'd always had over him yet again.

Marianne suddenly frowned, the smooth skin between her brows drawing together in a delicate furrow.

Forgetting that he was not supposed to be gawking at her, he tilted his head and asked, "What?"

She looked up at him, not seeming surprised at all by the query, but she did not say anything, her lips forming a thin line.

"Something wrong with your book?" he asked, prodding a little.

She shook her head, her bottom lip pulling as if she were chewing the inside. Again, she shook her head and returned to her book.

Kit frowned at that, but he could not exactly force her to tell him. He shrugged inwardly and turned his attention to his own book.

For a few moments, they did nothing but read in companionable silence, the only sound that of the pages turning.

"Kit?" Marianne suddenly asked in a timid voice.

"Hmm?" he replied absently, engrossed in his book for the first time that day.

There was the barest hint of hesitation, but it was enough to force him to look at her. She considered him with a curious, innocent look. "Where did you go after…?" She bit her lip and tried again. "That is, you were gone for a very long time after…"

He stilled as he realized what she was asking. She wanted to know what he had done those two years he had stayed away from England after his proposal. He'd never told anyone about that, not even Colin. Yet here she was, asking without any sort of demand or conceit.

He gave her a searching look. "Do you really want to know?" he asked her in return, reluctant to share that part of his past.

She nodded slowly, releasing a soft exhale. "Yes. I… I missed you. And I didn't understand then." She tilted her head a little and regarded him with another apology in her eyes. "And you were so altered when you returned."

Kit watched her for another long moment, then sighed and looked away.

"I went to find my father," he said in a low voice, ignoring her shocked gasp. "As ridiculous and idiotic as that seems, given Loughton's reputation, but I was desperate. I remembered that he had really loved my mother, and when we were children they'd had a relationship unlike anything I had ever seen. After she'd died, Loughton changed. He became hard and calloused. Nothing ever touched him. I did not know how someone could go from feeling so much to feeling nothing, and I wanted to understand. I wanted to do that."

"No," Marianne whispered, completely still.

Kit shook his head. "They were dark days, and I learned a great deal, hoping that my time apart from you would lessen what I felt. But Loughton… chooses another way to live his life than I ever would, and I learned very quickly that I was on my own. Eventually, I found ways to close myself off, and started to find the control I sought."

"Did it work?"

"Yes. And at the same time, no." He smiled humorlessly at nothing, lost in memories. "The first time I saw you again, I knew it hadn't worked entirely, but it was different. I was different. And that seemed to work, for a time at least."

For a long moment, there was no sound. Then he heard Marianne sniffle and looked over at her. She was trying, unsuccessfully, to wipe at her eyes without him seeing.

"I'm sorry," she whispered, grinding the heels of her hands into her eyes.

He sighed a little and sat forward, resting his arms on his knees. He shook his head and gave her a hard look. "Don't," he said roughly. "It was my choice."

She sniffed again and dropped her hands, looking at him with tear-filled eyes. "But my fault."

"It was a long time ago," he reminded her softly.

She shook her head, looking very young and very small. "Not for me."

Kit moved to the sofa and pulled her into a warm embrace. "That's enough," he soothed as she rested her head against his shoulder. "We need to move past it. We can't keep doing this forever."

She nodded against him. "I know, and I won't. But right now, I need to. Will you just hold me for a while?"

He smiled and tightened his hold. "Of course."

He didn't know how long they sat like that, but he would have done so for much longer. Only when Marianne drew away did he remove his arms, and even then he gave her thorough look. "Better?"

She nodded and offered him a faint smile. "Thank you for humoring me. I can't imagine it's pleasant for you."

"Reliving my past or holding you?" he asked, forcing himself not to smile, though his tone had turned playful on its own.

Her smile spread and she looked inordinately pleased with him. "Both, I should think."

He shrugged and took her hand in his, rubbing it gently. "The first is not pleasant, I will admit, but you were well within your rights to ask, and I don't mind sharing with you. And as for the second…" He let the suggestion hang in the air long enough for Marianne to blush a little. Then he grinned wickedly. "I doubt I shall ever mind that."

Marianne laughed and tried to pull her hand away, but he held it fast. "And just when I can't be more embarrassed, I remember you're the only man alive to see me in my altogether," she muttered, her cheeks coloring further.

He chuckled and released her hand finally. "Best not to mention your being in your altogether, my dear. The servants may get the most shocking ideas." He winked and returned to his chair, picking up his book once more.

Before his eyes had settled on the page, there was a knock at the door. "Come," he and Marianne called at the same time, sharing an amused look.

Reynolds entered, bowing with the faintest expression of surprise at seeing them in the room together. "Sir," he said to Kit, then turned his attention to Marianne. "Madam, the men have finished in the music room. Would you come and see?"

Marianne let out a delighted little shriek that was entirely inappropriate for a woman of her station. "Yes!" she squealed, leaping to her feet. She looked at Kit at once. "Come with me. Come see what I've done."

He gave her a bemused look. "I've seen the music room."

She sets her hands on her hips and huffed a little. "You've not seen it since I've had it redone. Now, come and see!"

He heaved a rather long-suffering sigh and looked at Reynolds. "You would think she'd torn down a wing of the house without my knowledge."

Reynolds's saggy cheek twitched but he only nodded in acknowledgement.

Kit got to his feet once more with much protesting and let Marianne link their arms and parade him from the room. She said nothing, but her expression said plenty. She was absolutely giddy and could hardly contain it, and it was surprisingly contagious.

The workers all stood within the music room, waiting for her verdict, and even when she was doing a fairly in-depth amount of inspection, she could not stop smiling.

"It looks much improved," she said with an approving nod. "The wallpaper is much better. Thank you for recommending the powder blue, Mr. Fields. I think the cream would have been too light for the wood." She ran a hand over the newly upholstered furniture, nodding slowly and smiling. She raised her eyes to the men and nodded more firmly. "Excellent work. If you will follow Mr. Reynolds there, he will take you to the kitchens where you might find something warm to eat."

The men bowed in an awkward unison and left them. Kit folded his arms and watched as his wife worked her magic on more unsuspecting men, shaking his head.

She turned to him, hands clasped before her. "What do you think?" she asked, eyes bright.

He smiled and took a moment to look around, and truthfully, it was a great improvement from the drab prospect it was before. Not that he had spent a great deal of time in the music room, but he could see himself rather enjoying this. "It's lovely," he said as he returned his gaze to hers. He glanced in the corner where the currently covered pianoforte sat, and gave Marianne a half-grin. "Have you played in here yet?"

She smiled and wandered over to the instrument. "A little here and there. I was distracted by the abysmal artwork, but now I think I could play with great pleasure." She tugged the sheet off of the pianoforte and rubbed the gleaming surface lovingly. "I was quite pleased to find such a fine instrument in the house, Kit. And it is remarkably in tune, considering you don't play."

He smirked a little and followed her. "How do you know I don't play?"

She scoffed and sat down on the bench as if she would play, but her hands remained in her lap. "Well, I would know if you did…" she started, then took in his expression and her eyes widened. "Wait, you play?"

He smiled and shrugged one shoulder. "Not often, but I can."

"You're musical?" she gasped.

He grinned at her aghast face and chuckled. "That would be a stretch."

She shifted on the bench and turned more towards him. "But you can play. Can you sing?"

"Yes."

"Kit!" she screeched, smiling broadly. "Why don't you?"

He cocked his head, his smile fading just a little. "Why don't you?"

She sobered at once and looked down at the piano, her fingers brushing the keys noiselessly.

Part of Kit wanted to brush off his impertinent question and talk about something else, distract her, make her smile again, but the larger part told him to wait a moment longer, just to see if she might share a bit of herself with him. If they had come that far.

"I am…" she said slowly, her voice low and rough, "remarkably insecure. Far more so than anyone would ever think."

"I don't believe that," he murmured, hooking a nearby chair with his leg and bringing it forward to sit before her.

She glanced at him briefly. "Don't you remember that day when I came to you after my first Season? I told you I had no accomplishments and nobody wanted anything to do with a girl with no accomplishments."

He nodded carefully, but did not see how that related. "You are quite accomplished musically."

She snorted and shook her head. "I am capable musically, and that is all that can be said for me. I can play, yes, as you said, and I can sing a little, but one could hardly call what I do accomplishment. I possess desire and ability, but lack the technique and the grace that define accomplishment in music. I will never be an accomplished musician; it is simply not in me. I never had the patience to put in hours of practice as other girls did. At anything. I wasn't a vain child, but I couldn't manage to excel at any particular accomplishment, and that unsettled me. I have always only been considered good enough, and I wanted more than that, but I was impatient and impulsive, and never put forth the necessary effort. I never wanted anything badly enough to work for it. Why couldn't it come easily for me as it did for so many others?"

Kit watched her, mesmerized by the words from her perfect lips, by the soft turn of her throat as she spoke, by the subtle, barely perceptive quiver in her fingers as they noiselessly stroked the keys. He had never imagined Marianne would feel anything like this.

"My first Season, when I was so disappointed, I realized that I had put myself in that position. Sweet girls with no talents get nothing. And with everyone in the world telling me how much I looked like my mother, knowing what a fine creature she was… Why, she was the envy of all in Europe." She broke off for a smile. "Well, at least Scotland and England, but in my mind it might as well have been everyone. I could not bear to be Eleanor Bray's daughter and embarrass my family and myself by completely lacking in everything. I had to live up to her, you see, and I couldn't do it. I couldn't do anything well. And if I could not do something perfectly, I wouldn't do it at all. So instead of letting myself be judged and criticized for my lack of accomplishment, I celebrated the fact that I had none. No one can judge what they cannot prove. I spend a great deal of time pretending, and am now very good at it. Most people simply think I am being modest, or some such, though modesty has never been a virtue I have displayed, for surely I could not be so unaccomplished as I declared." Her smile turned sad and she shook her head. "It was probably the truest thing I have ever let the world know of myself."

"You played at Tibby's musicale year the autumn before last," he reminded her gently.

She gave him a wan look of amusement. "And I was so distressed beforehand, Duncan nearly called for a physician. I managed well enough, as it was a small setting with people I was comfortable with, but my nerves and my fears nearly swayed me from it. That was the first time I have ever performed for anyone outside of my family, and even then, I never played on display. They had only heard me practicing." She cleared her throat and looked down at the keys once more. "I can play well enough for myself, and for those I trust, but if you put me out on display with the Lady Whitlocks and Lily Ardens and Mary Harrises and Mariah Ketterings and Phoebe Rouschs of the world… My fingers freeze and tingle at the thought, my stomach clenches, my head swims, and I can barely breathe. I would be a laughingstock by comparison."

"Hardly," he murmured.

The look she tossed in his direction let him know what a stupid thing that was to say. "You know Society, Kit. And I know Society. Comparisons are all they live by. I should not care what everybody thinks, but I do. I have little enough opinion of myself to supplant them, so I thrive on the good opinions of others. The less I can give them to find fault with, the safer I shall be. What if I did something wrong? What if I could not play as well as I practiced? What if my voice should crack when I sing? What if…?"

He moved closer and rested a hand on the bench near her, afraid she would recoil if he touched her. "What if you do splendidly?"

She sighed and closed her eyes, then rested her hand on top of his. "I don't think I could. With nothing to steady me, I have only my own abilities to depend on, and those abilities are sadly lacking."

He could barely breathe for the revelation she had heaped upon him. The shy, retreating girl of their youth had been cowering behind her insecurities and pretending to be this grand creature that was so admired.

He should have seen that.

"Marianne," he said gently, giving her a disbelieving smile, "you don't need anybody else's opinion. I know you love music, you always have. You should play for others, share that gift you have, even if someone else's fingers might fly a little faster."

"A lot faster," she muttered with a snort, but she smiled all the same.

"And anything else you want to do, you should do it," he continued, feeling rather bold at the moment. "Don't be ruled by fear anymore, Marianne. You're too strong for that."

She gave him an amused, slightly bewildered look. "Well," she said on a heavy sigh, still smiling, "perhaps one day I will." She looked at the pianoforte for a long moment, assessing it carefully. "Lily gave me some new songs when I left; I should look through those and see what I can manage."

Pleased beyond words, he nodded and sat back in his chair. "That sounds like a prudent beginning."

She looked at him once more, took in his comfortable position, and shook her head. "No, you have to go."

"What?" he cried with a laugh. "You just said…"

"I said one day," she interrupted, still shaking her head, "but I cannot play something new with you looking at me. Go away, if you please."

He chuckled and rose, putting his hands on his hips. "I will be able to hear you from the hallway, you know."

She nodded, a smile tugging at the corners of her mouth. "Yes, but you won't be looking at me. That is what makes the difference."

He smiled fully and shook his head at her. "Very well, I will see you when I am next permitted to do so." He bowed and turned to exit the room, as she requested.

"Kit?"

He turned on his heel and tilted his head in response.

Her expression was fraught with inquiry. "Why don't you play or sing?"

He chewed the inside of his lip for a moment, and exhaled slowly. "I suppose we share something in common after all, Marianne. Insecurity is a tricky business, and my reserved nature does not lend itself to much by way of frivolity. I may be an enthusiastic admirer of music, but never a participant." He shrugged one shoulder as if that explained everything. It was hardly a good excuse, but it was all he had.

"I understand," his wife murmured, and in her eyes, he could see that she did. She straightened a little, her smile turning shy. "Will you take me to the opera when we go back to London, Mr. Gerrard?"

He fought a grin, and lost. Giving her another, far more dignified bow, he inclined his head. "It would be an honor, Mrs. Gerrard."

Chapter Sixteen

*L*ater that same day, feeling much lighter and far more at ease with herself, Marianne went out in search of her husband. She had no particular reason, except that she wanted to see him, which was becoming a rather usual feeling for her.

And why shouldn't she? After all, her husband was a very attractive man, and his looser appearance in the country made it quite impossible to *not* enjoy looking at him. And she rather enjoyed being held by him, on those occasions he saw fit to do so. That night he'd come back after Fanny's departure he had held her all night, but had left before she had woken. No doubt, he had wanted to spare her the embarrassment and awkwardness of waking up next to him. That would be Kit, for certain, retreating from the discomfort of strong emotion, and now that she understood a bit more about his control, she admired him all the more for it.

In fact, she was coming to appreciate her husband more and more every day. Why, their conversation today alone had been revelatory for her. What else could there possibly be to this man she had married? He was patient and kind, he could not see suffering without wanting to relieve it, he had a strength of will and character that was awe-inspiring, and he did everything with honor and dignity.

So what exactly had she despised so about him?

Oh, right, he did not like her.

Well, she could hardly blame him for that. She barely liked herself, as she had been. And yet, things were changing. She did not have to pretend here, not with him. He liked her more for it, and she felt rather the same way.

How fast life could change, and how subtly, too. She would never have imagined that a quiet life in the country would suit her so well, or that she would enjoy reading in the library with her husband, or visiting tenants in the village. There were no neighbors within ten miles being in residence, and she did not mind.

Good heavens, who in the world was she?

She hid a smile in her hand as she realized her husband was probably thinking the same thing. The poor man, no wonder he was so changed. And somehow so unchanged. This was the Kit she had known so long ago, but grown up and matured, intensely male and unnervingly steady. Her thoughts were turning to him with increasing frequency, and there was something in the way he smiled at her that felt like a ray of sunshine.

But more than that, there was a comfort with him now. A sense of ease and warmth, something that made her want to do nothing more or less than walk the gardens with him by her side. Or feed the ducks in the Serpentine at Hyde Park. Or race the horses across the estate, as they had done just the other day. She enjoyed having fun with Kit, even if it were the most innocent of diversions.

She wondered if he might consider riding out with her again. Perhaps to the shoreline, as he was so wary of her going there herself. If he would show it to her, let her explore while he was near, then she could finally see it for what it was, and spend time with her husband at the same time.

A smile spread across her lips and she almost missed him, but her eyes were quick, and she stopped suddenly as she nearly passed the small drawing room at the back of the house. It was well within listening range of the music room. He would have heard every note she played, even the ones she wished he wouldn't. And here he sat, small fire crackling in the hearth, leaning back in a chair, fast asleep.

She entered the room as softly as she could, smiling as she took in the sight of him. His jacket was gone, as was his cravat, and somehow his hair had become less than perfect, and lounging as he was, his boots propped up on an ottoman, his hands folded together on his stomach, he looked more like a rake who had endured a very long night indeed.

And yet, he was anything but rakish. He took such care with

everything he did, and everything he felt. He'd even taken care of Marianne, despite all he had suffered at her hand and for her sake. He had somehow found a way to forgive her, and when he held her, he did so with such gentleness, but with a strength that soothed and assured her.

Her husband. This man, extraordinary and complicated and confusing and a thousand other things, was her husband. And her future.

He exhaled audibly, so perfectly at ease that she smiled even more. She approached quietly, carefully, suddenly desperate to study him as much as she could. To know his face and his features, every line and scar, every angle and facet. She wanted to brush the errant lock of chestnut hair off of his brow, knowing now how thick and lush his hair was, and her fingers itched to feel it again. She wanted to run a finger or two along his jaw, and feel how perfectly sculpted it was. She wanted to rest her hands on his shoulders, to feel the strength and power that resided in their broadness, though he was trim enough everywhere else. Where Colin had always looked lankier, Kit had been built for power, and though it would never be expected when one looked at him, it emanated from him still.

Drawn as if by some impossible force, Marianne found herself looking at his lips. They held power, too. Power to wound her, power to soothe her, the power to make her laugh… What other powers could they hold for her?

What would it be like to kiss him? She could hardly dare to approach him with such a question when he was awake, alert, and fully himself. But here, like this, in this moment…

She held her breath as she rested her hands on the arms of the chair, her heart pounding furiously in her ears, and leaned down to brush her lips across his in a feather soft caress.

A whisper of a gasp crossed her lips and she hovered barely above him, savoring the tingling sensation from so brief a connection. She could do it again, risk another venture into a world that she might never know otherwise. She swallowed silently, and prayed for strength, only to feel him shift beneath her.

She reared back and gasped in mortification as his eyes fluttered open. Flinging herself off of the chair, she retreated to the furthest corner of the room from him, clutching her arms as if she were cold.

"What are you doing?" he murmured sleepily, his penetrating eyes fixed on her with more intensity than his voice contained.

She thought about denying everything, surely he had been dreaming, but one look at his face told her he knew it all.

She swallowed hard, her face flaming. "I'm sorry," she whispered. "I just… wanted to know what it was like."

His eyes never left hers, and nothing in his posture or expression changed, but there was suddenly a new tension between them. A ticklish sort of fire somewhere in the pit of her stomach that spread to her fingers and toes, and grew warmer with every passing second.

"Well," Kit finally said in a low, rumbling voice, dragging his legs from the ottoman and slowly rising to his full and impressive height, "if you're that curious, it had better be properly done."

The ticklish fire burst into a rapid burning that encompassed every inch of her skin and her heart galloped on the backs of a thousand stallions as he came towards her, his eyes searing hers in a way that left her breathless and thoughtless.

Gingerly, as if she would break, he cupped her cheek, the skin of his hand barely grazing it. His thumb stroked her softly, drawing with it a shaky breath. His palm exerted the slightest pressure to her jaw, tilting her head back, bringing her lips into perfect alignment for his, and they parted under his gaze.

With infinite gentleness, Kit bent and touched his lips to hers, brushing against them with all the patience in the world, then sealing over them with exquisite tenderness. His lips eased pleasure from her, a slow, simmering heat that swirled about them both, and her hands slid from her arms and fluttered to his waistcoat. Softly, sweetly, he kissed her, again and again, a never-ending series of brushes and caresses, a conversation for which she had no translation, and needed none. Her breath snagged and her toes curled, and the teasing friction against her lips became an intoxicating sensation.

Just as she began to grow impatient, yet yearned for more of the same, he pulled back, his thumb stroking her cheek again. His eyes met hers, and she found his breathing to be as out of sync as hers was. Before she could blink, he pressed another hard kiss to her lips, then just as suddenly, he was gone, striding from the room with an exhale she could hear from her place.

Slowly, she brought her fingers to her lips, where a faint buzzing had begun, and she found herself smiling quite broadly as her breathing slowed to a more normal pace.

So… *that* was what it was like to kiss Kit Gerrard.

She could quite get used to that.

Still smiling, she tapped her chin in thought, and fairly skipped from the room, turning in the opposite direction Kit had gone, and strolling out into the gardens. She had a great need for some fresh air at the moment.

Kit was having a little difficulty breathing as he entered his study and closed the door firmly behind him. Was he a coward for having fled his wife's presence? Probably, but self-preservation was his first instinct, and he had known that he'd had to get out of there before he lost himself entirely.

Never, even in his wildest fantasies, had he imagined that Marianne would kiss him.

He couldn't recall what exactly he had been dreaming about in the drawing room, only that listening to Marianne play had lulled him into such comfort that he had drifted off before he'd known what he was about. And to wake to such a feeling… He'd been aware of her long before she'd ever touched her lips to his, but her silence, and her nearness, had rendered him immobile. He'd waited, wondering what she was about, knowing that she would never have been so bold had he been awake.

How he'd managed not to gasp himself when he'd felt the soft brush of her lips was astonishing. Never had any kiss affected him more.

When he'd stirred and asked what she was doing, he'd caught the embarrassed blush on her cheeks, the nervous and demure attitude as she avoided his gaze, and how tightly she clung to herself, as if to make her seem as small and insignificant as possible. Shy and retreating? His wife? It was hardly fathomable, and yet the evidence had been before him. And her revelations only a few hours before had proved to him that she was not so changed as he had once thought. She had never fully been the creature he had so detested. The thrill of pleasure at that knowledge was potent indeed.

Stripped of artifice, innocent as in years past, his wife had admitted to wanting to know what it would be like to kiss him.

What had transpired then had seemed a dream to him. He had to kiss her himself, and properly at that. He could not let her think that simple contact, stirring as it was, would be all there was. He had to taste her, to know if the lips he had so often dreamed of were as fine and delectable as he'd always wondered.

Now he had done...

What was one to do when one's reality far outstripped one's imagination?

How was he to keep from kissing her at every opportunity?

He leaned his head against the door, inhaled slowly, and exhaled the same. Control... He must find the control he had cultivated so carefully for years. Rather than fighting a creature he loathed, he must protect against a woman he wanted. Was he strong enough for that?

He had to be. He *had* to be. For a time, at least, he must have restraint. He was not prepared for this, not ready for the change in her.

And yet...

There was a knock at the very door he was leaning against, jolting him out of his dismal reverie. He stepped back and adjusted his waistcoat, ran a smoothing hand over his hair, and opened the door.

Reynolds was outside and bowed. "Mr. Jennings is here, sir, and says he would meet with you at your convenience."

Ah, work would be a most pleasant distraction right now. He could quite easily turn his mind to matters of business, and most efficiently address any difficulties.

At the moment, he could have climbed the highest peaks in Switzerland without feeling the least bit fatigued.

"Bring him here, Reynolds," Kit ordered with a firm nod. "We have matters to attend to."

"Yes, sir. And sir? Erm... your jacket? Or cravat?"

Kit looked down at himself and realized how he looked, but oddly enough, he found he did not care. He shook his head and met his butler's surprised look. "I think not. Jennings is a country man himself, we need not stand on ceremony."

"Very good, sir."

Kit exhaled slowly as the butler left, and shook his head as if to rid himself of thought. Kit Gerrard receiving an associate dressed as he was? The world would stand still in shock.

Fighting a hint of a smile, he glanced out of the window and caught a glimpse of Marianne wandering through the garden. A shiver raced up his spine and he wrenched his gaze away, moved behind his desk, and sat, taking great pains to reign himself back in, restore his right mind, and find some particle of sense.

He could withstand her. He could be friends with her and not drive himself mad.

He could.

When she had exhausted the gardens, Marianne turned her attention to the village, having been told that Kit had entered a meeting with Mr. Jennings and would not be done for some time. It was a quaint little town, and she saw a number of their tenants while she ventured into shops and along the cobblestone.

It occurred to her as she returned home that she'd not even considered changing out of her dress when she had known she would be out in public. She'd simply donned a spencer and bonnet, fetched a footman and the coach, and been on her way. It never crossed her mind that she might not look like the wealthy landowner's wife she was. But as she considered herself upon reentering the house, she thought she had done quite well enough anyway.

"I heard you went into the village," called a warm voice.

Marianne turned as she handed her bonnet off, and smiled when she saw Kit ambling towards her easily, no trace of awkwardness at all. She brushed a strand of hair away from her face and unbuttoned her spencer. "I did, and you were right, it's a delightful little place."

He smiled and leaned against the marble stairs. "You went alone?"

She raised a brow. Really, who did he think she was going to go with? There were hardly friends to call upon here to accompany her. "Yes. Well, no, I made Thomas go with me."

Kit shook his head slowly. "Poor Thomas."

Marianne rolled her eyes, smiling. "It was hardly so bad. We spent most of our time conversing with tenants and shopkeepers."

"And which shops did you like best?"

She shrugged out of her spencer and handed it to the maid with a smile. "Well, the milliner had some lovely things that I did not expect to see outside of London, and the modiste was quite as skilled as anything I could find on Bond Street, but I hardly needed anything from either of them."

He smiled at her warmly. "The bank will be delighted to hear it."

She smirked in response and rubbed her hands together to warm them. "The confectioner's shop was rather delightful, and he insisted I sample several things at no charge. I don't know that I shall be able to eat supper at this point." She grinned at the memory and looked up at him. "Your sisters will run ragged over him when they come and stay with us here."

His face became slightly arrested, and then eased back into the warm smile that had become her favorite thing. He looked far too pleased with her statement for her comfort, and yet she craved more of the same.

She had to look away, and chose her fingers for an intense study. "Other than that, I mostly explored the area. I had several small tour guides willing to show me all the fascinating, and some not so fascinating, details."

He chuckled softly. "I bet they did."

She glanced back at him with a hint of a smile. "I did buy a book though."

He looked rather impressed and folded his arms. "Did you indeed? What, pray tell, warranted the pleasure of being your purchase?"

"The last book by Miss Austen," she retorted with a sniff,

clasping her hands behind her and taking a meandering path towards him. "It has been out for some years now, but I have never gotten around to reading it. And Mr. Henderson gave me quite a good price."

Kit snorted and shook his head. "That woman's work will give women an unrealistic expectation of men in general."

Marianne bit back a grin and nodded sagely. "Too right, and it's about time someone held you all to a higher standard."

He looked playfully shocked, and pushed off of the stairs. "Oh, really?"

She tilted her head back to look at him with a teasing smile. "Yes, really."

He gazed down at her, smiling in his eyes and on his lips, and he gently touched the line of her jaw, tracing it down to her chin. She nearly shivered at the contact, and forced herself to remain still beneath his fingers.

"And what if I rose to that higher standard?" he asked in a very low voice that made her heart skip a beat. "What if…?"

An insistent pounding at the front door interrupted him, and Marianne had never been so inclined to curse in her entire life. Kit looked much the same and she leaned forward to rest her head against him. They were so close to something…

Reynolds answered the door and had to almost jump back as the impatient rider burst into the house. "Mr. Gerrard?" he asked the butler, panting and covered in travel dust.

"Here," Kit said with firm command, stepping forward.

The rider swept of his hat and handed a note from his pocket to him.

Marianne took in the state of the lad, surely no more than twenty, and wondered if she ought to offer him something. What was a mistress of the house supposed to do for an express rider? Send him to the inn down in the village? Some protocols she just could not remember, no matter that she ought to have.

Kit sighed heavily and nodded. "Very well. Thank you for your speed. Please, go on down to the village to the inn, and have yourself a hot meal and a room, if you like. Tell the innkeeper I have sent you."

"Thank you, sir," the lad replied with a relieved smile, bowing to him, then to Marianne as well, before sweeping back out, leaving Reynolds to shake his head at the dust that had settled in the hall.

Kit turned slowly to face Marianne, his expression a bit dark.

A jolt of concern hit her somewhere below her ribs. "What is it? Is something wrong?"

Kit shook his head and a reluctant smile formed. "Not really, no. In fact, it should probably be regarded as excellent news."

The discrepancy between his words and his expression confused her and she folded her arms. "Tell me, then."

"Susannah's pains have started."

Marianne's brows shot up in surprise. "Colin sent you a missive about that?"

"He's very nervous."

That did not surprise her at all, given Colin's manner and excessive devotion to his wife. She tried not to laugh. "Doesn't he remember that she has done this before?"

Kit seemed to be having the same trouble restraining himself. "Yes, but he was not there for that, so it doesn't count. I daresay the physician will have to tend to him just as much as he does Susannah." He looked down at the note and exhaled again. "I suppose I must be off soon. I could make it to Amberley before dawn if I push hard."

"Surely the baby will already be born by now," she said, taking the note from him, looking for some indication of time. "If this was sent this morning, surely…"

"Apparently, Susannah takes quite a while," Kit replied with an uncomfortable clearing of his throat. "With Freddie, it was nearly two days."

Marianne blanched and put a hand to her throat. "Good lord…" Then she shook her head, smiling. "Colin will be dead before you get there."

Kit barked a laugh and started for the stairs. "Undoubtedly. I'll be just a moment, don't go anywhere."

Within a few minutes, he was back down in fresh clothing, appearing perfect and pristine, as he was every day in London. And appearing just as untouchable. He hardly looked like the man who had kissed her so thoroughly mere hours ago, and impossibly, she felt her old defenses rising to the surface.

But then he saw her, and he smiled.

And just like that, her knees quivered and her breath caught and her walls came tumbling down.

"You didn't actually have to stay in the same spot," Kit told her as he came down, nodding at the nearest footman, who then went out to the stables.

Marianne couldn't resist smiling at him, shrugging a little. "I didn't. I walked the entire perimeter of the room a time or two, and you are quite right."

He cocked his head, looking amused. "About what?"

"The statues. They're dreadful."

He grinned and glanced at the nearest one. "I'm sure someone somewhere is very proud of them, but they hardly lend themselves to much praise, in my opinion."

Marianne snickered and shook her head. "No, indeed, nor in mine. I think I shall get rid of them after all."

"I wondered if you were keeping them to spite me."

"Of course I was."

He reared back in shock at the simplicity of her answer, then laughed heartily. "Why?"

She grinned and stepped closer to him, her fingers itching to toy with the buttons on his coat. "You glared so fiercely every time you saw them, and you started to develop a tick in your right eye whenever you walked through the great hall. How could I resist that?"

Kit's smile faded into something warm and almost tender, and he reached up to cup her cheek. He said nothing, but his eyes searched hers with an intensity that stole her breath and had her leaning closer, laying her cheek more fully into his hands, her own hands finding their way to his coat after all.

His lips parted as if he wanted to say something, but no words came out. His brow furrowed, and his fingers curved slightly against her skin.

"What?" she asked softly, curling her fingers into his coat.

"This is mad," he half-whispered. "I'm about to ride across two counties as fast as I can to attend my brother while he waits for the birth of his child. He'll be surrounded by friends, all of us men who can do nothing but wait with him. It makes no sense, and yet..."

She smiled a little and nudged him softly. "Yes, it is mad, but you would be mad *not* to do it. He's your twin brother, and you have to go. Go, and then come back and tell me everything."

He stared at her for a long moment, his hand settling more firmly against her face. He shook his head ever so slightly. "Don't change while I'm gone," he murmured.

She jerked a little in surprise, then smiled up at him. "Into what? I'll be here all alone, so unless Mr. Reynolds and Mrs. Dinstable corrupt me…"

That produced a faint smile. "I wouldn't put it past them." Then his smile faded and the furrow returned, and he could not seem to find the words he wanted.

But she understood. They had both changed so much, and so quickly, it seemed. They hardly knew who they were at any given moment, let alone who the other was. But the last few days had been fairly perfect, and if he were gone for a while… If she changed… Or if he did…

She was afraid of it, too. But she could promise him one thing.

She tugged on his coat a little. "I promise that the wife you leave is the wife you will return to." She smiled at the relief she saw in his eyes, and gave an impish wink. "Perhaps even a little better."

"Better?" he asked with disbelief, his eyes twinkling. "How so?"

"Well, absence supposedly makes the heart grow fonder. You'll likely think better of me for having not seen me."

Kit nodded thoughtfully in understanding. "You think I'll miss you."

She gave him a wry little smile. "Won't you?"

He smiled, but said nothing. He leaned forward and gently pressed his lips to her forehead, lingering a while. "Don't change," he whispered against her skin.

She inhaled a shaky breath and gave the barest hint of a nod.

Somehow staying in contact with her skin, his lips moved down to the corner of her mouth, and pressed the gentlest of kisses there. His fingers brushed her cheek tenderly, and then she was slowly, and very reluctantly, set back from him.

Her eyes fluttered open and caught sight of his face, handsome and warm and studying every feature as if she would not be here when he returned. Then he smiled, nodded, and turned from the house.

Marianne followed on unsteady feet and leaned against the door as she watched him mount his horse. He saw her there and waved, grinning when she returned it. Then he turned towards the road and galloped away very fast, looking effortless and powerful all at once.

Unable to keep from smiling as she watched him, a rather fluttering sigh escaped and she settled more heavily against the doorframe.

If that was goodbye, whatever would he do for hello?

Her smile broadened and her heart pattered in anticipation. Hope was alive and well within her, and ready to burst into flame at the slightest encouragement.

Chapter Seventeen

"A daughter."

"Yes, so you've said."

"It's a girl."

"That would follow, yes."

"I haven't the faintest idea what to do with a girl."

Kit shook his head and rubbed at his eyes, grinning. "Colin, you've spent quite a long time with our sisters, I think you can manage a girl of your own."

His brother rolled his head to look at him blearily, striving for his usual sardonic glare. "A daughter is not a sister, Kit, and you know what a muck I've made of the girls."

Kit snorted and took a drink of the brandy before him. He'd already drunk too much, but not nearly as much as Colin had. Colin had been so anxious for the entire duration of Susannah's labor and progression that his friends had plied him with the stuff, and still he had not been himself. When the word had come of the successful and healthy delivery of a daughter, and of Susannah's own health and safety, Colin had sunk into a chair and sobbed like a child. Only after he had calmed himself would he go and see his wife and daughter, and he'd stayed for hours, leaving Kit with his friends.

"Is that a normal response?" Kit had asked them with a wry smile.

That had prompted stories of their own reactions, some of which were far more amusing than he had expected.

Colin was away for most of that day, tending to his wife and child, and probably making himself quite a nuisance. Kit had spent the time with his sisters and nephew, once the guests had departed for Nathan's estate only a few miles away. They'd come back the day after for more visiting and well-wishes, and the ladies had wanted to check on Susannah, as well as spoil the other children in the house, much to their delight and Kit's hesitation. But he was assured that it was their duty, and he really had no choice in the matter.

The children were all in lessons now, some attempt at reestablishing normalcy, and Colin had descended from the upstairs rooms with a peculiar sort of grin and said that he desperately needed a drink with his brother, and here they had sat for the last hour, at least.

Kit shook his head as he looked at his brother once more. "You've not made a muck of anything, Colin. We have delightful sisters, and between the pair of us, we do a fair job of raising them."

Colin considered that, then leaned his head back and squeezed his eyes shut. "I'm a father, Kit."

That drew a smile from him. "God help that poor thing," he muttered good-naturedly, to which his brother merely held out his glass for Kit to clink with his own. "She's a pretty lass, if I do say so myself."

"The most beautiful child on the face of the earth," Colin announced with an imperious finger in the air. "No matter what Derek or Kate have to say on the subject."

"And you know," Kit said slowly, swirling his brandy carefully, "you already were a father."

Colin opened his eyes and looked over at Kit in confusion, then his expression cleared and a warm smile spread. "Yes... yes, I was, wasn't I?" He laughed softly and sipped from his glass. "Freddie. There's a lad after our hearts for you. He's got your brains and honor, yet my knack for mischief and fun. He'll either become Prime Minister, or a pirate captain. And he'll do a fine job of either. Perhaps both."

Kit chuckled and sat back in his chair, looking up at the painting that hung above the mantle. "He's a fine lad. He'll do you proud."

"Aye, he will. And he's already asking when he can read to Olivia." Colin grinned and shook his head. "I love him as if he truly were mine, Kit. No father could be prouder of his son." He bit his lip for a moment, his brow furrowing in thought. "I don't think I really understood until now. Seeing Olivia, knowing that she is mine… It changes a man, Kit. I never even dreamed what this would feel like. I'm destined to be a much better father to Freddie for feeling what Olivia has brought me." He shook his head and leaned it back once more. "And if she's half as pretty as her mother, I will have a devil of a time in about sixteen years."

"She'll have Susannah's wit and intelligence, too, if God is merciful," Kit reminded him ruefully. "That will save her a lot of trouble."

"Or give me more."

"Well, if she needs some help, I am sure her uncle Derek will prove quite a powerful ally."

Colin shuddered and downed the last of his drink. "He'll be a duke by then. Can you imagine?"

Kit actually could, but he thought it best to keep silent about that.

"How is Marianne?"

He couldn't keep from jerking a little at the sudden question, somehow managing to feel guilty being asked about her. "What?" he asked sharply, his voice several notches too high.

Colin gave him a curious, slightly devious look. "Do you normally look like a poorly behaved schoolboy when asked about your wife?"

Kit glowered and sat forward, setting his glass on the table nearest them. "No."

Colin smiled briefly. "So how is she? Well, I presume, as you are alive."

"She is very well. She is…" He trailed off, wondering how he could possibly describe what exactly his wife was now. He'd thought of her a thousand times at least since being here, wondering what she was doing, how she fared, remembering how she'd looked when he left, curious if she missed him… Something about seeing his niece, holding her in his arms, had tugged at something in his heart, and he wanted Marianne by his side at that moment more fiercely than he'd wanted anything in his life. Bitty had even asked him about "Mrs. Kit" and if he thought she'd like her new dress, and he'd fumbled his way through an answer, which apparently had delighted her.

Marianne had told him before she was not particularly fond of children. Could that change?

He'd never thought himself particularly partial to them before his sisters had dropped into his lap, but now everything was different. Suddenly he wanted what his brother had, was envious to an untold degree. He wanted to be a father.

Could Marianne experience the same change?

"I've lost you, haven't I?"

Kit shook himself and looked back over at his brother with a half smile. "Sorry."

"Don't be," Colin said with a slow shake of his head and a bit of a smirk. "I enjoy seeing you like this. It's not often you look so completely lost and indecisive. I like it."

Kit groaned and rubbed his hands over his face, then glanced at Colin. "Things are complicated. With Marianne."

"I rather expected they might be."

Colin's drollness made him laugh and he shook his head. "Not in the way you think, actually. The last week… perhaps two, have been quite enlightening."

"You've only been there three, how could two of them be so illuminating for you?"

Kit shrugged and attempted to explain things to Colin, without giving him too many details. Colin was really only seven years of age and would not properly handle the information. But he could tell him about the horse racing and their dealings with the tenants and the statues and the music room, about their times reading in the library, about Marianne's unfortunate incident in the rain, about his venture to save Fanny Hayes, and then, quite suddenly, he was talking about how Marianne had changed. How *he* had changed. How it was harder and harder to find fault with her, how much fun he was having… well, having fun with her. And how he'd found himself confiding in her without fear or resistance.

"I don't know what happened, Colin," he said with a hoarse whisper. "I don't know what *is* happening. All of a sudden, I'd rather be home than anywhere else. I know who and what she is, I always have, but it suddenly doesn't matter anymore. Or, at least, it's mattering less and less."

"You like your wife."

The soft murmur from his typically ebullient twin caught him off-guard, and he had to fight the tightness in his chest. "You know how I feel about her, Colin," he scolded with a derisive shake of his head.

Colin sat up and was also shaking his head, but he also bore a soft smile that Kit did not like. "You have loved her, yes. You have hated her, and you have hated that you love her. You loved her with such single-mindedness that you've forgotten to even like her." Colin tilted his head a little, letting the smile spread, as if something amused him greatly. "Now you are enjoying the great privilege of both. When the passion in your heart combines with the friendship you treasure… real friendship, separate and distinctive from all of the romance and flowers and madness… that is when the beauties of life truly unfold before you."

Kit stared at him in awe for a moment. He *did* like his wife. Very much. And he had not liked her in years, and certainly never while he had been in love with her. And now… now…

He shook his head, then cleared his throat and took a swift drink from his glass. "I still don't know if I can stand her," he muttered.

Colin laughed once and sat back again. "Yes, well, that comes with it, right up until you accept it and just enjoy it."

"It's too soon to trust it," Kit said with a wince. "I may go back to Glendare and find her completely changed."

An echo from two nights ago came back to him. Her face in his hand, her eyes warm and bright, telling him that she wouldn't change. She knew his fears before he ever had to voice them. Their friendship, their… attraction, dare he call it, was too fresh, too new, and what if it slipped through their fingers?

"I promise that the wife you leave is the wife you will return to… Perhaps even a little better."

He could hardly imagine better. He barely comprehended the wife he had now, but if she was willing to try for it, he would encourage it.

With open arms.

Wide open.

Suddenly, he didn't want to be sitting in his brother's drawing room, comfortable and content with brandy in his hand. He wanted to be at home with his wife. He actually wanted to ride the mad distance across two counties to see her, to tell her everything, and hear her laugh when he told her of the girls' antics, of Colin's behavior, of Susannah's droll wit... She would love every detail, and he had to commit them all to memory. The way he presented them would be just as important as the details themselves, and he'd never been a particularly good storyteller. Still, there was time enough for that.

"I would pay an absolute fortune to know what is going on in your head right now," Colin said, shaking his head and grinning like a cat with a bowl of cream.

Kit raised a sardonic brow and grinned. "I am not inclined to let you know."

Colin's face changed in an instant to surprised delight. "Bravo, Kit, you look positively wicked at the moment. There's hope for you after all."

"That makes one of us, then," he muttered as he drained his glass. "I think I'll be heading back to Glendare now."

"Already?" Colin laughed. "You've only been here less than two days, what's put you in such a rush?"

Kit rose and gave his brother a knowing look. "Time, Colin. And too much brandy. Your wife will have to wring you out before you'll be of any use to her."

"She's abed for the rest of the week, at least," he retorted. "She'll be fine."

"It's Susannah. She'll eat you alive."

Colin shuddered delicately. "Says the man who's married to Marianne."

And for the first time in his life, Kit grinned at that.

Colin's eyes widened and he sat up eagerly. "One question before you go. Does your wife still come to breakfast *sans* proper attire?"

Kit folded his arms and smirked a little. "I am not telling you."

A slow smile crossed his brother's face. "You just did. And I can see you are no longer shocked by it."

"No."

"Good heavens…" Colin breathed slowly, eyes widening further still. "You don't even care anymore."

Kit fought a smile and shrugged. "Not particularly."

"You enjoy it, don't you?" Colin hinted with a devious grin.

"I am leaving now," Kit announced as he turned on his heel, striding from the room.

"It's perfectly natural, you know!" Colin called after him. "A man should enjoy seeing his wife in all states."

"Goodbye, Colin," he retorted over his shoulder. He couldn't help but grin as he strode from the house at a rather easy lope, going to the stables himself rather than waiting for his horse to be readied for him. The sooner he could be off, the better. Colin would make his excuses to his sisters, and things were so brilliantly confusing at Amberley at this moment, anything would be permitted.

He could make it home tonight. Very late, but he could.

Home. What a peculiar idea. He hadn't had a true home in years.

He would have laughed had he not been suddenly breathless.

And there was a bit more quickness to his step as he neared the stables.

Marianne couldn't sleep. She had spent two days refinishing every room that was left, visiting every tenant she had not yet managed to, read four books, and played hours of the pianoforte, and still she couldn't manage to fully occupy herself. She was filling her days with more activity and occupation than she had in her entire life, but still it was not enough.

Still she lay here, entirely awake and alert, and entirely unsatisfied.

She knew what the problem was, of course. She'd known it the very first night.

She missed Kit.

Which seemed all too bizarre a thought. She'd gone ages without Kit before. She'd gone days without him even while they'd been here without any sort of twinges.

But that was before she actually enjoyed having Kit around. Before he'd become a fixture in her days.

Before he'd kissed her.

She groaned and buried her face into her pillow. She was going to become completely addled if she kept this up. Imagine centering one's days and life around a single person! What a waste of time and energy! And yet, here she was, unable to sleep for the wandering nature of her thoughts, and the dissatisfaction with her days. What else could she do?

She rolled over and flung the heavy bedcovers off of her with a dejected sigh. She would just have to do what she had done the last two nights, and read in the library until she could not keep her eyes open.

If she kept this up, she would get through all of the novels in the Glendare library before they returned to London, and what would Kit have to say then?

She grinned and clambered out of bed, fetching Kit's thick dressing gown that she had purloined from his room two nights ago. It was warm and comfortable, and it smelled like her husband.

She inhaled softly as she wrapped it around her, smiling to herself.

What a girlish sort of fool she was.

With a nonchalant shrug, she tied the sash, took her candlestick from the bedside table, and quietly ventured out of her room. She hardly expected to meet anyone on her way, given she had gone to bed so very late, but late night escapades always seemed to require stealth in tread and manner.

The hallways were dark and vacant, as she expected, and her path towards the back stairs was virtually clear. It was nearly a straight line from them to the library, and the fire should still be burning well enough there for decent light.

Encouraged by the ease of her way, she hurried a little faster down the hall.

She reached the top of the stairs and started quietly down the massive set, only to hear a faintly echoing set of steps from somewhere beneath her. The servants had long been abed, and they had their own stairs to use, which led exactly where any of them would wish to go. Why should anyone approach the back stairs, particularly so late at night?

She hesitated nearly halfway down the stairs and pressed herself against the wall, hoping to see a little better this way, and held her candle up higher.

A strong hand came into sight first as it grasped the railing of the bottom stairs before the first turn, and then a dark head with tousled, windswept hair. He trudged up the stairs wearily, and seemed unaware of the light, or her presence. Then he came fully into view as he turned on the landing and raised his head, squinting a little in the candlelight.

"Kit!" Marianne gasped, grinning broadly.

A tired smile spread across his face and he ventured up the stairs towards her. "Marianne."

She lowered the candle to the steps behind her and folded her arms, leaning back against the wall once more. She looked him over with a cursory eye, taking in the lines on his face, the disarray of his clothing, the weariness in his body, and shook her head. "You look terrible."

He laughed low and leaned against the wall a few steps below her. "I feel terrible, come to think of it. The ride is not nearly so pleasant at breakneck speeds on horseback." He tilted his head back against the wall and sighed. "But it is good to be home at last."

Her heart gave a faint little leap at his words, for she, too, thought of this as home. "How is everyone?" she asked quietly.

He smiled again and tugged at his wilting cravat, loosening it and pulling it out completely. "Very well, and they all send you their best. Bitty has a new dress she thinks you'll approve of, and asked me at least a dozen times if I thought you would."

Marianne smiled and shook her head. While she might not know anything about Rosie, and may never, given the girl's temperament, Bitty was the sweetest, most endearing creature on the planet. They would have their hands full with her.

"The baby is healthy," Kit continued, brushing off the jacket over his arm, though his eyes stared ahead at nothing, "and in possession of some very powerful lungs. Given that Colin is the father, that is to be expected."

That drew a giggle from Marianne and she watched Kit with fondness. "And what is it?"

His smile grew soft and he looked up at her. "A girl. They've decided to name her Olivia Eloise."

"For your mother?" she asked, remembering how fondly everyone had spoken of the late Eloise Gerrard, Lady Loughton. When they recollected her.

He looked surprised, and nodded. "Yes. How did you know?"

"You told me once," she replied with a faint switch of her hand. "What does she look like?"

"She's two days old. She looks like an infant."

Marianne rolled her eyes and snorted. "Kit… Who does she favor, Colin or Susannah?"

He shook his head, his smile turning quizzical. "I have no idea. By the time I see her again, she'll be more in possession of features to determine that. Right now, she looks like a new infant. Though she does have some pert little lips, and fairly rosy cheeks, and a very fine head of thick, black hair."

"All Gerrard, then," she murmured, her smile warming at the thought. "I am glad to hear it. I'd never put much thought into what those features would look like on a girl, though I doubted they would suit. But having seen your sisters, my doubts are unfounded. They are beautiful girls, and I have no doubt Miss Olivia will be quite as pretty as her aunts." She chuckled and paused in thought. "Livvy Gerrard? Good heavens, we've quite the stock of nicknames, haven't we?"

Kit was watching her with apparent interest, a faint smile on his lips. "How so?"

"Freddie, Rosie, Bitty, Ginny, and now Livvy, if they choose to call her such." She shook her head. "Adorable names, all. And you, sir, are Kit and never Christopher. We shall have to think of some clever names for our children. At least one of them should have a name that cannot be shortened."

She did not miss the slight stiffening of Kit's frame, nor how his breathing had gone still. Perhaps it was too soon to talk about children, but it seemed almost appropriate now.

Pretending she had not seen, she continued. "I rather like the Gerrard features, come to think of it. I would not mind if all of the children took after you. The girls would be quite pretty, and the boys would be very handsomely featured. I'll have quite a bit of trouble with the lot of them, being so attractive, and no doubt witty as well. Perhaps none of them will take after me, and I can't find anything wrong with that. Imagine smaller versions of me running about." She shuddered and grinned playfully. "I do hope at least one of them is a little plain. I think it would do her a world of good, and I'd love her better for it."

She fell silent as she looked at Kit again. He had gone completely still and his expression was perfectly arrested. Gone were the lines and strain of the day, gone was all sign of weariness or fatigue. He was thriving with energy, and the sight of such intensity in her direction was enough to steal her breath.

She swallowed with difficulty. "H-how is Colin?" she half-whispered, suddenly desperate for a more comfortable topic.

Kit blinked at the change, but he did not move, nor did his expression alter. "Colin is still half-drunk," he murmured, one side of his mouth finally giving way to a small smile, "but I think his bliss will far outlast his hangover." His eyes lowered in thought. "I've never seen him so at ease, and it had nothing to do with the drink. He's so... contented. I didn't think he could become more so after his marriage, but he's changed again. He is more, somehow."

"More Colin?" Marianne murmured with wry amusement. "God save us."

A low chuckle escaped Kit and he looked back up at her with a smile. "I saw this part of him when he adopted Freddie, and we've all seen the change since the girls, but..." He shrugged and shook his head a little. "I can't explain it, I've tried all day. And I find that I am..."

"Envious," she whispered, hugging herself more tightly.

His gaze sharpened on her. "Yes. Exactly."

She nodded, all too familiar with the sensation. When her brother and Annalise had Tillie, she had felt something stir in her. Nothing she could have identified then, she was far too proud and set in her ways, but now she could freely admit a pang of longing when she had held that darling child in her arms, when she had seen the indescribable joy in her sister-in-law's face, how tenderly Duncan had seemed to worship Annalise and his daughter… So many things that had never occurred to her to want.

And now…

Now…

"And Susannah is well?" she asked faintly, no longer looking at him, feeling unable to.

"Perfectly. She was a little put out that I did not bring you with me."

Marianne made a soft noise of amusement and tucked a strand of hair behind her ear. "She shouldn't worry about such things at a time like this. Perhaps we might go for a visit soon, when she is more recovered."

"Yes, that would be lovely."

"I want to see Susannah, and to try to make amends. I want to be her friend, and I want to hold Olivia, and I want…" She broke off as she realized she was rambling, and had been nearly about to confess all sorts of things she wanted, none of which should dare to be spoken aloud yet.

"What do you want?" Kit asked very quietly, his tone low and rumbling.

Something in his voice was doing strange and delightful things to her, and the effect was disconcerting. "Did you notice the great hall when you came in?" she asked quickly, feeling her cheeks heat.

His voice did not change in the slightest. "I did, and I was delighted by the new amount of space. Ten statues gone, but not the other two? Are you fond of them?"

She giggled and ventured a glance at him. "I thought you might feel the need to hit one of them with something sometime. Perhaps when I have driven you to a breaking point."

He tilted his head in consideration, his eyes and expression all warmth, and dare she call it tenderness? But with an underlying tension that sent her pulse racing. "How very considerate of you, but I hardly need two."

She smiled and shook her head slowly. "No, the other is for me. When I need to hit something. For when you drive me to my breaking point. One good swing and who knows what damage will occur? Perhaps we should have a contest to see who can completely demolish their temper statue first. It may take us several months, given their weighty mass and size, but I think…"

"You're wearing my dressing gown."

Marianne's voice faltered to a halt at his low interruption and her eyes widened even as her breath caught in her chest. So she was, but she had completely forgotten about it, and now she was standing here before him in it. Mortified, she ducked her head. "Yes," she replied as softly as she could.

"Why?" His query was just as soft as her reply, and full of some unspoken emotion that she felt surrounding them both.

"It's warmer than mine," she murmured, her suddenly shaking fingers moving to push another lock of hair behind her ear. "And it's thicker, softer, better quality…" She didn't have to look at him to know he was waiting, that he knew there was more to it than that. She closed her eyes and turned her face away as her cheeks heated. "And it smells like you. I… I missed you."

She was suddenly, and forcefully, pushed back against the wall with a gasp, as Kit bracketed her with both arms and his body. His breath snagged in his throat as his mouth found her hairline, and there he waited, each frantic pant of breath sending fire racing across her skin.

He smelled of road and sweat, and of brandy, and through the sudden fog of her emotions she wilted a little at the implication of that. "Kit," she gulped anxiously, "are you drunk?"

He shook his head almost imperceptibly, his lips moving just enough against her skin to give her answer. His body trembled and she felt an echoing tremble course through her, drawing with it all ability to breathe.

"Kit?"

With sharp exhale, his mouth moved to her ear and he leaned a little more against her. "Don't talk," he rasped, scorching the rim and lobe of her ear. "Don't think." His lips slowly danced down the side of her neck, wringing another potent shiver from her. "Don't say anything…"

The button at her throat was suddenly popped open, and Marianne gasped as Kit's clever mouth found the frantic beating of her pulse there. She had never felt more raw or exposed than she was now, yet she was perfectly covered and decent. But this was no mere matter of fabric or skin, this was far, far deeper.

She felt herself arching her neck as he lingered there, his mouth drifting back up towards her jaw. She was lost and falling, wandering in all the sensations he was provoking. And suddenly, it was not enough. Suddenly, she wanted more.

A hoarse moan rose within her and her hands, once trapped against his chest, now rose and slid themselves forcefully into his hair, tangling in the sweat-dampened chestnut locks. She tugged his face up and fused her mouth with his, straining upwards against him, sighing in relief when one of his arms locked around her and helped her to meet him.

Her pulse heightened, her toes curled and flexed, and there was no need for air, or thought, or anything else in the world but Kit. He was a man lost to everything, wild and frantic, yet so focused and intense, it consumed them both. His passion fueled hers, his need gave hers voice, and a clawing, clamoring ache was swiftly and steadily rising within her. Something only he could soothe.

She whimpered as his mouth left hers to play at her throat again. She toyed with his hair, holding him to her, eyelids fluttering as she was awash in a sea of sensations and feelings. Her skin was aflame, her lungs scorched with each breath, and her legs shook wildly beneath her.

"Kit," she managed to gasp as he found a particularly sensitive spot below her right ear, eliciting a sharp shiver from her.

Somehow, that broke through his haze, and he froze. His mouth lifted just enough to no longer touch her skin, yet he made no move to leave her. His breathing slowed and steadied, and she felt the hand locked around her tighten into a fist, gathering the slightest bit of her nightgown with it. A slow tremor crossed his body, and slowly, agonizingly, he lifted his body away from her.

She exhaled a half-sob of disappointment.

Slowly, almost apologetically, he nuzzled against the last spot he'd kissed, then softly kissed her jaw. As if in a daze, he grazed his face and brow against hers, his lips brushing hers faintly, and then he was gone, trudging unsteadily up the stairs into the darkness, never once looking back or saying a word.

When she heard his bedchamber door close, her legs finally gave out on her and she sank to the stairs with a hoarse, "Whuff."

It was entirely dark now, her lone candle apparently having gone out, but she barely registered that fact.

She pushed her hair back from her face and clenched handfuls of hair at her neck, staring at nothing, willing her body to cease its onslaught of torment.

She swallowed several times, with great difficulty, staring off at nothing between the spindles of the stairs. Slowly, she drew in a long, shaking breath, then said, to the emptiness of the dark, "What the *hell* was that?"

Chapter Eighteen

What in the world had gotten into him?

It was probably the four hundredth time he'd asked himself that question since his unexpected attack on Marianne the night before, pressing her against the wall and treating her, for all intents and purposes, like some common doxy behind the closed doors of London's tasteful Society. He could not explain it. He had been neither drunk nor too fatigued to not account for his behavior.

He'd slept well enough, as exhaustion had overtaken him, and he'd completely slept through breakfast, which was unheard of and which he was disappointed about as he'd been looking forward to Marianne's usual breakfast ensemble. But the lack of such pleasures was good for him, and he'd spent the entire morning furiously castigating himself and worrying about what Marianne would say or do when he inevitably faced her again.

He was ashamed to admit that he had avoided her these last four hours, and he knew he would have to face her soon.

But how could he? She deserved so much more than his behavior last night, though she had responded rather delightfully.

He'd had a hard enough time focusing his thoughts while she had been so dressed, in that pure white nightgown and her hair loose and streaming about her shoulders, and wearing his dressing gown, remembering all too well the last time he had seen her in it, and all the pleasure he had forgone then. And when she had spoken of their children and admitted to missing him… Surely what happened could not have been helped.

But what good was his control if he could not exercise it over himself in her presence? That had been the whole purpose for his securing it, though it had proven useful and important in many other aspects.

How was he to begin to apologize to her?

He wandered out of his study and into the library, stunned to find Marianne within, lounging on a sofa and reading, looking as light and innocent as she ever had, one hand drawn up near her mouth with a finger absently trailing across her lips as she read.

He was as transfixed with her now as he had ever been, and he found he didn't want to apologize for last night. He rather wanted to repeat it. Perhaps tonight.

She smiled faintly at something she read and turned the page, and his hands tightened into fists at his side. Or now. He could repeat it now.

She looked up at him, and he could have blushed at the frank appraisal in her eyes. But she tilted her head, softly smiled, and said, "Are you coming in or aren't you?"

He forced himself to smile back and nodded, taking only a second to pick a random book from the shelf nearest him, knowing he would barely get a word read. He situated himself on the sofa opposite, and made a show of reading it. But every fiber of his being, every hair on his head, was attuned to her. He could count the breaths she took, noted the pages she turned, the subtle taunting he felt each time her finger passed over her lips. Could she possibly know what she did to him?

Seeing her like this, elegant and refined, reminding him of who she really was, started that flicker of guilt to flare once more. She hadn't turned pale or gone still at seeing him, but who was to say what lay beneath the surface? She could be mortified, embarrassed, confused...

He had to know. He had to understand how to proceed here.

"Marianne," he began reluctantly, almost timidly, keeping his eyes down at his book.

"Hmm?" she replied rather faintly, but with an edge of something that drew his gaze.

She was watching him with an air of amusement and fascination, as if he were a puzzle she were trying to solve. Her hand now rested against her cheek in a thoughtful pose, and her lips were curved in a half smile that was somehow secretive, seductive, and sweet.

Whatever he was going to say vanished in the face of such a look.

She raised a questioning brow even as her smile spread further still.

There was no apology needed, he realized a bit breathlessly. He might not know exactly what she thought, but she certainly wasn't upset with him.

He could live with that.

Frantically, his mind raced for another topic. "Have you heard from your friends in London?"

The slight tightening of her lips informed him that she was quite positive that was not the question he had initially devised, but she sighed a little and dropped her hand. "I have, actually. Lily wrote me last week, but I have not heard from her since. She is much occupied with her sister, who seems interested in Robert Kent, which I cannot believe. Gemma writes almost every other day, and she is desperate for me to return. It seems there is no one else of any interest to her. And she says she has something rather vital to tell me, but she cannot put it on paper." She shrugged mildly and rolled her eyes. "One can only imagine what that is." She returned to her book, shaking her head. "I swear, that girl is just another Tibby in the making, though perhaps more sensible."

Kit frowned in thought, uncomfortable with the idea of returning to London. That was the source of all their troubles. Marianne had never given him the faintest idea of wanting to return, but he knew how she had once adored the Season and all its ridiculousness.

"Has Miss Templeton given you any indication of events taking place in London?" he asked carefully, keeping his voice calm and polite.

Too familiar with that tone, Marianne stilled and looked up at him. "Not really," she said warily, "though most of the events do not start for another week or so. Nothing too important for a fortnight, perhaps. She mentions a musicale being held at Miranda Ascott's that she has been invited to perform at, but that's got a few weeks yet. Why do you ask?"

He exhaled slowly, measuring his breath. He owed it to her to be honest, if nothing else. "I was simply wondering if you were wishing to return to London. For the Season."

Her brow furrowed a little and she closed her book with a soft snap. She considered him again, her mouth pulling a bit, as if she gnawed gently on the inside. "To be perfectly frank and honest, yes," she replied simply and without passion. "I think I would like to go back, if the rumors have settled. But I hadn't given it that much thought."

His frown grew and an uneasy weight settled upon him. "Why?" he asked, his voice harsher than he intended. "After what we left for, why?"

Her brows rose in surprise and she tilted her head at him, no doubt confused. "I just said I hadn't given it that much thought."

He closed his eyes and fought for calm. This wasn't Marianne's fault, he could not lash out at her. And yet he could not pretend to be pleased. "When would you prefer to be in London?"

"Next week," she murmured softly, sounding hurt, "but it can wait until later."

Kit couldn't bear it. He nodded sharply and rose. "We will leave at the end of the week, then." He strode from the room, wincing a little as he made his way back to his study.

London could mean the return of the creature. It could uproot everything they had gained here. And he would know that the glorious vision of a woman he had grown so fond of remained somewhere inside of her, and how that would burn. He would ache for quite some time for the loss.

He sank into his chair and put his head into his hands, filled with dread for the possibilities ahead.

Hours later, forgoing dinner in favor of work, which had seemed mountainous in the face of a departure, Kit sat back with a groan. It had been an excellent diversion for him, but with time had also come sense.

He was being ridiculous. They had four days before his declared date of departure. Would he really waste what time remained wallowing in resentment for something that had not happened? There was no guarantee that she would change back. And what of her fears? Surely she would wonder about him, as he had always been silent and disapproving where she was concerned.

He didn't want to go back to the way they had been. He wanted her just as she was now. Warm and inviting, coy and playful, engaging and fascinating and enchanting, and the most beautiful being on earth. The woman he could make plans with instead of plan around.

He looked out of the window of his study, which allowed him a view of the gardens and the terrace, now lit with the evening torches. The night was clear, and stars were aplenty, but they were only a faint acknowledgement to him. He was far more focused on the solitary figure on the terrace, leaning against a balustrade, looking up at the sky and out across the expanse before her, where the faint lights from the village festival could be seen.

She was dressed elegantly, as usual, in a gown of deep midnight blue, with a cream shawl about her, but her hair was in a surprisingly loose style, though still upswept. It was, to his mind, the perfect representation of what she had been here. Still containing the form and shape of days past, but with an ease that provided movement, and inspired warmth. She was the same as she had always been, and yet not the same at all.

Any more than he had been the same Kit Gerrard.

He watched her for several moments, wondering at the smoothness of her expression, seemingly so at peace out in the night air, despite his outburst. He'd had no reports of her retreating to her room in distress, had heard no raging about in a high temper, and she bore no hint of strain in her features now.

He exhaled and turned from his office, down the hall and towards the glass doors leading out to the terrace. The night was cool, but pleasant, and he took a moment to observe Marianne. How could a woman contain so much grace in such a simple, unmoving state? Even when he had been furious with her, hated her, as Colin had put it, he could not deny that she was a graceful and elegant creature. But something about the way she was now, the turn of her neck and the way she leaned without appearing casual, the tilt of her chin...

He *couldn't* waste their last days here. Not while she was here, not while his heart raced at the sight of her, not when she brought smiles to his face and lightness to his life...

Not while he loved her.

He softly approached, but made enough of a sound with his tread to not startle her. "I'm sorry," he murmured before he came into her view. He exhaled sharply and fought the desire to run his hands into his hair. "I don't know what came over me, Marianne, and I apologize."

She half turned and looked at him, her eyes containing all the light of the torches and the stars within them, and she smiled softly. "I know."

His jaw dropped in shock. "You do?"

She nodded, still smiling. "I knew it the moment you left the room. You would seclude yourself for some time, perhaps the rest of the day, until you had been calm enough, or felt badly enough, to do something about it. But you needn't have fussed so, Kit."

He felt rather tossed about by her astute description of his behavior. "Really?"

She shook her head, folding her shawl around her a little more securely. "You hate London, Kit. You've always hated London. But your family is there, so you go. Well, this year they are not, so there is no reason why we should venture in."

He stepped closer and leaned his hip against the balustrade nearest her, facing her, and crossing his arms over his chest. "What do you mean?"

She sighed a little and a strand of hair dislodged in the breeze and danced faintly against her cheek. "We don't have to go to London, Kit. In fact, I've decided that we won't."

"But you love London," he reminded her rather brusquely.

She met his gaze steadily, no hint of resentment or distress anywhere in her features. "I do. Or rather, I did. And I've always loved the Season, silly as it seems, but I refuse to do something that is going to make you so unhappy just for my own personal gratification." Her brows suddenly rose and her lips turned into a quizzical smile. "Good heavens, did that just come out of my mouth? Who am I, and what have I done with the real Marianne?"

Kit barked a laugh and suddenly felt such ease and comfort that his course was clear before him. He reached out and pretended to fuss with her shawl, enveloping her more warmly within it. "It's kind of you to offer, Marianne, given your fondness for the flurry of London at this time," he murmured softly, his hands wandering to her upper arms and rubbing gently. He slowly shook his head. "But we will go, as I said, at the end of the week."

She tilted her head at him, eyes curious. "Are you certain? I am perfectly content to remain."

He pushed the errant lock of hair behind her ear and took the opportunity to stroke her cheek. "I am certain. I don't want you to miss something you love so much just because I am ill-favored towards it. Besides, we cannot hide away here forever."

He let his hands fall away and turned to lean his forearms on the terrace railing, looking out at the grounds and the night sky. Marianne did the same, settling close enough to him that their shoulders touched.

"True," she admitted on a heavy sigh, "though it is a sad thought. I know we will have to visit all of your estates, Kit, but I can't think any will truly be home but this."

He smiled softly and felt himself nodding. "I know. But you'd like Cheshire well enough. It's practically a castle. Surrey we already know you're destined to barely tolerate, though it might grow on you." Here he smirked at her soft snort of doubt. "Yorkshire you've seen, though I doubt you were paying attention. And there's still Aunt Agatha's house in Devonshire..."

Marianne gave him a look fraught with amusement. "You have a house in Somerset *and* Devonshire? That seems rather excessive."

He shrugged, smiling back. "My father loved the coast and had no fondness for the north. I believe Mother tried to convince him to get some Scottish property, but I don't think he ever did."

That drew a louder snort from Marianne. "I can get you a Scottish property quite easily, if you like. My cousins have been trying to get me up there for years."

"I've heard stories about your MacLaine relatives," Kit teased with a nudge. "Are they true?"

"My cousins are exactly what everybody thinks of when they speak of Highlanders," she said with a shake of her head. Then she sighed and grinned. "And we love them for it. They are completely incorrigible. You'd be torn between love and hate the entire time."

"Then maybe it is time we do get some Scottish property," he mused thoughtfully. "Family connections are always worth preserving, yes?"

She rolled her eyes and looked up at the stars for a moment. "May I ask you something?"

"Of course."

She glanced over at him, a slight furrow between her delicate brows. "How is it that your father, a lord with relatively little influence in the peerage, should have so many estates? I know that you and Colin have divided them amongst yourselves for care, but why so many?" She cocked her head and frowned in thought. "I've tossed it over and over in my mind, and I can't make sense of it."

"That's because there is no sense to it," Kit told her bluntly. "On his own, Loughton had an extensive fortune, the Devonshire house… that would be Aunt Agatha's, and the house in London. He married my mother, somehow managing to find both love and an heiress, and found a passion for estate management in the process. Not only that, but he was good at it. Between the pair of them, they could outshine a duke and duchess in their own way. And Loughton knew he would never go further in the peerage, so he could only grow in fortune and influence. They started buying estates, or building estates, wherever they fancied, hired talented and capable estate managers, and each became profitable and enviable, so they kept at it. I think they were in the process of procuring one in Norfolk when Mother passed away."

"What happened to her?" she asked softly, somehow inching even closer to him.

"Childbirth," he murmured, shaking his head. "We were supposed to have a sister, but she was a stillborn. Colin and I were seven, and we'd already decided that if it was a girl, we were naming her Catherine and calling her Cat." Kit suddenly found himself lost in memory, remembering those dark days, losing mother and sister all in one day. He'd snuck a glimpse of the baby before she'd been taken away, and that memory had haunted him. She'd been just like any other baby he'd ever seen, only somehow better.

"And what if the baby had been a boy?" Marianne pried gently, nudging him out of his sudden melancholy.

"Charles," he recollected with a smile. "We were rather fixed on all of us having names beginning with the same letter."

"Where were you all when this happened?"

"Cheshire. That's where they are buried."

He felt Marianne's hand slip into his, and the warmth from it washed over him. "Then our next estate visit is Cheshire," she said firmly. "I want to pay my respects to Lady Loughton and to Cat."

Kit smiled and tried to pretend there was not a lump in his throat. "We never actually named her. It's a simple enough grave, with only the word 'infant' on it."

She shook her head fiercely. "No, she's Cat, just as you boys planned. Aunt Catherine to the children, and the girls ought to be told about her. They can make flower wreaths for her and your mother." She looked at him with a smile that wrinkled the corners of her eyes. "And what became of the impending Norfolk estate?"

Kit shrugged and looked up at the stars, marveling at the woman beside him. "Loughton let it fall through. He lost his desire for everything after that."

"I can hardly blame him for that," Marianne murmured, "though it does seem rather beastly to abandon the two of you. He had not lost everything, and had much to remain for."

"Well, as he was, he wasn't any good to us, so it was far better that things occurred as they did. He managed to set up our inheritance and responsibilities with the solicitors before he left the country, so we were not completely neglected by way of fortune and situation, but Aunt Agatha may have pressured him into that one." He smirked and rubbed Marianne's hand in his. "We turned out all right."

She laughed softly and leaned her head on his shoulder. "Yes, I suppose you did. Do you ever think about the fact that you will be Lord Loughton someday?"

"Not particularly," he admitted with a slight wrinkle of his nose. "My duties won't be any more or less than what they are now, I will simply have to get used to being called 'my lord' all the time. I'll have to prove myself better than my father, but that shouldn't take long. But you will be a lady, you know, and no one remembers Lady Loughton, so you can do whatever you like with that."

She lifted her head and pursed her lips in thought. "I hadn't thought of that. Well, if we can bring respectability back to the title, it would certainly help the girls' future."

Kit squeezed her hand tightly, unable to put to voice the feelings that currently constricted his heart. He looked over at Marianne, whose gaze was fixed on the distant lights of the village festival with a soft sense of longing.

"It's the festival," he told her quietly. "Lord knows what they're celebrating now, but I have heard it's quite the spectacle."

"It would be," she murmured with a hint of a smile.

He hesitated a moment, looking down at their twined fingers. "It is not so late. I can take you down there."

Her smile turned wistful. "No, I think that shall have to wait for another time. Perhaps once we are better known and not quite the oddities we are. I think it would take away from the celebrations to see us and draw attention." She looked at him and her expression turned impish. "And you know how desperately I hate to draw attention."

He chuckled affectionately and couldn't help himself; he leaned forward and slowly, tenderly captured her lips with his. It could not have been more different from their frantic kisses the night before. These were slow, leisurely, gentle kisses that had nothing to do with passion or need. These were kisses for the unhurried lovers who had all the time in the world.

And at this moment, they truly did.

The next four days would be counted among Kit's favorites in the history of his life. His friendship with Marianne continued to blossom into something he treasured beyond words, to say nothing for their familiarity with displays of affection. Every kiss warmed him to the tips of his toes, and seemed to last a little longer. Nothing had delighted him more than the day before their last, when Marianne had boldly initiated a kiss in the library that had resulted in a few books being knocked from their shelves, and ended in stitches of laughter for them both.

One of the days they had walked to the shoreline together again, taking the time to explore it and enjoy the sounds and smells and all it had to offer. Marianne had been the picture of a perfect country lass, but as she had wandered along, without bonnet or finery, her hair whipping wildly about in the breeze despite her coiffure, she had never been lovelier. He would remember her thus for the rest of his life.

They paid calls to tenants together, explored nearly every nook and cranny of the house together, and had even slid down that most excellent railing, at Marianne's insistence. "Just so we can say we have," she'd told him with a childish gleam. "We can't let Colin have all the fun."

On this, the last day, they loaded into the carriage, having bid farewell to the servants and all who fell under their care. Marianne gazed out of the window, looking utterly forlorn as she stared up at the house, and only shifted her attention when Kit had joined her within. She raised a perfect brow in question, a smile tugging at one side of her mouth.

Kit shrugged and closed the door, leaning back against the cushioned seats. "I have no desire to ride my horse all the way back to London. He doesn't converse nearly as well as you do."

Marianne grinned swiftly and crossed her ankles on top of Kit's knees. "Well, well, my husband is determined to be useful today. I am quite amenable to that."

He laughed and slid her legs from him, though not before stroking them a little. "You, I know very well, will sleep the entire way, and don't bother pretending otherwise."

Marianne winked and turned to wave goodbye to the servants, all lined up for farewells. "Perhaps. But I had a thought, Kit."

"I am afraid to ask…" he drawled, folding his arms and waiting patiently.

She gave him a look and then became very interested in her gloves. "What would you say to not going directly to London?"

He gave her a bemused look that she couldn't see. "Where else would we go?"

"Amberley," she said softly, wincing just a little as she met his eyes.

He reared back. "You want to see Colin and Susannah?"

She nodded quickly. "But more than that. I… I want to see if they would let us take the children to London with us."

His mouth dropped open in shock.

She smiled broadly and then bit her lip. "I see you weren't expecting that. But I've thought about it, and Susannah can't have much rest with the whole brood running about, no matter how capable Mrs. Creighton and the staff is. You know Susannah, she'll be pushing herself too much and driving Colin mad trying to mother everybody. She ought to focus on herself and Olivia. And I need to know the children better, so why not bring them back to London with us?"

"And if they want to stay in Hampshire?" he asked, somehow finding his voice again.

She shrugged lightly and folded her hands in her lap rather primly. "Then, of course, they may stay. I've no intention of dragging them around if they are unwilling." Her smile turned devious and he was suddenly nervous. "But if I know Bitty, and I think I do, she will not want to pass up an opportunity to get an inside view of a real London Season with someone who knows how to do it. And Rosie will come to keep Bitty in line, and Ginny will follow wherever the others lead, so the only thing to decide, really, is if Freddie wants to come with his aunts or stay with his parents and sister."

Kit felt a smile slowly spread and he took in his wife with new appreciation. "You have thought this through, haven't you?"

She nodded once, looking far too pleased. "I can be quite devious when I put my mind to it."

"So can I," he murmured a little too roughly.

Marianne's eyes widened and she giggled nervously. "What are you thinking?"

"I'm wondering how much trouble it would be to kiss you senseless in a moving carriage."

Her laugh turned wild and she settled herself in the corner furthest from him. "You stay right there, Mr. Gerrard, and let me have my nap. It's a long drive, and you do not want to have me irritated further by lack of sleep."

"I think I could amuse you well enough to deal with it."

She covered her face with her hands as more laughter escaped. "Good lord, my husband has turned rake."

"Have not."

"Have too."

"Not yet."

Her hands dropped and she gasped in both shock and delight. "Christopher Gerrard!"

He winked and laughed, and continued to provoke her until they were both exhausted enough to finally doze off, still smiling.

Chapter Nineteen

$\mathcal{A}$s she had expected, Amberley was a very active sort of place, despite its tranquil outer appearance, and it was evident that the four very active children within ruled over all. Colin, for all his attempts, only made things worse, which was rather expected. No one believed his pretended authoritative persona, and he was soon dragged into the dispute as a participant rather than the mediator.

As all of this was taking place within full sight of the front door to Amberley, Kit and Marianne had a perfect few of the fracas. Kit had quietly asked housekeeper taking their things what the trouble was, and she had relayed what she could, but she had wisely decided to stay out of it.

It seemed the finer points of pall-mall were being disputed, as the Gerrard children had formed their own version of the game, and someone, it was not entirely clear who, had broken one of the more serious parameters. Whether it was an actual pall-mall rule or a Gerrard rule was also unclear, and Marianne watched with fascination as the children argued viciously, even the usually silent Ginny was red-faced and indignant. Colin looked utterly lost amidst the strife and his voice could be heard among the din of the others, though it was hardly a voice of reason.

Beside her, Kit heaved a long-suffering sigh and shook his head as he ventured into the melee.

"Can I fetch you some refreshment, Mrs. Gerrard?" the kind housekeeper asked as she took Marianne's bonnet and cloak, perfectly poised and acting as if this were a perfectly normal occurrence for the house.

Then again, perhaps it was.

Marianne smiled and said, "No, I thank you. If you might only tell me where I may find your mistress? I should like to visit with her."

The housekeeper smiled warmly. "She and the little lass are in her chambers, madam. I'd have a girl take you, but…"

"No need," Marianne interrupted gently. "There is quite enough to be getting on with. Give me the direction and I shall find it well enough."

The directions were given and Marianne made her way up the stairs, brushing at her skirts a little. She wasn't so dusty, but it was hard to avoid it even with the carriage. She perhaps ought to change, but she would rather not stand on ceremony for the moment, and she doubted Susannah would mind very much.

She took stock of the comfortably situated house, everything warm and cozy, perfect for raising a family destined to be a bit wild, yet it was all with enough finery to be admired, even if reluctantly by those with more elaborate tastes. There were windows in abundance, flooding the entire house with natural light and conflicting with the more gothic exterior delightfully. She would get a better look at the house in its entirety later, but thus far, she was quite impressed.

She reached Susannah's chambers and knocked softly, gaining entrance at once.

Susannah was reclining on the bed, her honey colored hair loose in long waves about her, dressed in a comfortable day dress, and still a little pale, but altogether looking well and whole. She grinned in delight at seeing Marianne there, and made to rise.

"No, don't you dare," Marianne scolded immediately, entering the room fully and closing the door behind her. "I will come to you."

Susannah lifted a brow and sat back with a grunt. "I *can* do things, you know. Colin has me practically confined in here, and I am likely to go mad from it."

"For once, I am in agreement with Colin," Marianne replied airily coming to the other side of the bed and sitting next to Susannah, taking her hand. "But don't you dare tell him."

Susannah laughed warmly and leaned her head back against the pillow.

"How are you?" Marianne asked her, squeezing her hand. "I

heard it was a rather long time for you."

"Yes, longer than even Freddie," Susannah said with a wrinkle of her nose, "and I never thought that was possible. But I am very well, truly. I tire easily and my sleep is frequently disturbed, as you can imagine," her blue-green eyes turned soft as she looked over at a nearby bassinet that Marianne had missed, "but my little angel makes it so hard to resent that."

Marianne could not take her eyes off of the bassinet. Her heart suddenly pounded with too much difficulty and her breath caught. She got to her feet awkwardly and made her way to it, unaccountably choked up by the dear little infant sleeping contentedly within. Wide eyes and delicate lashes rested upon round cheeks and above a pert little nose, and those perfect lips Kit had mentioned were parted ever so slightly as faint puffs of air raced passed them. Her hair was dark, but it was too soon to say if that would be her actual color. She hoped it was. A darling little dark-haired girl with plentiful curls driving Colin mad for the rest of his life.

She smiled as she touched a finger to an open, tiny palm, and nearly laughed when the delicate fingers curved around it. "May I hold her?" she asked Susannah softly.

"Of course."

She lifted the infant into her arms and was struck by how comfortable it felt, how right. Even when she'd held Tillie it hadn't been like this. But then, she hadn't been the same woman then.

"She is beautiful, Susannah," she murmured, coming back over to the bed. "Absolutely perfect."

"Thank you," Susannah replied as she dusted a fond finger over her daughter's cheek. "You should hear Colin go on about her. One would think we had done something rare and extraordinary."

"Haven't you?"

The question seemed to catch Susannah off-guard and she cocked her head. "I suppose," she said slowly, watching Marianne carefully. When she didn't respond, Susannah sat up a little bit and pulled her hair behind her. "How are you, Marianne? How was Glendare?"

Marianne suddenly became very focused on Olivia and turned a bit away, unable to help smiling. "It was lovely, thank you. It was just what I needed."

"Are you… are you blushing?" Susannah suddenly asked, incredulous.

Marianne felt her face heat even more and her smile deepened.

"Marianne Gerrard! You *never* blush!" Susannah gushed, swinging her legs to the side of the bed like a child. "You tell me right now what that is about! What happened?"

Marianne shook her head and bounced the baby. "Nothing happened."

"That sort of nothing is just the sort of nothing that positively begs to be spoken of."

Again, she shook her head, raising her eyes to meet Susannah's reluctantly.

Her sister-in-law looked determined to a fiendish degree and her eyes flashed. "You tell me everything now, or I will go to Colin and tell him you have a secret about his brother, and you know what that means."

Marianne's widened as she blanched in horror. Colin would be insufferable and annoying, poking and prodding and raising all kinds of hell until she was too embarrassed to do anything but give in. At least Susannah had some measure of sense. And she knew Kit as well as anybody, perhaps she could offer some insight.

With a resigned sigh, she sank back onto the bed and tucked Olivia against her as if she could shield her. Slowly, but honestly, she revealed everything from their weeks at Glendare, the good and the bad, the embarrassing and the delightful, far more confusing and emotional in the telling than she'd thought possible.

They'd been here one afternoon, a night, and a morning, and already Kit had resolved more fights than he'd ever been in with Colin, he was sure of it. He loved his sisters madly, but they were also conniving and brilliant and impossible.

That was what they had inherited, or learned, from Colin.

The trouble was that they appeared so innocent and sweet, and no one suspected they could possibly be so much trouble.

That part might have been a little bit him.

He sighed as he wandered the halls a little, wondering where his family was at this moment. It was too quiet, but Mrs. Creighton was a stern taskmaster when it came to lessons. She might not know how to corral the children when it came to pall-mall, but no one could hold that against her. They were Gerrards, after all. Even Freddie, though not a Gerrard by birth, had exhibited all of the finer qualities, and most of the lesser ones, of the family.

And Marianne... Marianne had...

Well, somehow she'd settled the most violent of disputes between the girls not that long ago, and had done so with ease and grace, listening to all sides with far more patience and understanding than he could ever have managed. He had been unable to comprehend the argument at all, something to do with dresses and combs or some other girlish nonsense. But it must have been serious, for Marianne had never once quivered with any hint of amusement. Bitty and Ginny had heeded her with respect and adoration, and then proceeded to regale her with tales of their country adventures.

Rosie had moodily left the room and he'd not seen her since, but neither had he been paying attention. He and Colin had escaped the gaggle of females for a ride across the estate, and he'd only just returned, Colin having rushed up to check on his wife and daughter for the twelfth time.

Kit frowned in thought. Rosie needed to get over her dislike of Marianne and accept her, respect her as she did Susannah. She might never be a motherly type to her, and he did not expect that, but she was his wife, and as such, she deserved some regard.

He nearly missed them, quietly sitting on the floor together in the drawing room, and pulled back to remain out of sight. Not that they would have seen him, as their backs were turned. Rosie sat rather mulishly, picking at the embroidery on her skirt, and Marianne sat far more elegantly beside her, looking at the younger girl with concern.

At one time he would have bet money that Marianne would never sit on the floor regardless of the situation, and more recently he would have bet more money that she would never elect to be alone with Rosie, yet here she was doing both, willingly and without anyone else around.

"Perhaps you'd like me if you got to know me," Marianne was saying softly, a small smile on her lips. "It might not be so bad, you know."

Rosie shrugged a little, not meeting her gaze. "Maybe. Kit likes you now, so that says something."

Kit winced as Marianne leaned back in surprise. "How do you know he likes me?"

Again, Rosie shrugged, but she tossed her hair a little, as if what she was about to say was common knowledge. "He used to not smile. Now he does."

She had a point.

"Oh…" Marianne murmured, her eyes widening.

Rosie brushed at her skirts and folded her fingers together, looking down at them. "Can I ask you a question?"

"Of course."

If Marianne knew Rosie better, she would not dare to consent so easily.

"Will you answer it honestly?"

"Yes."

Rosie finally looked up at her, cocking her head slightly. "Why did you and Kit get married so fast?"

Marianne's brows rose slowly and Kit held his breath, knowing he ought to interject before this got out of hand, but at the same time wanting to see how it played out.

He watched with anxiety as Marianne sighed softly, her expression taking on a faraway look. "We got married in the manner we did because… I needed saving. From myself. I had behaved very badly indeed, hardly the behavior of a proper young woman, and it got out of hand. Your brothers came to save me, and rather than having me endure punishment and ridicule, Kit offered to marry me. And it was better for all if it was very fast and without any sort of fuss. I didn't even have a proper trousseau, and you know what a shocking thing that is for any bride." She shuddered and smirked a little.

Rosie cracked a smile at Marianne's suddenly sarcastic tone, and

Kit felt all of his breath escape in one massive rush of air, surprised that no one heard it.

Marianne reached out to pat Rosie's knee, knowing better than to be too familiar with her. "I wish we could have had the time to do things properly. I would like to have met you girls and let you get used to the idea, and to me, before all of that, but it wasn't possible. I am sorry for that."

Rosie nodded, looking thoughtful. "If you could change things," she asked in a surprisingly mature tone for a girl of ten, "would you?"

Marianne sat back, suddenly seeming almost wistful. "I would change me, and my decisions. I would most certainly change myself." She slowly shook her head, smiling. "But those decisions led me to this marriage with Kit, and I wouldn't change that."

Rosie's smile grew and she sat up a little taller, apparently having decided on her feelings at last and a much more animated discussion of books began.

Kit slid even further out of sight and rested his forehead against the wall, trying to process what he had just heard, and what had happened.

Marianne was making a conquest of everyone, even his stubborn little Rosie. She was open and artless, warm and encouraging, and utterly unlike any version of her he had seen before Glendare. Gone was the prim and proper heiress who had barely tolerated the children before, and barely tolerated anyone at all, despite their admiration, or lack thereof. Somehow, she'd always been able to draw people in. Even as a young girl, when he had first loved her, she'd had an air of something rather hypnotic that dared others to follow. Once she had learned how to harness and control that power, she'd unleashed it to all of London freely and without restraint.

Now it was reined in once more, but no less potent.

Better still, she had found a heart, or ceased hiding it, and she was a creature reborn. Something pure and delightful and winsome, a breath of spring air in a field of wildflowers. He wanted more and more of this, days and weeks and years of it. Slowly and steadily, she was melting away the last edges of his resistance to her.

What would become of him then? If she managed to ensnare him once more, would he be lost to everyone in the world but her?

Would he mind so very much?

If she remained as she was, it might not be so bad. But if she changed once more, if she became caught up in the spirit of London, as she had done before, it would be the bitterest form of torment.

How far did he trust her?

How far did he trust himself?

For a man who made a concentrated effort to feel nothing, he felt his emotions with surprising strength and depth, with an intensity that was a damned nuisance. He had loved her with a passion, and he had hated her with one just as strong. If he let himself go fully now, when things were beyond his wildest imaginations, it would consume him, whole-heartedly and without restraint. There would be no recovery, and if this did not last, it would shatter everything that made him who he was.

He thanked God his control was as strong as any of his emotions, for the fear of losing himself was paralyzing.

It all came down to trust. Belief. Confidence in the course before him. He could not properly act until then.

Perhaps Rosie was more like him than he'd ever thought.

"Kit?"

He made a face at Colin's voice, low and bemused.

"What are you doing?" his brother asked, coming to lean his back against the wall next to him.

"Trying to figure out to whom I am married," Kit muttered.

"You've forgotten?"

"Yes."

"That's a shame. I rather like her."

Kit cracked an eye open and looked at him. "Do you? You warned me off enough."

"Yes, well, she was not the same person then, and nor were you."

"Hence the problem," Kit groaned, closing his eyes again.

"If she can manage little Gerrards so effectively, you've married the right woman. Circumstances or not, Kit, this is turning out rather well. For both of you."

Kit squeezed his eyes shut against the burst of pleasure and pain that seared him. If only he knew what the future held. If only he weren't such a coward. If only...

Colin let out a low chuckle. "Why is your face in the wall?"

Kit released a short, irritated sigh. "Because at this moment that is the best place for it."

"Right…" He shifted uncomfortably. "Susannah says you want to take the children to London with you. Are you mad?"

"Probably. But it was my wife's idea."

Colin choked on air, and grabbed his shoulder, forcing him from the wall and shoving him down the hall towards the study. "Now *that* is something I need to hear. Go."

Chapter Twenty

*I*t was going to be a disaster, and she hadn't even left the house yet. Worse than that, she was not even dressed yet. Her first event back in London, a ball hosted by the duke and duchess of Eastbourne, of all people, and she could not find a single thing to wear. Literally every appropriate gown for a ball that she owned was strewn about the room, either on her bed or on the floor, and nothing was even tempting her. Not the scarlet with gold trim, not the cream muslin, not the blue silk brocade, not even her old favorite, the vibrant purple muslin with the sheer overlay, and none of the others either.

She ought to have thought about this beforehand, but there had hardly been time.

They'd been back in London three days, and the children were quite accustomed to the house and the situation, and were delighted by the amount of space in their rooms and in the garden behind the house. They'd kept her and Kit quite occupied, so much so that they'd barely seen each other but for meals. She caught the flash of heat in his eyes when she came to breakfast in her nightgown and wrap the first morning, but that had been before she had realized the children would wake early and dine with them. Since then, she had taken care to dress appropriately, at least until they were used to her and more accustomed to her ways.

But what Marianne wanted most desperately at this moment was to see her husband look at her, in all her finery and elegance, and to know what he was thinking. He'd grown so familiar to her recently, she could see the slightest flicker of emotion in his once unreadable face. And he'd become such a tease, so delightfully witty, sometimes even shocking her, that she'd begun to wonder if she had married the more playful and sly Gerrard twin. And she adored every moment.

She would know if he approved of her look within a heartbeat. Assuming she found something worth wearing. The Eastbournes were very respectable and she must look the part, as Kit Gerrard's wife, but everything she owned was so blatantly Marianne Bray that she hesitated. She was so changed now, they did not even seem like her gowns.

Bitty had suggested that Marianne wear something with frills tonight, as she currently thought anything with frills must be the height of finery, and at this moment, she was tempted to bring her up here to pick something out for her. Bitty would be very decisive and have no prejudice to any gown in the room.

Marianne could use such a perspective.

Then she would not be standing here, hair completely unbound, half-dressed, straining against her corset with her irritated breathing. There was not time for this madness. They would be late if she did not come to her senses and pick something. It was too late for regrets, even if she could believably feign a megrim. And rather like with the Rivertons, there was no refusing the Eastbournes. Not if one wanted to conceivably remain in Society.

She turned to the long mirror, holding up a moss-colored green silk, smoothing it against her hip and legs, cocking her head. Almost, but still not quite right. She huffed in irritation and flung it back on the bed. "No, no, no," she groaned as she rubbed her temples. "This is not going to work!"

Anna clicked her tongue sympathetically, but she looked beyond exasperated. "You have so many gowns, madam, surely…"

Marianne shook her head and adjusted a chemise strap that had slid off of her shoulder. "It is not the number of gowns, Anna. I have no qualms repeating an ensemble. The trouble is that I feel so different now, nothing seems to suit."

She reached for her gold-embroidered muslin and looked at herself in the mirror, holding the dress up. She shook her head again, and sighed. "Everything I own for a ball is so bold and brazen, and I do not feel like that girl anymore."

"Personally, I would go with the blue."

They both whirled to see Kit leaning rather rakishly in the doorway, half-dressed himself, and watching with interest. His shirt was open at the neck, exposing his throat rather temptingly, and he suddenly seemed taller, more imposing, even more dangerous.

Marianne clutched her dress to her more tightly to cover herself, as she was fairly exposed thus. She had no idea how long he had been there, or how much he had seen, but propriety suddenly seemed important. Her cheeks heated and she was, for the moment, entirely without words in the face of his attractiveness.

He smirked a little and raised a brow at her.

She cleared her throat faintly. "The blue?" she managed, sounding too breathless and too slow.

He nodded once, a sultry hint of a smile on his lips. "Indeed."

She started to smile, then tucked it back to play a little. She gave him a look of disapproval as if she would scold him for such a suggestion. "But is that not rather bold?"

Again came his slow nod. "It is, but so are you. Be bold, Marianne." He pushed off of the doorframe with a wink and left, but not before taking in her current state with too much thoroughness.

Marianne bit her lip, buried her face in the gold dress with a faint squeal, then turned to Anna. "Let's try the blue again."

The Eastbourne ball was nearly as important as Almack's to the opening of the Season, and they could always boast the best company, the best refreshment, and the best décor, should they have boasted at all. Which the Eastbournes, as a rule, never did.

The Eastbourne events were not as ornate or elaborate as the Riverton's, but hardly faulted for it, and far less scandalous things occurred there. One entered the Eastbourne home and found themselves growing more respectable by the moment. It was for that reason, and the duke's rather imposing glare, that all rakes, scoundrels, and rogues kept far from the premises.

There was always a dinner before the dance, and Marianne had been a little disappointed to find herself seated next to Lord Blackmoor, but she was determined to make the best of it. And one look at her husband had given her the confidence to do so, as even that brief of a glance had given her an echo of the scorching approval she'd seen when she finally descended that evening. He'd not managed a single word beyond a hoarse "good", but his eyes had said so much more, and she'd barely managed to make it steadily to the carriage, even with his arm.

Kit had given her a very small smile over the dinner table, as more would be unlike him in public, but she returned it and inclined her head, then turned to the man beside her in an attempt to converse.

It had not gone well.

He'd been polite, but cool. Reserved, aloof, and even arrogant. She knew how highly Kit thought of him, but she had yet to find any legitimate reason why. The man might have been one of the marble statues at Glendare.

But try she did, and she could not call him rude, technically, as he'd somehow managed to be polite amidst the rest of his qualities. Hardly a proper dinner companion, but still a gentleman.

The finest of cuisine had been at their disposal and not even Lord Blackmoor's surliness had been enough to render the meal a waste. Neither too rich nor too bland, and such a selection that it was nearly as troublesome as her dress selection to determine just what she would eat and what she would not. Compliments flowed to the host and hostess as freely as did the wine, and the former became more elaborate as the latter increased.

Soon enough, they were dismissed to the ballroom, and there, at least, Marianne felt in her element. She was immediately set upon by Gemma, who had not been able to find her before, and she was tugged aside before the usual throng could form.

In rapid, low tones, Gemma related details that she could not have put into a letter, as it was simply too shocking, she claimed. It seemed that Lily Arden had been settled into a hasty engagement with Thomas Granger, who was pleasant enough, if a bit reticent, all for the sake of saving his fortune. Lily's parents, absent from her life but for the business details, had practically sold her off to their old friend, and Lily was heartbroken. Despite having carried a *tendre* for the man secretly for some time, this was hardly the situation she had wished for.

"Well," Marianne said rather coolly, squeezing Gemma's hand, "we shall be her steadfast friends, and do our part. If we cannot save her from him, we can at least save her from gloom."

Gemma's eyes blazed and she nodded. "Exactly. I knew you would see it properly." She glanced to the side, and looked back at Marianne with a smile. "I think your coterie is waiting."

Marianne saw them and grumbled, "Only a few weeks ago they despised me."

"Yes, but that was before Fanny Hayes's incident, and James Harper's ill-timed proposal to Georgina Whittle, and before Penelope Davies tore her dress at the theater and exposed some very bowlegged knees." Gemma grinned swiftly and kissed her cheek "You are back on top, my dear. Don't forget me."

"Never," Marianne insisted. She winked and then turned with a sigh to the gathering people and began her rounds with them.

Kit watched the people surround and nearly engulf his wife, and further watched with a hint of pride at how smoothly she managed them all. While he may have wished his wife had been a bit more of a meek creature at times, there was no denying her skills when it came to people. She was efficient and brusque and never tolerated nonsense, and she did it all with such charm.

It might drive him mad, but he could not deny that he was impressed.

He mingled a little with some of the guests, the Bevertons and Whitlocks primarily, as well as Blackmoor, who had said nothing about his dinner conversation with Marianne, which Kit supposed to be very telling. Marlowe was nowhere to be seen, but Kit had learned never to expect anything with him. The Duke of Eastbourne had paid his respects, and Kit had conversed with him politely, having always held the man in high regard, but not in depth, as the man was the host and monopolizing him would have been rude.

It was some time later when he caught sight of Marianne again, this time dancing with one of her silly admirers. Apparently her sins had been forgiven and her reputation quite recovered. Her waiting throng was as massive as ever, and anyone looking on would never have guessed at her misfortune, or that she had married him.

Was that not what they had all wanted? For her to not feel the effects of her poor decisions?

So why should he suddenly be so very cross?

And as he glowered at the man now making his wife laugh, seeing the youthful and handsome face gazing down at her with such ardor, he could also admit to severe pangs of jealousy.

Had he ever been jealous before?

Of course not. He'd never had a reason to be.

Grinding his teeth together, he found himself wishing most heartily that he hadn't a reason now. The moment the dance ended, he strode across the ballroom and placed himself directly in front of the man whose hand was outstretched and waiting for Marianne.

"I say!" the idiot protested when Marianne reached them.

Kit did not even spare a glance for him, and kept his eyes on those of his wife, who tilted her head and smiled a little coyly. "This dance is mine," he said firmly, taking Marianne's hand.

"No, it's not. I've claimed the waltz!" the man cried.

"I don't care," Kit replied, feeling something quite powerful rising within him the longer he gazed at his wife. "I am taking this dance with my wife."

At least three people gasped, and Marianne's brow quirked just a little. "You can't!" the same idiot sputtered, sounding scandalized.

Now Kit did glance back, giving the puppy a withering look. "Are you telling me that I cannot dance with my wife?"

The man colored and fell back a step.

"My apologies, Mr. Banks," Marianne said in her best polite voice. "My husband has a prior claim." Her lips twitched into a smile that curled his stomach quite pleasantly. "He will always have the prior claim."

With as much flourish as he dared, Kit escorted her to the dance floor, and took up the proper position.

"You don't dance, Mr. Gerrard," Marianne murmured as her hand rested in his.

"No," he admitted as the musicians struck up, "but I daresay I waltz."

Marianne's smile would have spurred him into dancing the entire night if he were less of a man. As it was, he could barely speak for their entire waltz. He looked nowhere else but at her, and she was just as intent on him. He'd missed her these last few days, when duty and responsibility had forced them apart, and had longed for their ease and comfort of Glendare, when they could be absorbed in each other without seeming excessive. Holding her in his arms now, acutely aware of the perfection in their movements and their fit, he could not imagine ever being more satisfied.

Swirling about the room, seeming the only two there, he felt himself becoming lost, falling further and further away from anyone and anything else. He wanted to swing her up into his arms and beg her to remain. He wanted to crush his mouth to hers, even in this room, and to hell with the scandal. He wanted to give her children, scores of them, and start right away. He wanted to sit quietly in a library with her, stealing glances and smiling for no reason at all. He wanted to hear her playing music when she thought she was alone. He wanted…

Control. He wanted control. And he wanted time.

And damn it, he wanted her.

But not now. Not yet.

The music came to a close and applause filled the room. Marianne was a little flushed, and he was a little short of breath. He kissed her glove and led her back to her throng.

"You were right," she said, her words rushed.

"About?"

She glanced up at him slyly. "You do waltz. You most certainly do."

In lieu of carrying her off into the night, he gave her a very smart bow, and squeezed her hand, then left as soon as humanly possible. Only when he was a safe distance away did he breathe again.

"Did you see that?" a woman hissed from somewhere behind

the pillar he stood by.

"I thought you said theirs wasn't a love match!" someone else gushed.

"That's what we all thought!"

"If that wasn't the most outrageous display of passion confined to a ballroom, I will eat this fan."

"Positively smoldering."

"It will be all over London by morning. The Gerrards are not only a love match, but a shocking one. No wonder he saved her, I daresay the man cannot do without her."

"The way he looked at her, Cynthia! My goodness, what ardor!"

"I don't condone husbands and wives dancing for that reason alone. What were they thinking? And a waltz? Really."

"Don't be such a prude. They are young and in love!"

Kit was seething by the time the busybodies went away, and he wrenched himself out of his position. He knew he had not been controlled enough during that dance, and there was the proof of it. No one was ever supposed to know his true feelings, and they certainly were not to speculate that he loved his wife. Or that she might, impossibly, return the sentiment.

Could a man not dance with his wife and not be wild about her? Was that so unlikely?

He caught Blackmoor's eye, and they retreated together, finding the safety of the card room, and the men equally reluctant to dance and attention, much more to their taste.

It could not have been more than an hour and a half later when an agitated young man came into the room and looked around anxiously, seeming desperately relieved to find Kit within.

"Mr. Gerrard," he panted as he came over and bowed. "Please, sir, it's your wife…"

Kit groaned and looked up from his game. "What is my wife doing now?"

"She's all in a rage, sir, and it's drawing comment."

He snorted in derision. "Has she struck anyone yet?"

The man seemed to shrink back in horror. "No, sir."

"What's it about?" he asked reluctantly, praying it was something silly he could write off.

The young man shifted his eyes nervously to the man next to him. "Lord Blackmoor, sir. The subject of supper was brought up, and it was observed that he was her companion there."

Kit sighed heavily and hesitated to rise. There was no saying what Marianne would say or do here. A dozen possibilities rose in his mind, and each angered him more than the next.

Blackmoor surprised him by rising first. "I'll take care of this. I am the subject after all." He didn't wait for a response, and left the room quickly.

"Ridiculous," Kit muttered to himself. "Absolutely ridiculous." He waited what seemed an age, his mind reeling. He didn't want to know what had happened in the ballroom and he didn't want to interfere, especially when he considered what Marianne was capable of.

The creature formerly known as his wife had apparently returned. And with it, the return of everything dark and resentful he'd associated with her.

He nearly groaned when Blackmoor returned the room, his friend's expression blank. "Well?"

"It's handled," he said simply.

Kit winced. "Was it horrible?"

Blackmoor shrugged a shoulder as he picked up his cards once more. "Not really. She refused to dance with me."

Kit closed his eyes in horror. "Good lord, that woman." He shook his head, cursing under his breath, and looked back to his friend. "I hope you didn't take offense."

"Not at all. I didn't want to dance with her either." He suddenly seemed very pensive for a moment.

"Blackmoor?" Kit prodded.

Blackmoor came out of whatever stupor he was in and gave Kit a very frank look. "Why did you marry her? You said you had your reasons. What are they?"

At this moment, he didn't have a clue. He shook his head, considered the phrasing for a moment, then slowly shrugged. "I just… I couldn't let anyone else have her."

It seemed a weak reasoning in light of what Marianne had done, but it was the truth.

"Interesting." He looked out of the door towards the ballroom, as if something had caught his attention.

"Blackmoor?"

"Interesting idea, marriage," he mused, bringing his attention back.

Kit snorted a little. "Not really. You've done it before."

"I'm considering it again."

If Blackmoor had said he was considering becoming a vicar, he could not have stunned him more. "How seriously?"

He shrugged. "As I said, considering."

"Well, please consult me before you do something rash," Kit grunted, shaking his head. "Between my wife and my brother, I have access to more information on anyone than Scotland Yard."

"Duly noted." Blackmoor glanced out of the door again, brows furrowed, then he shook his head and went back to their game.

Chapter Twenty-One

$\mathcal{S}$omething was wrong. Something was terribly, terribly wrong.

They'd been in London just over a week, and Kit had spoken to her only a handful of times since the ball. Worse than that, when he did speak to her, it was in the cool, carefully polite tone from their past. He barely looked at her, even when she'd come to breakfast in her nightgown and wrap again. He'd always had *something* to say about that, even when they had been fighting. But now, it could not have interested him less.

She'd considered coming to breakfast stark naked to see if that would cause a flicker of any kind, but that seemed a little drastic.

Nothing she did interested him anymore. He was never around, and when he was, he was all indifference. Somehow, that wounded her more than his insults ever had. And she found herself growing more and more bitter, angered, and resentful. What had caused her husband to suddenly change?

She'd tried to speak with him about Lily Arden's engagement, but he'd brushed that aside with claims of how fortunate she was to have a husband who was respectable and honorable and, if Colin was to be believed, actually interested in her. He thought nothing about the manner in which the arrangement had taken place, assuring her that most of England's marriages in the upper classes were carried out the same way. And further told her not to create a mountain out of a molehill.

She'd tried to invite him on an outing to the park with her and the children, but he refused at once. There was too much for him to accomplish, he said, for such a pointless venture. Yet later that day, she had observed him out in the gardens with Ginny and Bitty engaged in some imaginary search for treasure.

She'd even asked him to listen and give him advice on her playing, which ought to have delighted him, given his previous passion on her playing and the interest he had wanted to take. But again, he had declined. She had thought, perhaps, he might have exaggerated his musical tastes and abilities before, but she'd seen him helping Bitty with her pianoforte lessons, singing the melody with her, and his voice had been utter perfection. The blending of their two voices as they sang and plunked had brought tears to Marianne's eyes, and the joy on Bitty's face had softened her bitterness.

Kit would be a marvelous father.

If they ever got around to that.

It became very apparent to her, after days and days of the same, that the problem somehow lay with her. He was just as attentive to the children and his associates, and behaved as he ever did when they were in public. He even glared at the attention she received, as he had before, but it seemed to go unnoticed by all but her. He was polite and respectful, and no one seeing them would find anything amiss at all. But the distance between them was greater than it had ever been, and she had no idea why.

She eventually decided that she could not wait for her husband to come to his senses and like her again. She could not spend her days lingering at home, anticipating the slightest bit of attention from him like some infatuated miss. She had to fill her days with better things, and hope that time would soften him again.

Today, she had been more productive than she had been since Glendare, and she felt better for it. She needed to find some useful purpose with her days, and her fortune, and her time, particularly when she would one day be a lady of title, and she might have done so after today. She sighed with satisfaction as she removed her bonnet and gloves upon reentering the house, handing them off to Mrs. Wilton.

"Have you had a pleasant day, Mrs. Gerrard?" the kind woman asked as she gestured for her spencer. "You've been gone almost the whole of it!"

Marianne smiled and started unbuttoning the garment. "Yes,

very much so. Now, if you don't mind, I promised Miss Rosie I would…"

"Marianne," came the sudden bark of her husband, silencing her and causing both women to turn in surprise towards the hallway, where his glowering form emerged.

Marianne swallowed and nodded to Mrs. Wilton, who took the bonnet and gloves only and disappeared. "Yes, Kit?" she asked softly as she rebuttoned her spencer.

He folded his arms in his most intimidating fashion. "Where were you today?"

She blinked and tilted her head, confused at what she was supposed to have done to earn this ire. "Excuse me?"

"You were gone all day. None of the servants or the girls knew where you were."

Again she blinked, and then frowned at this interrogation. "I was out."

His eyes flashed ominously. "That's not good enough," he growled.

She sniffed and brushed at her skirts with a careless shrug. "I was on several errands today."

She'd never heard her husband snarl before, but the sound that emerged from him was far too animalistic for it to have been natural. "You tell me your whereabouts right now, or so help me…"

"Are you threatening me?" she interrupted in disbelief, her voice rising with indignation.

His throat worked and she saw a muscle tick in his jaw. "Tell me where you were," he demanded in an only moderately calmer tone.

She shook her head, suddenly feeling very defeated as the realization dawned. "You don't trust me."

Kit's eyes narrowed. "Whether I do or not is beside the point if you do not tell me."

Something inside of her burst and she felt a towering rage come over her. "Fine," she snapped, throwing her hands into the air. "You want to know where I was? I spent the entire day trying to find something useful that I could do with myself, some difference that I can make." She smiled coldly, as if she didn't believe it was possible herself. "I went to three charity meetings where nothing was accomplished but gossip, and bad gossip at that, and then I went to call on Gemma Templeton, as she is so downtrodden about Lily's state, and then, if you can bear the suspense, I went to St. Ann's Orphan Home to speak with Lady Sprotmire about the work there. And if you have difficulty believing *that*, you may speak with your great friend, Lord Blackmoor, as he saw me leaving and was kind enough to escort me to Lady Whitlock's home where we discussed some new music."

Kit looked a little unsettled by her outburst, and looked away briefly. "That report was unnecessary. I only needed the basics."

Marianne shook her head slowly and took two steps towards him, then stopped when he took the same amount away. She wanted to cry, but there were no tears. She bit her lip, pleading with her eyes. "What's happened, Kit?" she whispered, feeling broken. "Why are we back to this? We were friends, becoming more than that even, and…"

He held up a hand to silence her. "In the future, please inform myself or one of the servants about your activities beforehand. This is London, and your safety is paramount."

The coolness… The sheer detachment of his manner killed whatever light of hope had ever existed within her. The wonderful, warm, charming husband she had known for so short a time was gone, and only this cold, immovable man remained.

She swallowed her grief and nodded. "Are you still willing to take me to the opera tonight?"

"Of course. We have a box, and your brother and his wife, as well as your aunt, will be joining us."

She smiled bitterly. "How wonderful. At least one of them is bound to be pleased to be seen with me." With a mocking curtsey, she walked passed him to the stairs and made her way up, praying she would not crumble.

Generally speaking, there was little about the opera that Marianne did not love. All of the finery and excitement of a ball, with all of the opportunities to see those of importance and influence, but in the sort of setting that required more subtle ways to make an impression, all while enjoying what was usually some breathtaking musical talents and engaging scores. The feeling and passion in opera was so lost on the world, and with the restrictions and confinement of English propriety and high Society, one could feel quite stifled. But at the opera, one could be transported to the emotional realms so foreign to one's life.

Tonight, however, there was little to find pleasure in.

The music was breathtaking, the arias perfection, the duets tormented, and the show itself quite engaging. She was even dressed in a new ensemble that was destined to make the fashion followers envious, a powdery blue silk with a sheer silver overlay that changed the tone of the blue with every flicker of candlelight. Anna had outdone herself with her hair, intricate curls and folds and decorative pins giving her a look that was nothing short of regal, and she felt as stunning as she looked.

But everything, even her new heights of popularity and the uninhibited looks of admiration she'd received from everyone, fell far short of the satisfaction she had wanted.

Kit had barely glanced at her all evening, though he sat beside her. Their hands had been near enough to touch initially, and once Kit had come to that realization, he had jerked the offending hand away and turned himself as carefully away from her as possible without letting anyone staring into their box know. And there were several pairs of eyes staring into their box.

Between Marianne and Tibby, who was shockingly dressed in all black silk and lace, though she had nothing to mourn, it was astonishing that anyone watched the stage at all.

The more people stared, the surlier Kit grew. His face was composed, but cold, and it was palpable.

Duncan and Annalise had tried to ease things before the show and during the first interval, and while Kit had answered their queries with all politeness, he had added nothing to the conversation and avoided anything to do with Marianne. Duncan had given Marianne several pointed looks, all of which she had pretended not to see.

She would have much to answer for if ever they were alone.

She could not keep the secret for long, not when Kit was telling quite enough for them both with his manner.

The curtain fell, signaling the second intermission, and Tibby whirled in her seat to look at them both. "You two need to go out and be seen."

"What?" Marianne all but barked, her gloves feeling very hot.

Tibby's eyes narrowed and her black feathers waved a little. "Go out of the box. Walk. Be seen. Smile pleasantly. Let the world observe you. They've done nothing less all night, and the pair of you are as stiff as statues. Get up and do it now, or I will do something that will really start some gossip."

That was all the encouragement either of them needed and they were suddenly on their feet and out of the box. Kit held out his arm and Marianne took it very lightly, both of them avoiding eye contact.

They smiled and nodded to several people, never pausing in their slow, apparently leisurely walk to refresh themselves. Whispers and smiles surrounded them, and Marianne waved to a few people she genuinely liked, smiling as easily as she could manage. She had no idea if Kit did anything of the sort, but neither was she going to look.

It felt ridiculous to parade this way. Why should they matter to anyone else now? They were married, they were back in London, and there were plenty of other scandals to remark on since theirs. She didn't want to pretend anymore, and neither did Kit.

That much she still knew about him.

When people started returning to their boxes for the last acts of the evening, a small burst of panic hit Marianne. She might never be this close to Kit again, not for a long while, if his behavior towards her was any indication. She had to say something, do something, now, while he was being forced to touch her.

Halfway back to their box, she pulled them both to a stop and yanked him into a small and abandoned hall just off of the main thoroughfare.

"Kit, I have to speak with you," she rushed in a low voice before he could protest.

The brow he raised was as taunting as it was imperious. "I gathered."

"Kit..." she began, her voice gentling.

"If you are going to speak on the same topics as earlier," he interrupted gruffly, "save your breath. I refuse to discuss it here."

She exhaled and barely resisted the urge to rub at her brow. If he was in a difficult mood, she couldn't approach a topic of emotions or any sentimentality. If she wanted to properly communicate with him, it would have to be something on which he would converse.

"Then maybe you'll discuss this here," she snapped. "I think we should send Rosie to school."

He went slightly slack jawed, and his eyes became colder. "Excuse me?"

"Finishing school," she elaborated. "I think she would benefit from it."

"You want to send her away?" he asked, his agitation rising.

Marianne huffed a sigh. "Just to school, not forever."

He set his jaw and firmly shook his head. "Out of the question."

"Why?" she demanded.

"No, Marianne."

"I am only thinking of Rosie," Marianne tried to reason.

"That is my job, not yours,"

Marianne paused, clamping her lips together hard as she considered him, and what he was saying. "So I am to ignore the girls in our house?" she finally asked. "Pat them on the heads and beg that they are seen and not heard?"

He seemed to shrug without actually shrugging. "You seemed keen enough before to do just that."

Marianne stepped back a little, shaking her head. "Not anymore. I love those girls, Kit. I want to be in their lives, and I want to help you raise them, but not like this."

"I thought you had no expectations of this sham of a marriage," he said, his words sending a chill through her.

She slowly shook her head, wanting to take his face in her hands and force him to really see her. "I have changed, Kit! Why can't you see that I have changed?"

"We all change, Marianne. It is a fact of life."

"I know," she whispered. "In a matter of days, you have gone from my husband to a stranger. I had hoped…"

Kit turned away and shook his head. "I was a fool," he muttered with heavy bitterness. "I thought that ignoring the world would be enough, but it is not. It is foolish to think that either of us could change enough for this to be… anything but what it was when we wed."

"Then why did you marry me?" she cried, a pair of tears finding their way to her cheeks. "If that is how you feel, why?"

He turned his head only and gave her a look that was half furious, half anguished, carrying the torment of the damned within its depths. "Because I couldn't help myself," he rasped. He flung himself out of their hiding place and down the hall, away from their box.

Marianne rested against the wall, listening to his angry footsteps fade, and letting more tears roll pathetically down her face. She knew enough of Kit to know that at least half of his words were spoken in anger. But which half? What was truth and what was heat of the moment?

The depth of his agony stole her breath and she cursed herself for having had such power over him. No one should feel that much when it is so little returned or even acknowledged. But how long would he punish her for that?

He deserved to be free of the torment of her, but she deserved the second chance he had vowed to give. If he let her, she could prove to him that his love had not been misplaced. She could not give him the distance he seemed to crave, not now and not yet.

But could he, perhaps, be reminded of why he loved her? He'd had his reasons for loving her before, and she'd been ignorant of them all. Now she was more aware of him than she was herself, and she wanted to earn him.

She wanted her husband to love her again. And she wanted to love him back.

She made her way back to the box just as the music started back up. Duncan saw her enter and frowned at her being alone.

"Where is Kit?" he hissed, leaning over to avoid being overheard.

Marianne smiled as sadly as she could. "He is unwell, I am afraid, and went home. I would accompany him, but he insisted that I stay, as I love the opera so." She bit her lip and forced down the lump of shame in her throat. "If you could perhaps see me home tonight, I would be most appreciative."

Her brother looked at her carefully, and she prayed she was enough of an actress to fool him. He pursed his lips a little and nodded. "Of course, minnow. I don't like your husband leaving you, but it is done now."

She nodded her thanks and focused on the stage, but noticed nothing at all as her mind whirled with how to put a plan into action.

When the opera reached its conclusion, their party made their way to the carriages, several admirers and associates slowing their way for final conversations and praises. But Duncan was imposing enough to ward many away, and Tibby was not shy about her desires for home either.

Marianne wrapped her cloak more tightly around her as they exited the theater, then came to a startled halt as her carriage and footmen waited there. It took her several moments to understand what that meant.

Kit, despite his fury, had hired a hack or walked to wherever he had gone, and left the comfort of the carriage for her.

Impossibly, her emotions welled within her at the sight. Still a gentleman after all. He had made sure she would not want for a way home.

Hope, that stubborn little flame, flickered again.

Chapter Twenty-Two

"And then she had the gall to tell me that she wanted to send Rosie away! After everything, after my sister finally started trusting her, she wants her gone! I don't know her at all!"

Kit ran his hands through his hair then tugged at his already mangled cravat. He was so enraged, so beside himself, that he was surprised at his coherency. He'd hired a hack to take him to his club, and had been relieved to find Blackmoor already within. It had taken only a little prodding from his friend for all of his frustrations and irritation and confusion to come tumbling forth.

Blackmoor sat at the table, boots propped on a nearby chair, watching him with interest. He was still impeccably dressed, even as Kit's appearance became more and more deranged.

"I thought finishing schools were fairly commonplace for young girls," Blackmoor mused thoughtfully.

Kit gave him a wary look. "They are…"

"And you do want your sister to be finished, yes?"

Now Kit glared at his friend. "Of course, I do."

Blackmoor wisely said nothing and only shrugged, looking down into his glass.

"I don't know what I'm doing, Blackmoor!" Kit moaned. "I want her, I don't want her, I hate her, I very much don't hate her… She drives me to distraction, from one end of my emotions to another."

"Sounds painful."

"She encourages attention, she finds offense at the most obscure things, and she seems to think that being married gives her some new means of independence." He shook his head and gestured wildly at his friend. "Good heavens, look what she did to you! And she barely knows you!"

Blackmoor frowned and tilted his head. "What are you talking about?"

Kit rolled his eyes and paced around. "The ball! When she got worked up into a frenzy, no doubt over some gossip surrounding you, and then refusing you! Such a ridiculous, vain thing."

Blackmoor's eyes widened and slowly he dropped his legs to the floor. "Kit, she was defending me."

Kit came to a very abrupt halt. "What?"

There came a slow nod and a pitying smile. "When I went out there? She was telling everyone that she was not going to play any games with me or let anyone else do so. I should be left alone to my own devices without consideration to anyone else. And she refused to dance with me because she knew I didn't care for it, and hardly cared for her. Suffice it to say, we have agreed to dance at another time when we feel more inclined."

Kit rather thought his heart was going to fly out of his chest and he had to press his hands into the table to keep from toppling over. "Why didn't you tell me?" he whispered painfully.

Blackmoor's thick brows rose in surprise. "It hardly seemed appropriate. I thought you knew your wife."

"So did I." He paused, letting the revelation sink in. Then he looked at him carefully. "Did you see her today?"

"Yes. Coming from St. Ann's, of all places." He snorted softly and shook his head in disbelief. "I thought it best not to ask, but I could hardly let her walk about London unescorted, and she had no carriage, so I offered to take her home, only to be told she was going to Whitlock's. I drove her myself, so if you hear of us having a mad affair, you'll know why."

Kit winced, sank into the nearest chair, and buried his face in his hands.

"Hmm," Blackmoor mused, propping his feet back up. "Maybe I won't get married again."

"I don't think all wives are like this," Kit muttered from behind his hands. "Just mine."

His friend barked a hard, mirthless laugh. "You should have met my first."

"I did."

"And that wasn't enough to scare you off?"

"Shut up." He dropped his hands and looked at him with a sigh. "What do I do?"

Blackmoor shrugged slowly, a secretive smile on his face. "I believe apologizing would be an excellent place to start."

"I was afraid of that." He heaved himself out of his chair and rubbed at his brow. "I still have to keep my distance. For my own sanity."

Blackmoor gave him a disapproving look, but only said, "That does not mean you cannot apologize, you stupid dunce." He grunted softly. "If you doubt her word, have Gent look into it. He loves gossip and intervention."

Kit shifted a quick glare at him. "I don't doubt her.

"No?"

"No…" Kit offered a very short sigh. "I think I doubt myself."

"Well, then Gent won't be much help at all, will he?" Blackmoor mused sardonically.

Kit nodded and then switched to shaking his head as he left, feeling like a heel of epic proportions. He'd overreacted. Again. And he had the suspicion that Blackmoor had meant his words far more than his careless attitude had portrayed. He couldn't have the Gent keep a watch on his wife any more than was already there. He couldn't ask that of his friend, and he couldn't bear the thought of reducing himself to such actions.

He didn't doubt his wife; he just didn't know what to do.

His wife had him tangled up in knots, and no matter how many times he caught her stroking Ginny's hair as the child fell asleep in her lap or wandering the gardens with a basket and clippings or reading herself in the library, it was easier to believe the creature had returned. It was easier to bear the old familiarity of hating her, resenting her, than it was to accept that he could have everything he'd ever dreamed and more.

She had changed. He knew that, had known it all along. And he hadn't really needed Blackmoor's confirmation on her location today. He just… couldn't believe his own heart.

And now, when he'd gone so far beyond his boundaries in the opposite direction, he had to make amends. She didn't deserve his resentment, nor his malice. He was better than that. Distance was all he needed. He could do that. He could maintain a safe distance without hurting her.

He nodded firmly and quickened his step as he hurried for home.

Marianne sat at her toilette brushing out her hair, lost in her thoughts. She'd sent Anna to bed ages ago, but she had remained here, scheming ways to win her husband back.

The first thing she needed to do was somehow force him to stop being angry with her. She would temper her finery, take more consideration with her words, and practice reserve in public. She really ought to have done so anyway, if she were being honest with herself.

After he could stand her again, it should be simple.

She'd written several notes tonight, none of which would be sent until morning, but she'd had to do *something* tonight. The first was to Miranda Ascott, asking if she might play at the musicale next week. She was terrified at the prospect, but surely Kit would approve, knowing her fears as he did. The second had been to Kate, Lady Whitlock, begging her to help her prepare something that wouldn't let her be embarrassed.

The third had been to Lady Sprotmire accepting the offer to volunteer regularly at St. Ann's. She'd felt something special in that place, and the desire to help had continue to build within her. She'd have the girls look through their things and see if there was anything they could spare for those poor children. It could be good for all of them to be exposed to those less fortunate than they. She touched the letters with a tight smile. This would help her, she knew it.

A soft knock sounded at her door and she turned in surprise. "Come in?" she called, unable to keep the curious question from her tone.

Her brows shot up when Kit entered, looking all too much like the man that had pressed her against the wall and kissed her wildly. Yet his expression was careful and composed, contrasting with his appearance starkly.

"I hoped you had not gone to bed yet," he murmured, shutting the door and leaning against it, his eyes trained on her.

She offered a very tremulous smile. "Not yet. I'm not as tired as I should be. The opera, you know. It energizes me."

He almost smiled, and she felt like wilting at the failure to draw one out. "I need to apologize, Marianne," he murmured hoarsely. "For today… for recently… but especially for tonight." He shook his head and she waited, hoping he would go on. He sighed and met her eyes. "That wasn't fair, what I said to you before. I couldn't let you think that I don't hold you in some regard, or that I disliked you. The words were very poorly chosen, and I wasn't thinking clearly. You know me well enough to know that I would never have married you if my feelings were so opposed to you as a wife."

The air seemed thick between them and she took a careful moment to consider her response. "I hoped that was the case, though I was curious. We had hardly been on speaking terms for years."

His brow furrowed a little. "But you should never have had cause to doubt… That is, I hoped you knew that I would come for you. With Colin and the rest. That I wouldn't sit by and let that happen."

"I didn't know," she admitted quietly, drawing her knees up beneath her chin. "I didn't know what you thought of me or what you would do."

That seemed to disappoint him. "I owe you an explanation. You asked me earlier why I married you if I was…"

She nodded and sat up straighter. "If you felt so against it. Yes."

He nodded and gave a short sigh. "The truth is, ironically, what I said to you before. I couldn't help myself."

Now it was Marianne who frowned. "I don't understand," she told him apologetically.

He shrugged his shoulders, his mouth tightening in another almost smile. "Neither did I." He sighed heavily. "The trouble between us has less to do with you and more to do with me. You see, something about you always has and probably always will test my resolve and control, and after what passed between us six years ago, I have learned, through much practice, how to exude comportment and control at all times."

"When you went to your father."

"Yes. But I never told you how I learned it, or what I did. Marianne, you unmanned me with everything that you were, and that was the most unsettling feeling of all. I couldn't let myself be so unguarded again, especially with you. So I went to Loughton."

Kit swallowed and shook his head. "He was not pleased to see me. He did not like being reminded of the life he'd left. But he let me stay, though he shared absolutely nothing with me. I learned by observation. My father chooses to go through life without feelings, without caring, drowning and ignoring any feeling except indifference in drink and women and gambling rather than be hurt again. And he became a monster. I spent months with him and never heard about his second wife or the girls. He didn't even live with them. They didn't matter enough to Loughton." He shook his head firmly. "I wasn't going to become that. So I left him, and spent time touring the Continent, filling my days with whatever I could, but nothing that would turn me into the wreck of the man I'd seen. I learned how to control my emotions, rein in impulses, find the power over my own will, and eventually, I was able to contain myself. Then, and only then, could I come back to England. And face you."

Marianne could barely move, and didn't even think of responding. Staring at her husband, seeing the depth of his emotions, knowing what it must have cost him to come to her and tell her… It moved her beyond belief.

Kit finally met her eyes once more. "I don't know what it is between us, Marianne, or why it torments me and drives me to such distraction. It might not even have words. But know this… I will never regret that I married you. I will always be loyal to you. I'm your husband, for better or for worse, and you will always be my wife. I still belong to you."

Marianne swallowed with some difficulty. "I'm sorry to torment you so."

He managed a thin, but sincere smile. "No. It's all right. I've grown accustomed to the sensation."

She could not help but to return his smile with a small one of her own. "Thank you for telling me," she murmured.

"I owed you at least that much," he replied, straightening against the wall. "And an apology for my behavior about Rosie."

She straightened up at once. "May I clarify what I said?"

He considered her carefully, then gave a short nod. "Of course."

Encouraged, Marianne let her legs fall down to the floor and rested her hands in her lap. "I never meant that we get Rosie out of the house or that we send her away tomorrow. I meant in a few years, perhaps when she is twelve, and only if she agrees. She will soon outstrip what Mrs. Creighton can teach her, and she deserves better than what I had. And I was not wanting to send her far, just to Miss Masters in Kent."

Kit seemed to relax a little and cocked his head, his eyes thoughtful. "What if she does not like it?" he asked.

"Then we pull her out and bring her home," Marianne said with an easy shrug. "No matter. But Kit, she is always going to be overprotective of her sisters, and a governess would only heighten that for her. She needs more than that. So all I thought was if she could get away, go someplace with other girls and be free to be herself without having to worry about anyone else, she might blossom further still. And she could come home whenever she wished; Kent is not so far."

Kit was nodding thoughtfully. "That sounds rather agreeable," he finally murmured.

She exhaled a sigh of relief. "Thank you."

He nodded once and turned to the door, then paused. "I do see the change in you, Marianne. And I trust you. It's just… London brings out the worst in me."

Marianne smiled at him, warmly and genuinely. "We can leave. We can go tonight."

He glanced back at her, smiling. "No, we can't. But it means a great deal that you offered."

Marianne sighed, drumming her fingers silently in her lap. "I miss Glendare," she whispered.

"I know," he said simply, his eyes meeting hers for a heated moment. Then he left her room and shut the door softly behind him.

Chapter Twenty-Three

Three days later, the longest of her entire life, Marianne sat silently panicking in Miranda Ascott's rather simply adorned music room, her palms sweating to an extent she had not thought humanly possible. The room was huge, far too audacious a space for a music room, considering the conservative size of the house itself, but Miranda had often considered herself at the level of Tibby or Lady Cavendish, if not the Rivertons themselves, and was never one to permit convention to stand in the way of her tastes.

The size of the room didn't make much difference at this moment, except that it permitted an inordinately large number of guests to attend events there. And every seat was filled. And more guests were standing by.

It was truly terrifying.

Worst of all, her husband was not even in attendance. She knew he was aware of the event, he'd consented to attend it. But when the time came for departure, he hadn't come, and she had been informed he was not at home. Now she had been here for half an hour, painstakingly waiting her turn, and she had not seen him. She had looked around so often she could have testified before a tribunal of every person that *was* there, and what half of them were wearing.

But her husband was most assuredly not among them.

Gemma was beside her, with Mary singing at this very moment, and Annalise and Duncan were somewhere nearby. She did not want for support, and she knew without a doubt that they would be proud of her even if she mangled the piece. But it was not enough.

It would never be enough.

Mary's song came to a glorious finish and the applause was effusive. She smile prettily and allowed Mr. Ascott to escort her back to her place, where Geoffrey defied decorum by wrapping an arm around her shoulder and kissed her cheek, whispering something in his wife's ear that made Mary grin and tighten her hold on his leg. Then Mary looked at her and winked, which Marianne acknowledged with a shaky nod.

Miranda rose with all of her practiced grace and smiled graciously at the gathering, as if their lingering applause was for her. "Dear friends, we now have a very special treat for you all. We feel Miss Arden's absence most deeply, and trust that her sister will convey our regrets to her."

Rosalind Arden blushed at being singled out and nodded once. She'd accompanied Mary, and while she did not have Lily's talent, she was certainly accomplished enough, and now she returned to her seat with a dipped chin and lowered eyes.

"At any rate," Miranda continued, "we will not want for fine performances. I know it will surprise and delight all of you, as it did me, to know that our next performance will be by none other than Mrs. Gerrard."

She could have done without the reference to Lily, that would only increase their anticipation as they compared the two, and she hardly needed that. Still, she managed to rise without tripping over her gown and made her way to the pianoforte as the gathering clapped a little and whispered a great deal.

Her legs shook, her head swam, her stomach roiled, and her fingers were beginning to lose feeling. This was going to be a disaster. She knew the song inside out and backwards, she had played it perfectly ten times in a row today, but suddenly she couldn't even remember how to play the instrument at all.

She sat down at the bench as gracefully as she could manage, exhaled a quick, soft breath, and looked to her friends for the last reassurance.

But something else caught her eye. Standing in the back of the room, in the only opening with a clear view of her, stood Kit, his eyes steady on her, confidence and reassurance evident in his features. He calmly held her gaze, then nodded once.

Her nerves melted in an instant, and she felt her smile becoming less forced. She turned to the instrument and began to play.

She focused intensely, forbidding her mind to stray in any direction as she poured her heart and soul into the piece, emphasizing certain points for emotion, and pretending she was alone in her music room. It was the only way she could think to manage this.

Impossibly, it seemed to work, and her fingers flew with the grace and skill she had always wished for. It wasn't a difficult piece, and she wouldn't impress anyone with a true knowledge of music, but considering where she had come from, it was a feat indeed.

She held her breath as she came to the most challenging, yet most emotional part of the song, and felt a burst of joy when she made it through, though it hadn't been perfect and her tempo had faltered a little, she pressed on as if that was how it ought to have been done, keeping her composure all the while.

Slowly, gently, she moved into the end, and let her fingers remain on the keys longer than normal to draw out the last lingering tones as far as she could.

Applause surrounded and filled her, seeming nearly thunderous in her ears, though she knew it was no such thing. She turned with a beaming smile she could barely restrain and saw her friends in tears, but she only gave them a cursory glance. Her eyes found Kit at once, and the approval and pride in his eyes was potent in its intensity. He applauded with the rest of them, smiling as if he couldn't help himself. He held her gaze for an eternity, then nodded slowly, once, and then again as his smile grew.

She could have burst into tears at the sight, but managed just to exhale a delighted sigh of relief as she let Mr. Ascott take her back to her seat, her eyes never leaving Kit's until she was forced to.

He had come. He had heard her. And he had smiled.

Now, perhaps, they could get somewhere.

"And I wanted to take some of my dresses, too, but Marianne

said that wouldn't be sensible," Bitty said with a scowl. "Why is that not sensible?"

"She told us, Bitty," Rosie said as she rolled her eyes. "We don't have enough dresses for all of the girls, so not everyone would get one. That's why we went and got fabric the other day, so the seamstress there could make all of the girls a new dress."

"And new trousers for the boys!" Freddie broke in with a grin.

Bitty frowned and sat back against her chair. "Mine would be prettier."

Kit bit back a laugh and gave his sister a consoling look. "Of course, Bitty, but for little girls with no dresses, I am sure they will be very grateful for their new ones. And I am sure you made sure it was a fabric of a lovely color."

She grinned and nodded quickly. "I did! It's a pretty blue and the seamstress promised me the skirts will twirl. That way when they dance it's more fun!"

Kit shook his head and saw Rosie and Freddie do the same.

There had been a change in the children since Marianne started her work with orphans at St. Ann's. They had offered suggestions and gifts and now clothing without a second thought, even asking if they could go and play with the children.

Ginny had talked endlessly about giving a doll to them and a few other toys, without the barest hint of regret. Rosie and Freddie had given some books and primers they thought could be of use, and Bitty, naturally, could only think of dresses. They loved hearing Marianne's stories from her visits, and from what he could tell, had only been told good things.

Who knew what else Marianne would see and experience there.

He frowned as he looked at the clock and down the table at her empty seat. Dinner was always prompt and she was never late, often being seated before he ever came into the room. It was now ten minutes past, and that was more than unusual.

"Has anyone seen Marianne recently?" he asked of the children.

Four sets of shrugs met his query and he sighed.

"She went to see the orphans today," Freddie said with a frown as he thought.

"But she's always back by the late afternoon," Rosie broke in.

Kit looked towards the doorway and saw Mrs. Wilton subtly gesturing him to come to her. He nodded and rose, smiling at the children. "You all may eat without us. The footmen will help serve you, and they will report to me on any mischief. Understand?"

Four heads bobbed quickly and the footmen smirked a little in amusement. They knew the children well enough by then to be well equipped to deal with them.

Kit moved out into the hall and indicated for Mrs. Wilton to tell him whatever she wished.

"Your wife is upstairs, sir," she said in a subdued tone. "She went directly to her rooms after returning from St. Ann's. She said she was not hungry, and repeated the same when I offered to have a tray brought up."

Kit did not like the sound of that. Marianne was always hungry, and never let anything get in the way of her appetite. It was one of the things that amused him most about her.

"What was her manner and temperament?" he asked the housekeeper. "Was she distressed? Was she ill? Was she raging?"

Mrs. Wilton shook her head, her lips forming a tight line. "No, sir. She seemed... weary. And distracted. She barely heeded me at all. But, sir, I think... I think she was going to cry."

He nearly groaned, but bit it back. He wanted to go back into the dining room and let her be, but he knew he couldn't. He could not leave her like that.

"Thank you, Mrs. Wilton," he murmured. "I will see to it."

She bobbed a curtsey and left him, and he turned to the stairs and headed up, reminding himself of the distance and control that he needed to maintain. It was growing harder and harder to do so, for Marianne was becoming more and more vital to his life. She had shocked him by performing at Miranda Ascott's musical evening, and had done so with perfection. He could have burst with pride, and not for the skill, but for braving the attempt. He had heard her endlessly practicing newer and harder pieces, and seen Gemma Templeton coming to advise her, and knew how she had struggled and toiled.

Had she ever worked so endlessly for anything?

But that wasn't all. Marianne was always with the children now, whether it was playing on the piano or dressing in frilly gowns with

Bitty, reading or debating with Rosie, or acting out all sorts of imaginary things with Ginny. She had even been coaxed into hiding games that Freddie had concocted, and Marianne had laughed louder than any of them. And lately he had seen her sacrifice calls and shopping and visits in favor of giving her time and service to St. Ann's, always with the sort of passion she had once reserved only for the ballroom.

He had watched her unobserved enough to know that none of this was an act.

How could he resist a woman so blasted irresistible?

He knocked on her bedroom door, and heard a soft, unintelligible response, which he took to be an invitation to enter. Marianne sat on the divan on the far side of her sitting room, rather simply dressed, still wearing her pelisse, and her face turned away from the door.

"Mrs. Wilton says you will not eat," Kit said quietly as he came towards her, noticing how she stiffened slightly at his voice. "What is that all about?

She shook her head and turned her head further away as he came around to the front of the divan. He heard a faint sniffle and sighed as he sat down beside her. "You are upset," he murmured. "What is it?"

She turned towards him and he could see where tears had been, but no longer remained. She was a little pale and drawn, and as Mrs. Wilton had said, weary. "I am fine, Kit. Please don't distress yourself."

"I'm not," he replied simply, "but you can hardly expect me to leave you when you are in distress."

She blinked rapidly and looked down at her hands, curled up in her lap. "I will be well enough," she ground out, as if to herself.

He hesitated, then laid a hand over hers. "Marianne."

She clamped down hard on her bottom lip. "I don't know if I can tell you without becoming emotional."

Against his better will and judgment, he stayed put. "I'm not afraid of tears. Shall I hold you?"

She nodded and leaned into him, and gingerly he wrapped an arm about her. "There," he soothed a bit awkwardly. "Tell me."

He felt her nod against him and then exhale. "There was a new little girl at St. Ann's today. Jane. She was four years old, and no one knows her story. She hardly speaks at all, but she looks around the room every so often, her eyes filled with tears. I asked her what was wrong for perhaps the tenth time, hoping she would open up."

Her voice sounded hollow and vacant, and he found himself holding her closer. "And did she?" he prodded as gently as he could while still maintaining politeness.

Marianne did not seem to hear him. "She looked up at me and asked, 'Where's my brother? Where's Caleb?' And she sounded so scared, Kit. She cried for her brother. And she was the very image of me as a child." Her voice became choked with tears and she paused for control. "It scared me how perfect a likeness she was. And I couldn't help thinking that would have been me if anything had happened to Duncan. She is exactly what I would have been."

"You had Tibby," he reminded her.

Marianne's fingers clenched together more tightly. "What if Jane has an aunt as well? Any relative? What if she had anyone to look after her? Could her fate be less dismal than what she will get in her present situation?" She shook her head against him and sniffled. "I wanted to bring her home so badly, to make sure she knew what a real home was, to give her a future. But I couldn't. I know for every Jane there are twenty more just like her."

The harsh bitterness in her voice struck something with him, and he looked down at the top of her head. "Is this too difficult for you?" he asked softly. "Seeing those children and those conditions?"

Again, she shook her head, this time with vigor. "No, it gives me purpose and perspective. I want to do more for them, but I have so little to give. I want to see Jane become something great, something better than I have been with all of my opportunity. But circumstances dictate our future, and unless she is adopted, or we find the truth about her family, all she can achieve is the height of a lady's maid, and that breaks my heart."

Kit held her a few moments more, his heart somewhere in the vicinity of his throat. He, too, could have been cast off by his family if it were not for Aunt Agatha and whatever shred of paternal duty remained in Loughton. He and Colin could have been left for some foundling organization, they would have been apprenticed off, separated, and who knew what would have become of them? He had never really considered himself as fortunate in his circumstances before, but now he could hardly believe the luck.

Marianne pulled away, suddenly stiff, and rubbed at her eyes. "Thank you," she said tightly, averting her eyes. "You may go now."

Kit hesitated, looking her over. "Are you sure?"

She nodded, still not meeting his gaze. "Yes, of course. Go down to the children before the potatoes find their way to the ceiling."

He almost smiled at her attempt at humor. "Will you eat something?"

"Not tonight," she murmured, the words somehow seeming more than a simple denial.

He waited for her to say more, and when she didn't, he bowed slightly. "As you wish. Good night, Marianne."

He saw her throat work on a swallow, and then she nodded in acknowledgment.

Utterly helpless and feeling rather dismissed, Kit did as she bid and left, returning to the dining room a little more subdued and infinitely more grateful.

Perhaps he, too, could benefit from her time spent with the orphans. And benefit them in return.

Chapter Twenty-Four

$\mathcal{A}$ few days after her interaction with little Jane, Marianne returned to the St. Ann's for another afternoon of volunteering, grateful for the distraction. Kit's attentions to her the other night had her in such turmoil, she could hardly bear to think of him. He had listened and held her, which no doubt he thought quite enough, but the torment of being near him, being held by him, without actually being held… It ached in deep places within her to be held so lightly, so innocently, as if duty required it. It would have been better not to have been held at all.

But she couldn't fault him for trying.

She entered St. Ann's with a weak sigh, wrinkling her nose up at the faint musty odor. It was an older building that had been made over for the foundlings, but it was not particularly well-kept. When there were no real funds for upkeep, it was difficult to make improvements.

Lady Sprotmire and Mrs. Clarke, the two ladies who saw to the care and running of the place, approached her at once, beaming as if she were heaven sent.

"Mrs. Gerrard," Mrs. Clarke gushed, which was not a usual thing for her, as she seized Marianne's hands. "You must convey our heartfelt gratitude to your husband. An angel on earth, I swear it."

She reared back in surprise. "My husband? Why?"

Lady Sprotmire laughed and beamed further. "For his goodness and kindness, my dear! His generous donation to us!"

Marianne gaped, her eyes going wide. "His… his what?"

Mrs. Clarke gasped and her hands shot to her plump cheeks.

"You didn't know?"

She shook her head faintly.

Her hands were once again seized. "He came to us the day after your last visit. He toured the entire facility, saw every single room and broom cupboard, even the kitchens down below. He declared his intention to give a sizeable donation, which we shall not disclose as such things are impolite."

Lady Sprotmire rolled her eyes and squeezed Marianne's arm. "Then he said he would get others to do the same, and since then, we have not only received his, but donations from the Earl of Beverton, the Marquess of Whitlock, Lord Blackmoor, Lady Raeburn…"

"My aunt?" Marianne broke in on a weak gasp.

The two women nodded frantically, smiling. "And more and more keep coming!" Mrs. Clarke told her triumphantly. "We've been told by our board of trustees that we are now to expect workers for renovations and a full staff, among other things! It is amazing how he has transformed them."

Marianne frowned a little, her mind whirling to catch up. "Who?"

The women looked at each other, then back at her. "Your husband," they said together.

She fumbled for a seat and found a small bench behind her, then fell heavily onto it.

Lady Sprotmire knelt, amidst several small pairs of shoes, and took her hands. "Your husband also placed himself on our board of trustees, and demanded changes. Not only to the building, but to the opportunities presented to the children. He wants better apprenticeships and situations for all of them, and a complete history for each child to be compiled, as much as we know."

It was too much, too impossible, and Marianne shook with the force of her sudden emotions. Kit had not only listened to her far more intently than she believed, but he had acted upon it. He had seen for himself the conditions she could not bear to describe, and he was moving heaven and earth to improve everything he could.

How could she not love such a man?

She gasped sharply at the realization that suddenly burst into a shower of sparks within her. She loved him. Of course she loved him, she had done so for weeks, perhaps longer. She loved him for his passion, his determination, his steadiness, his unfailing generosity, and the hidden devil that he so rarely revealed. She loved him, not for what he had done, but for why he had done it.

She loved him for all that he was, even when he had wounded her pride and crushed her spirit. He was always there, as firm and calm as an anchor in a tossing, turbulent sea.

Tears rolled freely down her cheeks and she smiled through them, wondering if she could walk on air for the joy she felt coursing through her.

"And there's more," Mrs. Clarke squealed.

What more could there be? She couldn't bear what already was!

"We know who Jane is!" the woman continued, heedless to Marianne's bewildering ecstasy. "He arranged for an investigation into her, using his own resources, and only this morning we received the report! She has a second cousin in Brighton, a retired Naval captain, and he and his wife are coming up to fetch her! They have four children of their own, and are very respectable. Jane will be part of a real family!"

Marianne closed her eyes on her tears and bowed her head, fighting for control. He had done everything, and so much more.

"I think perhaps, Mrs. Gerrard, you ought to go home," Lady Sprotmire advised with a warm laugh. "You look quite done for."

"But there is work to be done," Marianne tried to protest.

"We have plenty of help today," she insisted, pulling her to her feet. "Go home and be with your husband, dear. There will always be work to be done here."

Somehow, Marianne managed to exit the building and make her way home, not caring at all about her appearance or the sight she must be to anyone seeing her. It all faded into the dim background of the torrent of love and gratitude and joy that consumed her.

She wanted to rush home and throw herself in her husband's arms, hold him close, and tell him just how deeply she loved him. He cared for her enough to do all of this, and that gave her hope as never before. She could wait for his love so long as she stood a chance.

She bit her lip on a wild laugh and nearly skipped the rest of the way home, her heart light and easy, and terribly anxious.

To her utter dismay, Kit was not at home when she arrived, and she was beside herself with the energy and eagerness bubbling up. The children were in lessons, and the house was quiet, and she could not stand to be idle now. So she sequestered herself in the music room, playing and singing anything she had at hand, and not caring overly much if it was well done, which was well, as she burst into laughter several times in the middle of a few songs.

She was utterly ridiculous, but there was nothing to be done about that.

When she had done all of the songs she could, and feeling more her usual self, she calmly made her way out of the music room.

She let out a brief shriek when she nearly ran into her husband in the hallway just outside, leaning against the wall, evidently having listened to several notes.

She clamped a hand over her mouth, her eyes wide, her cheeks flaming with mortification.

He smiled a little and her heart tumbled. "Enjoying yourself?"

She bit down on her lip hard. "I am so sorry," she whispered behind her hand.

He shook his head, still bearing that maddening hint of a smile. "Don't be. You have a lovely voice. I love it."

When at last Marianne could feel her missing kneecaps after that statement, she managed to clear her throat. "Thank you. Kit, would you mind if I spoke to you about something? It is… rather important."

He raised a questioning brow, but gestured towards his study. "Of course, after you."

She clenched her hands together, opening and closing her fingers as she made her way to the study. She could do this without losing composure or crumbling at his feet. She was too mortified to fling herself at him, but was she sensible enough for coherency?

Kit closed the door to the study behind her, then came to lean against his desk, folding his arms. "What can I do for you?" he asked with utmost politeness.

Love me? She nearly swayed to the side as the errant thought burst into her mind, and she took a long moment to steady herself. Exhaling slowly, gathering her courage, she met his eyes, and nearly lost it again.

She forced herself to swallow, then opened her mouth and found the words already there.

"All my life I thought I wanted an adventure," she began almost timidly. "A man who craved what I did, who felt and expressed everything as I did. I was reckless and carefree and thought I had no boundaries and would never need any." She shook her head and found her voice growing stronger. "Then I had my own adventure and it wasn't the thrilling ride I thought it would be. My world was turned upside down and I did not know who I was."

Kit looked a bit wary at this declaration, but she was bold now, and wouldn't stop.

"Then I discovered the truth," she continued. "I didn't need an adventure, I needed a ballast. I am emotional and excitable and a million other things that mean I will never be completely tame or controlled. I didn't need more of myself, I needed someone to steady me. I needed a rock."

She swallowed hard and seized the last of her courage. "I needed you, Kit." She bit her suddenly trembling lip and clamped her equally trembling hands together. "I need you. You make me the woman I always wanted to be, the one I never knew I could be. I love you. I loved you at Glendare and at Amberley, and when the carriage was still there at the opera, and when you told me to wear blue, and when you came to hear me play, and then today…"

Her voice broke and she suddenly gasped, unable to contain herself a moment longer. "Oh, Kit, if there is any chance that you could come to love me at all, even the slightest portion of what you once felt, then I am begging you to tell me so now. I can't breathe for the anxiety and…"

"Enough," Kit interrupted, holding a hand out as if to physically restrain her. "You have said quite enough. As you said, you are emotional and excitable, and I think you had better go to your rooms and recover yourself before this goes any further."

Marianne stared for a moment, fairly certain her heart would never beat the same way again. She was being dismissed? Just like that?

He inclined his head towards the door, otherwise unmoving

against his desk.

Her body moved slowly, sluggishly, as if it could not comprehend doing anything at all. She groped for the door handle and somehow managed to walk down the hall with only one hand gripping the wall. Her body trembled, and her head ached, and her heart was reduced to fluttering shambles within her. Tears coursed unchecked down her cheeks, falling onto her hands and skirts and the floor below. She felt for her heart with a limp hand, overwhelmed with the desire to take it out and thrust it away forever.

How could she bear loving a man this much, being near him daily, bearing his children and sharing his life, while knowing he had refused her love so easily? She would slowly wither away and become nothing under such a crushing blow of disappointment day after day. He would never love her as he once had, she was too late.

She found her way up the stairs and to her room, shut the door firmly behind her, and sagged against it, still clutching her chest, as loud and frantic sobs broke free. She blindly fumbled for the bed and collapsed onto the counterpane, her sobs becoming only slightly muffled against the bedcovers. Her fingers clawed and clutched at the fabric, desperately trying to lose herself into their depths.

What was left of her if the man she loved wanted nothing to do with her?

"God help me, I can't do it," Kit suddenly exclaimed as he burst into the room, causing her to rise up with a choked gasp of surprise.

He was to her in an instant, suddenly there on the bed and holding her to his chest. "I can't be strong and unfeeling and immovable anymore, not with you. I can't do it." He clung to her, shuddering and struggling for breath, as she was. "Forgive me," he pleaded, kissing her hair, then burying his face in it as he rocked her. "Forgive me, my love. I'm so sorry. I'm so very sorry."

"You love me?" Marianne cried as she pulled back, her hands going to his shoulders.

He kissed her hard, the taste of her tears mingling with that of his lips in a heady concoction. "Yes, you maddening, darling minx. Yes, I love you. I never stopped, I couldn't."

He shook his head and captured her lips once more, searing her with the passion simmering just beneath the surface. "I love you," he groaned as he touched his forehead to hers. "I love you and I am in love with you, and I love everything about you. Say you'll forgive me, and forget everything I have been and said and done and just put me out of my misery and tell me again."

She laughed breathlessly in delight and captured his face between her hands, took a lingering moment to kiss him silent, drawing another, more ragged groan from him. She broke the kiss, but left her lips close enough to brush his as she fiercely said, "I love you, Christopher Gerrard."

He kissed her gently, his hands suddenly shaking against her cheeks and moving to stroke her hair. "Let me start this marriage over. Let me love you as I always should have. Tell me that it is not too late for me. Tell me that…"

She cut him off with a desperate kiss, which he took in with enthusiasm and relief, and his hand on her waist tightened and pulled her ever closer, even as the other tangled itself in her hair.

"I love you," she whispered against his lips.

He returned the favor with recklessness, giving her a kiss so heated, so passionate, so filled with pent up emotion that her toes curled, and she gasped as his mouth slid to her throat, finding that vulnerable spot at the base at once.

Lost in the heady sensation of him, she wrapped her arms around his neck, heart and limbs soaring as he tumbled them both to the bed, and gave herself over completely to all that he was, and all the glorious things they could be together.

In the dark of her bedroom, some time later, they lay curled together, her head on his chest as she tucked against his side, his arms tight around her, one hand stroking the dark tendrils of hair down her back.

"We are moving your things into my room at once," Kit said authoritatively.

Marianne frowned in mock consternation and looked up at him.

"Why am I going to your room? This is a most comfortable bed."

He shrugged. "Very well then, I will move in here."

She grinned in the darkness and patted his chest. "How accommodating you are."

"It makes no difference to me where I sleep so long as you are there," he told her, his voice suddenly gruff.

Impulsively, she hugged herself close and sighed. "Now that is a sentiment we can agree on."

They were both quiet for a moment, reveling in their closeness and all that had been revealed. "When did you start feeling something for me?" he asked, his fingers toying with her hair.

She chuckled against him. "Well aren't we feeling proud of ourselves?"

He snorted and gave her a sardonic look. "I've dreamed of this exact moment for years, I think I'm entitled to enjoy it."

She snickered and kissed his bare shoulder. "I always felt something for you," she murmured. "I just didn't know what it was. But I looked for you, all the time. I always wanted to talk to you, see you, make you laugh."

She sighed and placed her hand over his heart. "I didn't realize how much you meant to me until I no longer had you near. And then I was halfway in love with you before I knew what I was about. I think you've always been the most important person in my life, Kit. I loved you without knowing it. Now I know it and I can't breathe." She gasped a little with the admission, her breathing growing uneven with the force of her newfound emotions.

"Shhh," he murmured, nuzzling her and softly feathering kisses along her brow, her ear, her nose. "It becomes more natural eventually."

She shook her head against him. "I hope I always burn for you like this," she whispered fervently. "I want to be breathless and aching and uneasy, I want to be surprised daily by your attractiveness…"

"So do I," he replied with a droll smile.

She rapped his chest sharply. "Shush! I'm complimenting you."

"If you go on," he warned, "I will have to take unscrupulous advantage of you."

She raised a brow and looked up at him with a wicked grin. "Promise?"

He groaned and threw an arm over his eyes. "I'm doomed. You are always going to test and tempt me, aren't you?"

"Of course I will," she replied lightly, feeling rather satisfied. She dropped her tone and looked up at him through half lowered lashes. "Every time I lose my breath with you, I fully intend to make you just as breathless, just as aching, just as empty, all the while testing that blessed control you love so much. But don't give it up completely. You'll need it."

He suddenly rolled over her, giving her a heated, hungry look as he pinned her beneath him. "Promise?" he murmured, leaning down to layer searing kisses along her throat.

"Oh lord…" she rasped, her eyes fluttering shut. "I love you, Kit."

"I love you, too, darling. Now be quiet and let me do this properly."

"Oh yes," she managed weakly. "We must be proper."

"Always," he replied as he took her lips once more, and Marianne was quite without words for some time as she and her husband made up for time they had lost.

Epilogue

"You look wonderful, Mary!"

"I look like a whale. I am convinced I was never so large with the twins."

"A whale? My dear woman, have you seen me?"

"Kate, you know very well you are tiny."

"Annalise is tiny."

"I am not. This one is far bigger than either of the boys."

"When that one grows up a little, she just might be half the size of mine."

Marianne scoffed and gave Moira a look. "Moira, you are barely showing."

Moira turned to her and raised a brow. "It is my fifth child, dear. I know how big they are by now."

"And I am on my seventh," Kate crowed, rubbing her swollen midsection.

"So yours should be well under control by now," chimed in Mary, by far the largest of them all, though no one was going to say anything about it. It was a miracle they had conceived again after the twins two years before.

"Ha!" Susannah barked, thrusting out her own expanded girth. "Control? Her children mind as well as the Gerrards."

"Which explains why you and Marianne are bringing more into the world," Moira muttered dryly, waving over a well liveried servant.

Kit shook his head as he watched the women debate over their size and forthcoming children. Somehow, impossibly, every couple here was expecting a child in the coming year. There had been several overlapping pregnancies as the years had progressed, but never had they all done so. All of the men had safely retreated to another corner of the room, observing their women warily.

"Geoff, I can't tell you how happy we are for you," Duncan said, clapping a hand on his shoulder.

Derek snorted softly. "Duncan, it's been several months, and now you're telling him this?"

That earned him a glower of massive proportions, though Kit noticed there was a glint of amusement in his brother-in-law's eyes.

"Yes, Derek," Duncan replied in a dry tone, "and it bears repeating for the unique blessing it is. If you took a moment's respite from overpopulating the world with hellions, perhaps you would see that."

Geoff grinned broadly, betraying the true joy he felt. "I don't mind receiving congratulations. I thought we were beyond fortunate with Will and Julianna, but to have another?" He shook his head and laughed. "This should be easier, yes? One instead of two?"

"Unless they're Colin's children," Kit muttered, surveying the screaming children racing around the room.

That drew a round of laughter, even from his twin. "I admit it, they're wild. Freddie and Livvy lead them, but Amelia and Matthew keep things interesting."

Nathan smirked as he watch his children try to herd the others. "Yes, I'm sure they do. And Ginny doesn't help matters."

Now Kit laughed loudly, as did Colin. Ginny had turned out to be more headstrong and willful than Rosie ever had been, and up to mischief more than not. But she was growing more sensible by the day, merely hiding her wildness better. Bitty was everything a girl of nearly thirteen could wish for, and loved being at school with Rosie, who had become a stunning beauty of remarkable wit and poise, and at sixteen would soon be finished with school herself and beginning her foray into Society.

Which terrified both brothers to the bone.

Thankfully, Freddie could still put Rosie in her place when they were both home from school, though he had yet to grow as tall as her, which she reminded him of at every opportunity. He was fourteen and growing finer and more impressive than any of them had dared to hope. And only his family could draw out his childish side.

"No, Charlotte, put John down," Nathan scolded as his only redheaded daughter tried to heave her husky toddler brother away from her playacting with the other girls.

She gave him a distinctly Moira-like look. "Papa, Tillie and I want to dress up in costumes with Grace and Emma. John is in the way!"

Little Grace folded her arms and looked at him with all the superiority of her marchioness mother shining through. "Yes, Uncle Nathan, John is in the way."

Nathan looked at Derek for help, but he only shrugged. "See if he will go play with David. He's got Simon and Will over there, or the little Bray boys seem to be creating a tower in the corner."

Emma wrinkled up her nose. "John won't want to play with David or Simon, Uncle Nathan. They're my brothers."

Derek grinned down at his daughter. "Ah, spoken like your aunt Diana. Fine, sweetling, send him over to Graham and Andrew, then. He'd love the block tower."

Emma, Grace, and Charlotte nodded and urged John away. Tillie, ever the miniature Annalise, looked concerned for the toddler, and turned to let her brothers know to be careful with him.

"Who would have thought that we'd have such a brood?" Nathan sighed as he leaned against the wall and shook his head.

Colin snorted and handed the box of celebratory cigars around. "Not I, certainly. I didn't think any of you would ever manage wives."

Geoff looked at him in disbelief. "What, but you would?"

Colin sniffed and raised his nose. "Of course, I would. Everyone knows I am the charming one."

"And modest," Kit added as he shook his head at the proffered cigars.

"Certainly the most handsome," Colin informed him with a nod.

That earned his brother a significant brow raise as the others laughed.

"You obviously have been listening to the wrong sort of gossip," Kit informed his sadly delusional brother.

"Tibby always said I was the most handsome man on earth," Colin protested.

Duncan roared with sudden laughter and cuffed the back of Colin's head. "You duff, she says that to everyone."

"And how is Lady Raeburn? Or should I say Lady Tinsdale?" Derek asked with a wry grin.

Kit and Duncan rolled their eyes and heaved nearly identical sighs. "Mad. Poor Tinsdale, two years of marriage and he still thinks he manages things."

"I think he's mad, too," Kit pointed out with a grin. "Mad for Tibby, mad for their travels, and mad for his new and exciting life."

"They are in Germany now?"

"Prague. But they are coming in for the Season."

"Anyone seen Harry or Robbie?" Derek asked, looking suddenly suspicious.

"Lost the heirs to Ashcombe and Beverton, have you?" Geoff asked with a laugh as he sank into a chair.

Duncan smirked and waved a dismissive hand. "I saw them with Freddie a few minutes ago, wandering around somewhere."

"At least they're assured of a good influence," Nathan sighed, shaking his head. "They need it." He settled more comfortably in his place, looking over at his wife with fondness.

All of the men turned to survey their wives, all of whom were engaged in an apparently serious conversation.

Kit marveled at Marianne, who had only just begun showing her own pregnancy, to his delight. Their marriage had been a perfect dream, far beyond anything he had ever imagined he could have. Not that it was all bliss, for she was a stubborn, headstrong woman, and he was a prideful man, and they fought often. The difference now was they made up fairly quickly, and they laughed far more than they argued. She was more beautiful and beguiling than she had ever been, and with the passing years he had seen her thrive and blossom in new and astonishing ways.

And somehow, she loved him with a fierceness that stole his breath.

They'd done everything they had talked about, visited every estate and seen them thrive more than they ever had in his father's care. Loughton was ill in France, apparently near to death, but letters had been saying that for years now and he was still here. Kit would inherit the title soon, but he could not have been more of a lord and master than he felt now. Title would not change anything, except their number of invitations would increase.

If that were even possible.

Marianne caught his eye and for a moment she looked mildly amused by whatever she saw. Then her smile deepened, her chin dipped, and she slowly stepped away from the other women.

Kit was moving before he recollected that he wanted to and was to her side in an instant. She had that effect on him.

Just as she always had.

She reached up a hand to his face and raised a brow. "You called?"

He smirked a little. "Did I?"

She tilted her head, her smile turning into a knowing one. "Didn't you?"

He grinned and kissed her brow. "Perhaps I did," he murmured against her skin, noting the warmth of it. She'd been under the weather before their journey here, and in her condition, he'd been rather concerned, despite her repeated assurances that she was well.

"I'm fine," she murmured, knowing too well why he lingered. "I think being here in Derbyshire is good for me."

"It was rather nice of the Whitlocks to invite us," he agreed as he pulled back to look at her. "Though I really think they are mad to have the lot of us here for the holidays."

She considered that with a smile. "True. Kate says the duke and duchess were more of a mind to stay with the Beckhams this year, as they only have four children, and David's family is in Scotland. We are the next best thing."

Kit looked beyond his wife to the other women, all of whom were giggling about something, and each had put their hand on their expanded stomachs.

He shook his head. "We have *got* to find ourselves some new friends, darling. Things are getting scary."

Marianne scoffed and tugged him a little closer. "You don't know the half of it," she muttered out of the corner of her mouth. "The women all just agreed to name our currently unborn children after the adults present."

Kit stilled and looked down at her in horror. "Marianne, my love, if you have any tender feelings for me at all, please do not name our son Colin. Or Derek. Or our daughter Moira. Or Kate."

His wife frowned and put one hand on her hip. "Christopher Gerrard. We have three children together and I have listened to your views on naming them all. Now it is my turn. I will name our child this time. And you will like it."

He swallowed harshly, feeling more than a little fearful. "So... I should tell the other gents that we have sold our souls and there is no escape?"

She nodded firmly. "Quite so."

Kit looked around the room, seeking out his children, and sighing. Rafe was playing animatedly with his cousin and best friend Matthew, as they were so close in age, while his younger sisters played with the adorable and sweet Julianna Harris. Cat and Daphne could not have been more different in temperament, no matter how eerily similar they were in looks. They would be Kit's torment, having learned far too many tricks from their aunts already, but they were surprisingly compatible and rarely fought.

"I suppose," Kit murmured with a good deal of faux reluctance, "that would be all right. Considering our other children seem to be doing well enough. And I suppose you may have earned it."

"May have?" Marianne sputtered with a jerk. "May I remind you what I suffered with Daphne?"

He winced and gave her an apologetic look. "I did apologize. Profusely. And Daphne is so sweet now, much sweeter than Cat, surely that softens it."

His wife gave him a derisive look. "Ask me in three months if it's softened."

He blanched and raised her hand to his lips, lingering as much as he dared.

Across the room, the other men watched them with interest.

"Did you ever think those two would have a marriage like that?" Nathan asked quietly of no one in particular.

Geoff snorted and shook his head. "Not at all. Nor that Kit's firstborn son would be more like Colin than Colin's sons."

That made Colin laugh and he looked at his nephew fondly.

"Rafe is a boy after my own heart. Kit needs him."

"With those beautiful girls?" Duncan scoffed, smiling as Cat waved at him. "He certainly needs something."

"How is it that they manage such a match?" Derek mused, still watching the couple in question. "I wouldn't have paired them together for the world, but they are one of the most enviable couples in England."

"He's always loved her," Colin said with a soft smile. "He just decided to let it show."

"But Marianne…" Geoff broke off with a wince and looked at Duncan apologetically.

Duncan shrugged, knowing full well what his sister had once been. "All it took was her marriage to Kit and suddenly her true self came to light."

They all fell silent as Kit and Marianne suddenly moved over to the pianoforte in the grandly windowed nook on one side of the room, gently ushering Helena and Lizzie from their gleeful plunking on the instrument.

"What are they doing?" Derek demanded, his brow furrowing.

Geoff rolled his eyes and gave him a look. "Music, Derek. You know, the pleasant sounds that your wife and daughter are so skilled at creating from that rather large instrument over there?"

Derek glared as the others chuckled, but all laughter stopped when Kit and Marianne were conferring together over the pieces.

"Wait, they're going to sing? Together?" Nathan asked, looking at the rest in shock.

Geoff shrugged, still smiling, but looking stunned himself. "So it appears."

"Can Kit sing?" Duncan asked faintly.

Colin grinned. "Actually, yes. He just doesn't."

Derek shook his head, his glower returning. "How much has he had to drink?"

Nathan laughed shortly and gave him an incredulous look. "It's Christmas, Derek. And it's your house, and your punch…"

The marquess paled and his eyes widened. "Oh dear."

Colin chuckled fondly and shook his head. "It's not the drink," he told his friends. "It's Marianne."

That got their attention and they stared at him in awe.

"Explain," Geoff said with a brief wave of his hand.

Colin watched his brother and his wife together, feeling the odd swelling of pride and contentment within him that was becoming rather common for him the more his family grew. His brother was his best friend, and he had a wife that was somehow, impossibly, perfect for him and made him more than what he was.

There wasn't anything else to wish for in life.

He cleared his throat a little. "He steadies her," he explained to the others. "He supports her, keeps her grounded…"

Derek huffed a bit. "All very well and good, but what does she do for him?"

Colin felt himself smiling like a fool. "She gives him wings." He set his drink and cigar aside and went to the pianoforte to join them in singing carols, and one by one, the others followed, until they were all together uniting their voices in the music.

Outside the grand and sprawling estate, the snow softly and steadily fell, ensuring some grand adventures for the days ahead and the chance to draw ever closer to those one loved, wrapping all within in the warmth of the Season, and the joy of such a family.